Merwan Gatignol

PISTOUVI

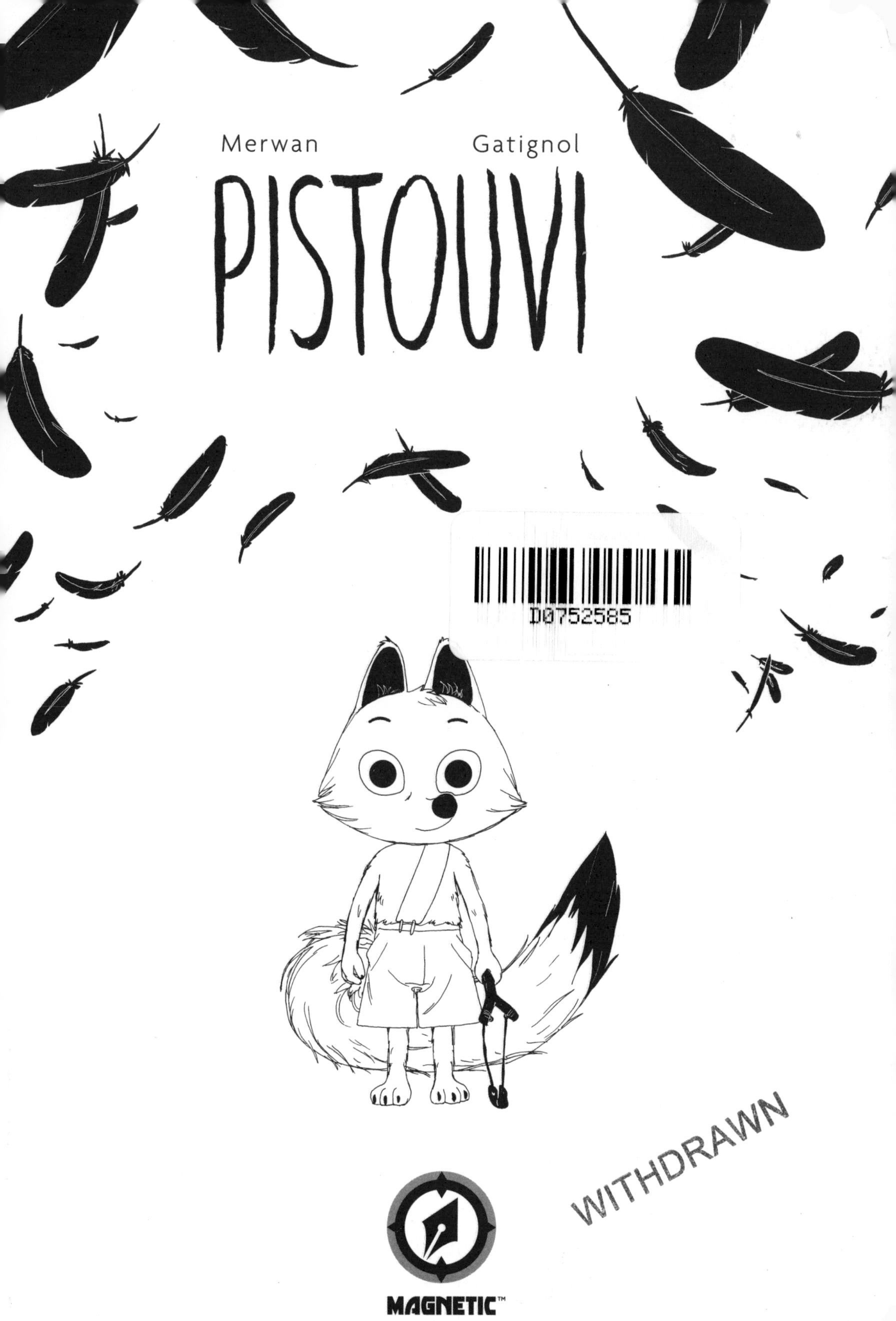

MAGNETIC™

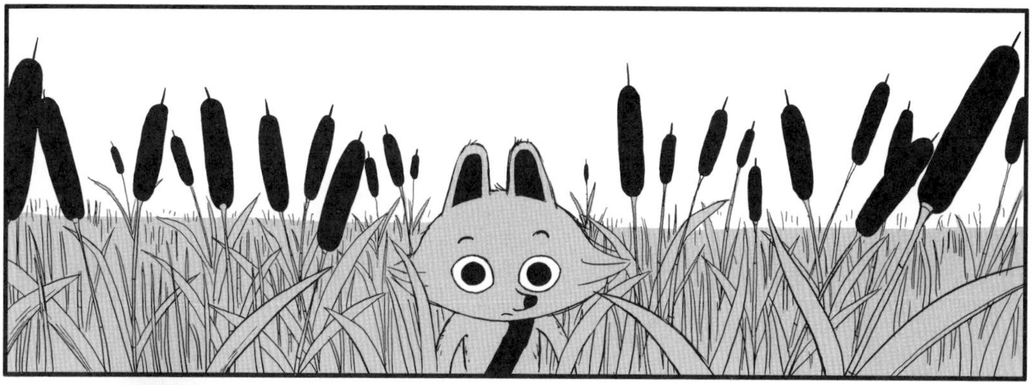

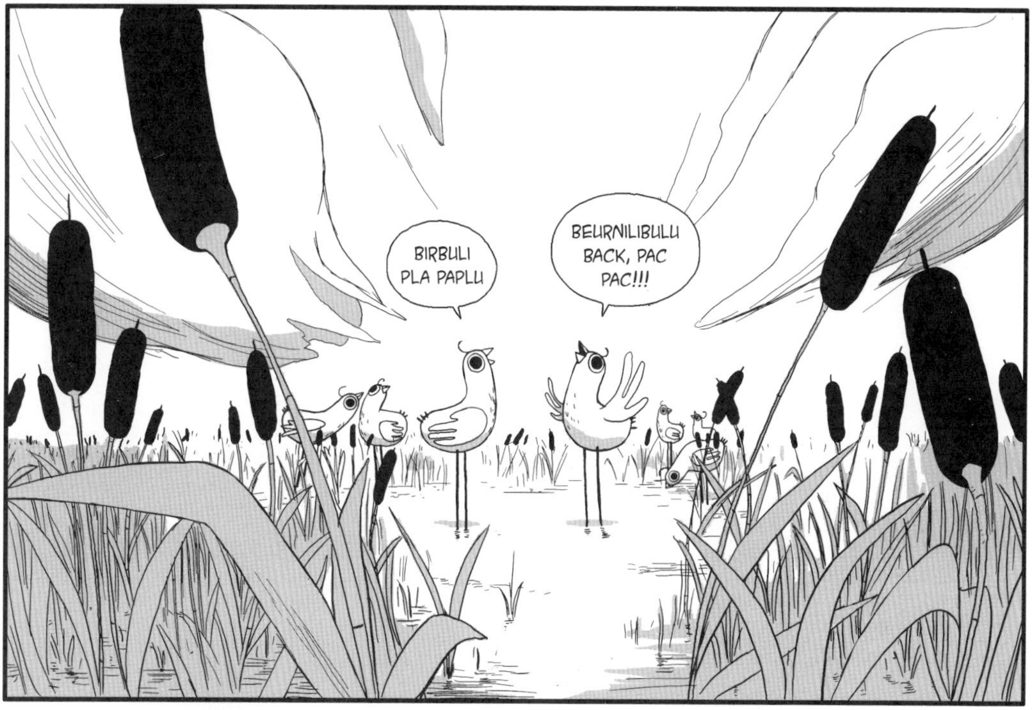
BIRBULI
PLA PAPLU
BEURNILIBULU
BACK, PAC
PAC!!!

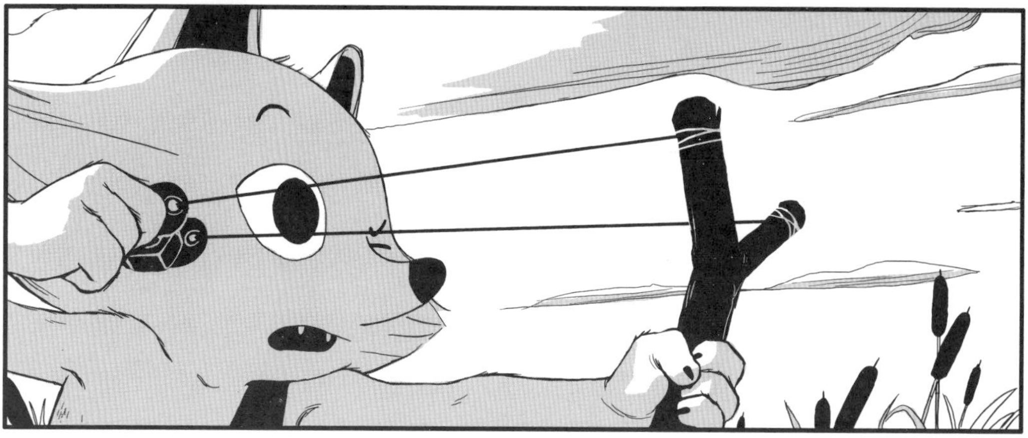

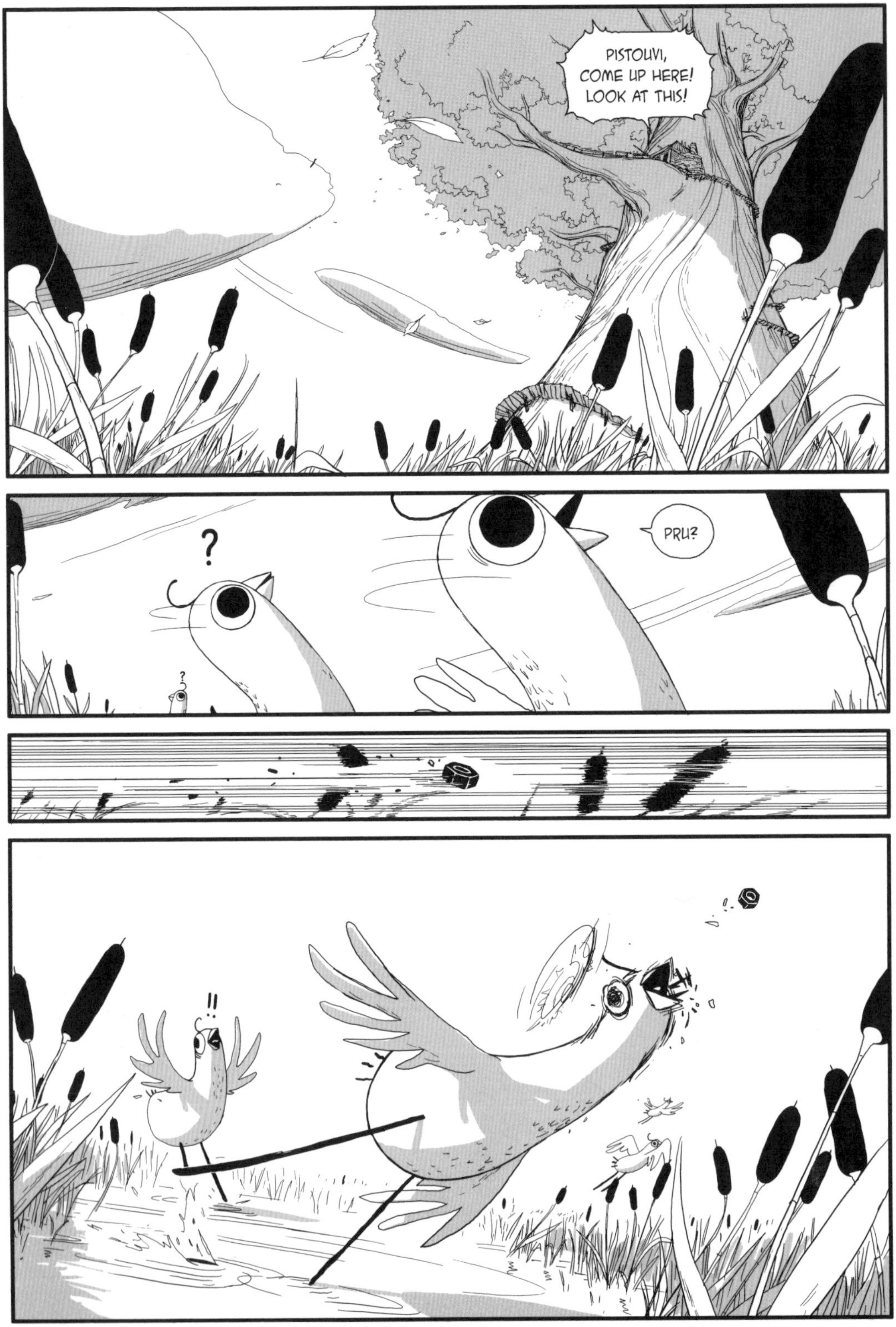
PISTOUVI, COME UP HERE! LOOK AT THIS!
PRU?

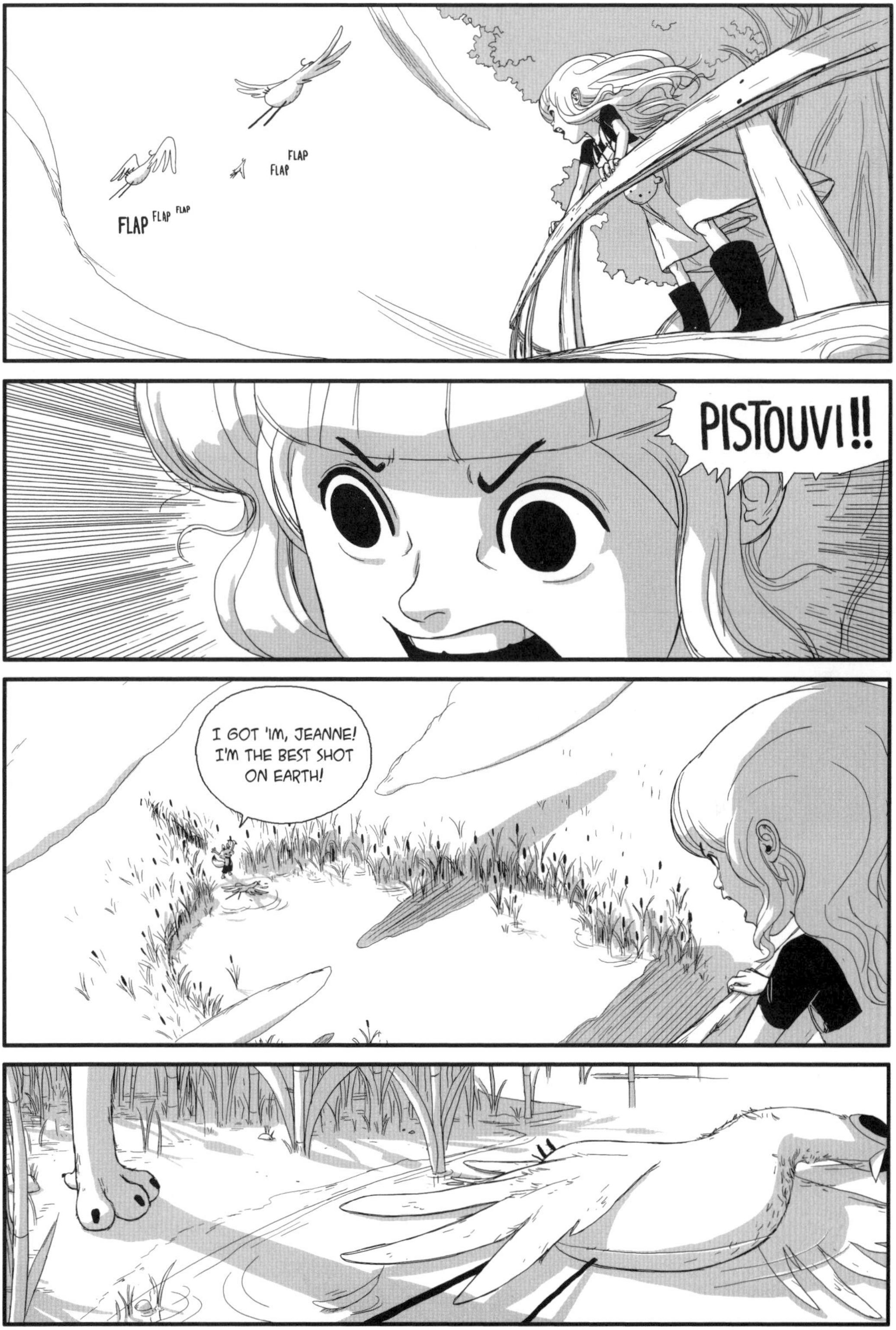
FLAP FLAP FLAP
FLAP FLAP
PISTOUVI!!
I GOT 'IM, JEANNE! I'M THE BEST SHOT ON EARTH!

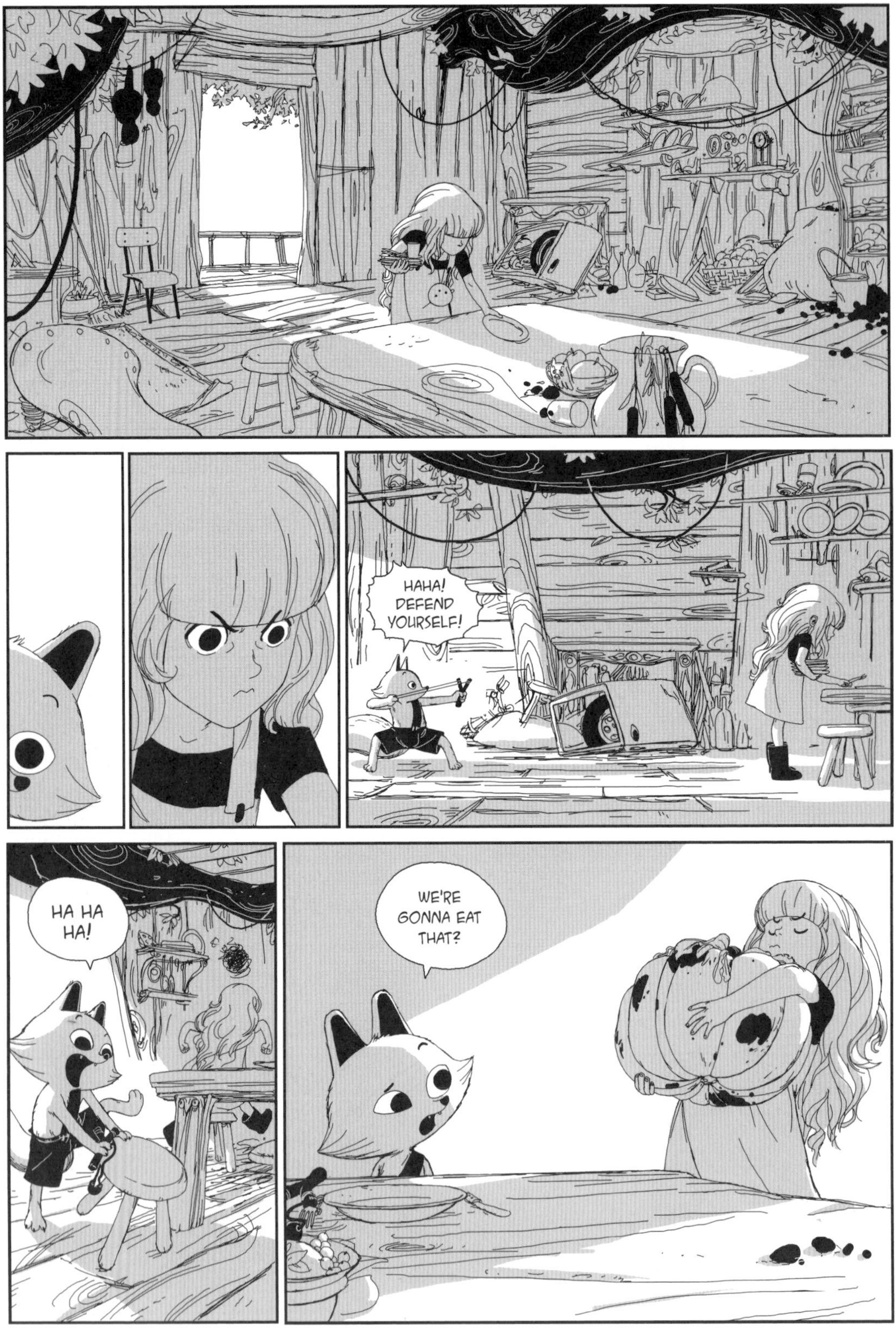
HAHA! DEFEND YOURSELF!
HA HA HA!
WE'RE GONNA EAT THAT?

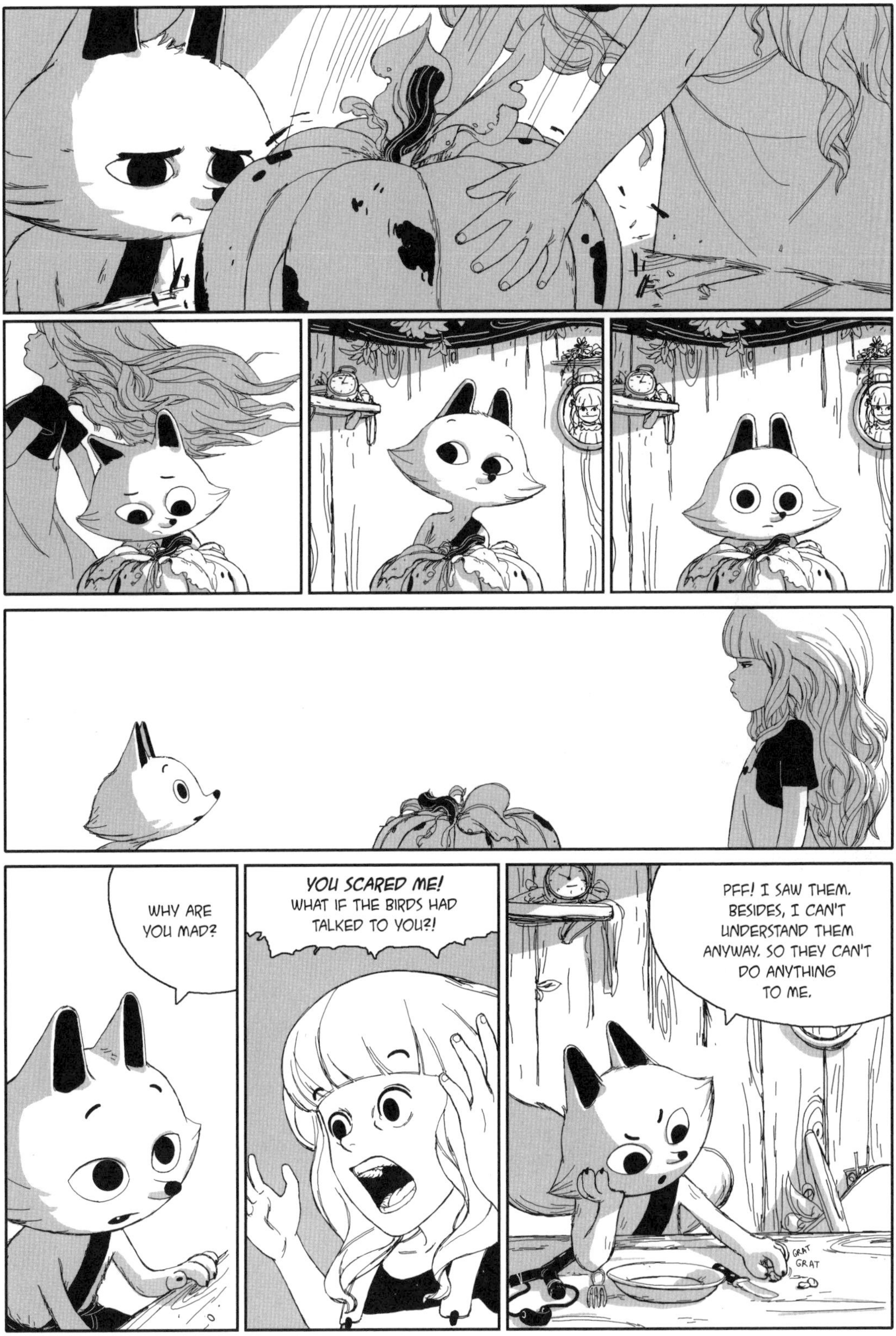
WHY ARE YOU MAD?
YOU SCARED ME! WHAT IF THE BIRDS HAD TALKED TO YOU?!
PFF! I SAW THEM. BESIDES, I CAN'T UNDERSTAND THEM ANYWAY. SO THEY CAN'T DO ANYTHING TO ME.
GRAT GRAT

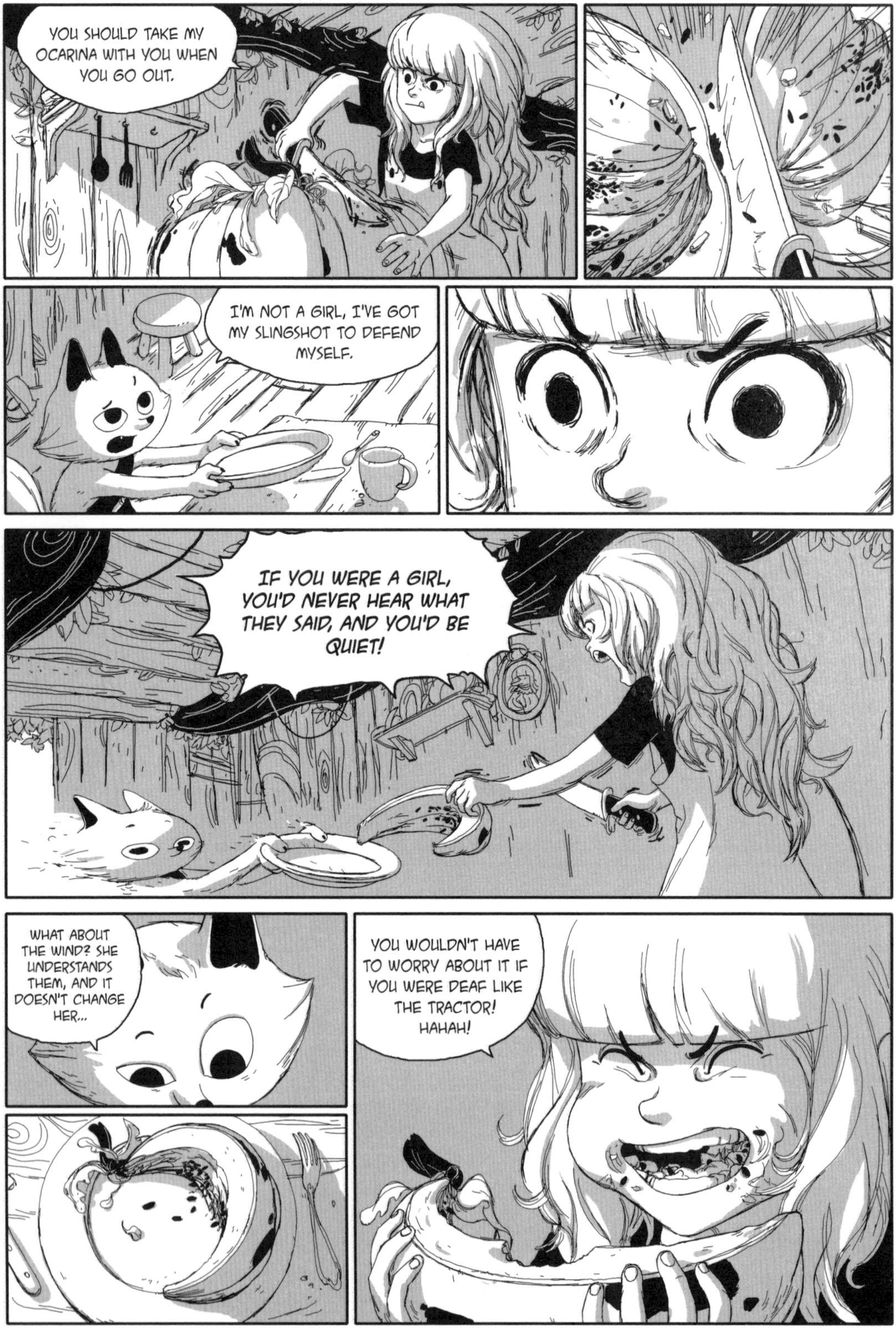
YOU SHOULD TAKE MY OCARINA WITH YOU WHEN YOU GO OUT.
I'M NOT A GIRL, I'VE GOT MY SLINGSHOT TO DEFEND MYSELF.
IF YOU WERE A GIRL, YOU'D NEVER HEAR WHAT THEY SAID, AND YOU'D BE QUIET!
WHAT ABOUT THE WIND? SHE UNDERSTANDS THEM, AND IT DOESN'T CHANGE HER...
YOU WOULDN'T HAVE TO WORRY ABOUT IT IF YOU WERE DEAF LIKE THE TRACTOR! HAHAH!

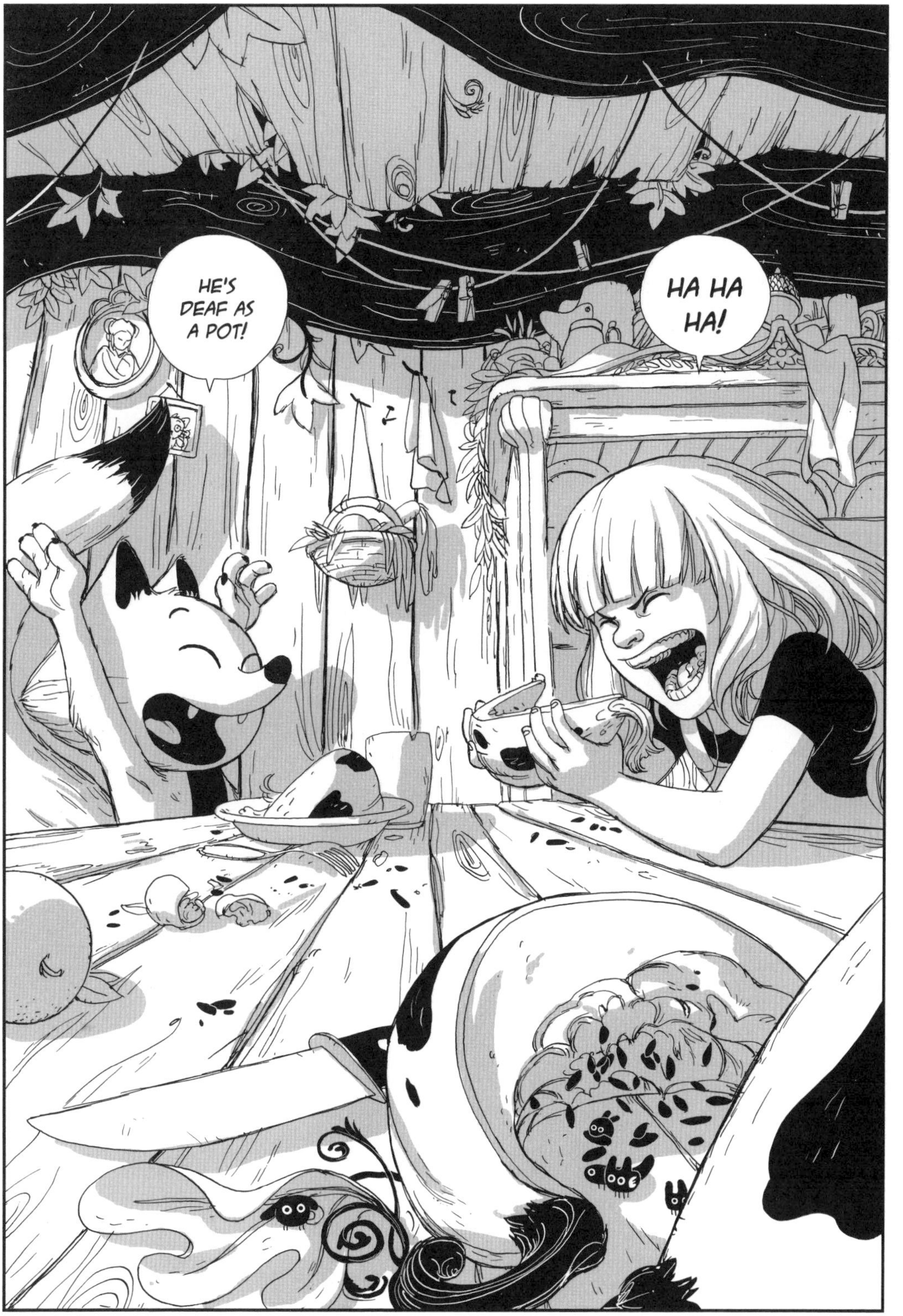
HE'S DEAF AS A POT!
HA HA HA!

Chapter 1

HERE

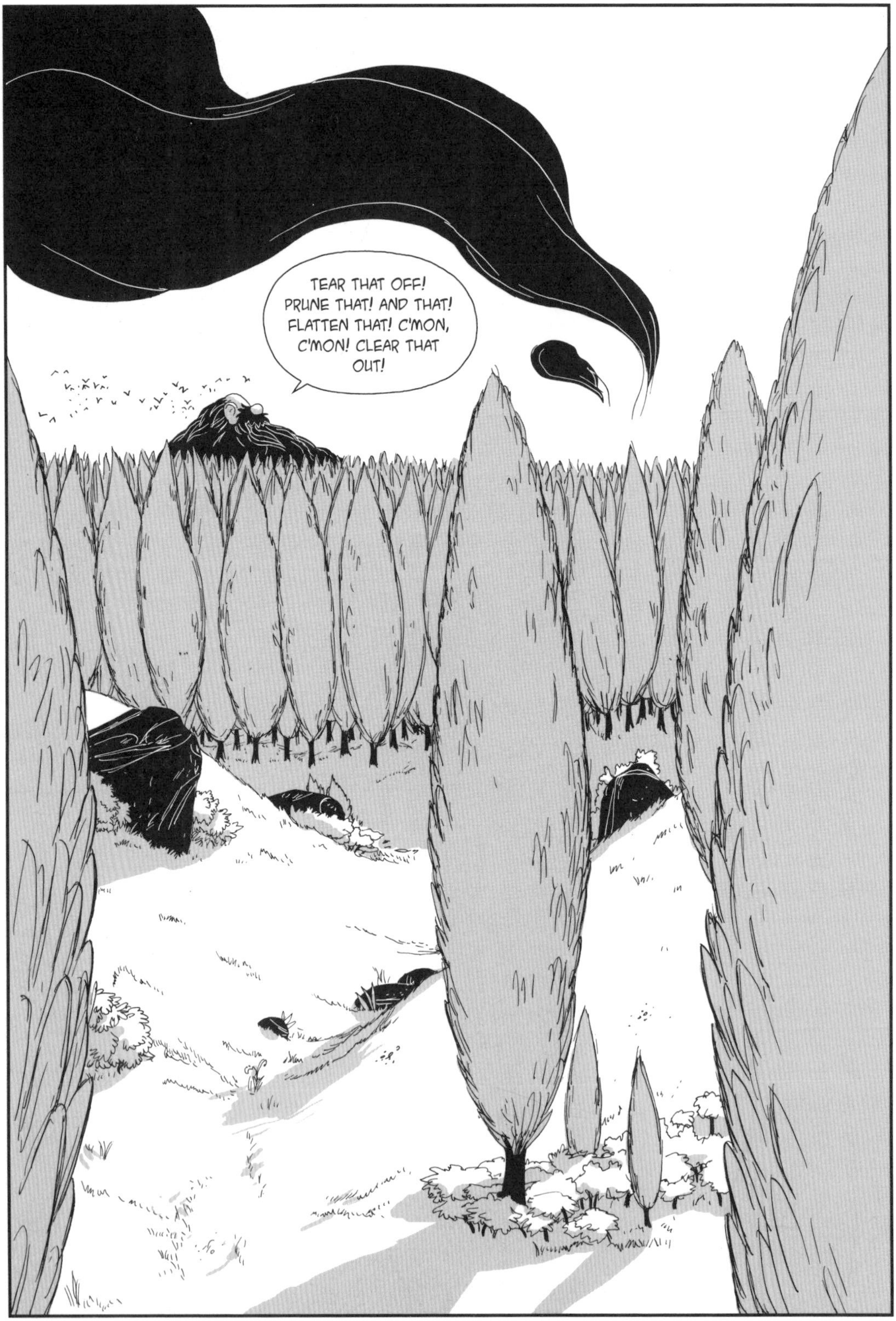
TEAR THAT OFF! PRUNE THAT! AND THAT! FLATTEN THAT! C'MON, C'MON! CLEAR THAT OUT!

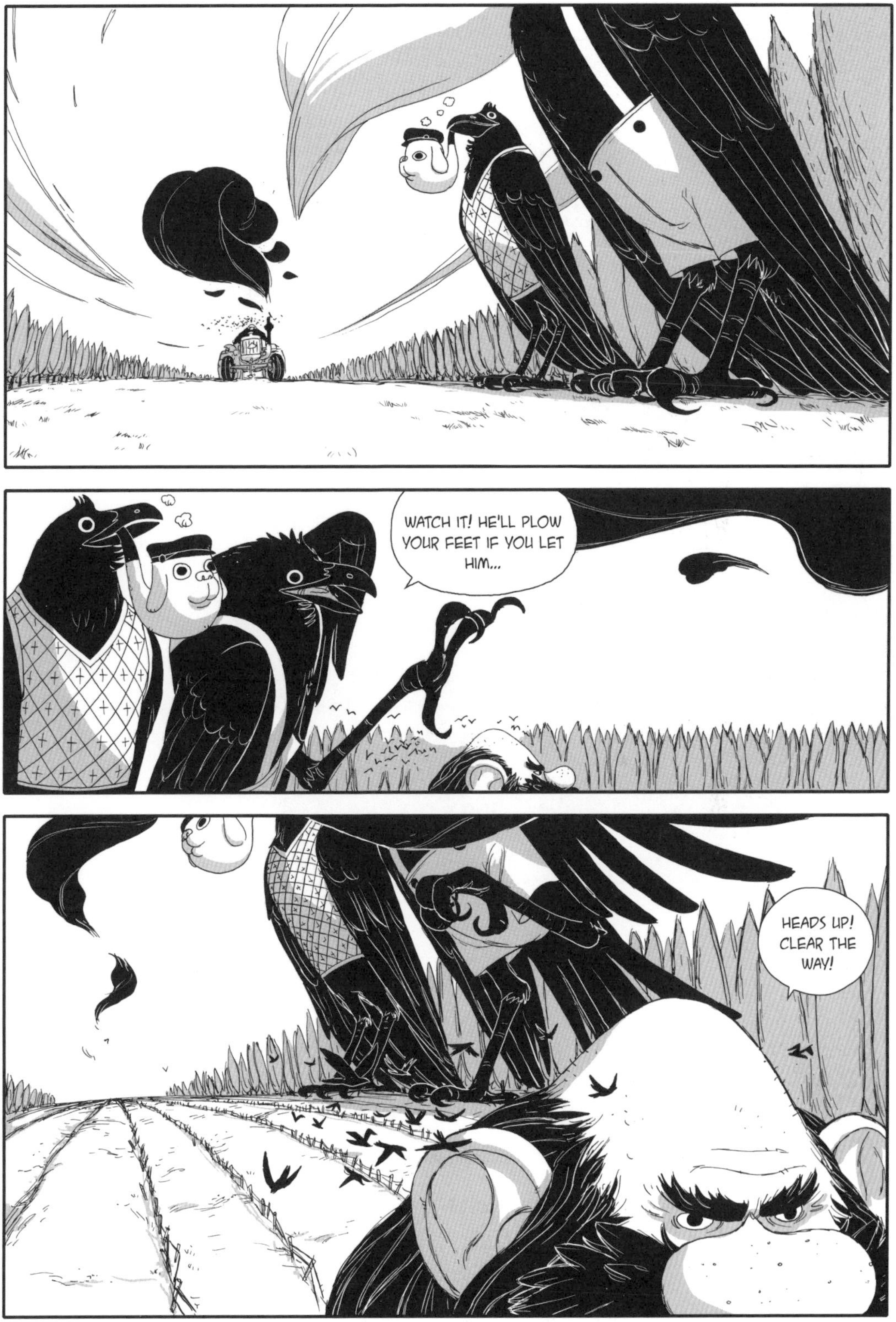
WATCH IT! HE'LL PLOW YOUR FEET IF YOU LET HIM...
HEADS UP! CLEAR THE WAY!

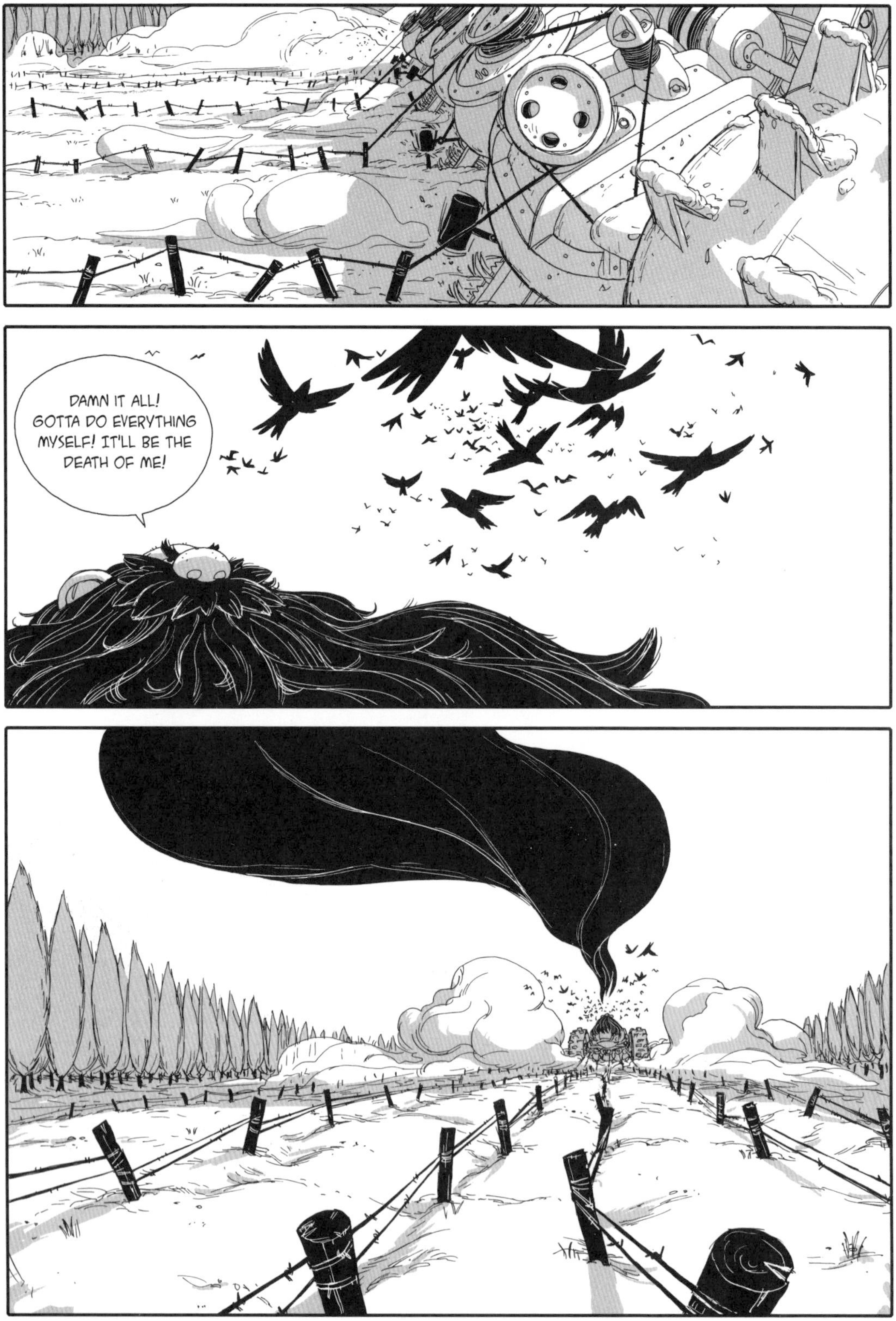
DAMN IT ALL! GOTTA DO EVERYTHING MYSELF! IT'LL BE THE DEATH OF ME!

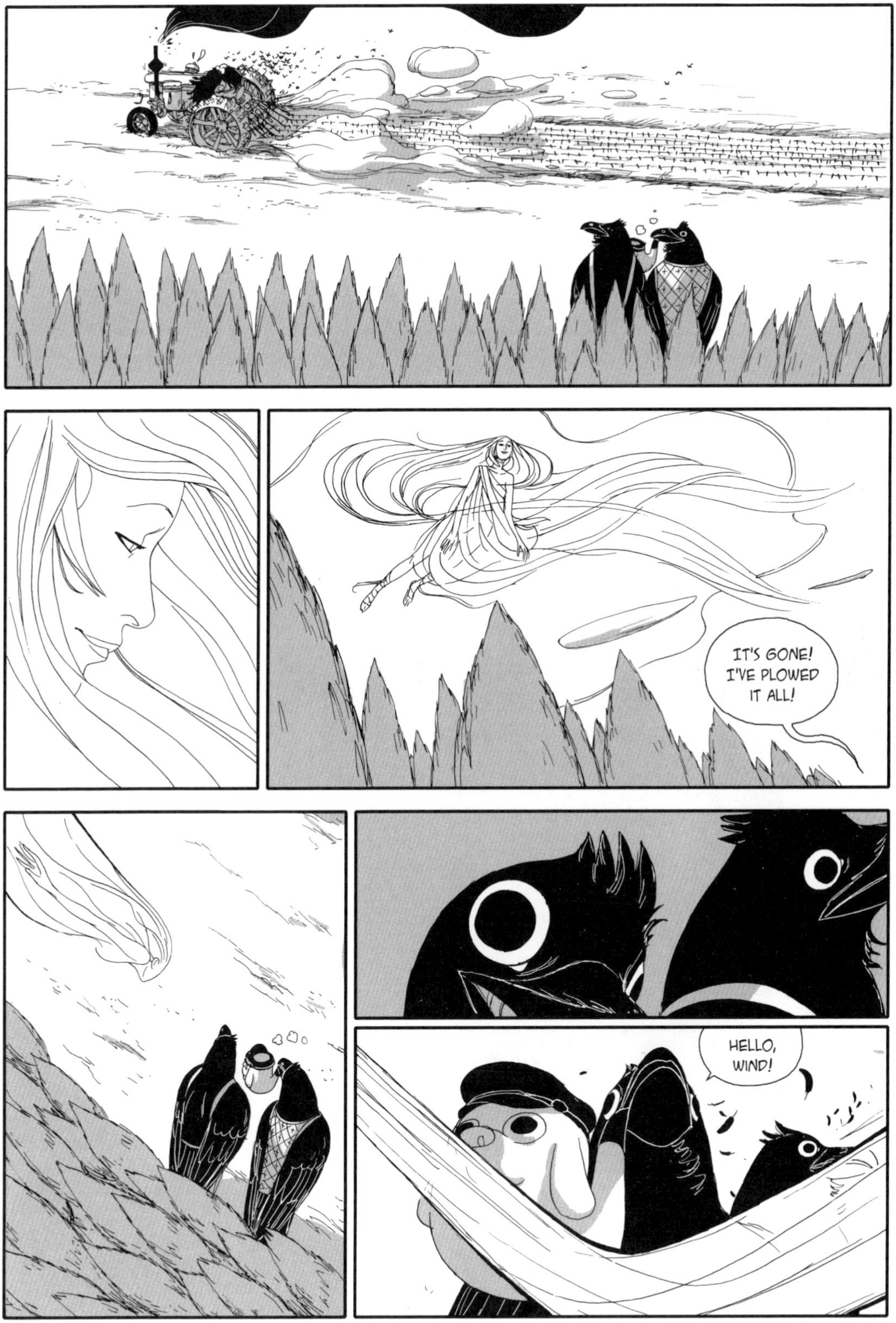
IT'S GONE! I'VE PLOWED IT ALL!
HELLO, WIND!

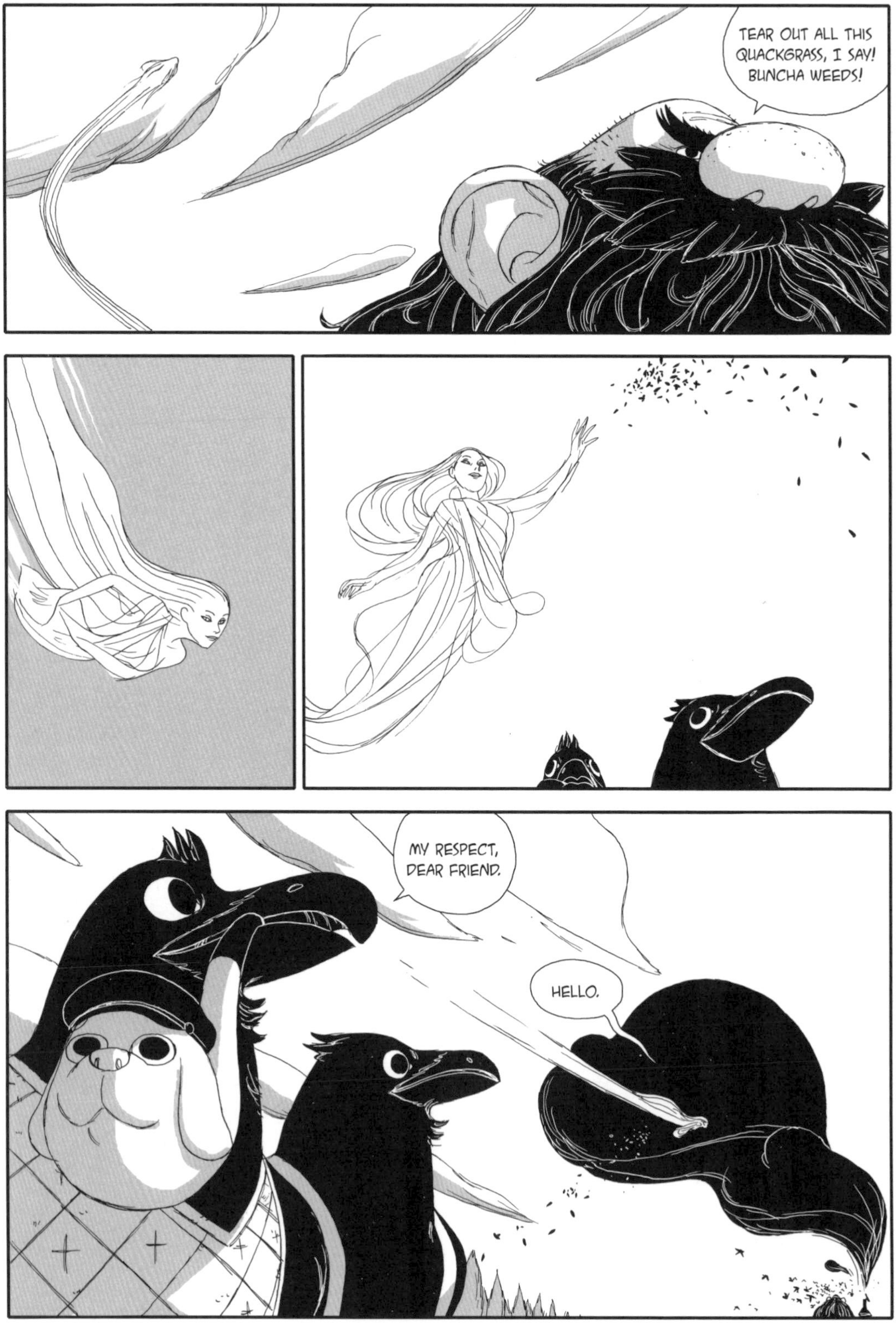
TEAR OUT ALL THIS QUACKGRASS, I SAY! BUNCHA WEEDS!
MY RESPECT, DEAR FRIEND.
HELLO.

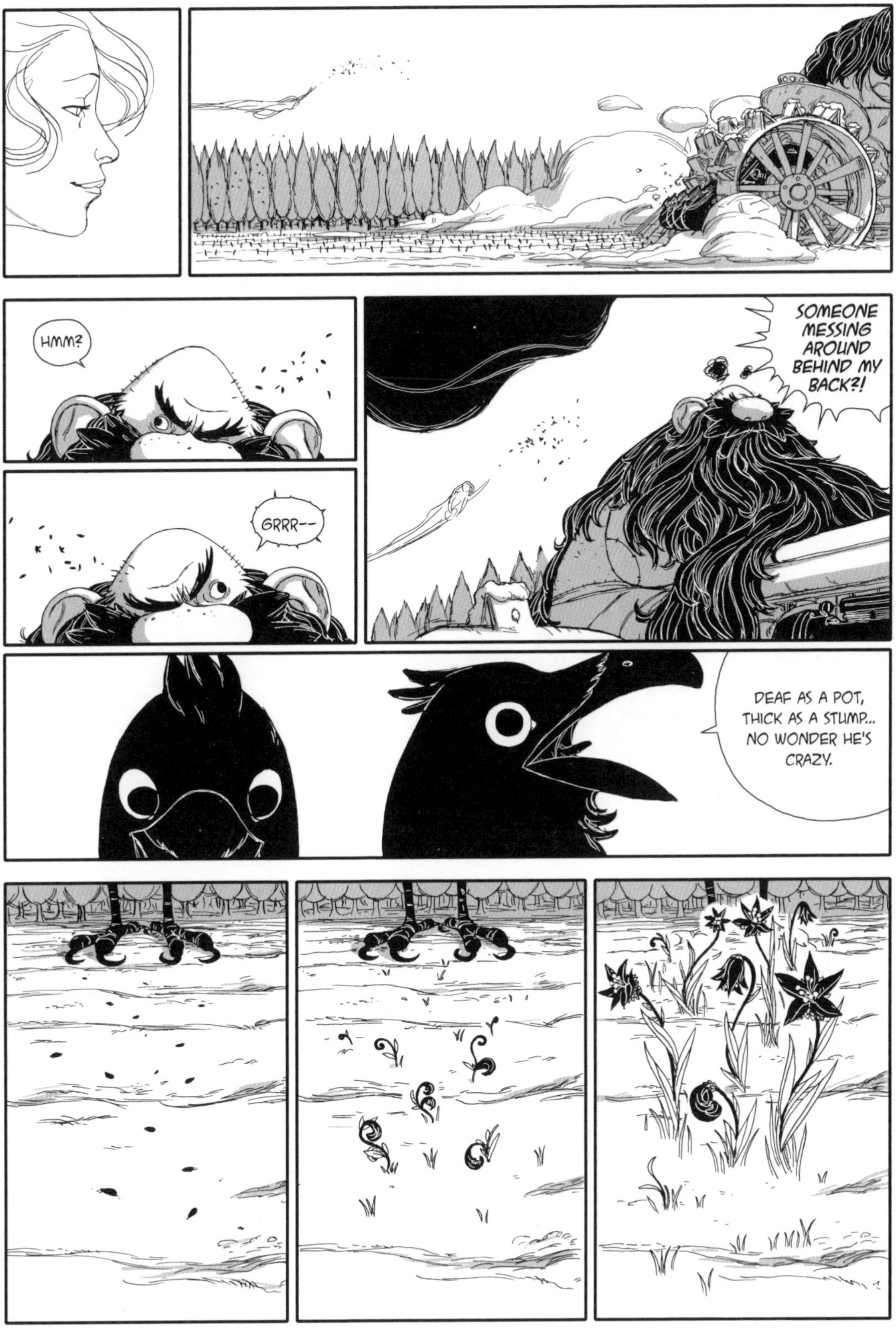
HMM?
SOMEONE MESSING AROUND BEHIND MY BACK?!
GRRR--
DEAF AS A POT, THICK AS A STUMP... NO WONDER HE'S CRAZY.

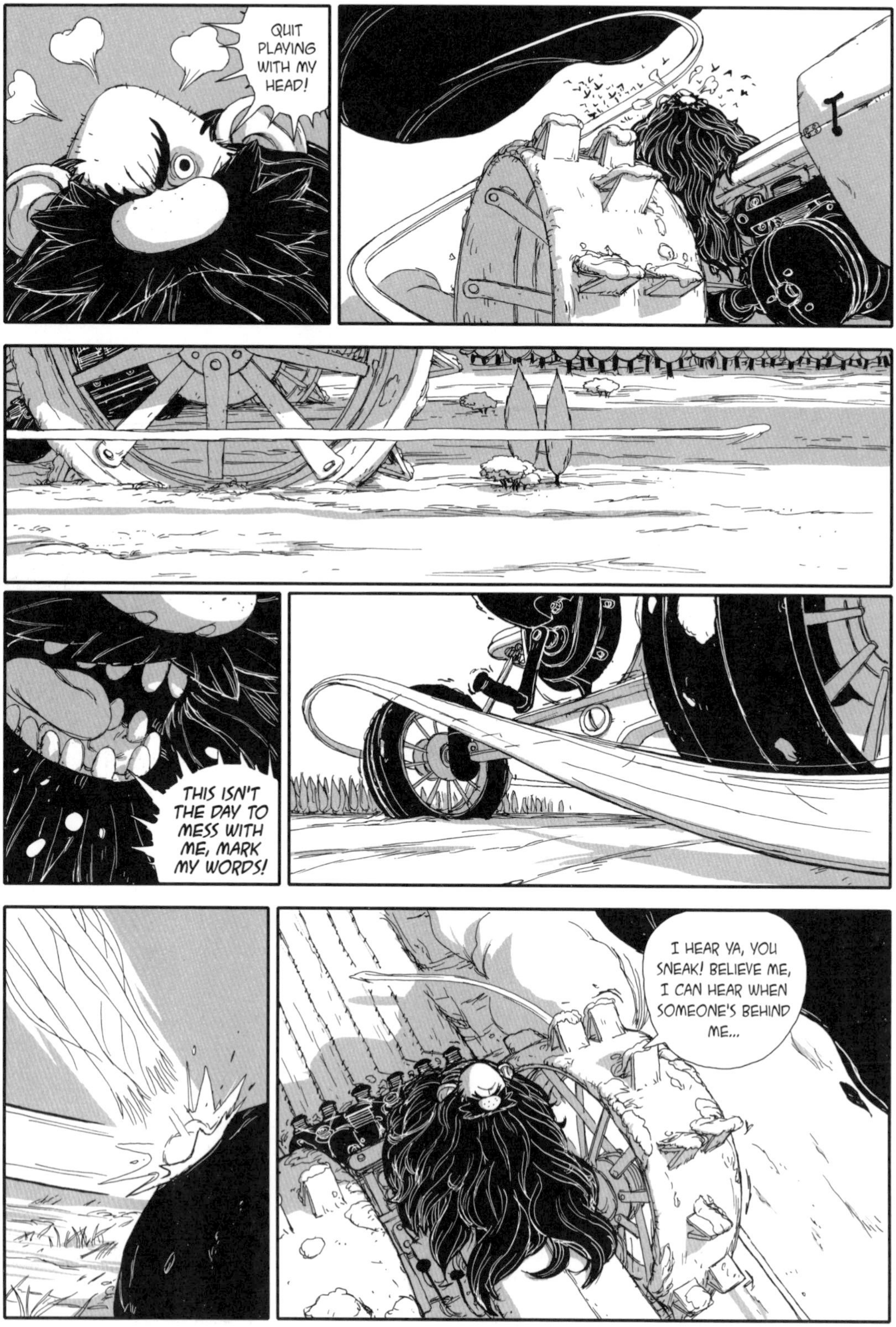
QUIT PLAYING WITH MY HEAD!
THIS ISN'T THE DAY TO MESS WITH ME, MARK MY WORDS!
I HEAR YA, YOU SNEAK! BELIEVE ME, I CAN HEAR WHEN SOMEONE'S BEHIND ME...

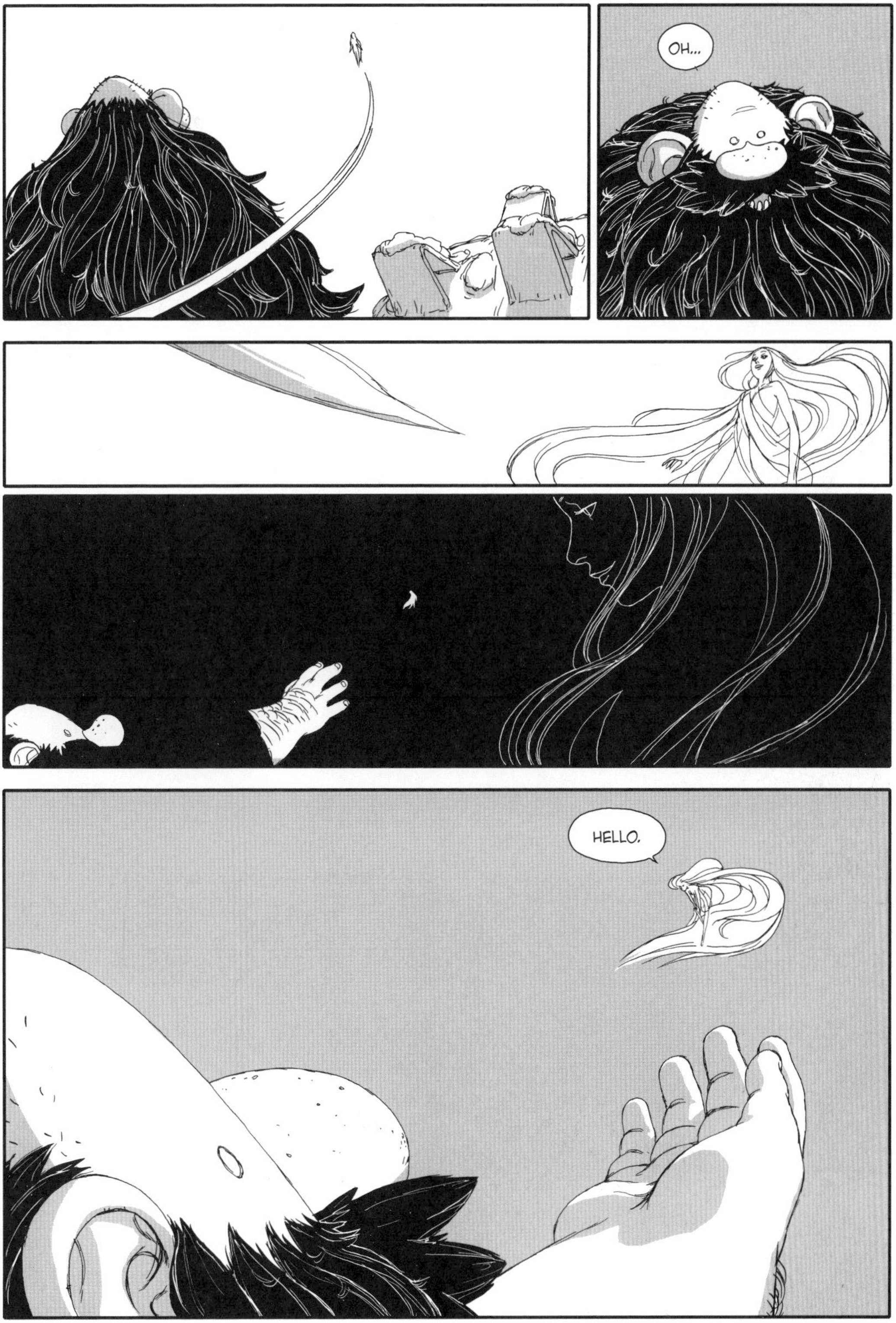
OH...
HELLO.

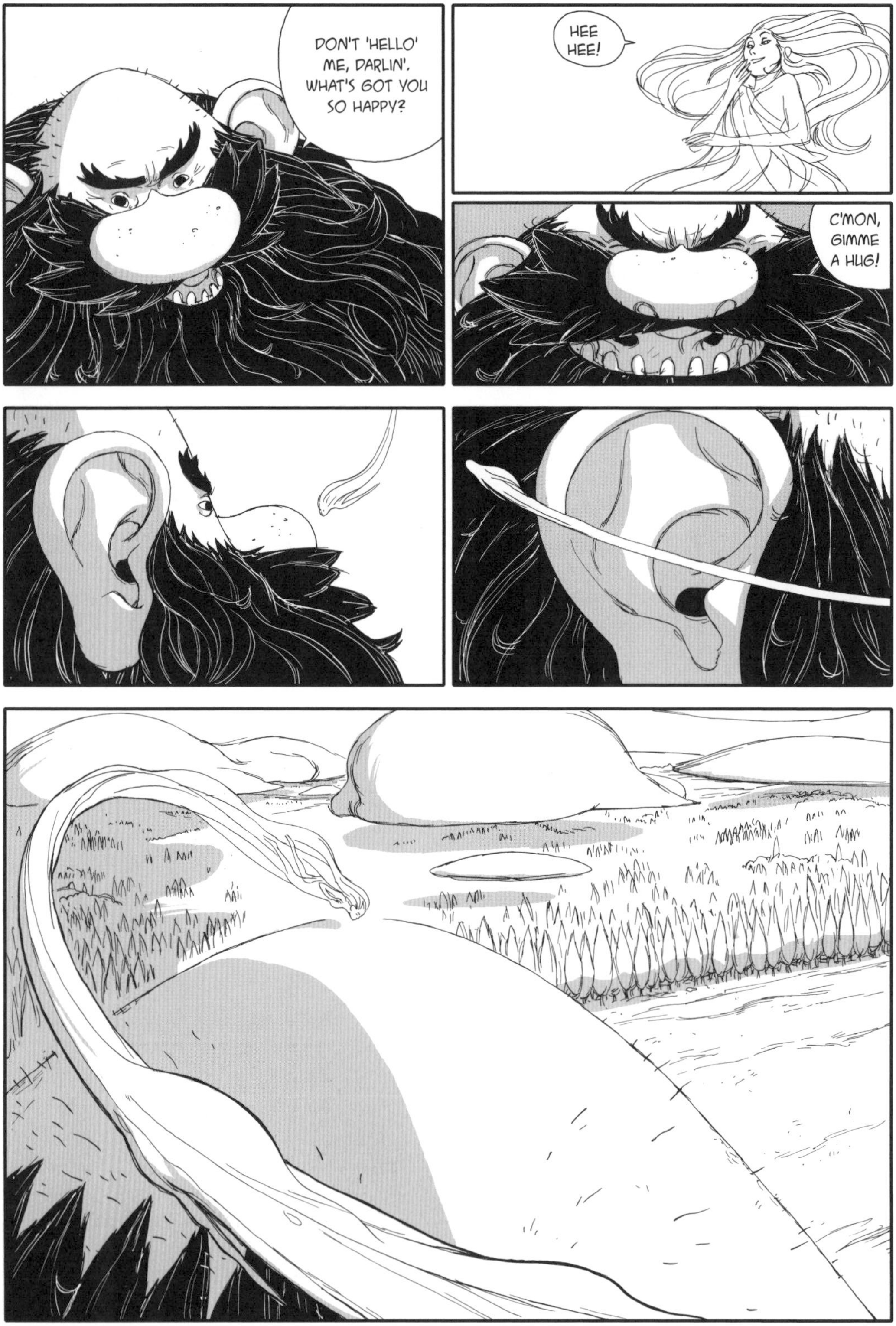
DON'T 'HELLO' ME, DARLIN'. WHAT'S GOT YOU SO HAPPY?
HEE HEE!
C'MON, GIMME A HUG!

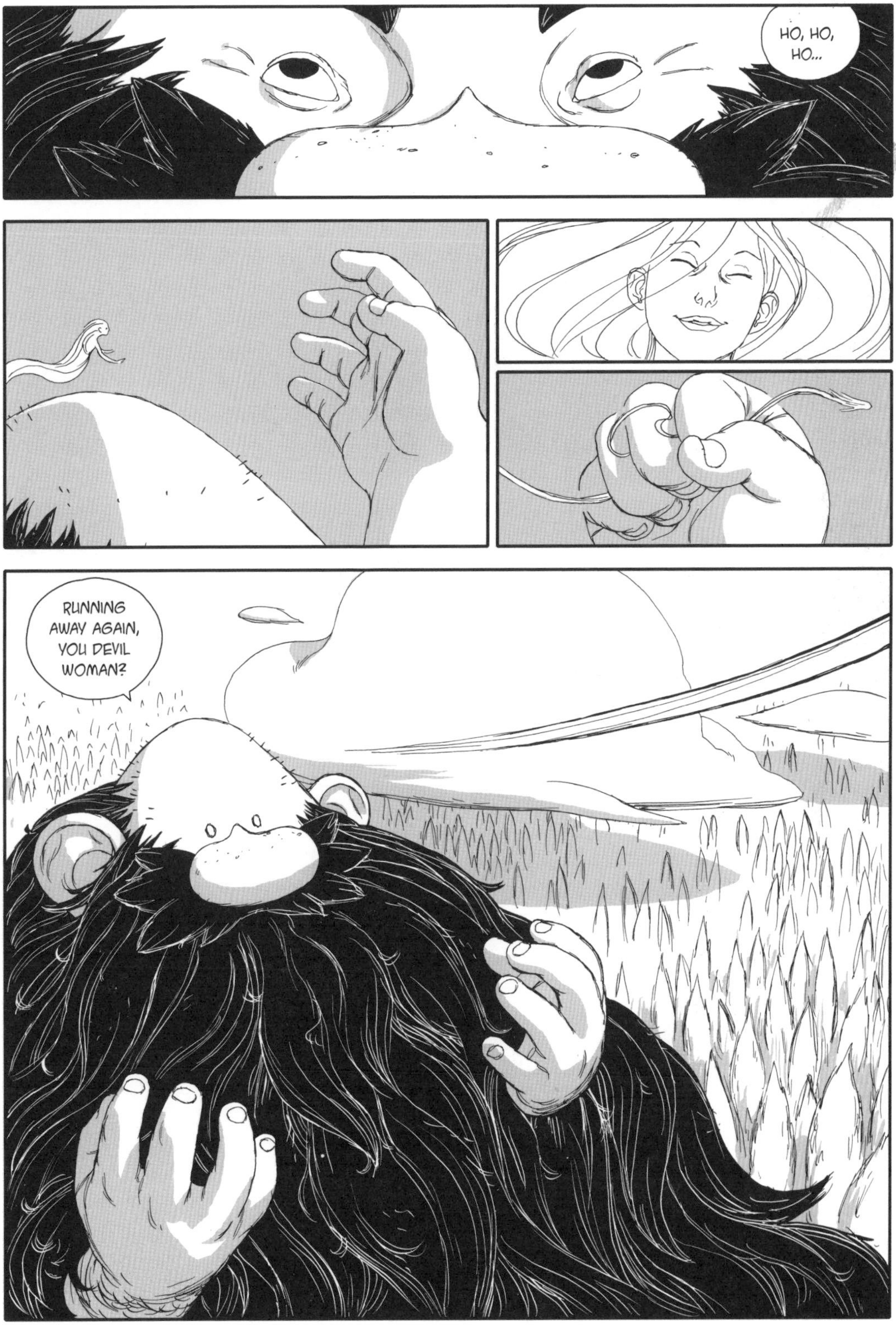
HO, HO, HO...
RUNNING AWAY AGAIN, YOU DEVIL WOMAN?

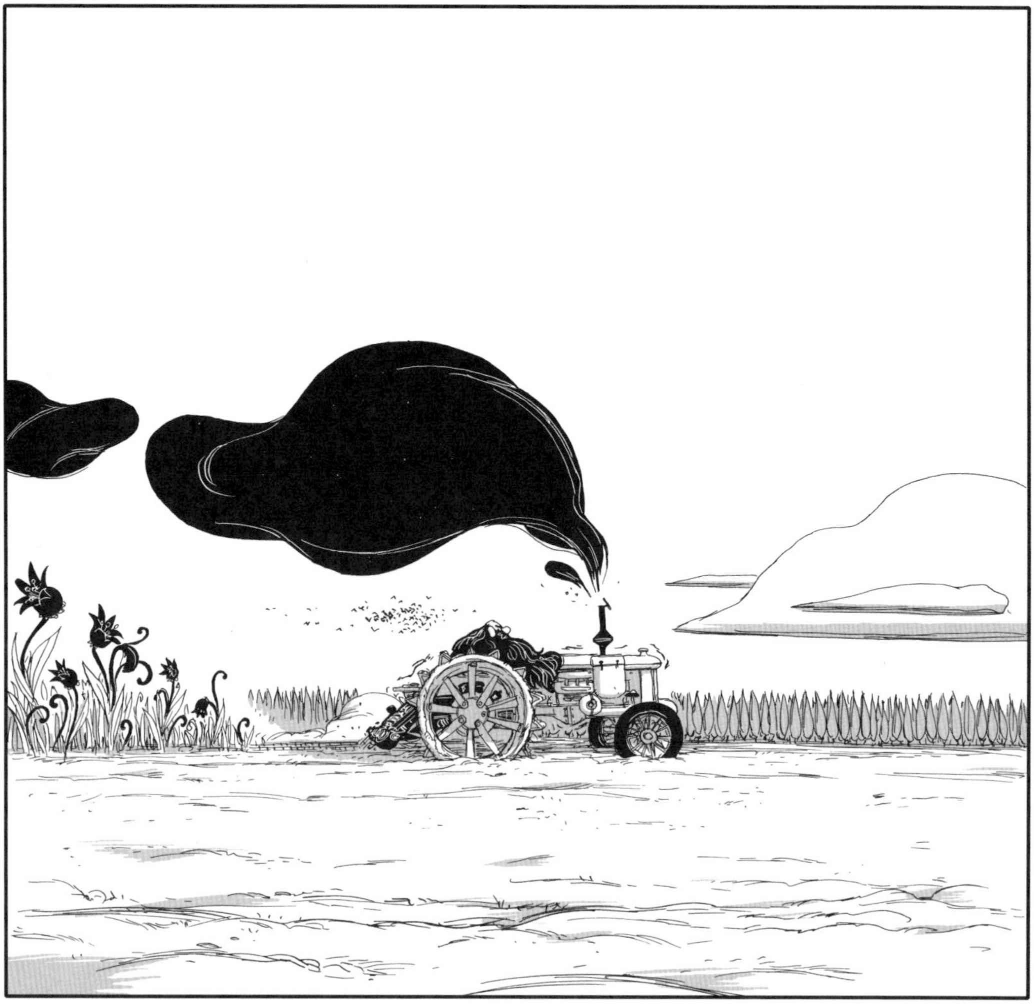

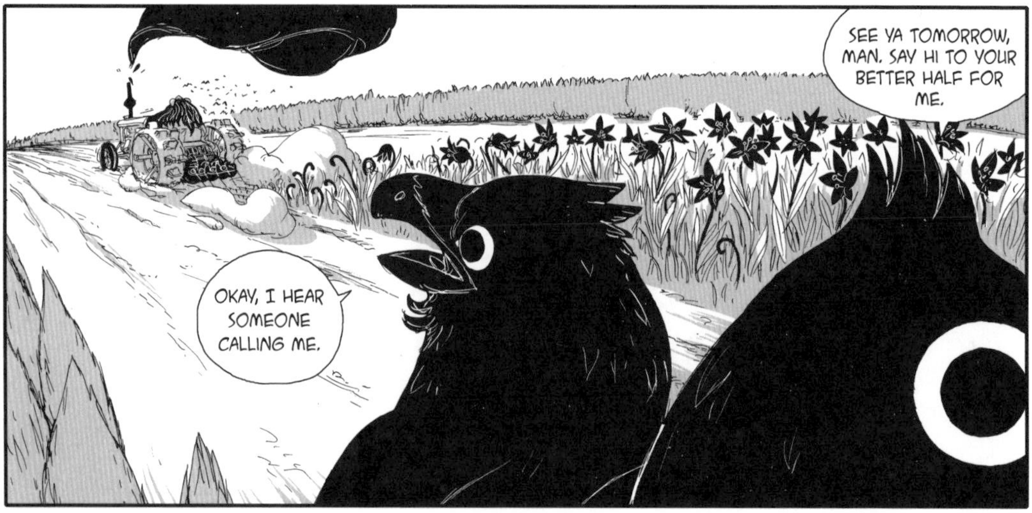

SEE YA TOMORROW, MAN. SAY HI TO YOUR BETTER HALF FOR ME.
OKAY, I HEAR SOMEONE CALLING ME.

Chapter 2

US

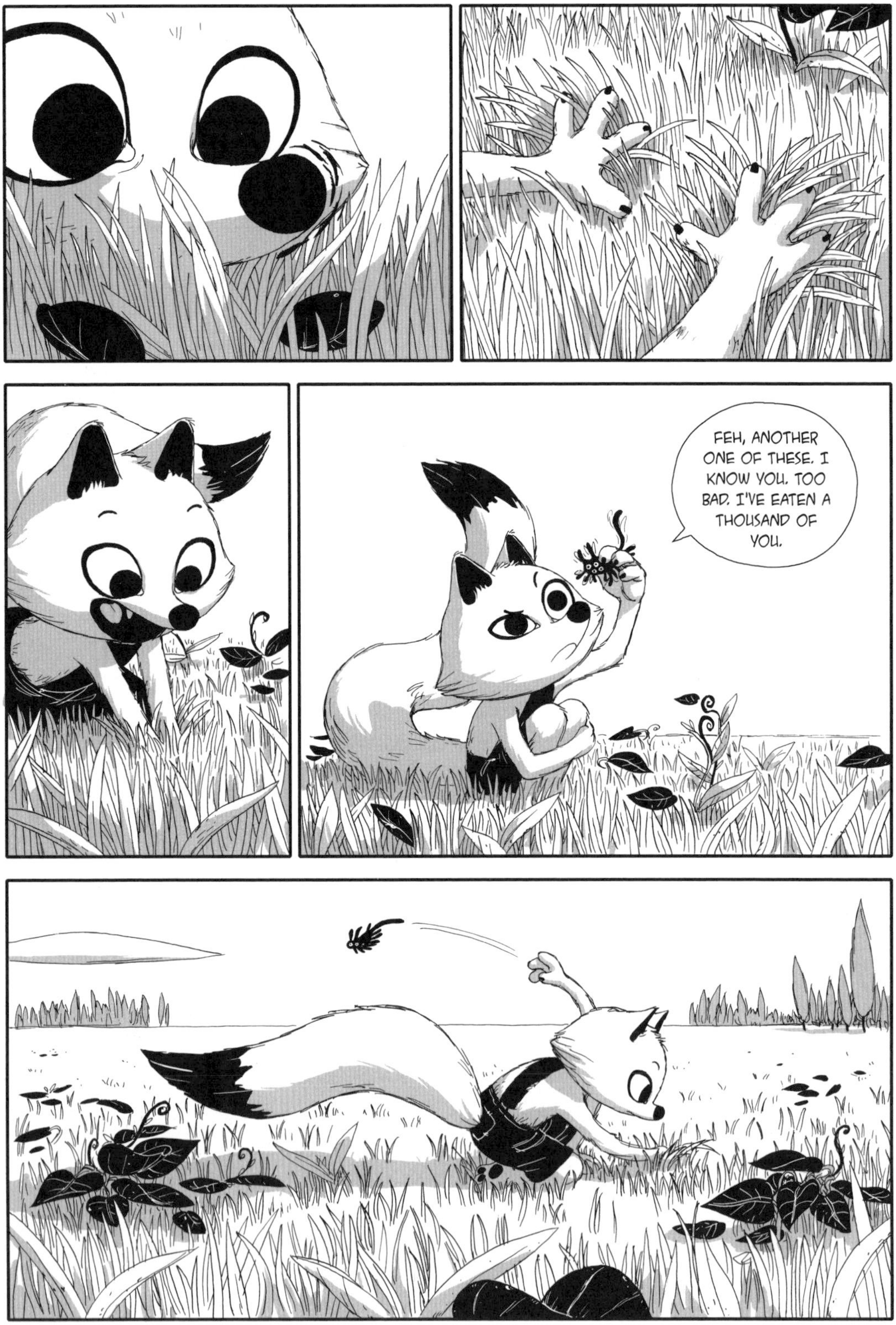
FEH, ANOTHER ONE OF THESE. I KNOW YOU. TOO BAD. I'VE EATEN A THOUSAND OF YOU.

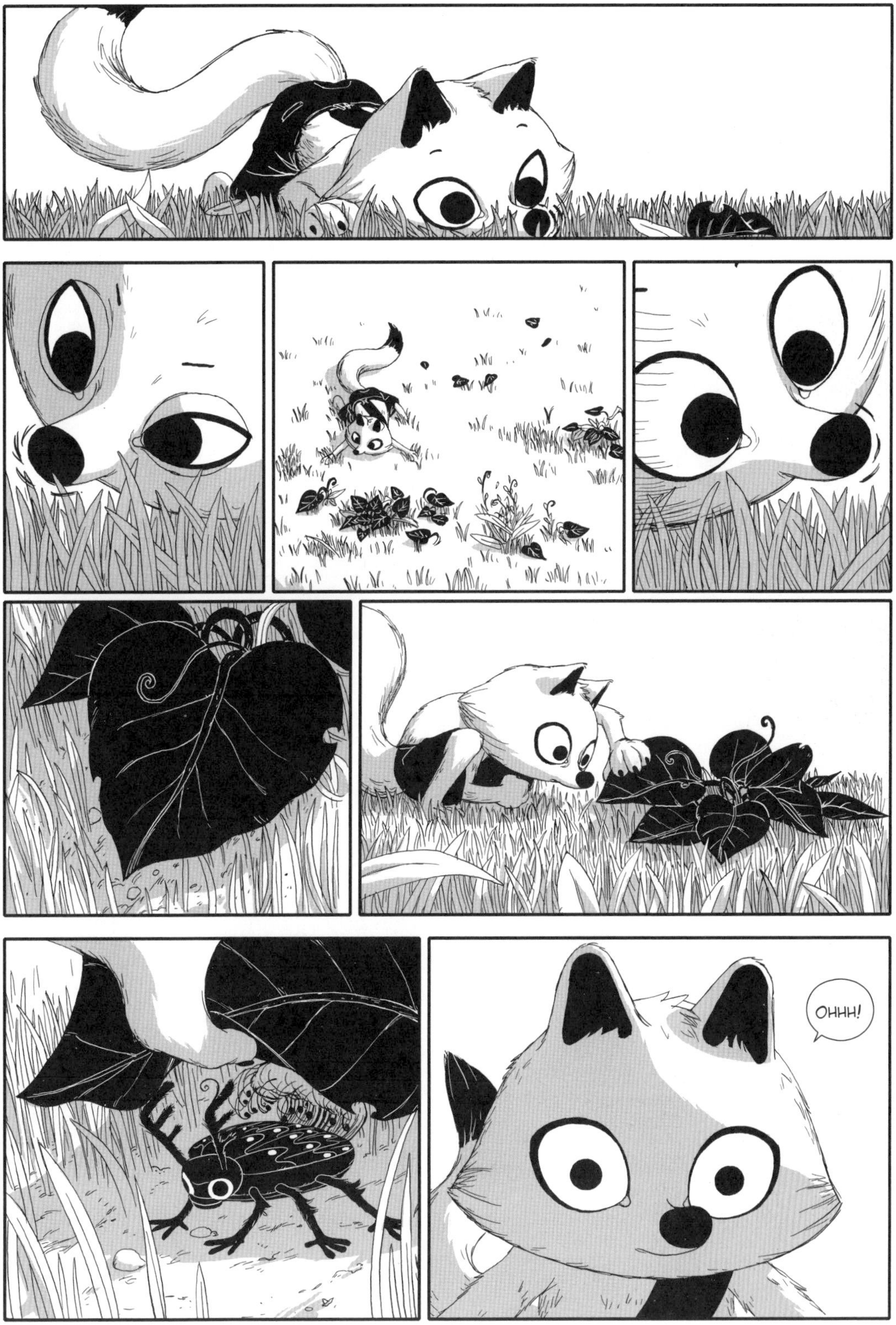
OHHH!

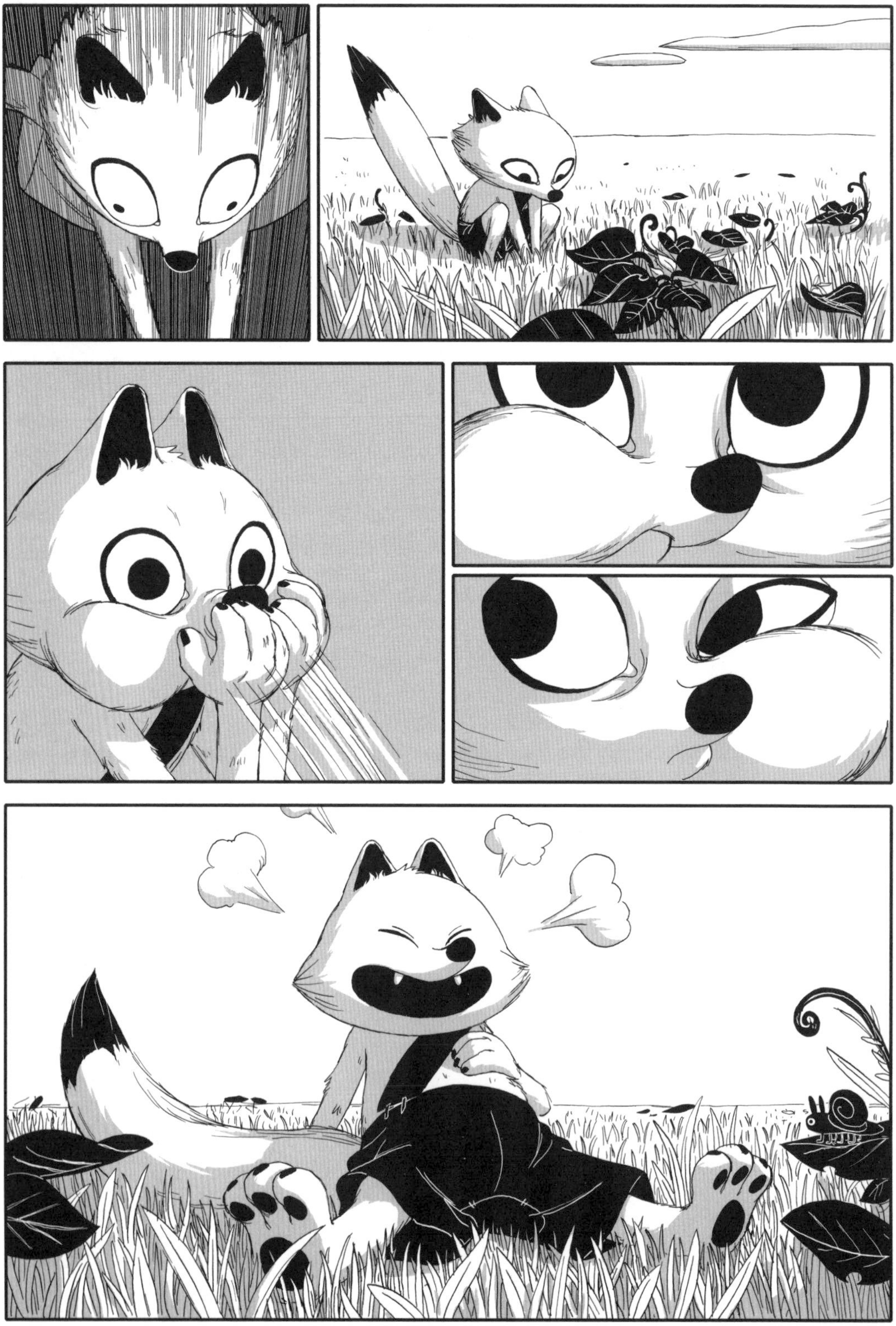

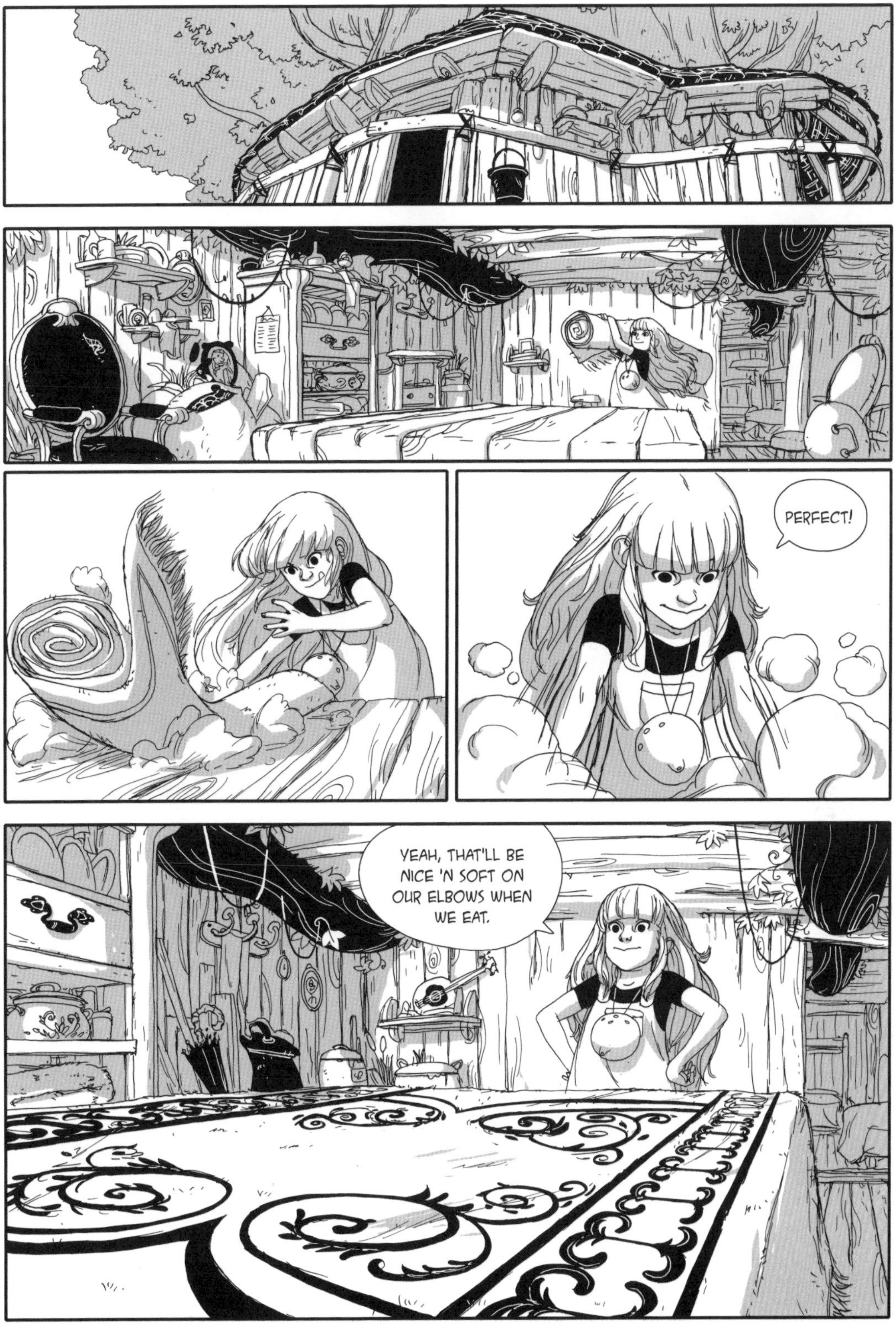

PERFECT!
YEAH, THAT'LL BE NICE 'N SOFT ON OUR ELBOWS WHEN WE EAT.

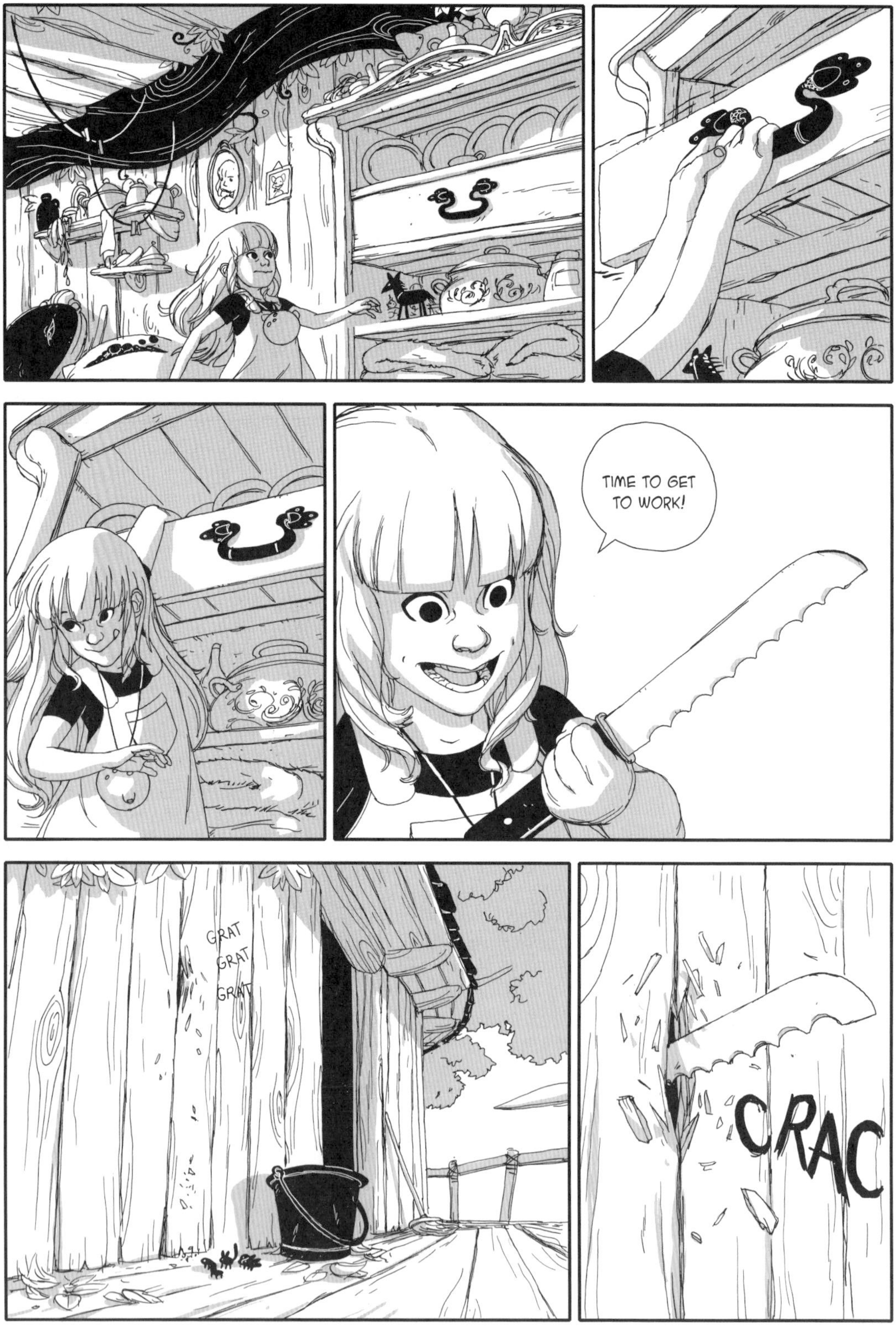
TIME TO GET TO WORK!
GRAT
GRAT
GRAT
CRAC

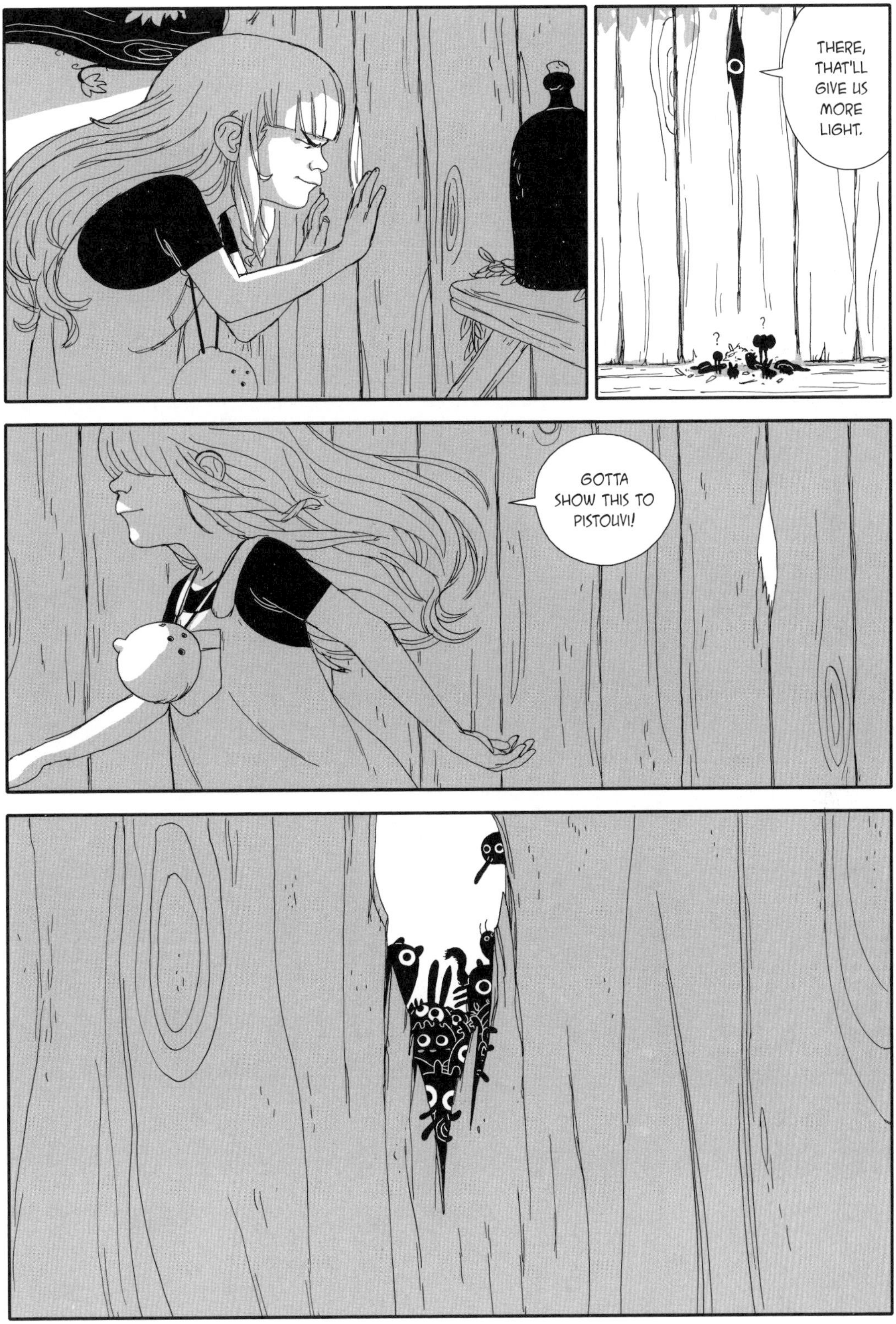
THERE, THAT'LL GIVE US MORE LIGHT.
?
?
GOTTA SHOW THIS TO PISTOUVI!

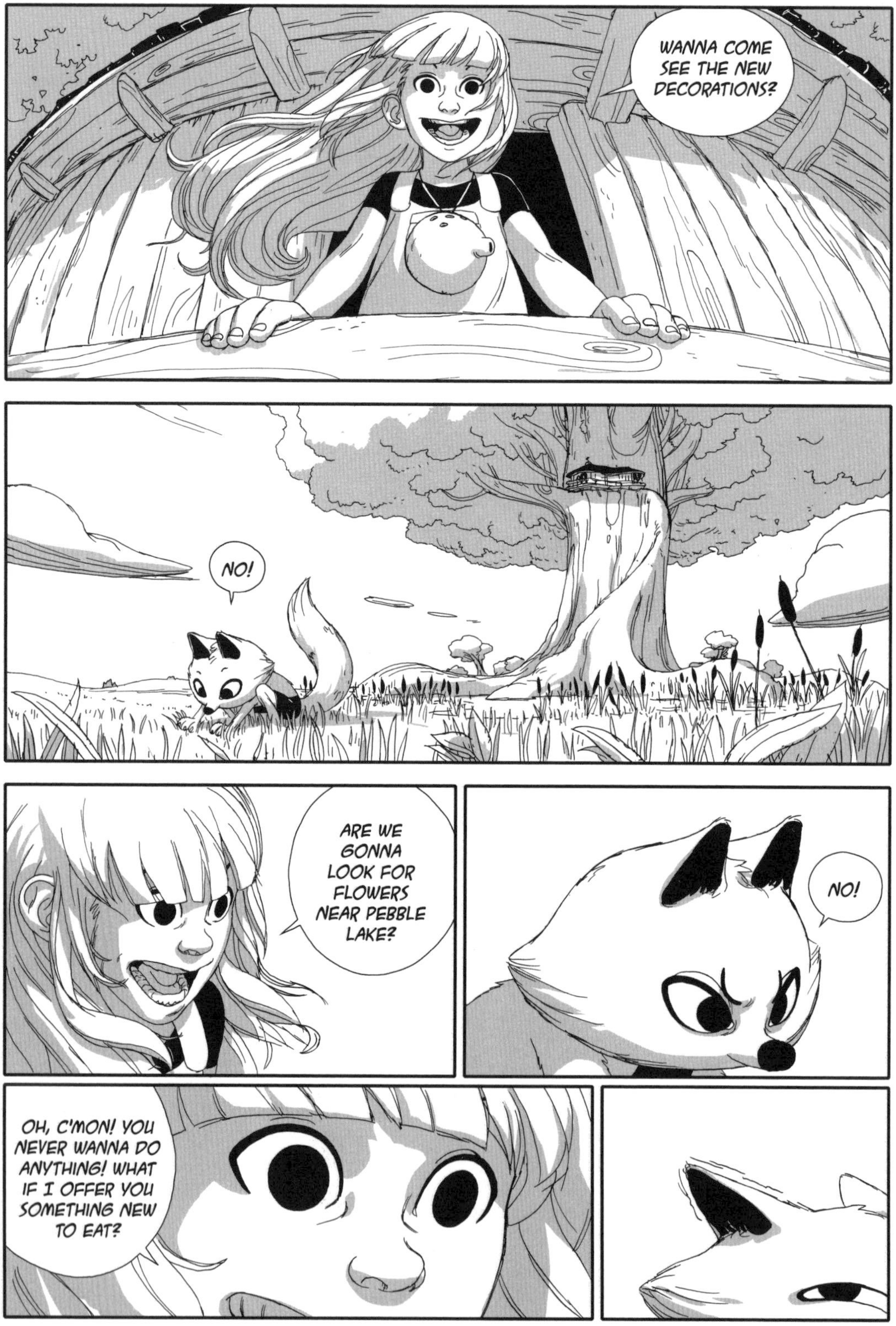

WANNA COME SEE THE NEW DECORATIONS?
NO!
ARE WE GONNA LOOK FOR FLOWERS NEAR PEBBLE LAKE?
NO!
OH, C'MON! YOU NEVER WANNA DO ANYTHING! WHAT IF I OFFER YOU SOMETHING NEW TO EAT?

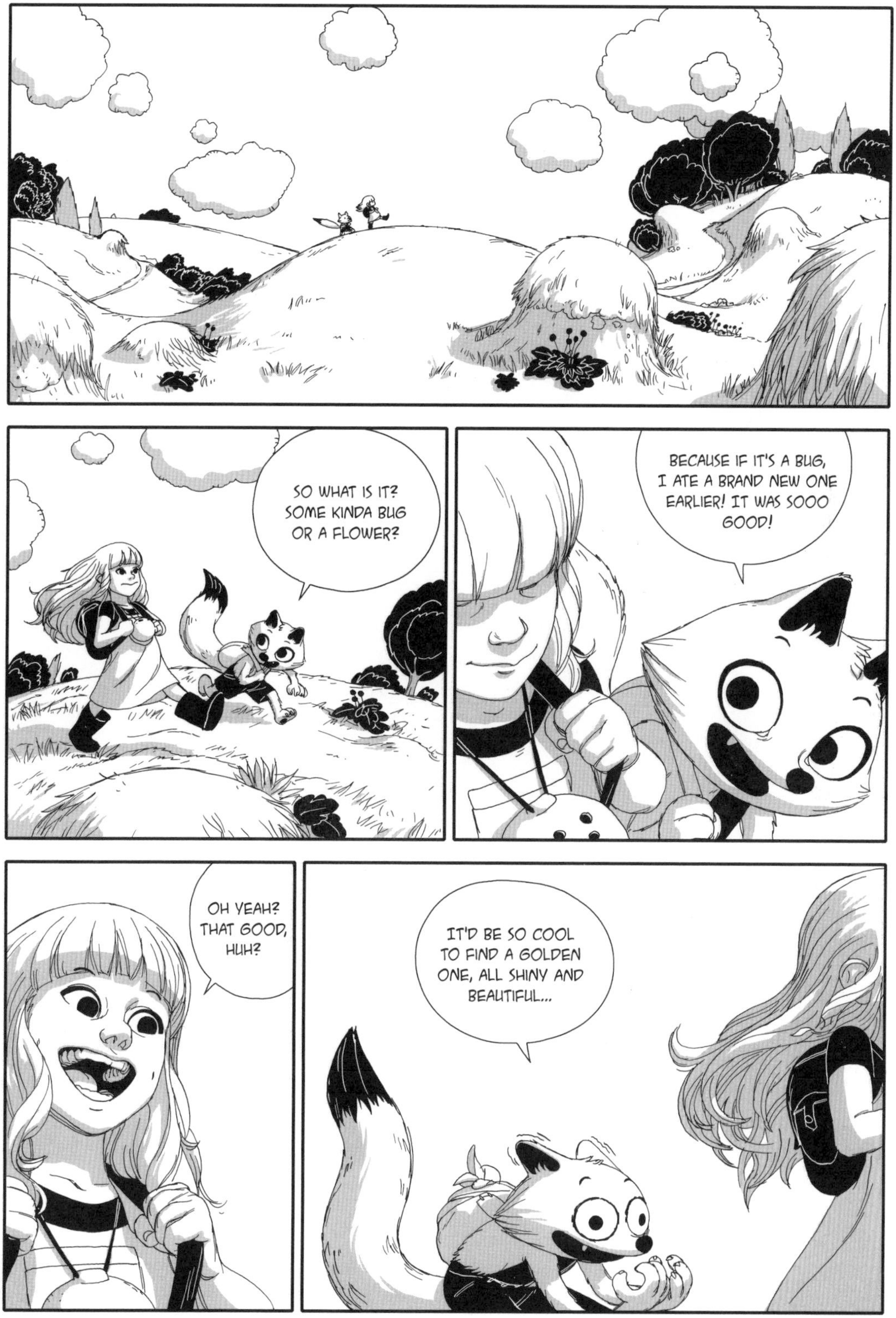
SO WHAT IS IT? SOME KINDA BUG OR A FLOWER?
BECAUSE IF IT'S A BUG, I ATE A BRAND NEW ONE EARLIER! IT WAS SOOO GOOD!
OH YEAH? THAT GOOD, HUH?
IT'D BE SO COOL TO FIND A GOLDEN ONE, ALL SHINY AND BEAUTIFUL...

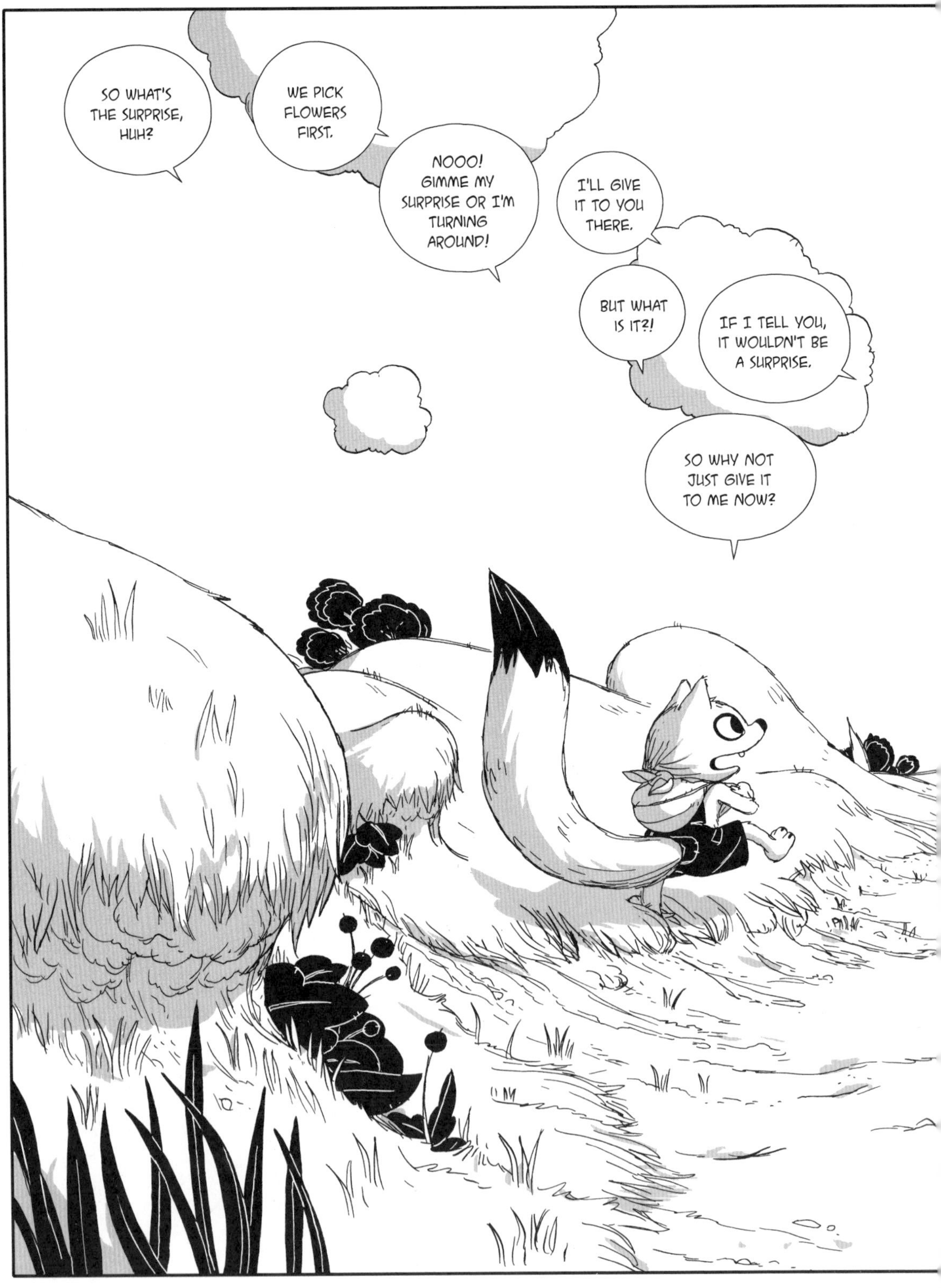
SO WHAT'S THE SURPRISE, HUH?
WE PICK FLOWERS FIRST.
NOOO! GIMME MY SURPRISE OR I'M TURNING AROUND!
I'LL GIVE IT TO YOU THERE.
BUT WHAT IS IT?!
IF I TELL YOU, IT WOULDN'T BE A SURPRISE.
SO WHY NOT JUST GIVE IT TO ME NOW?

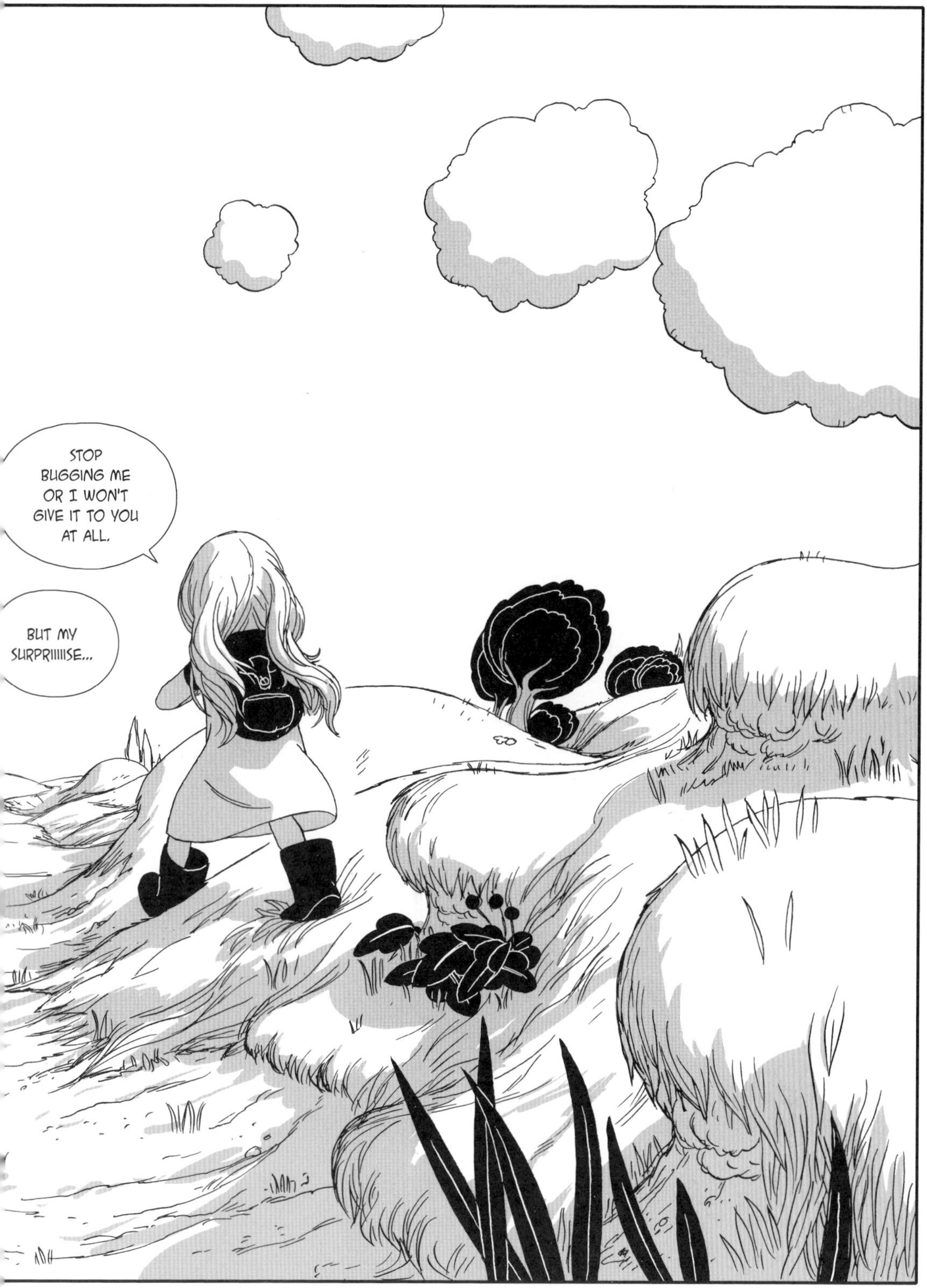
STOP BUGGING ME OR I WON'T GIVE IT TO YOU AT ALL.
BUT MY SURPRIIIIISE...

Chapter 3

THEM

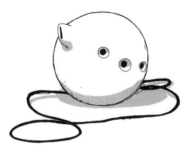

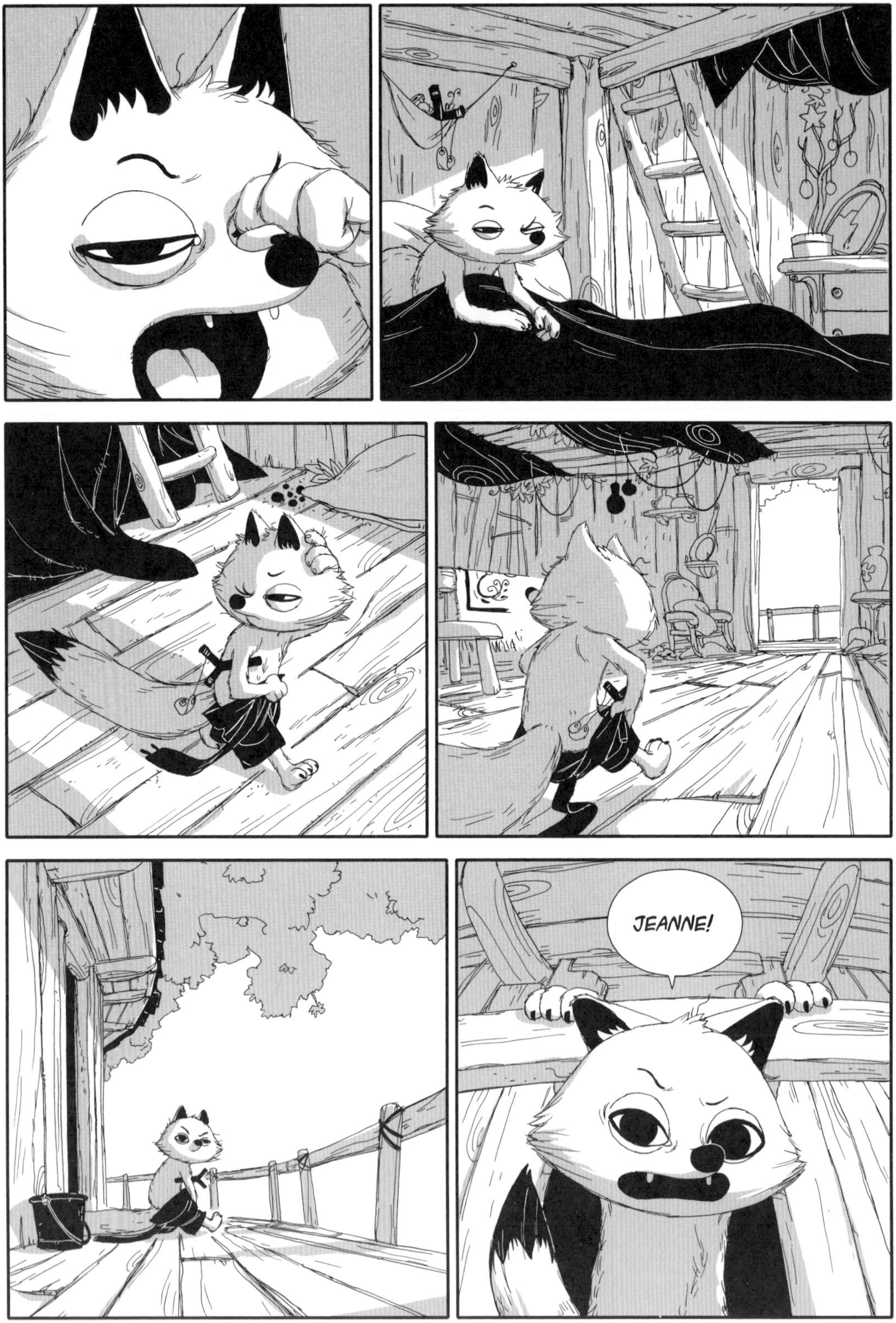
JEANNE!

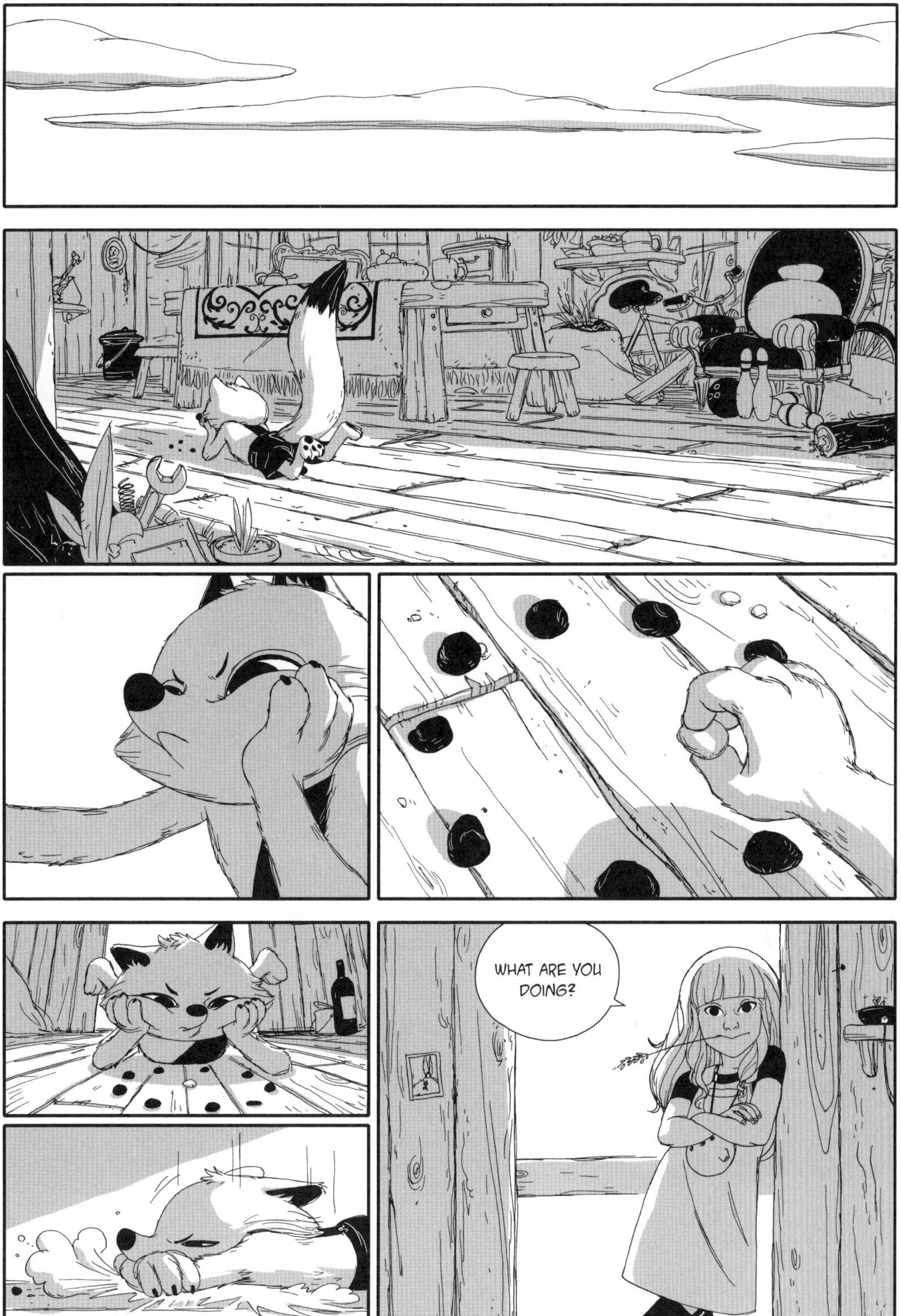
WHAT ARE YOU DOING?

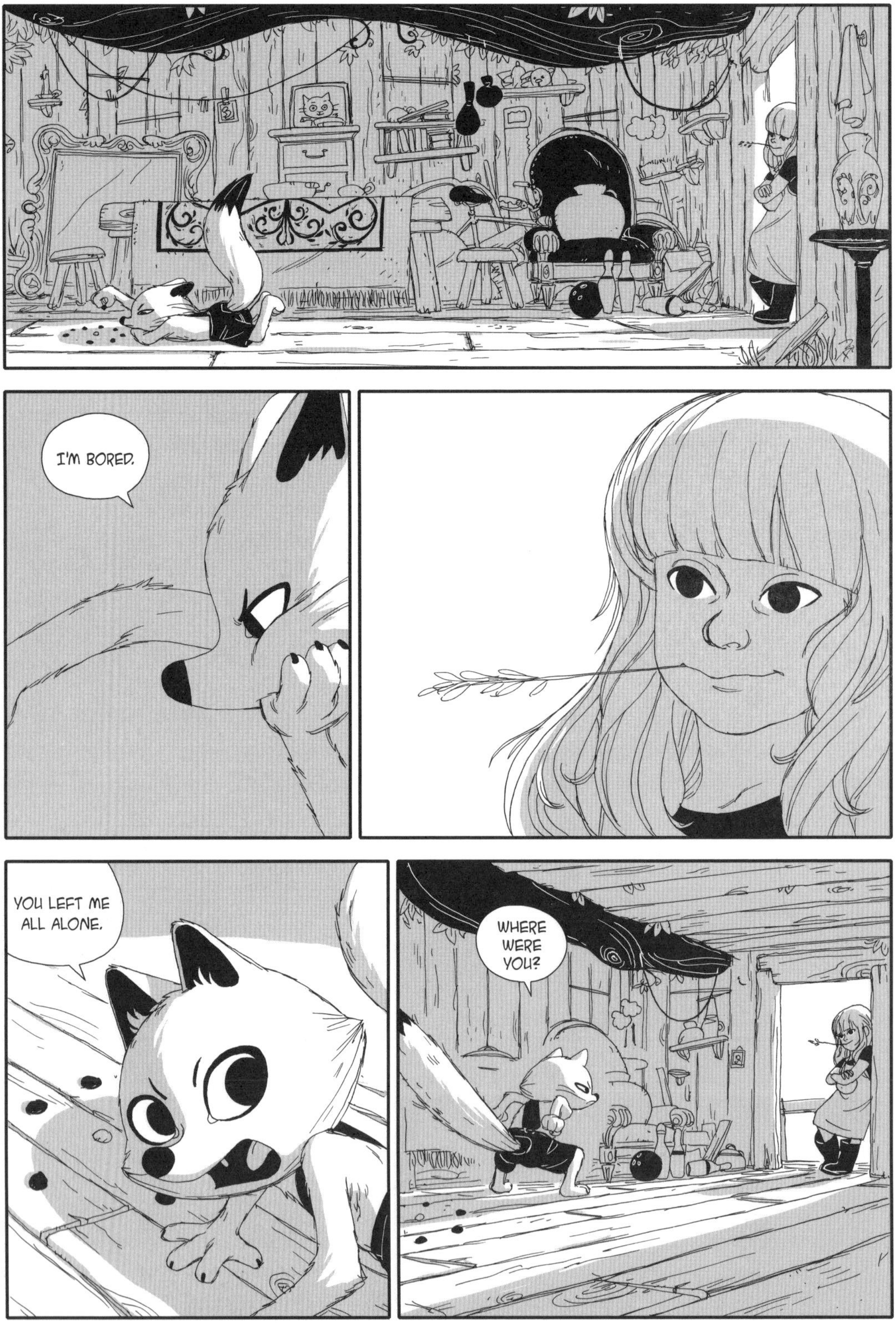
I'M BORED.
YOU LEFT ME ALL ALONE.
WHERE WERE YOU?

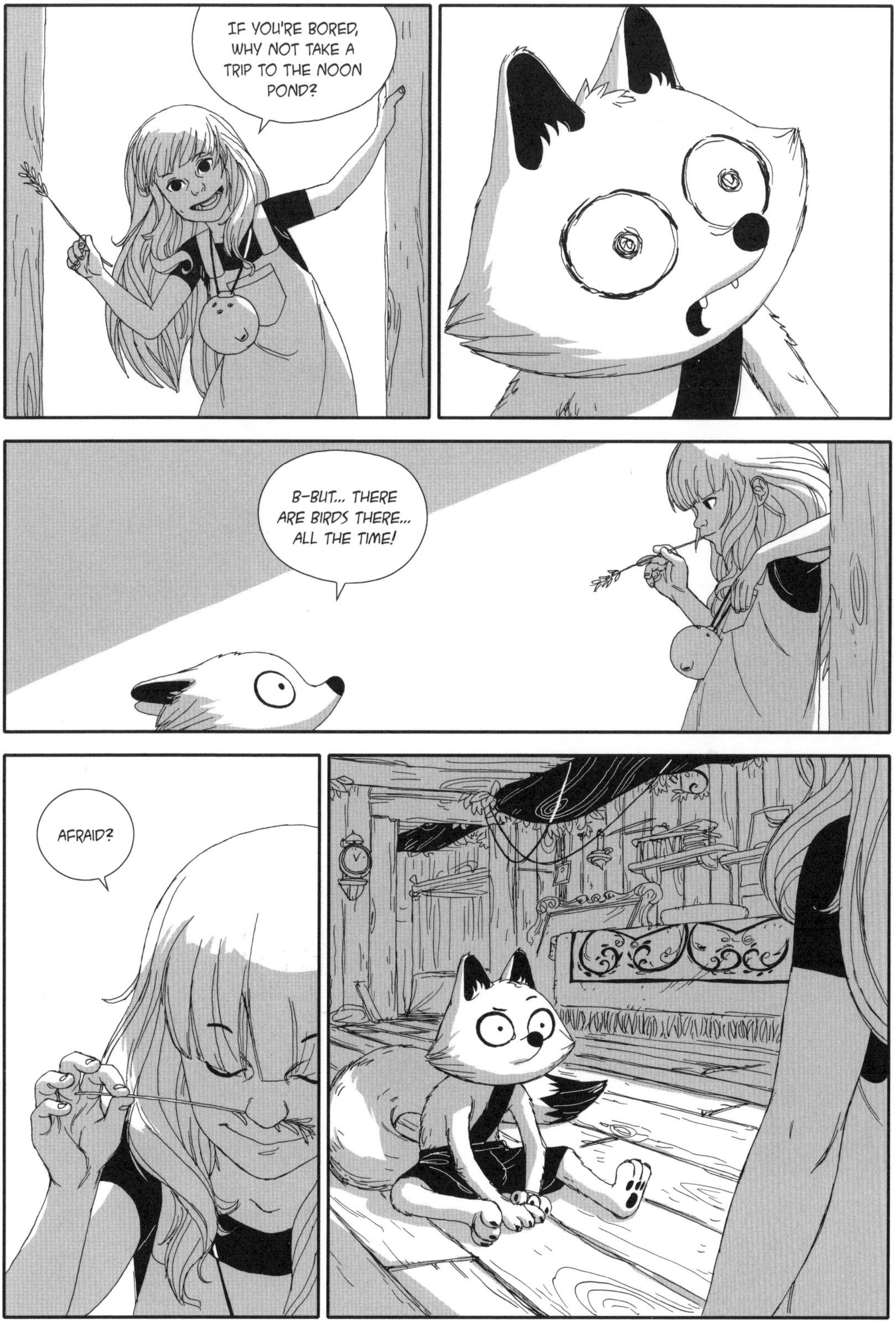
IF YOU'RE BORED, WHY NOT TAKE A TRIP TO THE NOON POND?
B-BUT... THERE ARE BIRDS THERE... ALL THE TIME!
AFRAID?

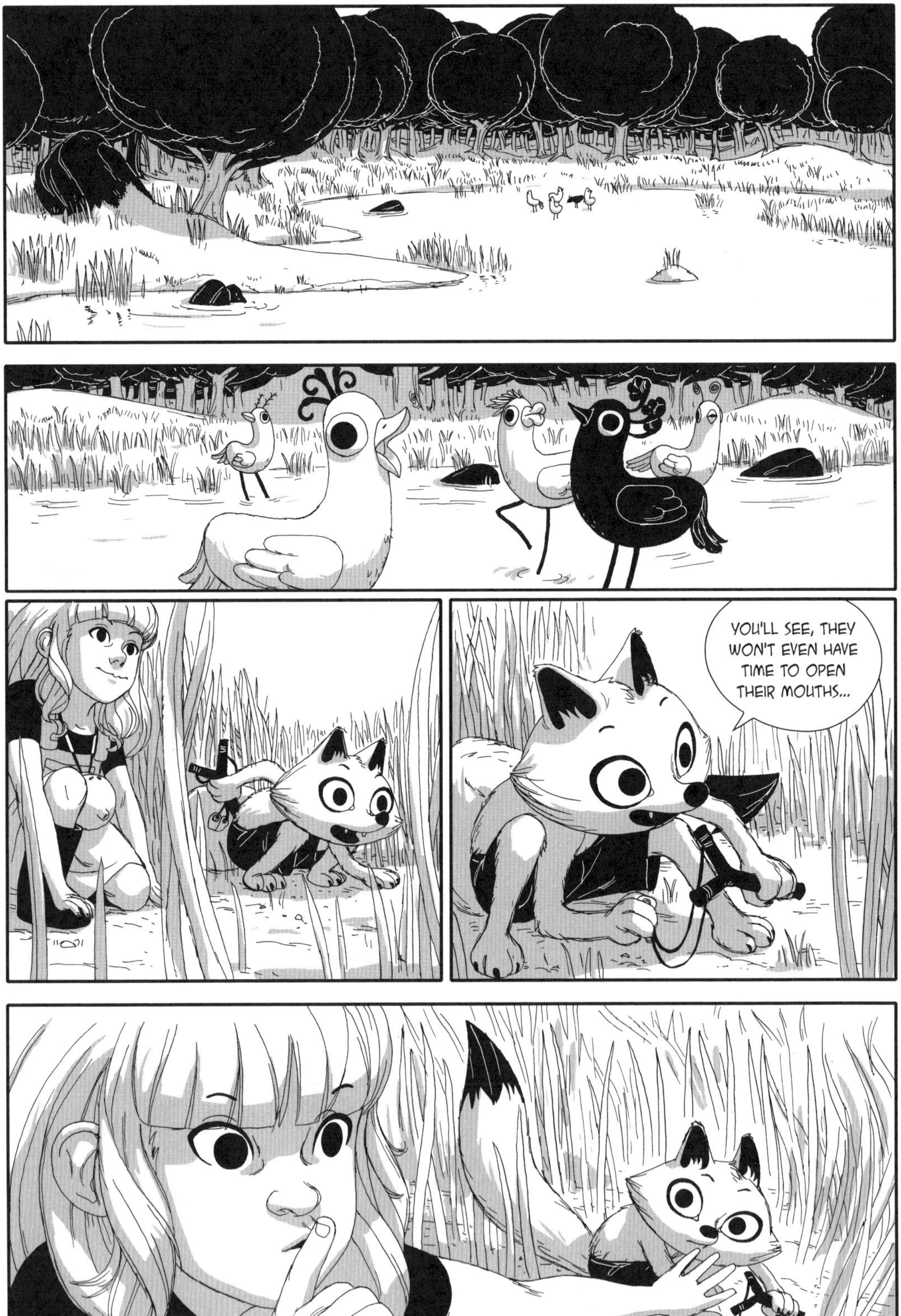
YOU'LL SEE, THEY WON'T EVEN HAVE TIME TO OPEN THEIR MOUTHS...

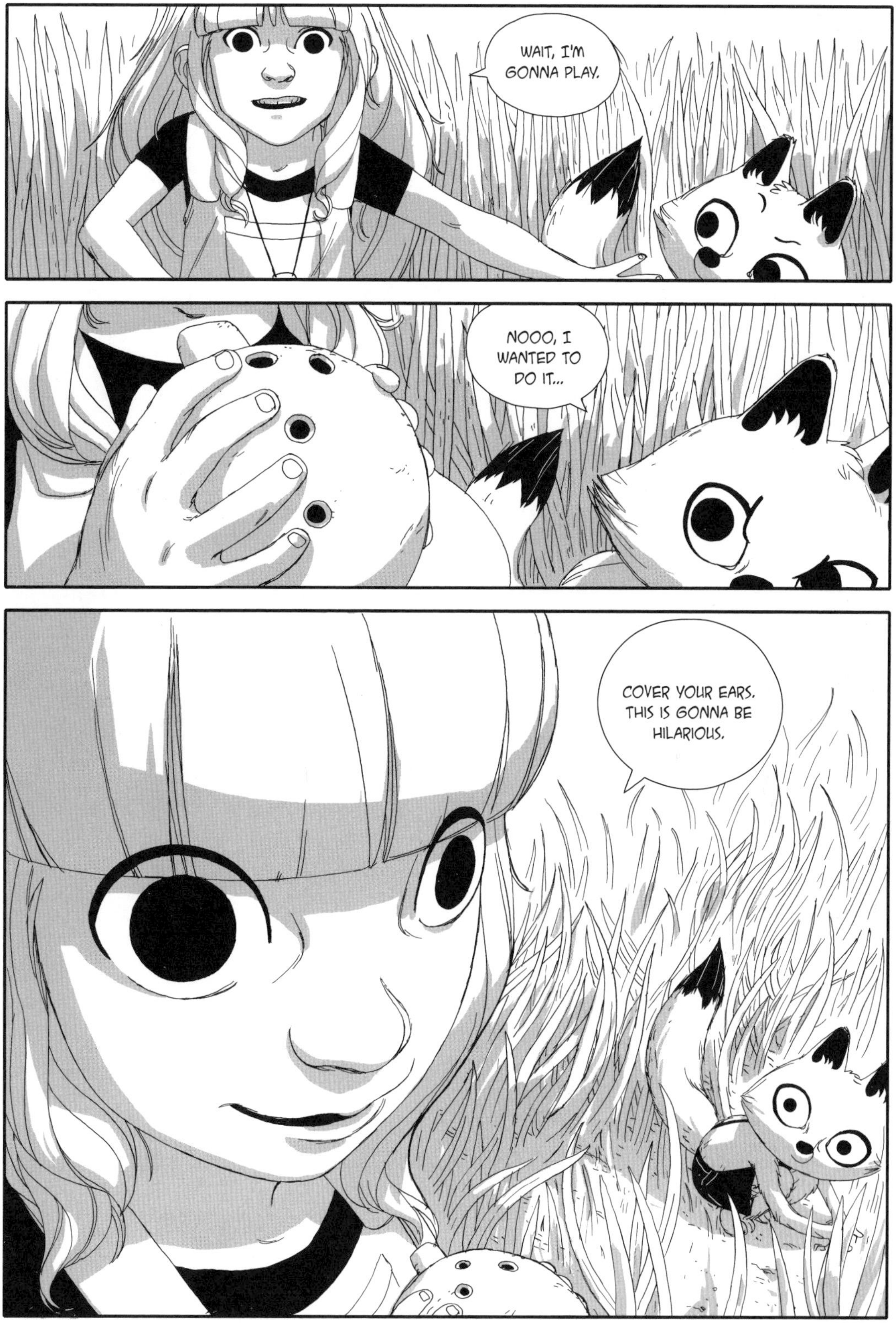
WAIT, I'M GONNA PLAY.
NOOO, I WANTED TO DO IT...
COVER YOUR EARS. THIS IS GONNA BE HILARIOUS.

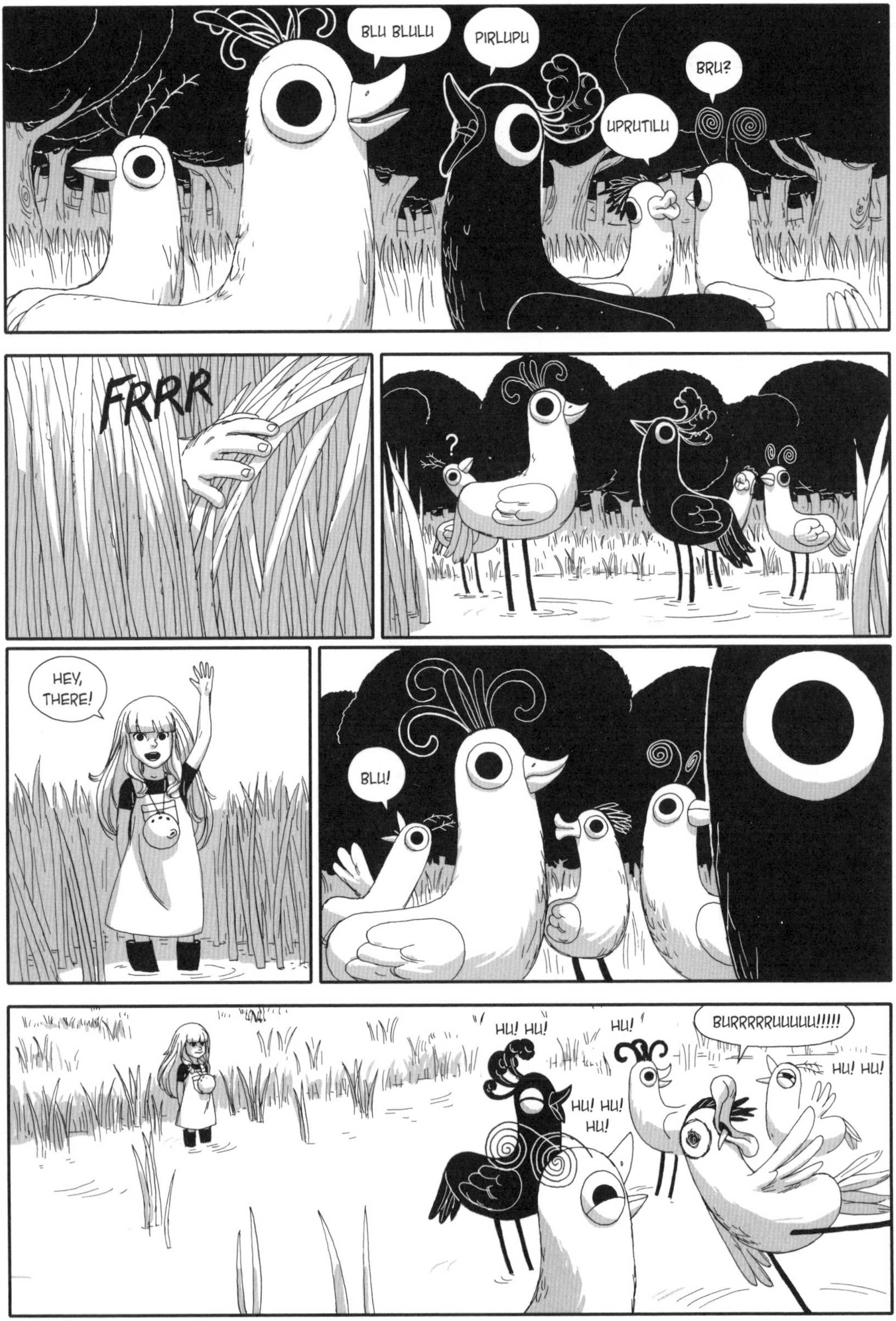
BLU BLULU
PIRLUPU
BRU?
UPRUTILU
FRRR
?
HEY, THERE!
BLU!
HU! HU!
HU!
BURRRRRUUUUU!!!!!
HU! HU!
HU! HU! HU!

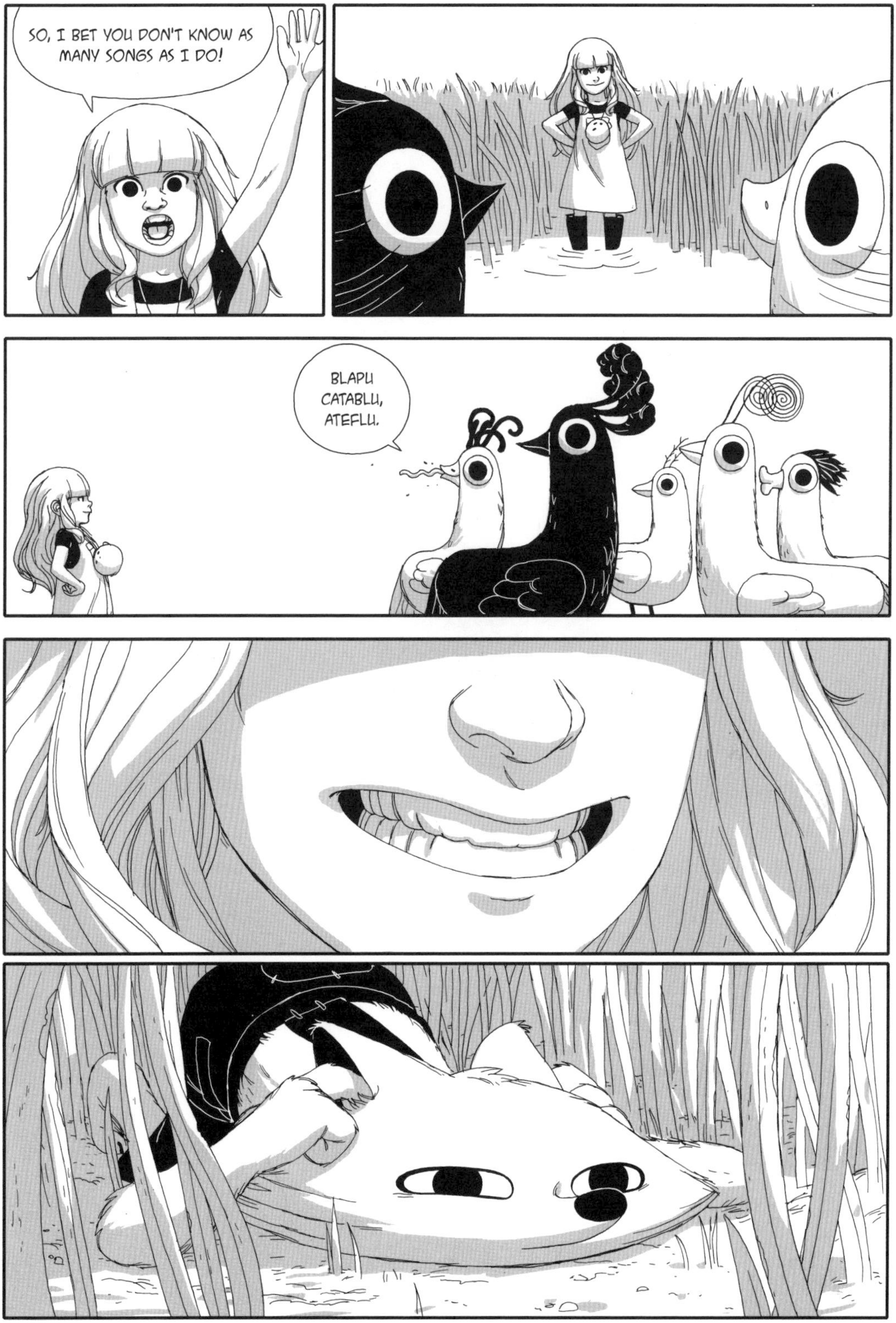
SO, I BET YOU DON'T KNOW AS MANY SONGS AS I DO!
BLAPU CATABLU, ATEFLU.

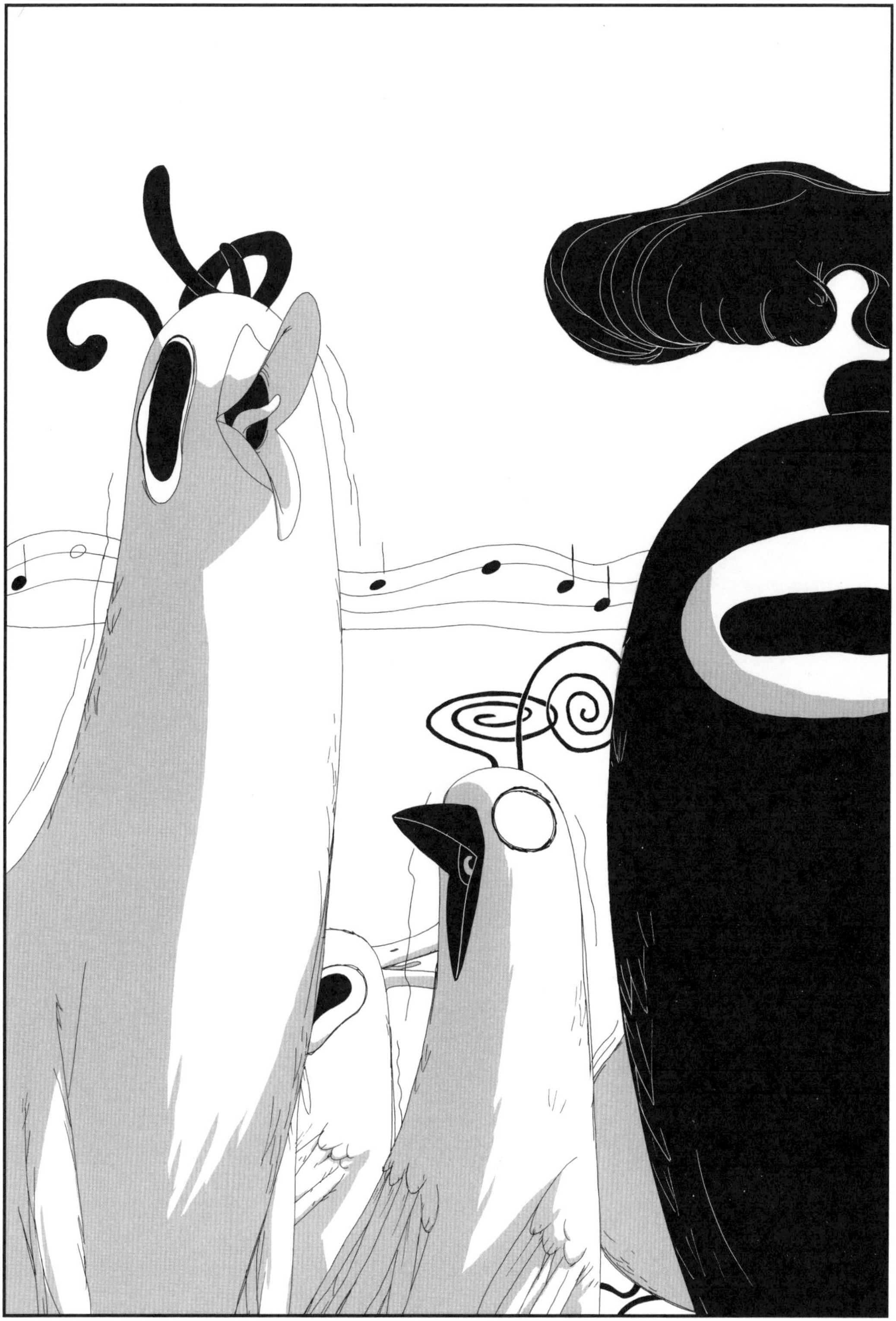

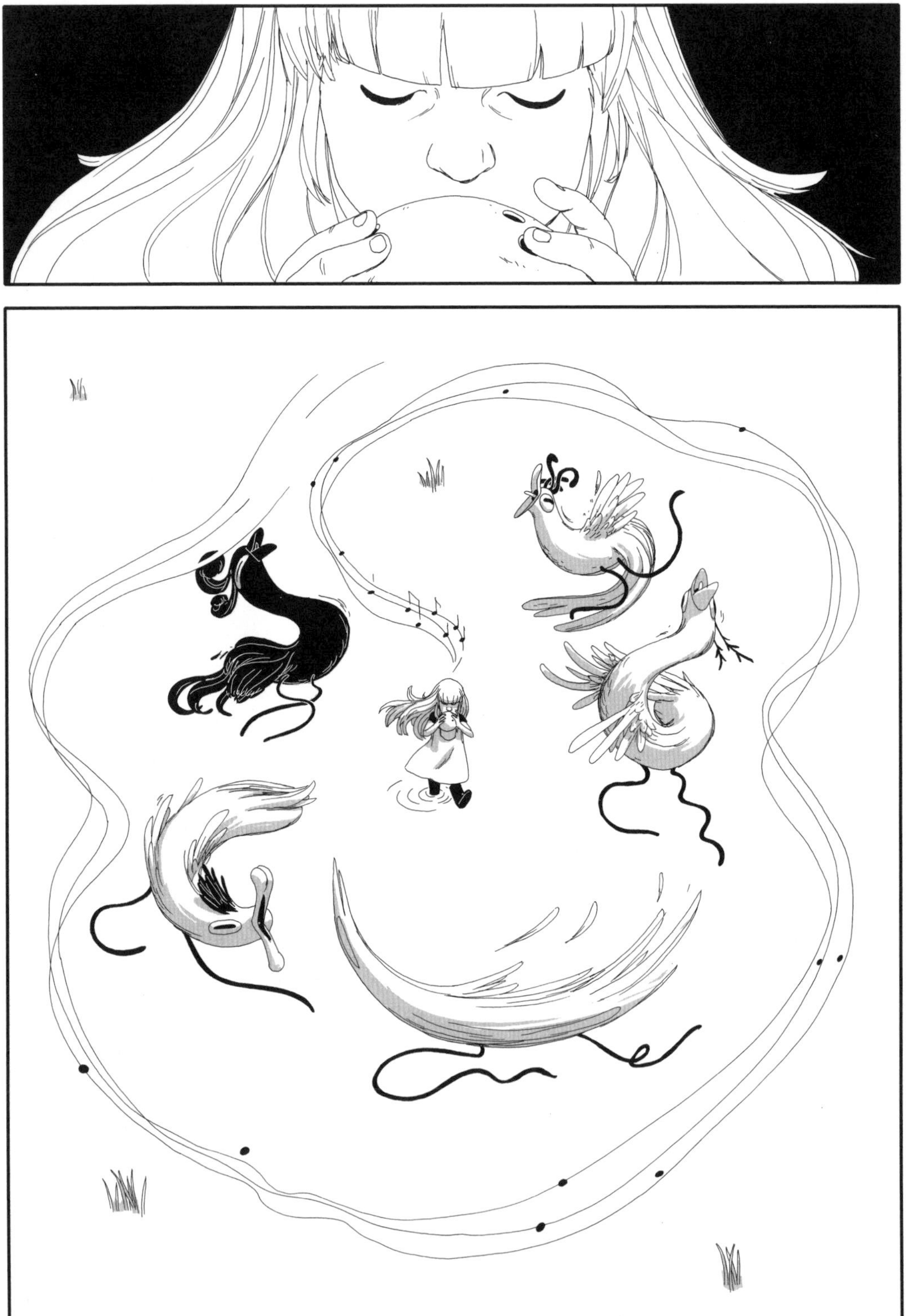

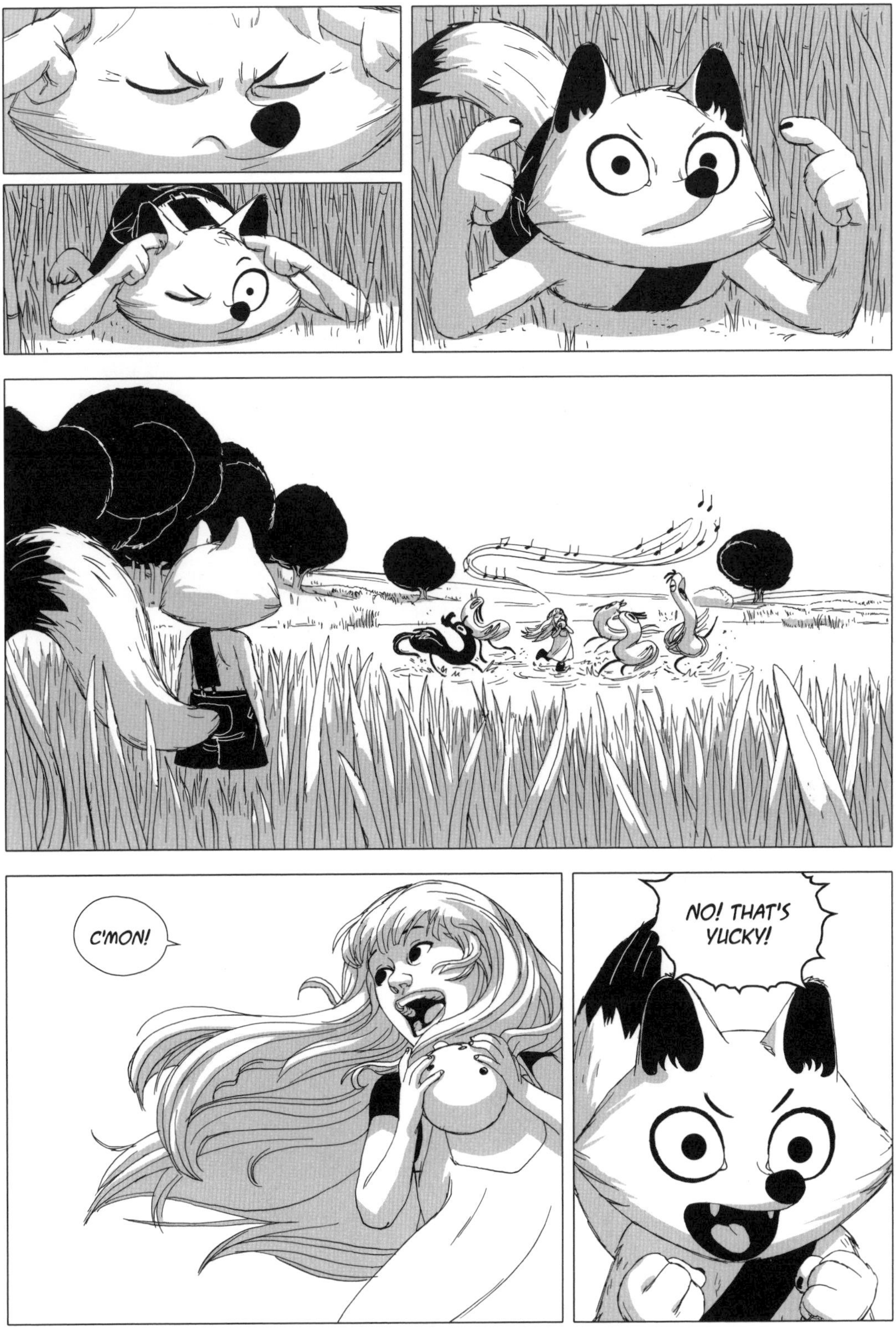
C'MON!
NO! THAT'S YUCKY!

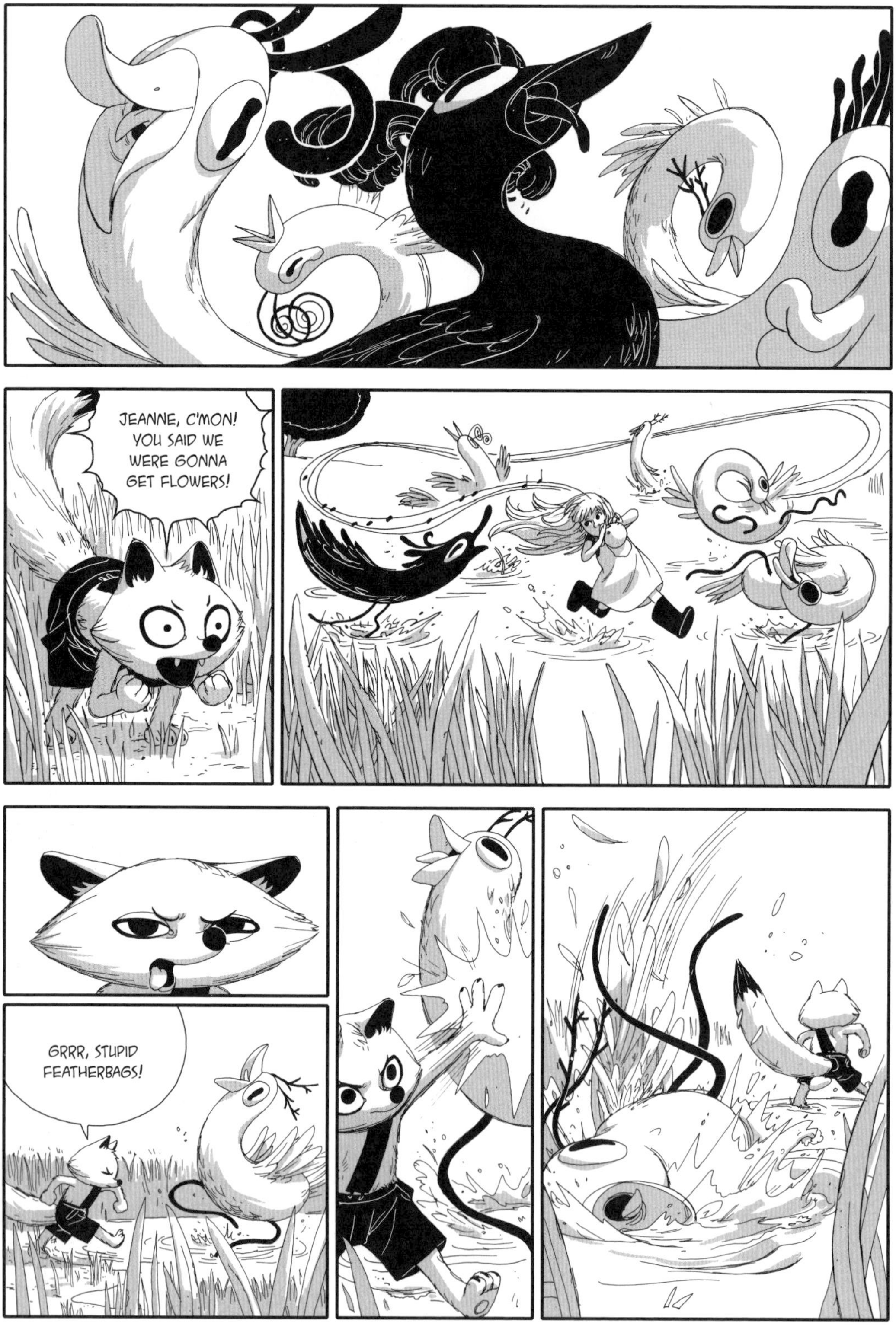
JEANNE, C'MON! YOU SAID WE WERE GONNA GET FLOWERS!
GRRR, STUPID FEATHERBAGS!

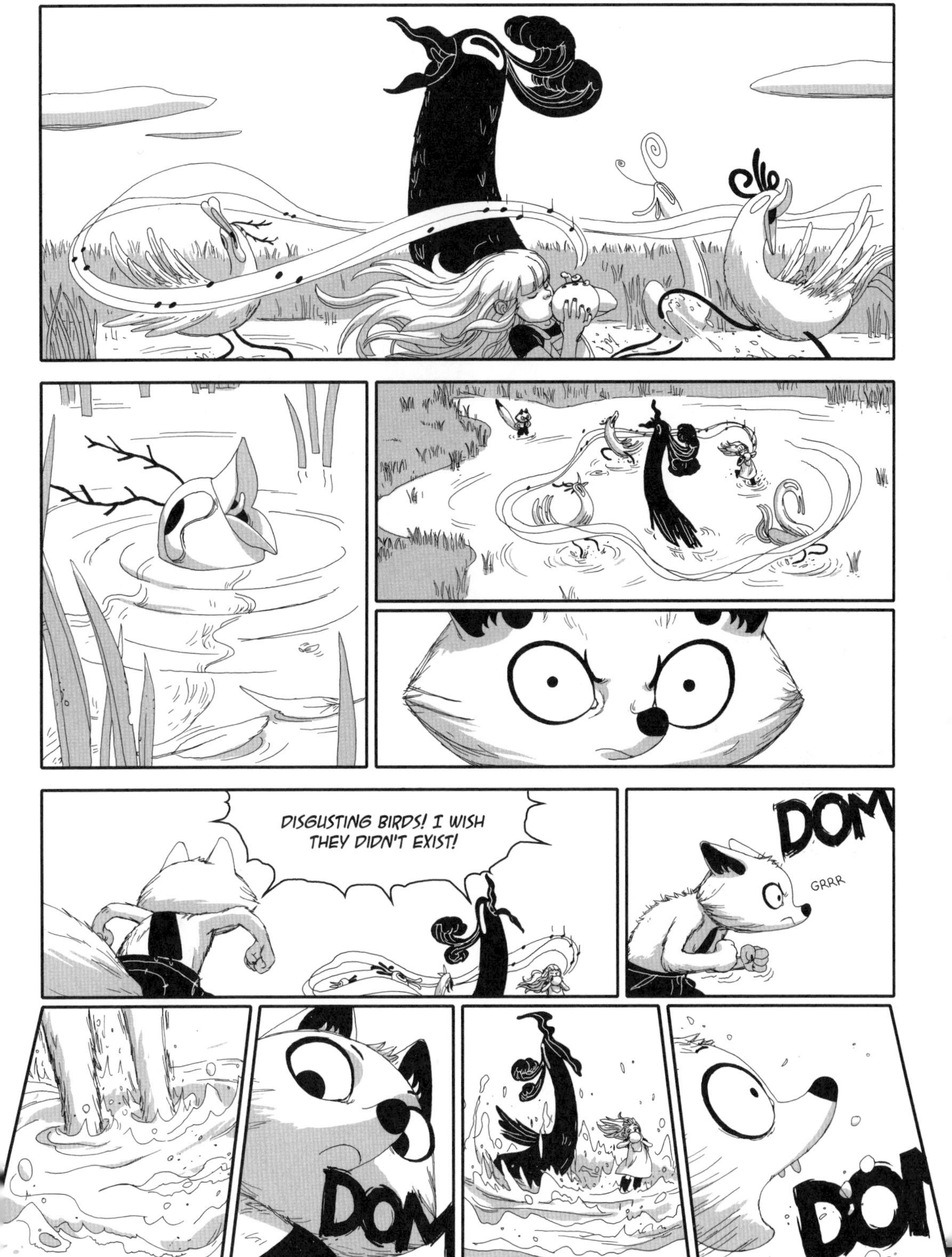
DISGUSTING BIRDS! I WISH THEY DIDN'T EXIST!
DOM
GRRR
DOM
DOM

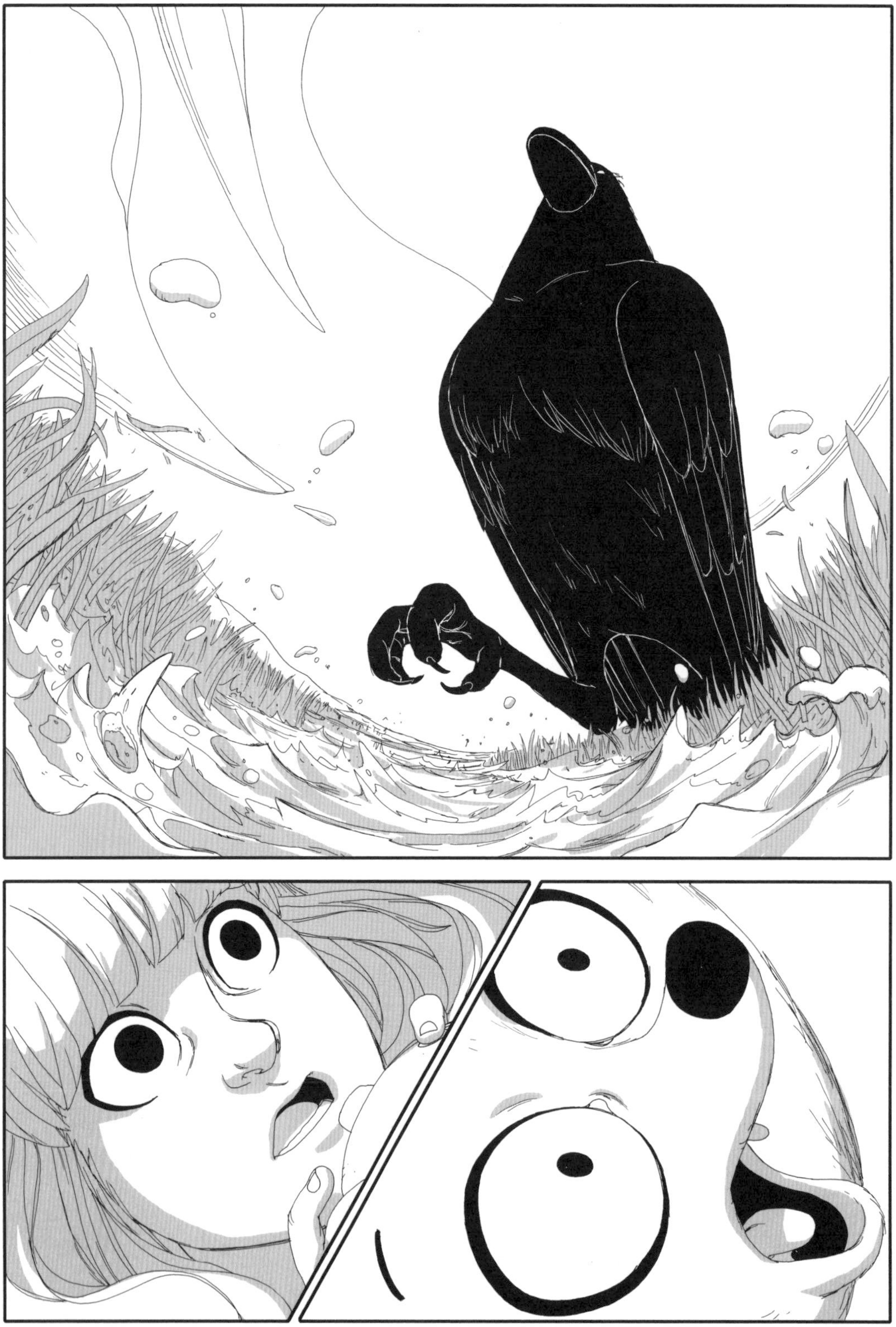

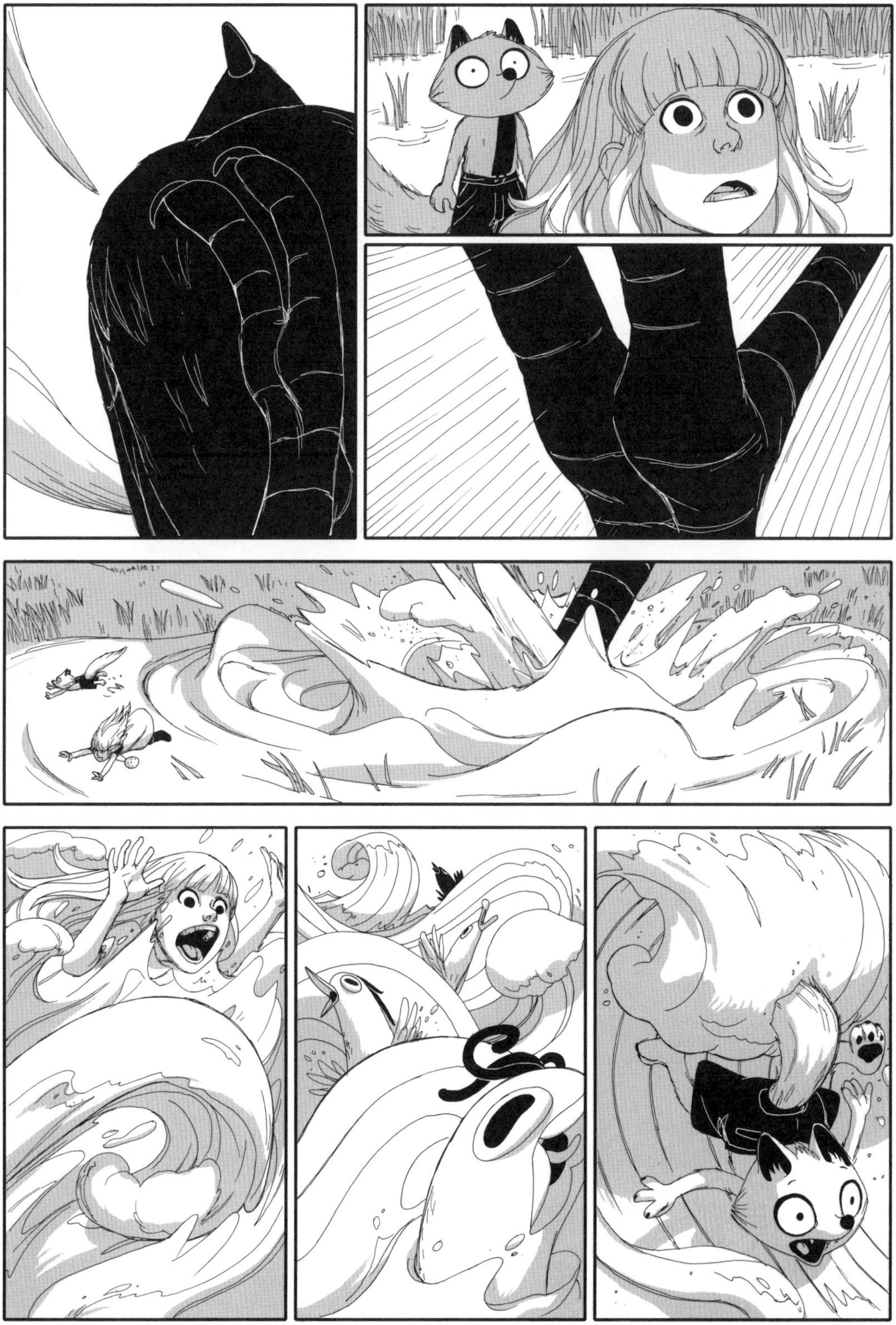

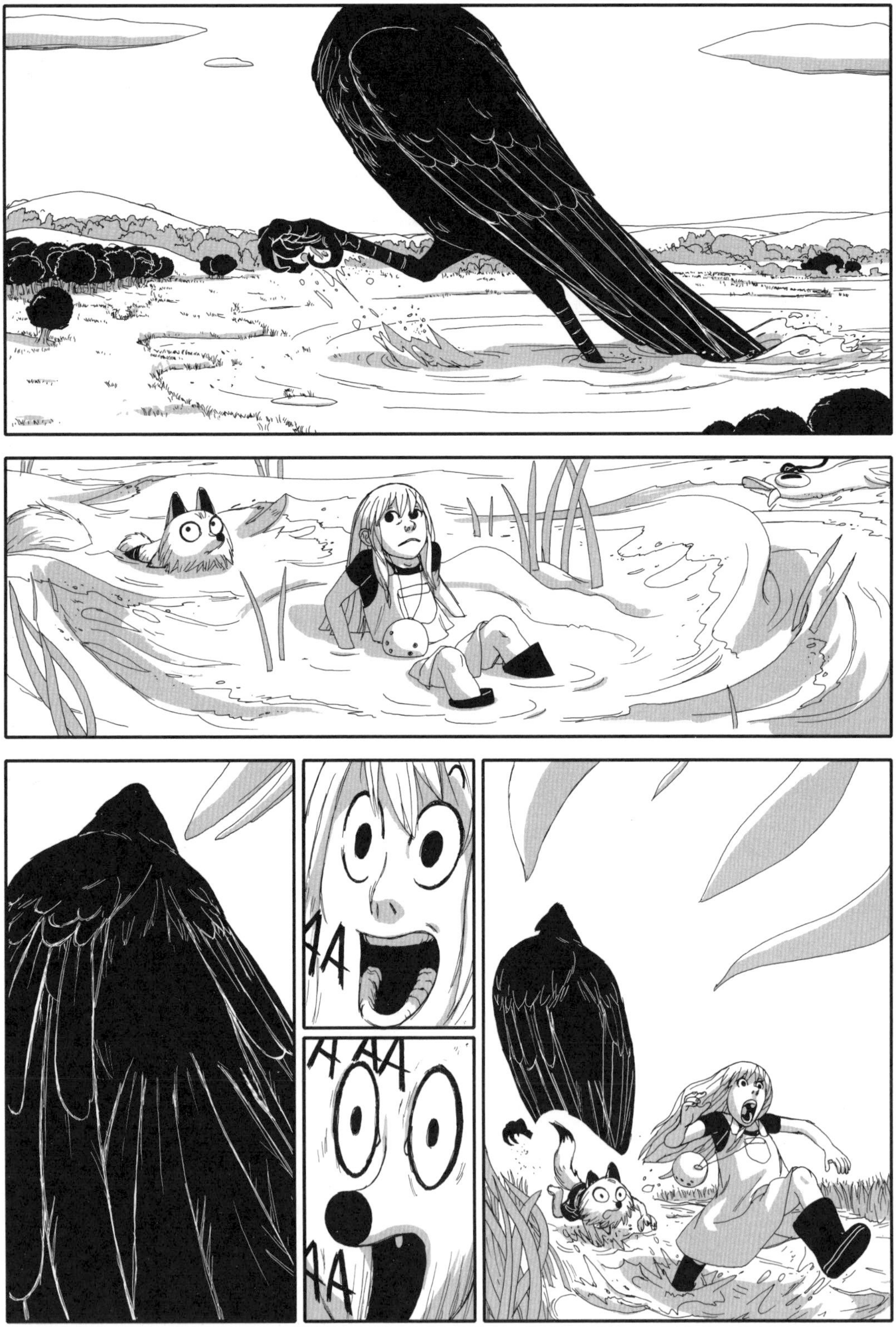
AA
AAA
AA

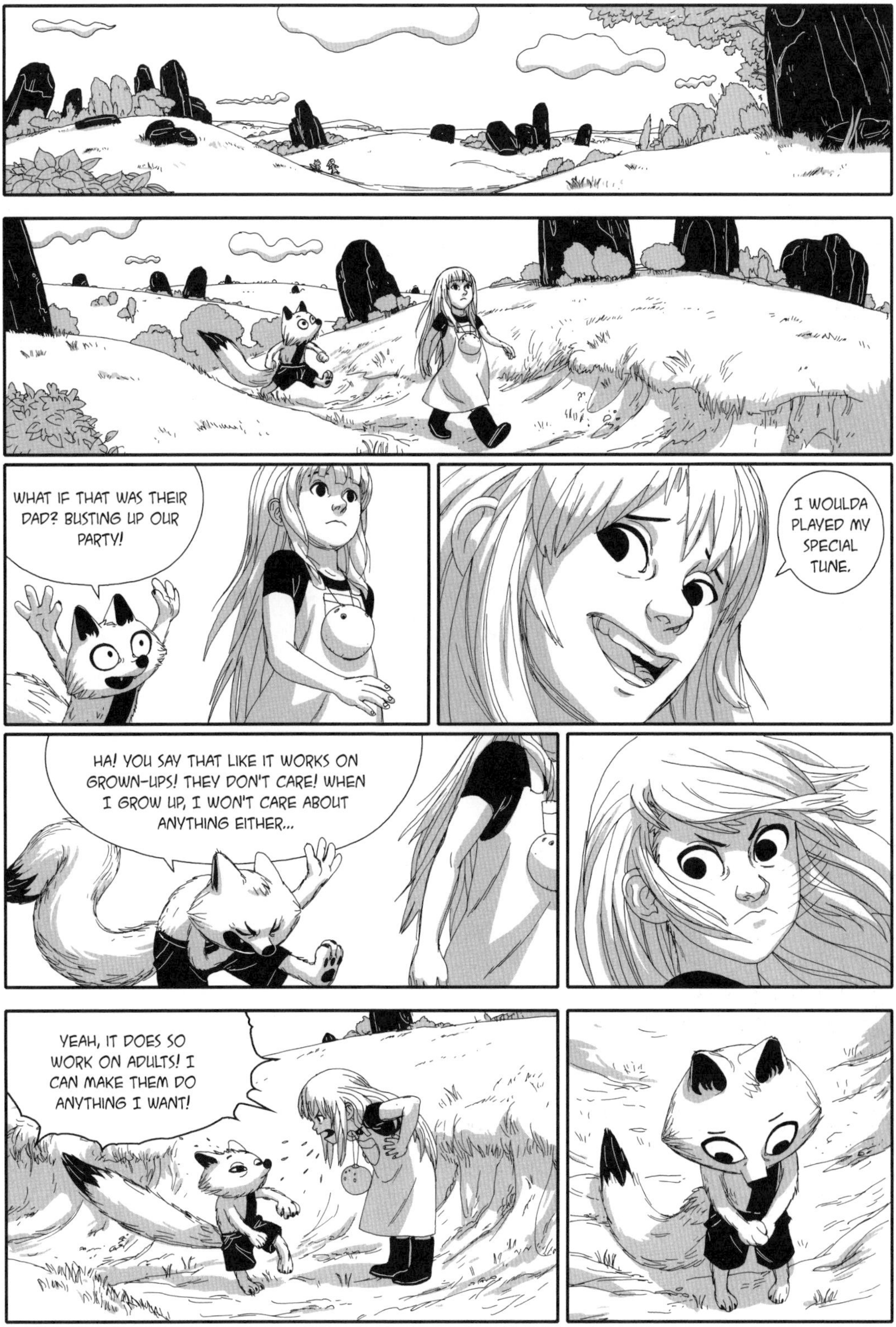
WHAT IF THAT WAS THEIR DAD? BUSTING UP OUR PARTY!
I WOULDA PLAYED MY SPECIAL TUNE.
HA! YOU SAY THAT LIKE IT WORKS ON GROWN-UPS! THEY DON'T CARE! WHEN I GROW UP, I WON'T CARE ABOUT ANYTHING EITHER...
YEAH, IT DOES SO WORK ON ADULTS! I CAN MAKE THEM DO ANYTHING I WANT!

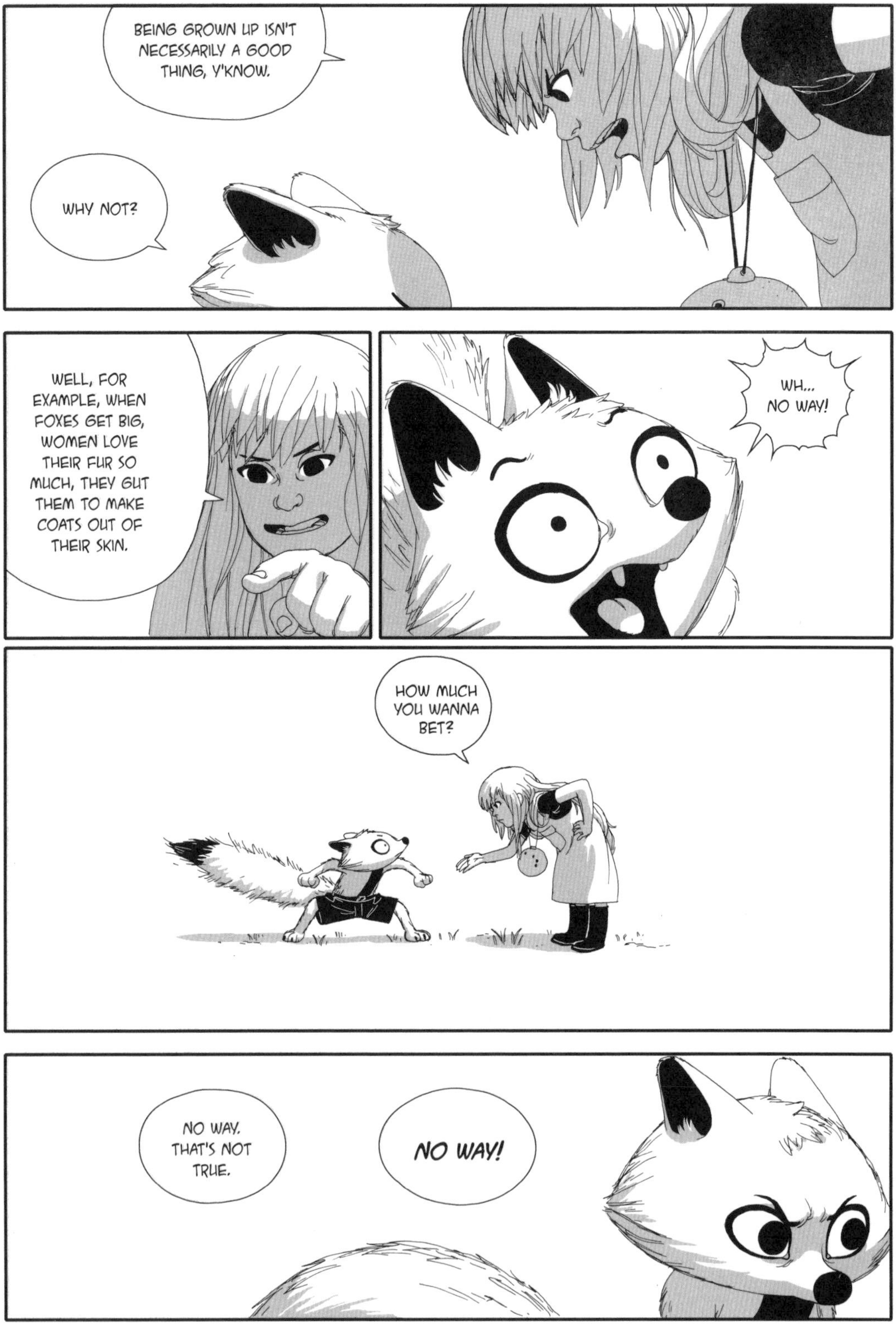
BEING GROWN UP ISN'T NECESSARILY A GOOD THING, Y'KNOW.
WHY NOT?
WELL, FOR EXAMPLE, WHEN FOXES GET BIG, WOMEN LOVE THEIR FUR SO MUCH, THEY GUT THEM TO MAKE COATS OUT OF THEIR SKIN.
WH... NO WAY!
HOW MUCH YOU WANNA BET?
NO WAY. THAT'S NOT TRUE.
NO WAY!

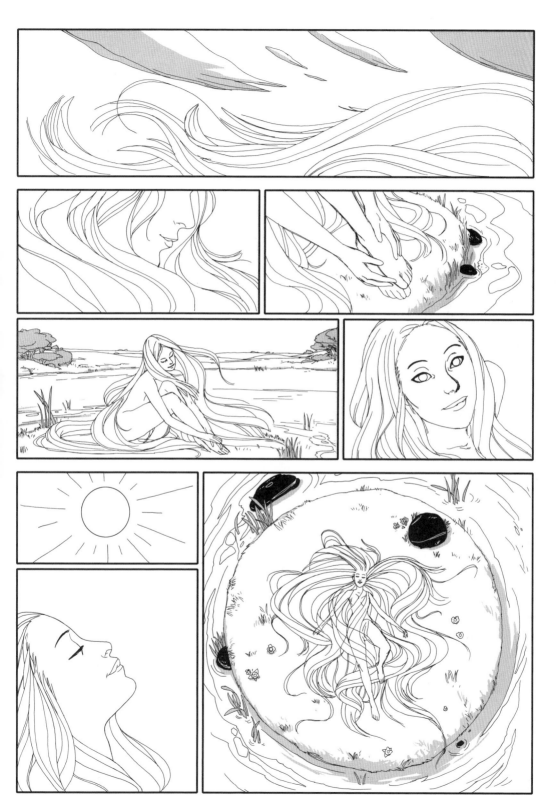

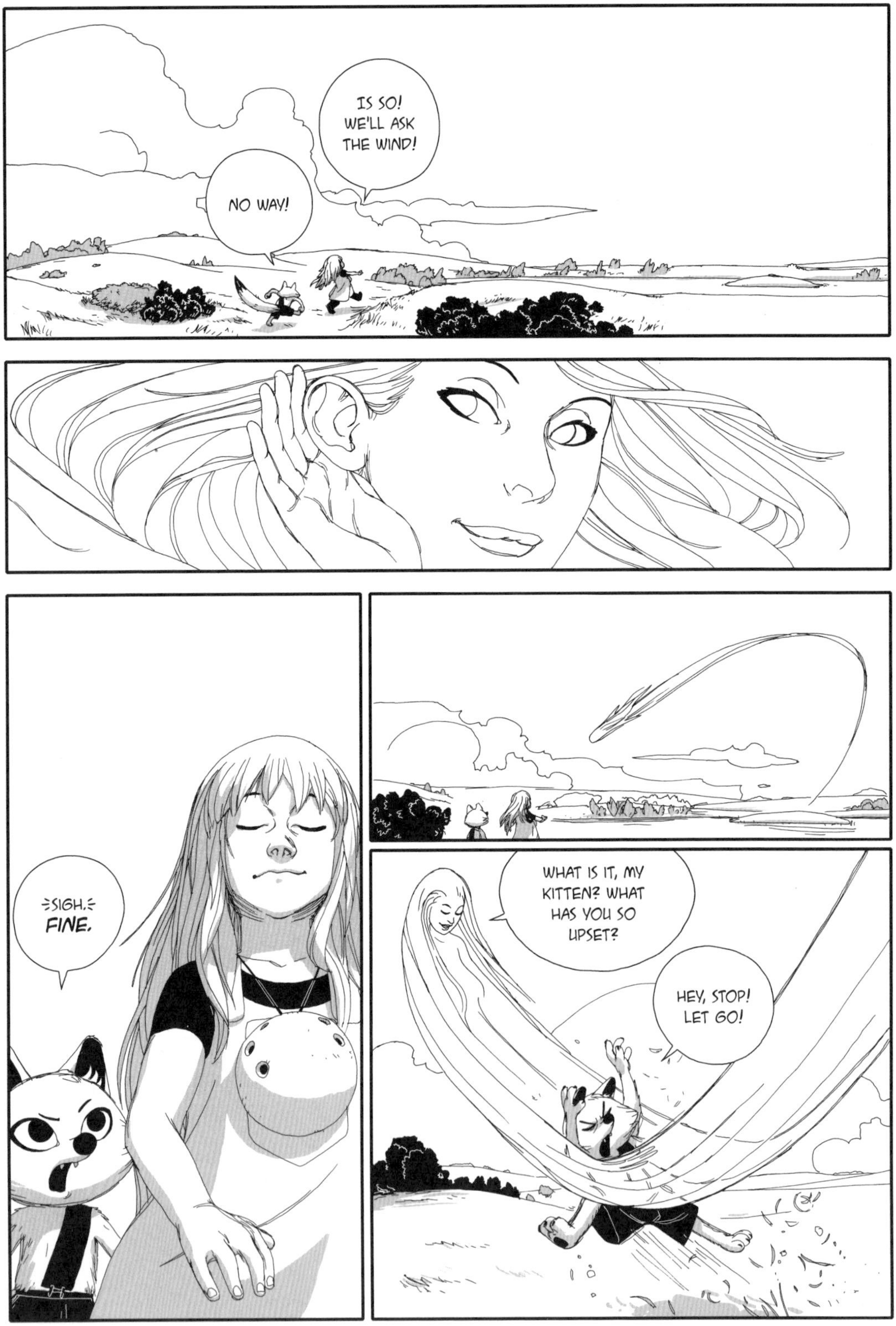
IS SO! WE'LL ASK THE WIND!
NO WAY!
SIGH. FINE.
WHAT IS IT, MY KITTEN? WHAT HAS YOU SO UPSET?
HEY, STOP! LET GO!

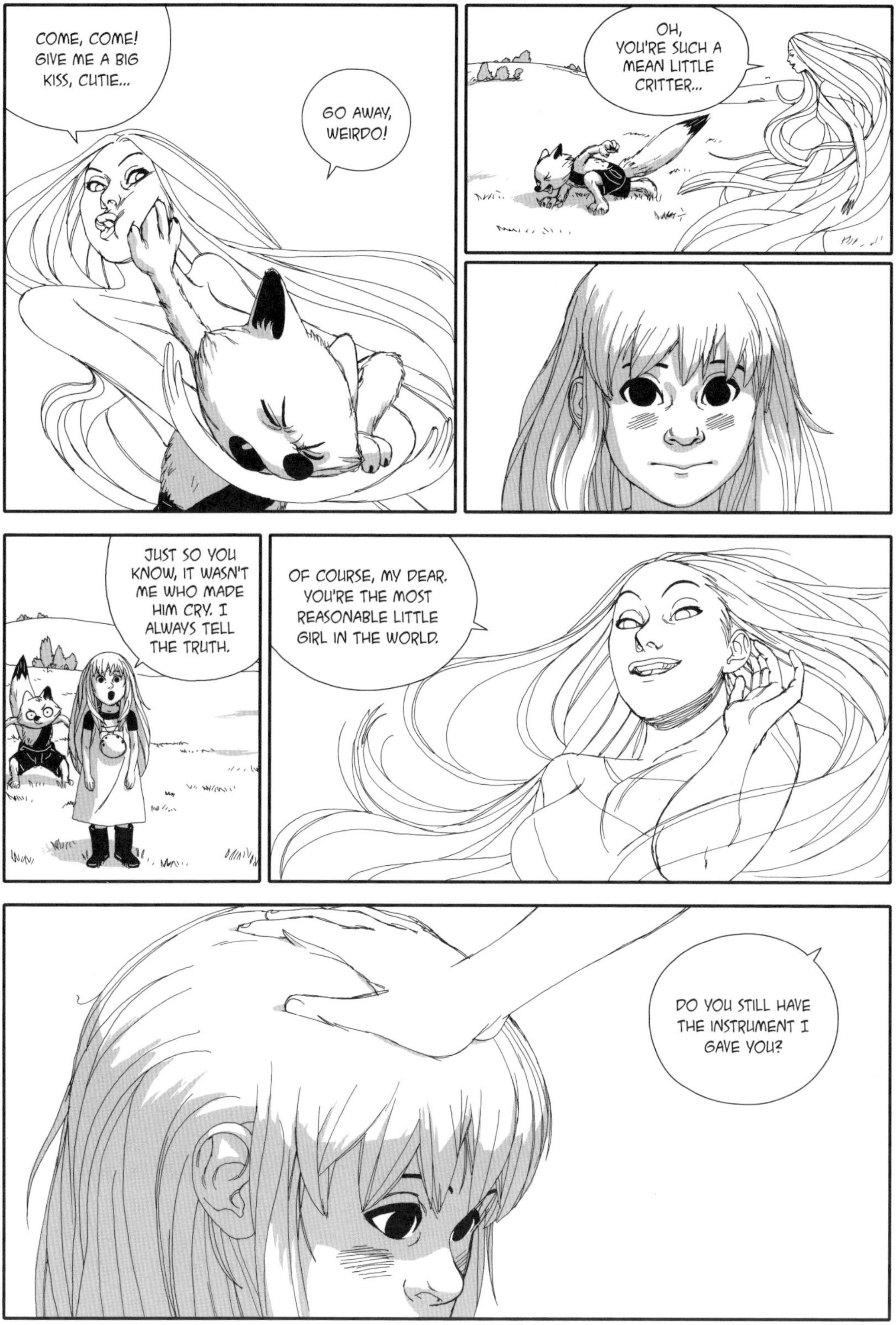
COME, COME! GIVE ME A BIG KISS, CUTIE...
GO AWAY, WEIRDO!
OH, YOU'RE SUCH A MEAN LITTLE CRITTER...
JUST SO YOU KNOW, IT WASN'T ME WHO MADE HIM CRY. I ALWAYS TELL THE TRUTH.
OF COURSE, MY DEAR. YOU'RE THE MOST REASONABLE LITTLE GIRL IN THE WORLD.
DO YOU STILL HAVE THE INSTRUMENT I GAVE YOU?

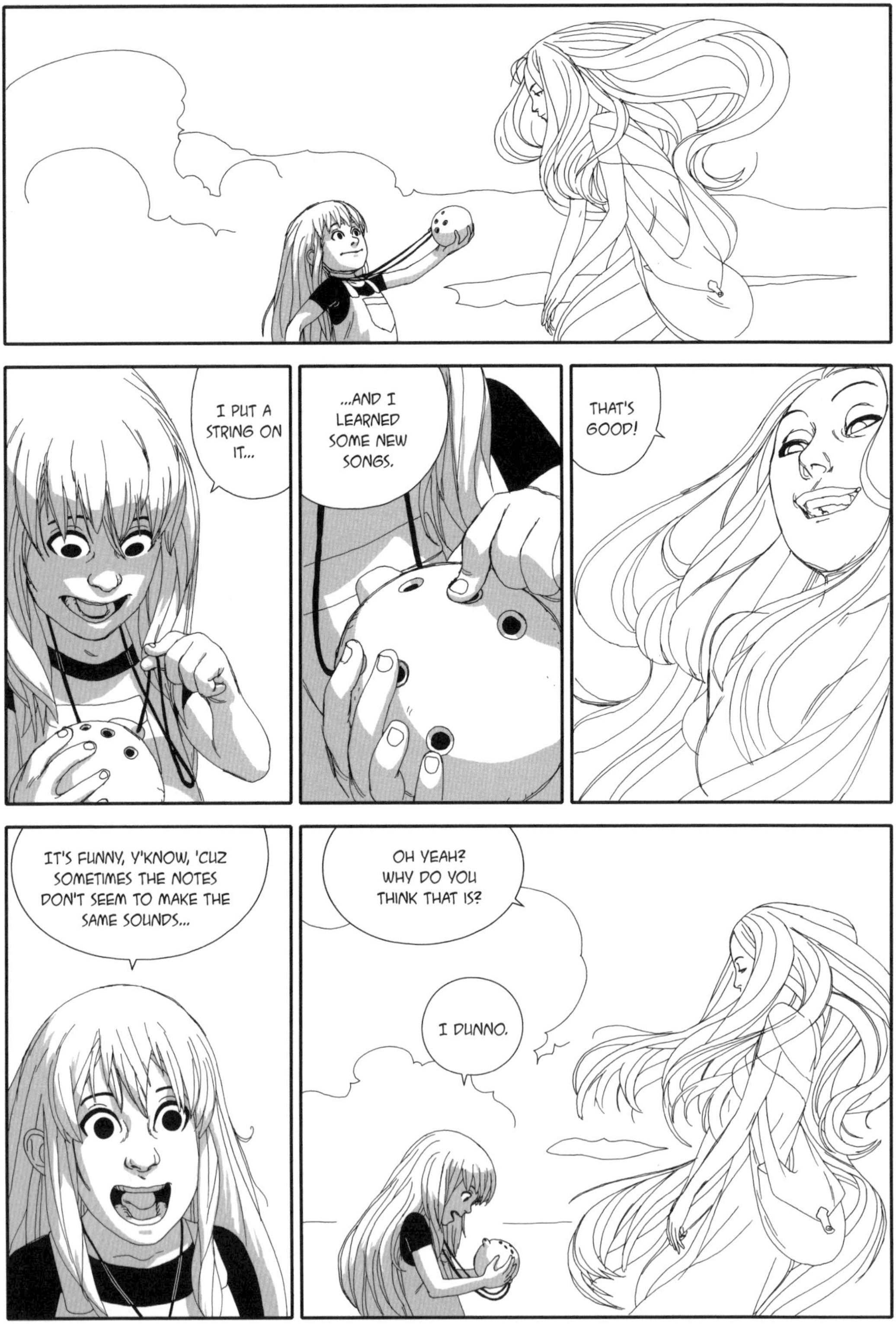
I PUT A STRING ON IT...
...AND I LEARNED SOME NEW SONGS.
THAT'S GOOD!
IT'S FUNNY, Y'KNOW, 'CUZ SOMETIMES THE NOTES DON'T SEEM TO MAKE THE SAME SOUNDS...
OH YEAH? WHY DO YOU THINK THAT IS?
I DUNNO.

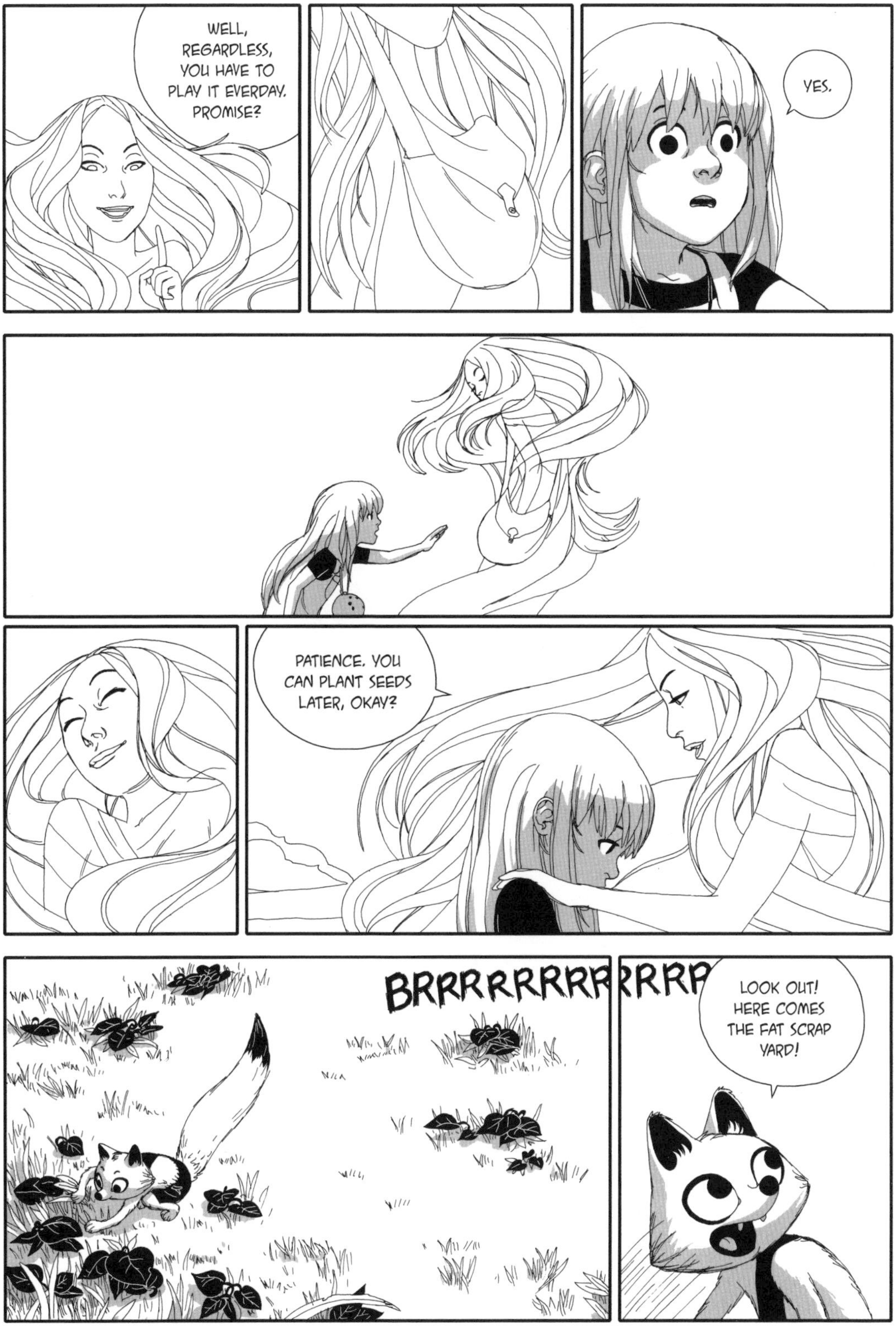
WELL, REGARDLESS, YOU HAVE TO PLAY IT EVERDAY. PROMISE?
YES.
PATIENCE. YOU CAN PLANT SEEDS LATER, OKAY?
BRRRRRRRRRRRRP
LOOK OUT! HERE COMES THE FAT SCRAP YARD!

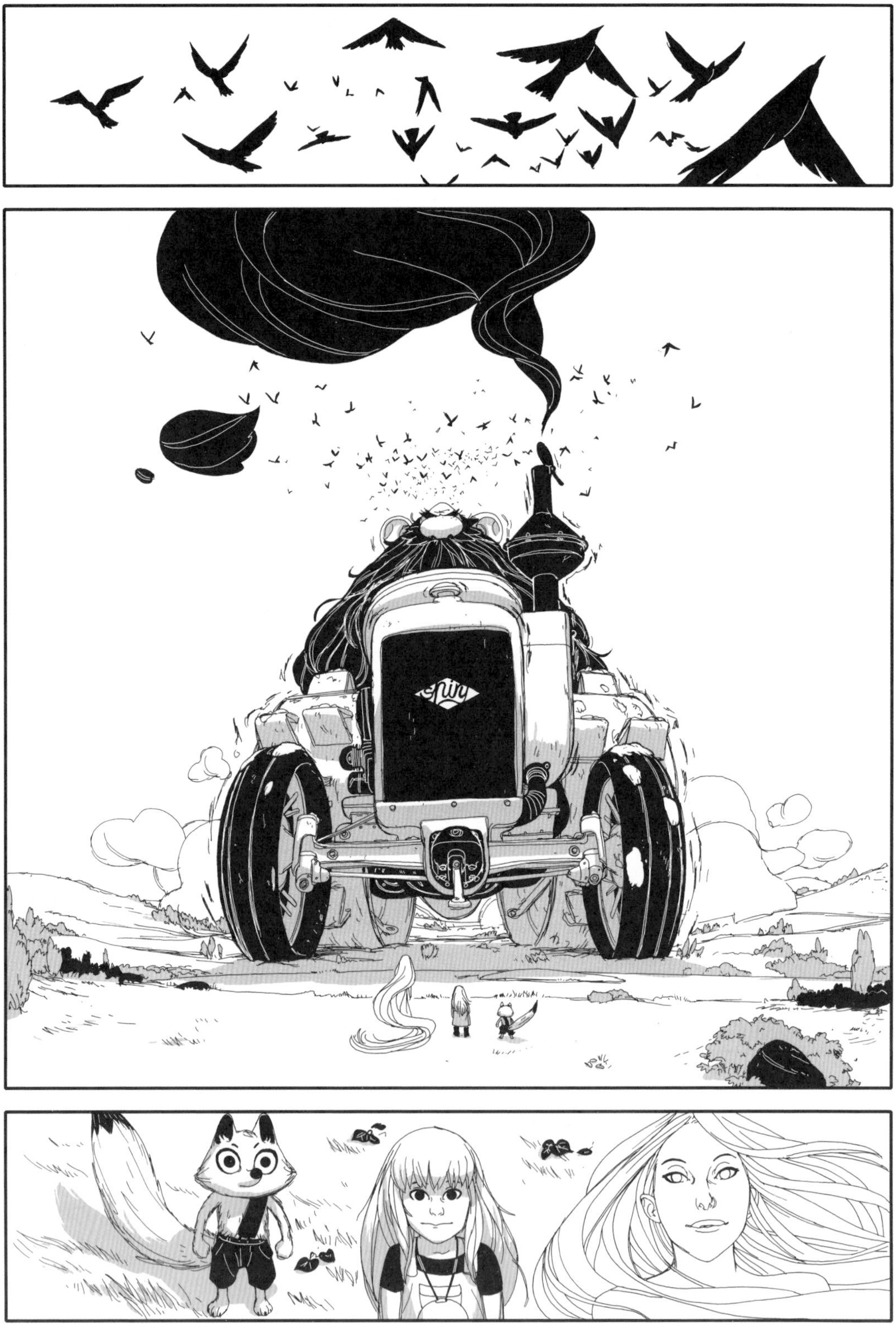

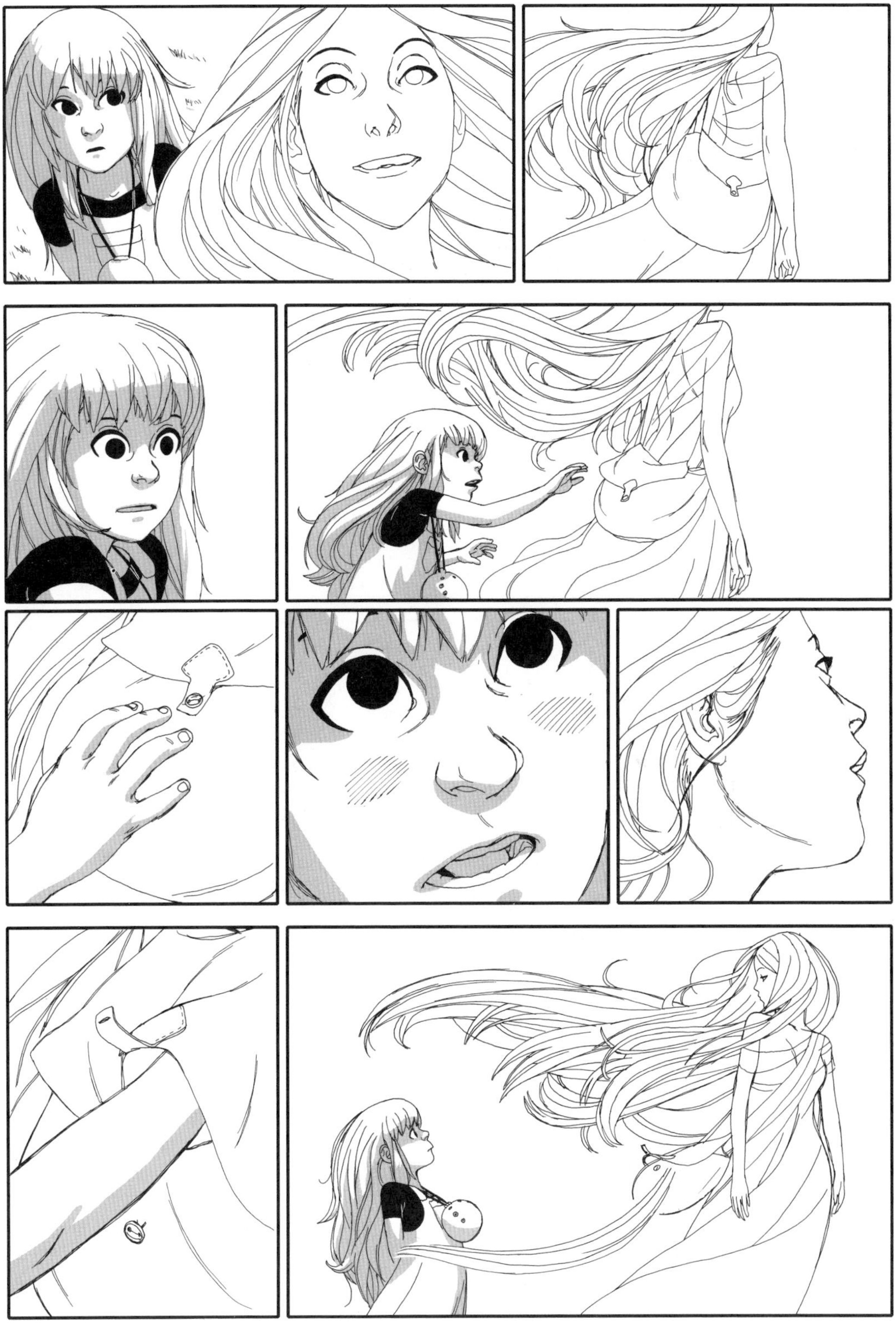

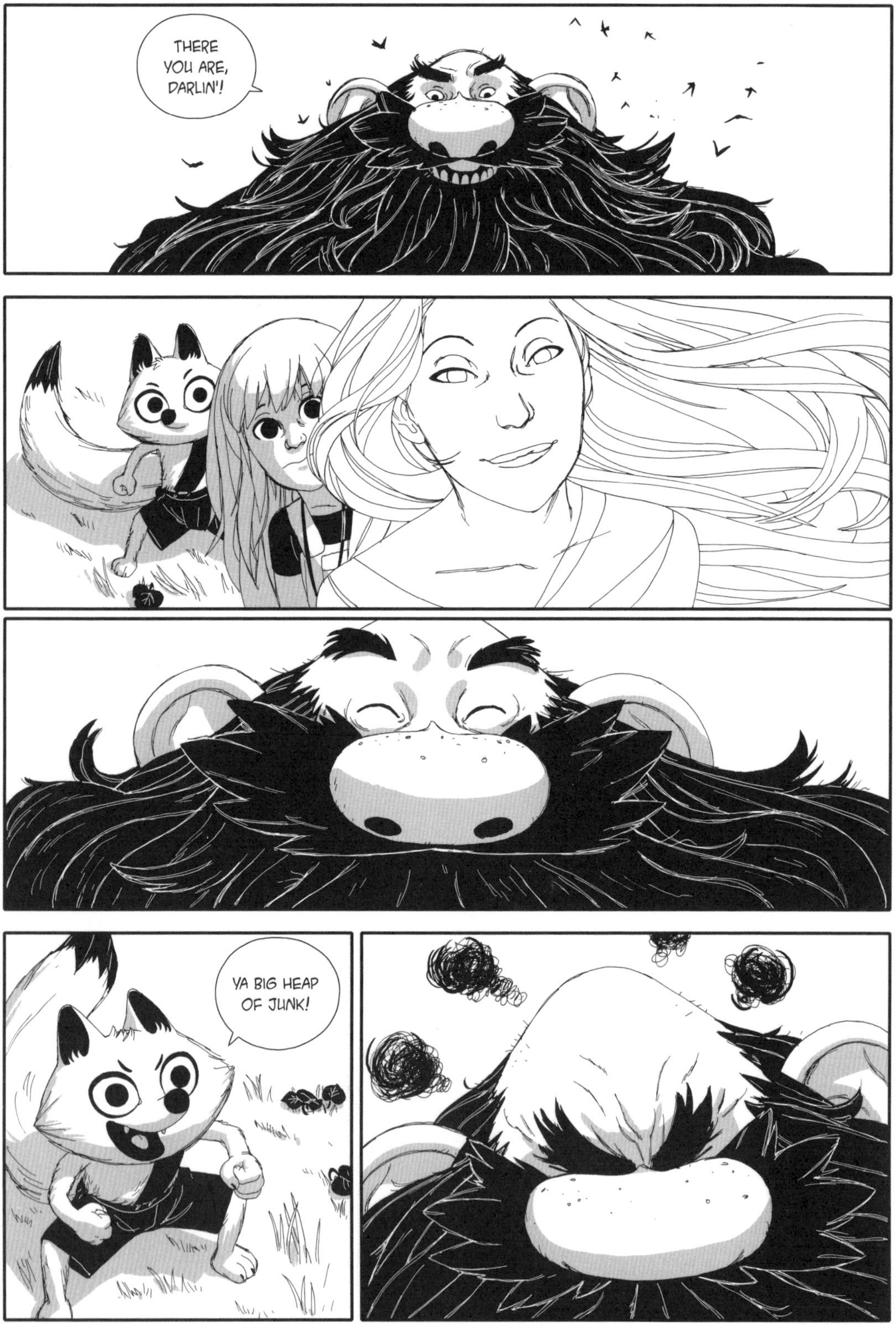
THERE YOU ARE, DARLIN'!
YA BIG HEAP OF JUNK!

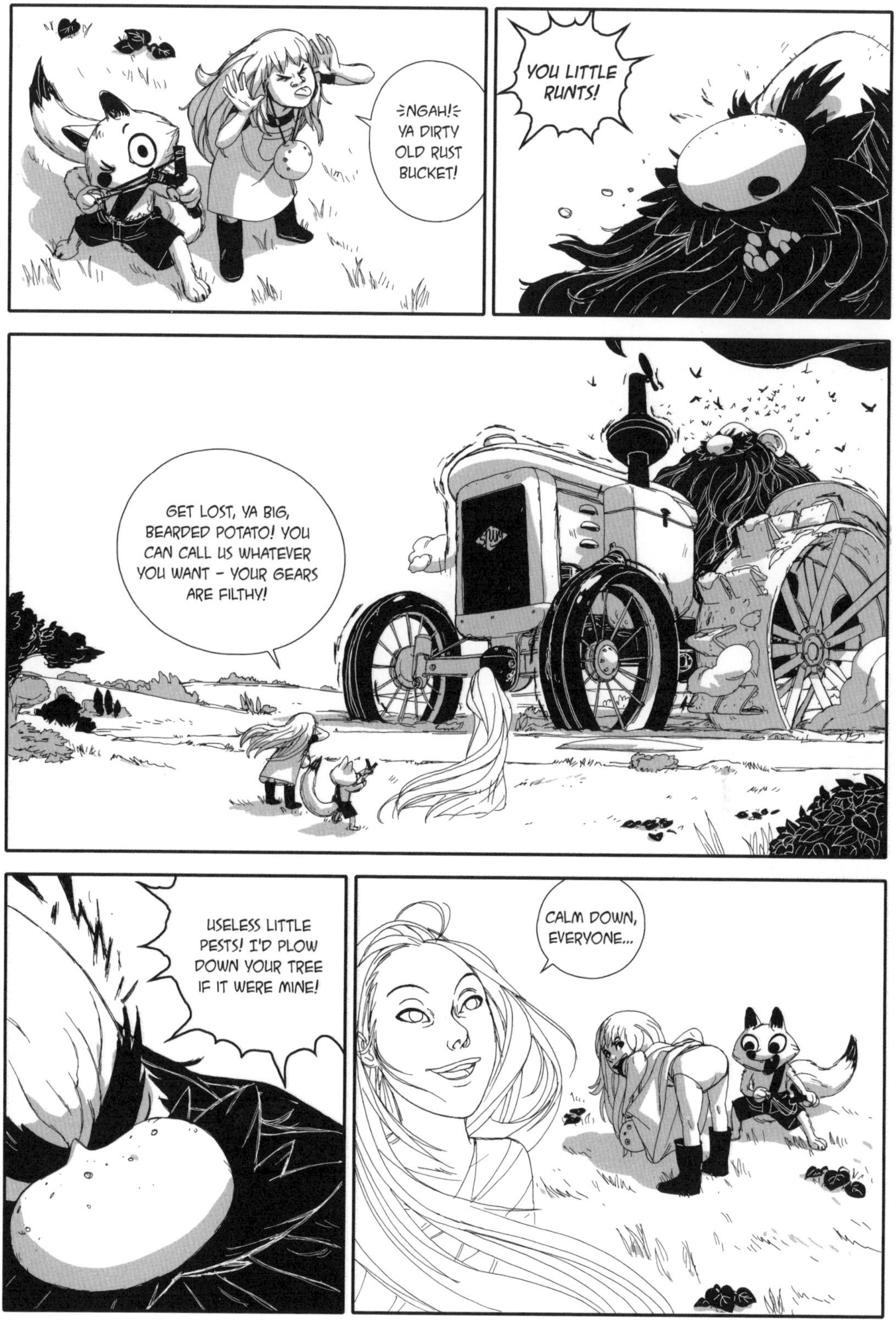

≶NGAH!≷ YA DIRTY OLD RUST BUCKET!
YOU LITTLE RUNTS!
GET LOST, YA BIG, BEARDED POTATO! YOU CAN CALL US WHATEVER YOU WANT - YOUR GEARS ARE FILTHY!
USELESS LITTLE PESTS! I'D PLOW DOWN YOUR TREE IF IT WERE MINE!
CALM DOWN, EVERYONE...

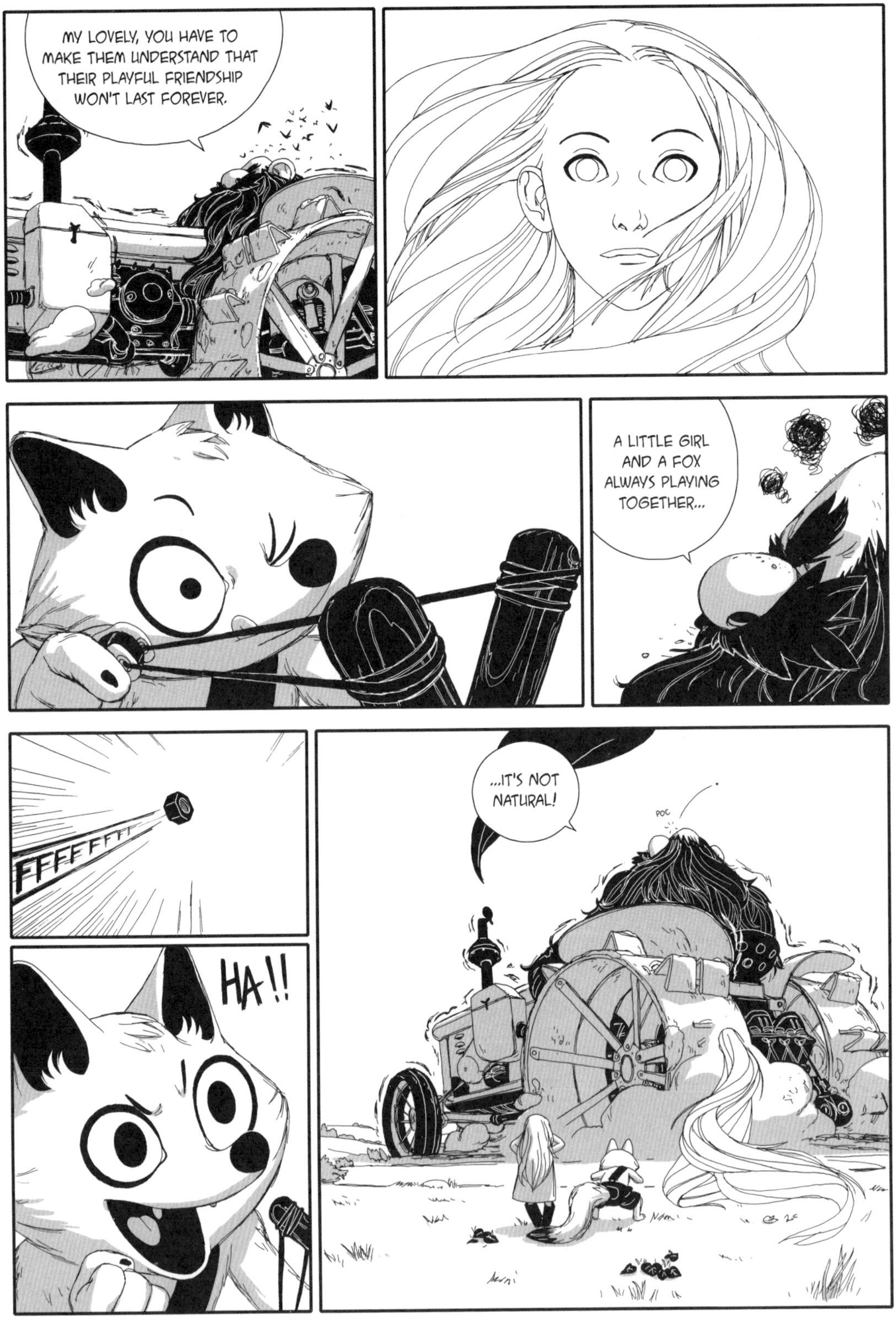
MY LOVELY, YOU HAVE TO MAKE THEM UNDERSTAND THAT THEIR PLAYFUL FRIENDSHIP WON'T LAST FOREVER.
A LITTLE GIRL AND A FOX ALWAYS PLAYING TOGETHER...
FFFFFFFF
HA!!
...IT'S NOT NATURAL!
POC

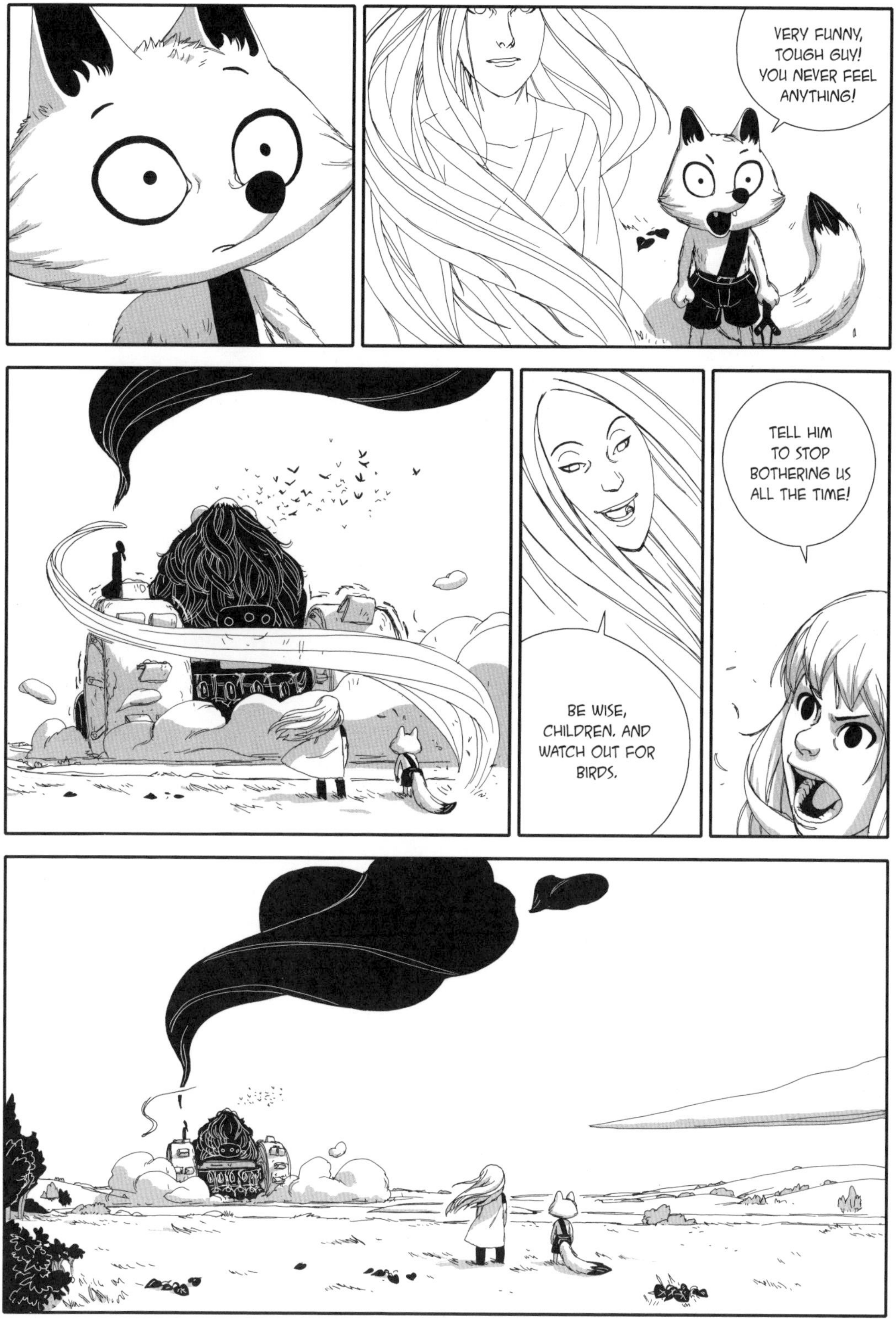

VERY FUNNY, TOUGH GUY! YOU NEVER FEEL ANYTHING!
TELL HIM TO STOP BOTHERING US ALL THE TIME!
BE WISE, CHILDREN. AND WATCH OUT FOR BIRDS.

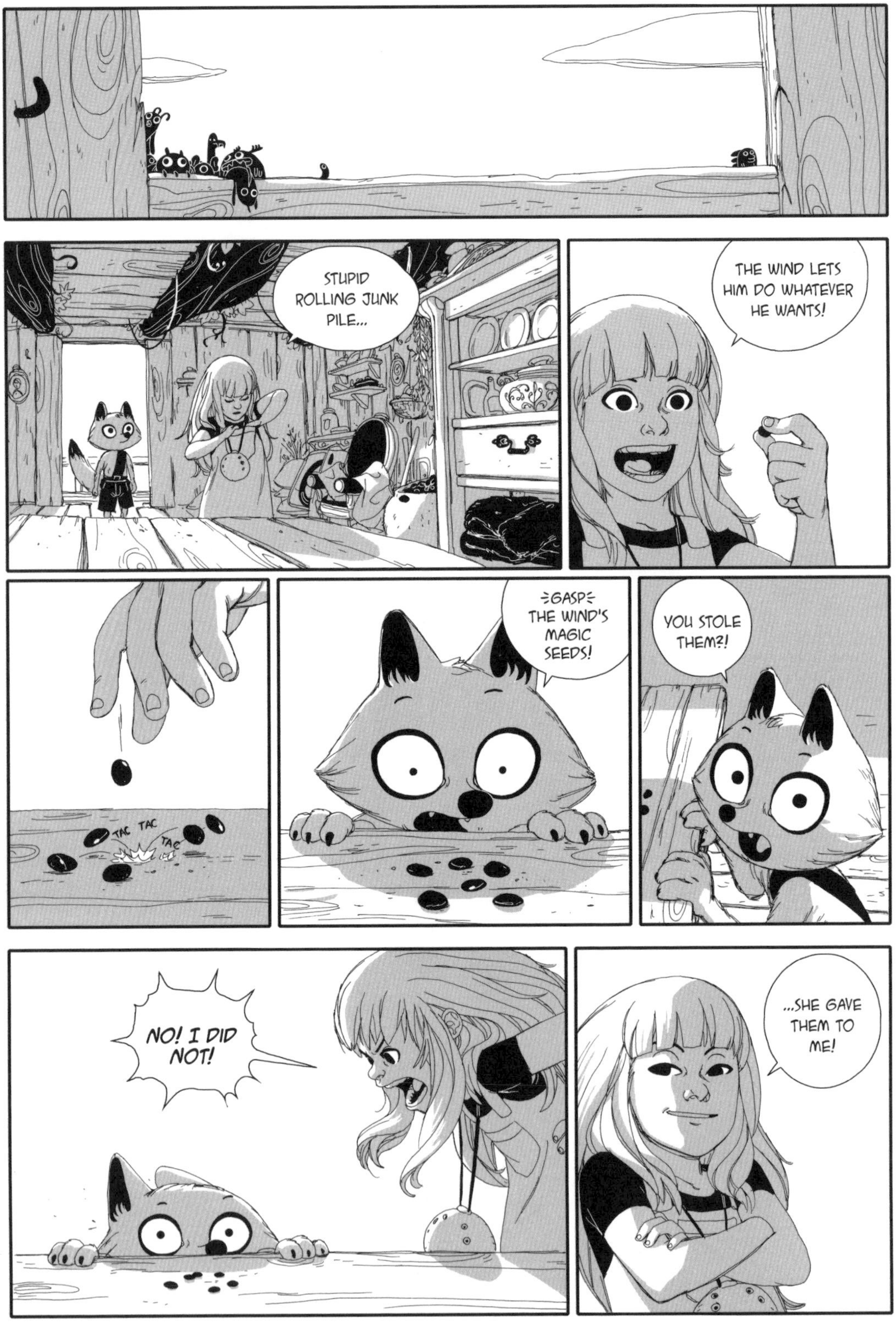

STUPID ROLLING JUNK PILE...
THE WIND LETS HIM DO WHATEVER HE WANTS!
TAC TAC TAC
≡GASP≡ THE WIND'S MAGIC SEEDS!
YOU STOLE THEM?!
NO! I DID NOT!
...SHE GAVE THEM TO ME!

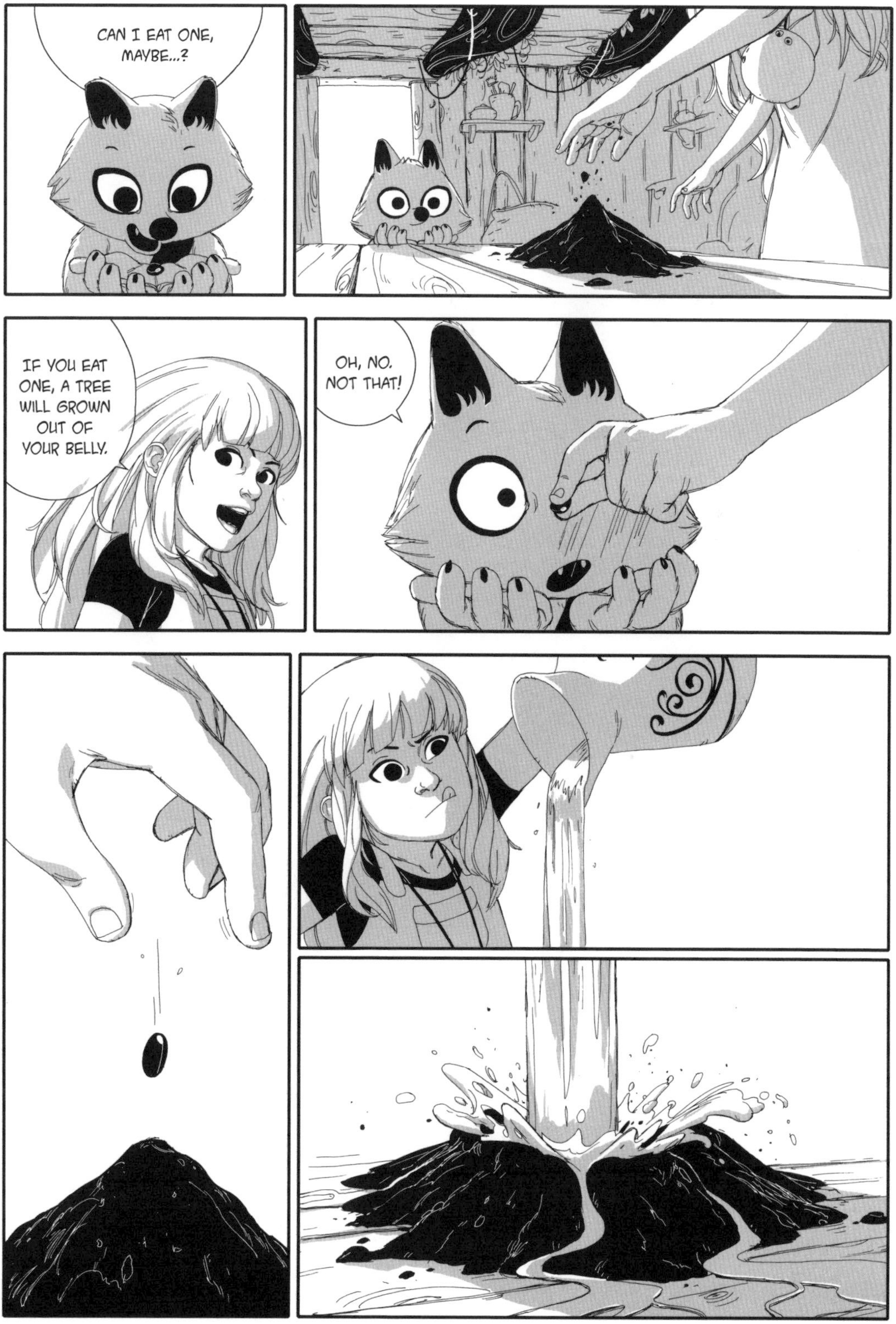
CAN I EAT ONE, MAYBE...?
IF YOU EAT ONE, A TREE WILL GROWN OUT OF YOUR BELLY.
OH, NO. NOT THAT!

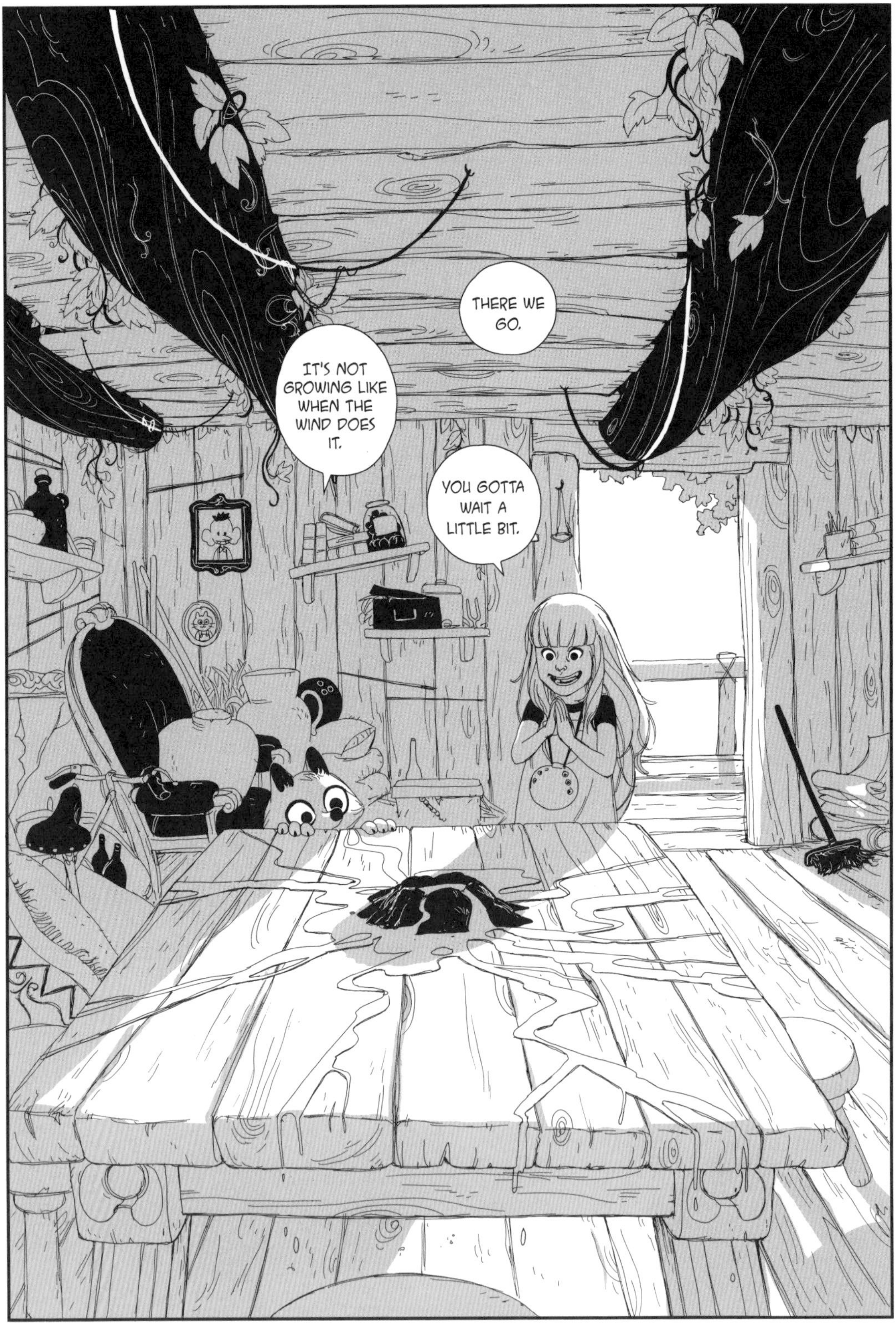
THERE WE GO.
IT'S NOT GROWING LIKE WHEN THE WIND DOES IT.
YOU GOTTA WAIT A LITTLE BIT.

Chapter 4

OVER THERE

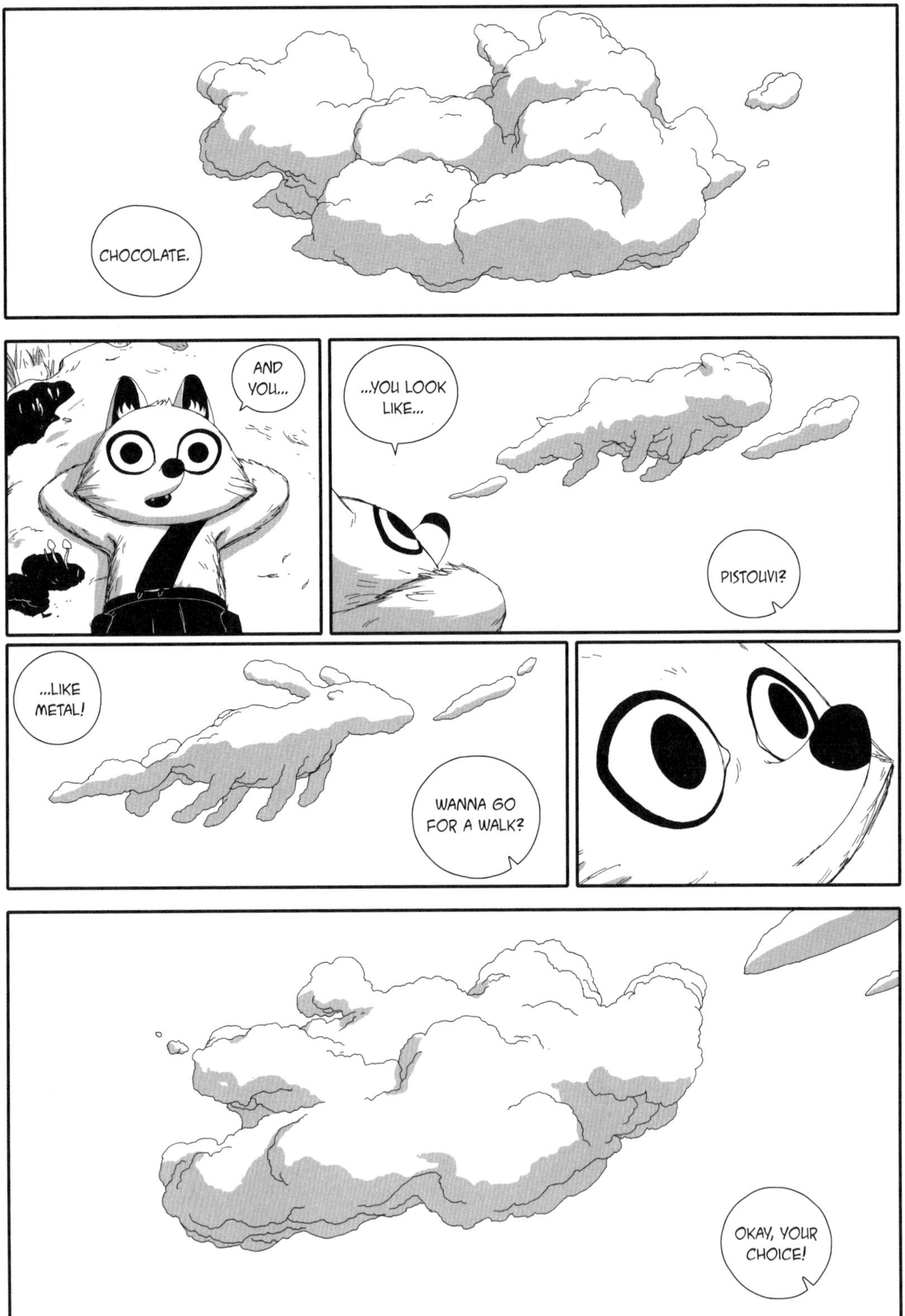
CHOCOLATE.
AND YOU...
...YOU LOOK LIKE...
PISTOUVI?
...LIKE METAL!
WANNA GO FOR A WALK?
OKAY, YOUR CHOICE!

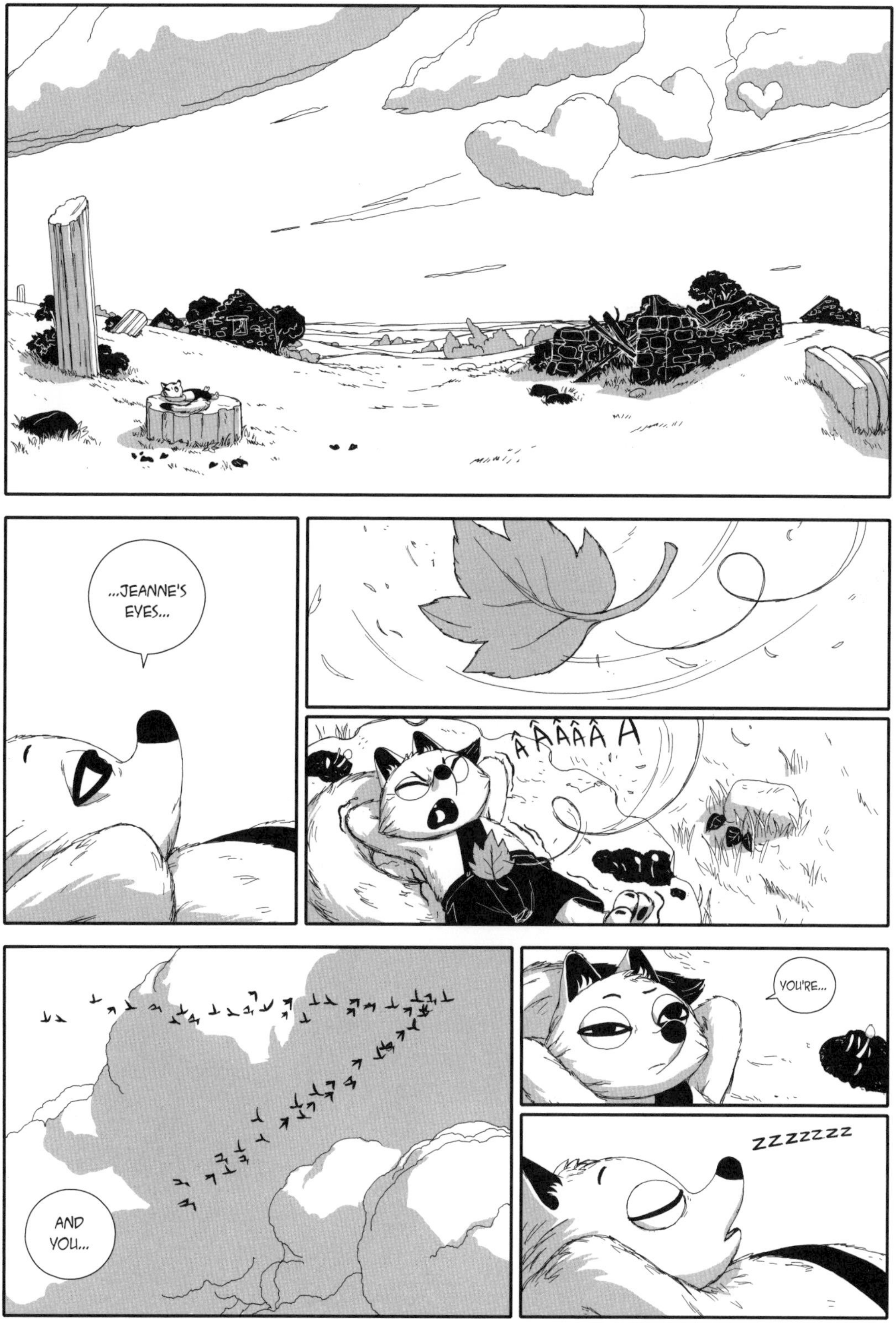
...JEANNE'S EYES...
ÂÂÂÂÂ A
YOU'RE...
AND YOU...
ZZZZZZZ

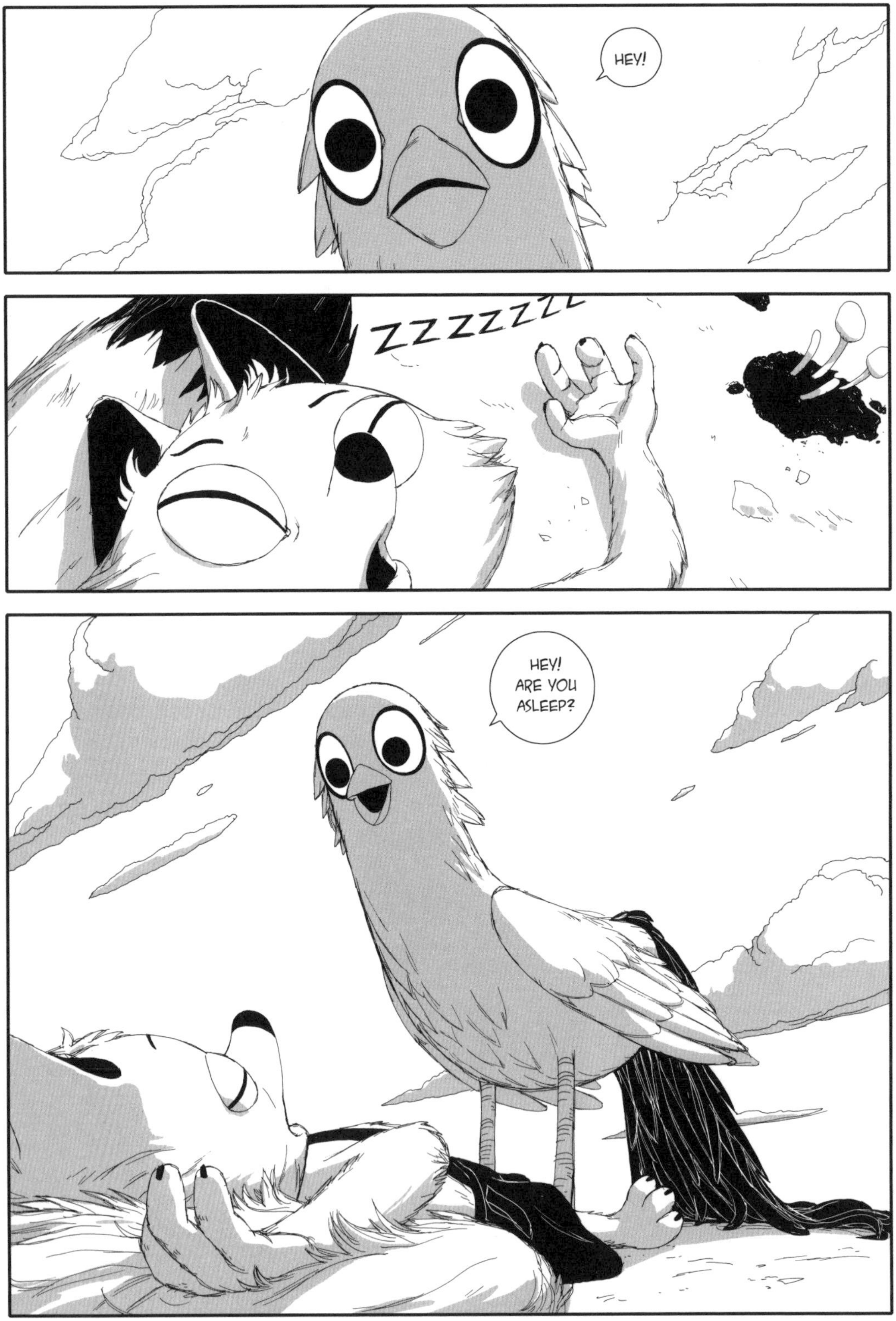
HEY!
ZZZZZZZ
HEY!
ARE YOU
ASLEEP?

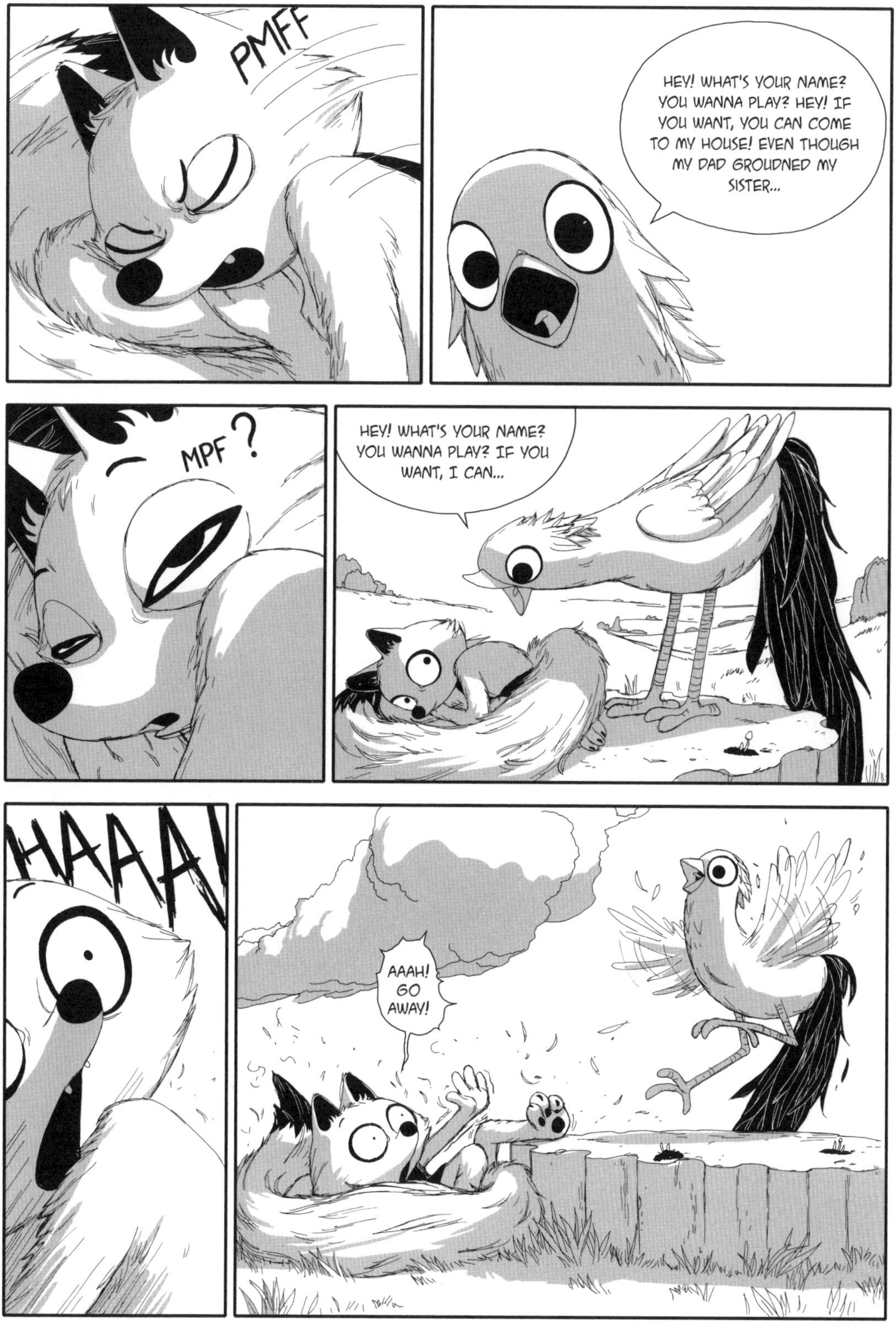
PMFF
HEY! WHAT'S YOUR NAME? YOU WANNA PLAY? HEY! IF YOU WANT, YOU CAN COME TO MY HOUSE! EVEN THOUGH MY DAD GROUDNED MY SISTER...
MPF ?
HEY! WHAT'S YOUR NAME? YOU WANNA PLAY? IF YOU WANT, I CAN...
HAAA
AAAH! GO AWAY!

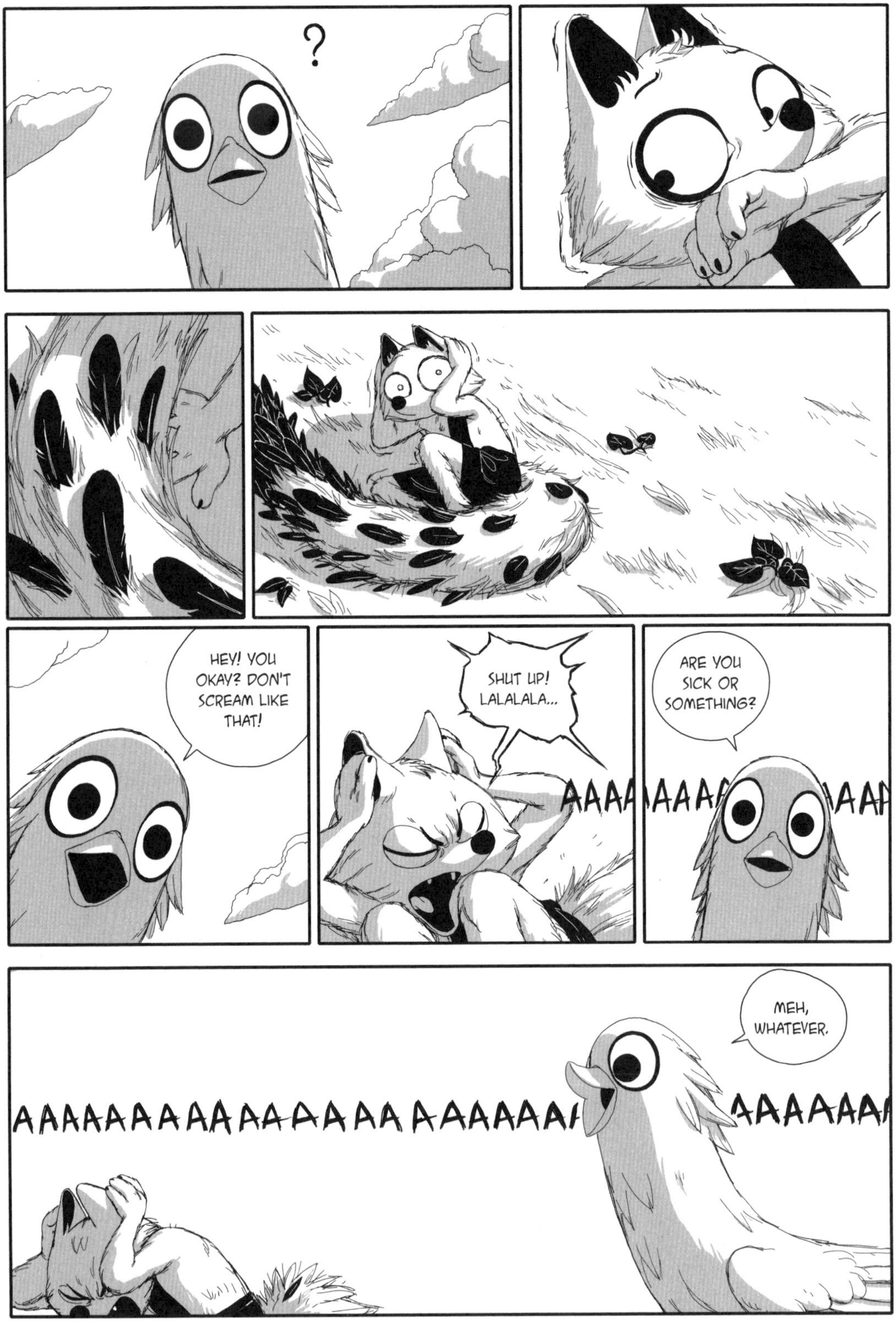
?
HEY! YOU OKAY? DON'T SCREAM LIKE THAT!
SHUT UP! LALALALA...
AAAA
ARE YOU SICK OR SOMETHING?
AAAA
AAAA
MEH, WHATEVER.
AAAAAAAAAAAAAAAAAAAA
AAAAAA

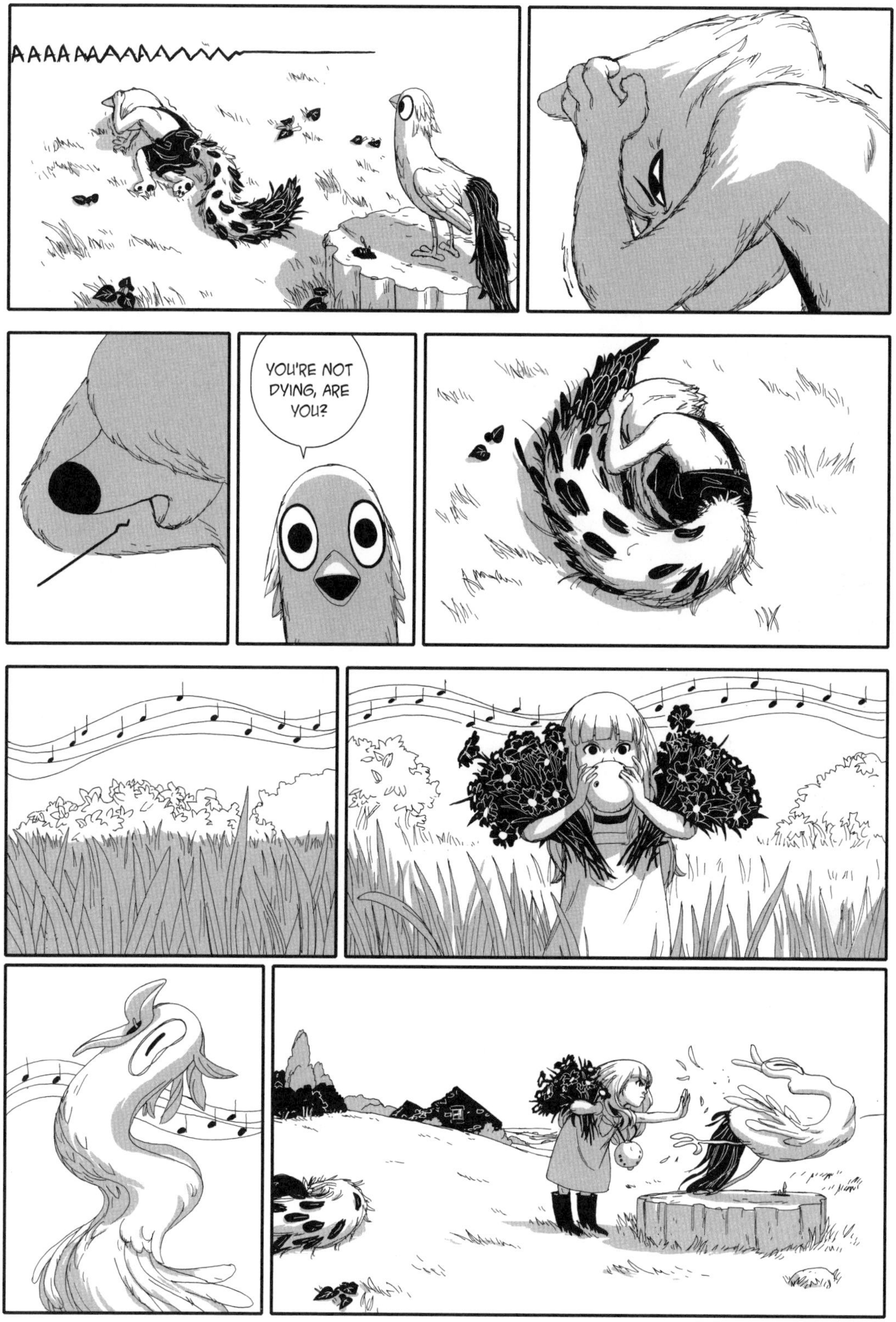
AAAAAAAAAAAA
YOU'RE NOT DYING, ARE YOU?

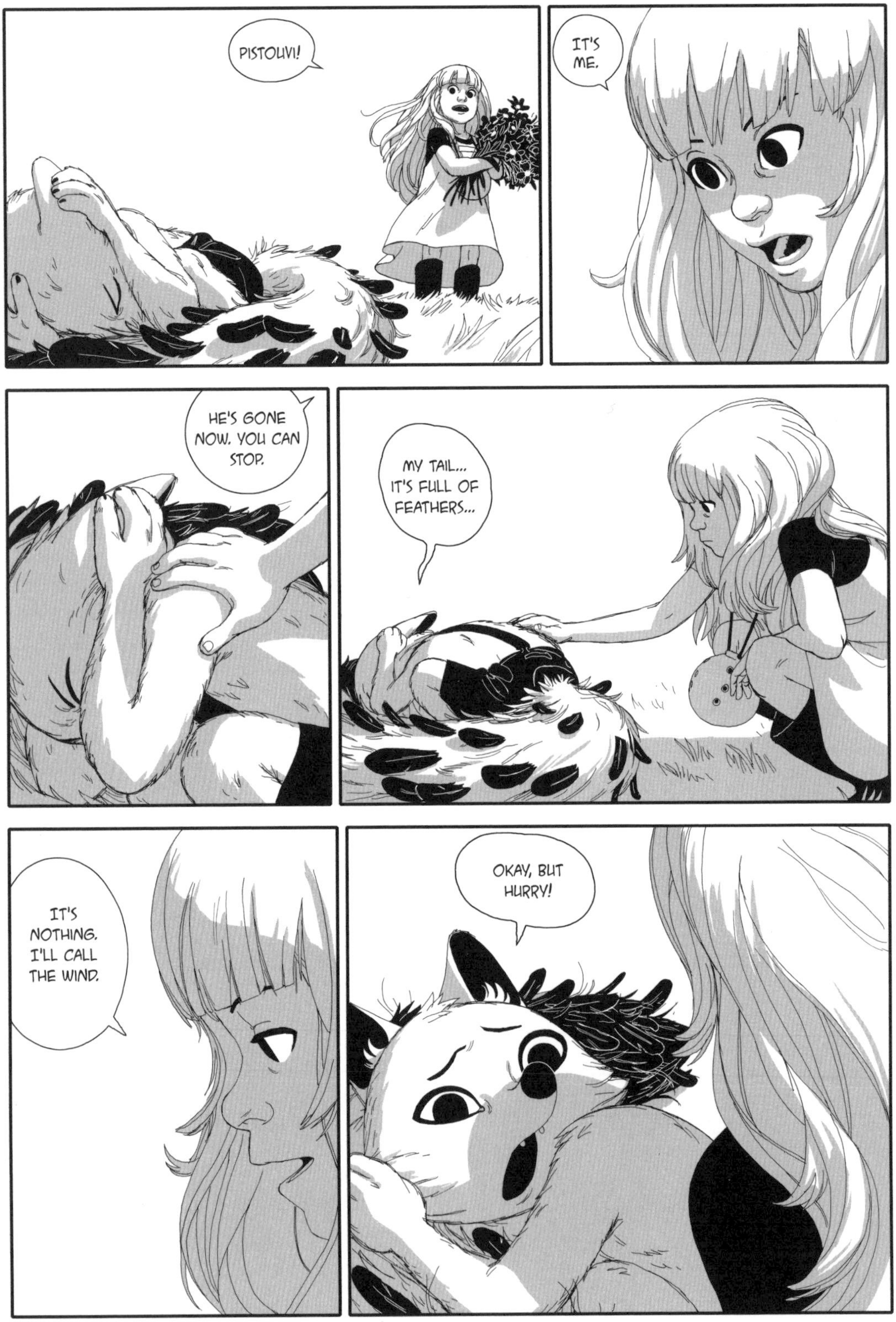
PISTOUVI!
IT'S ME.
HE'S GONE NOW. YOU CAN STOP.
MY TAIL... IT'S FULL OF FEATHERS...
IT'S NOTHING. I'LL CALL THE WIND.
OKAY, BUT HURRY!

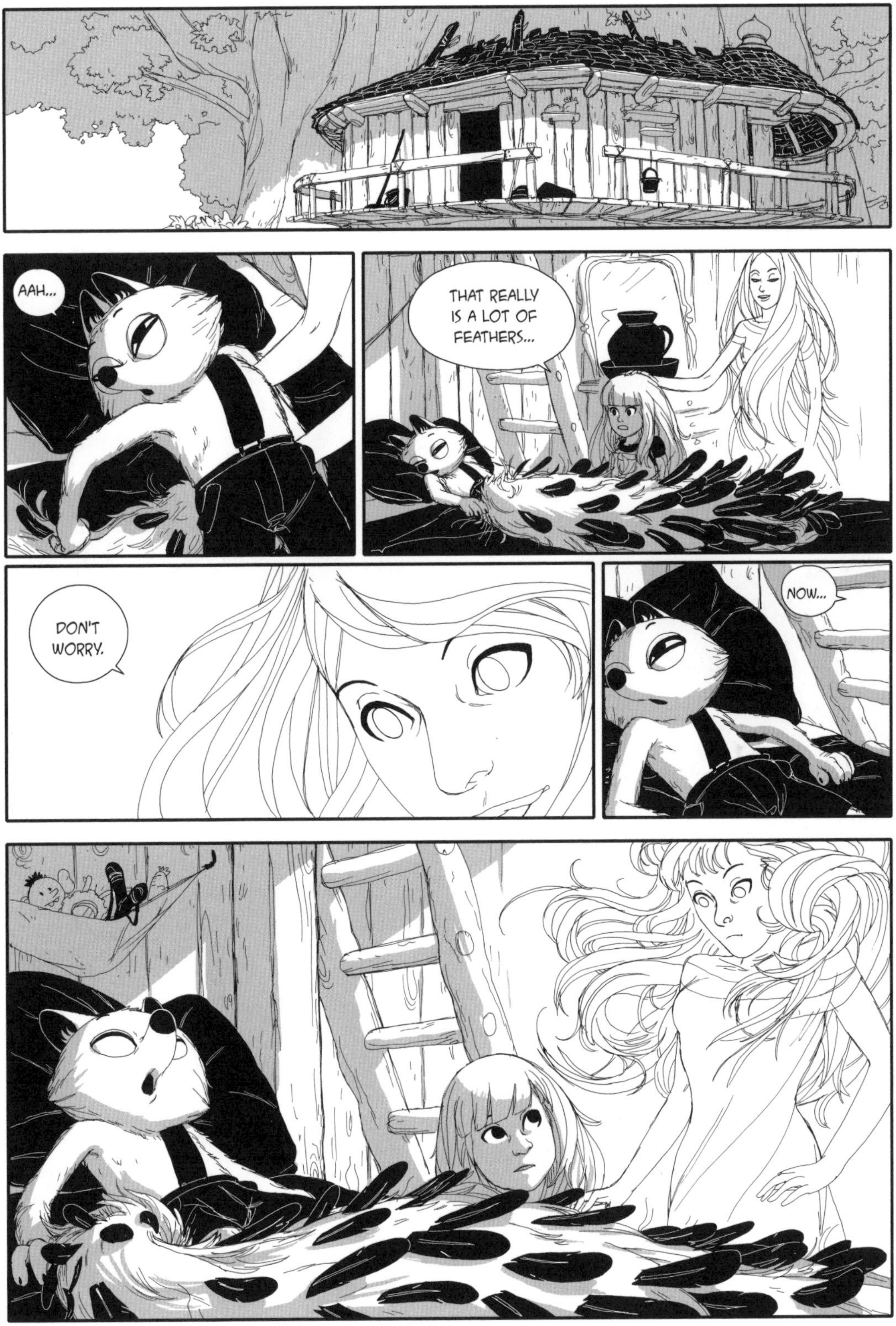
AAH...
THAT REALLY IS A LOT OF FEATHERS...
DON'T WORRY.
NOW...

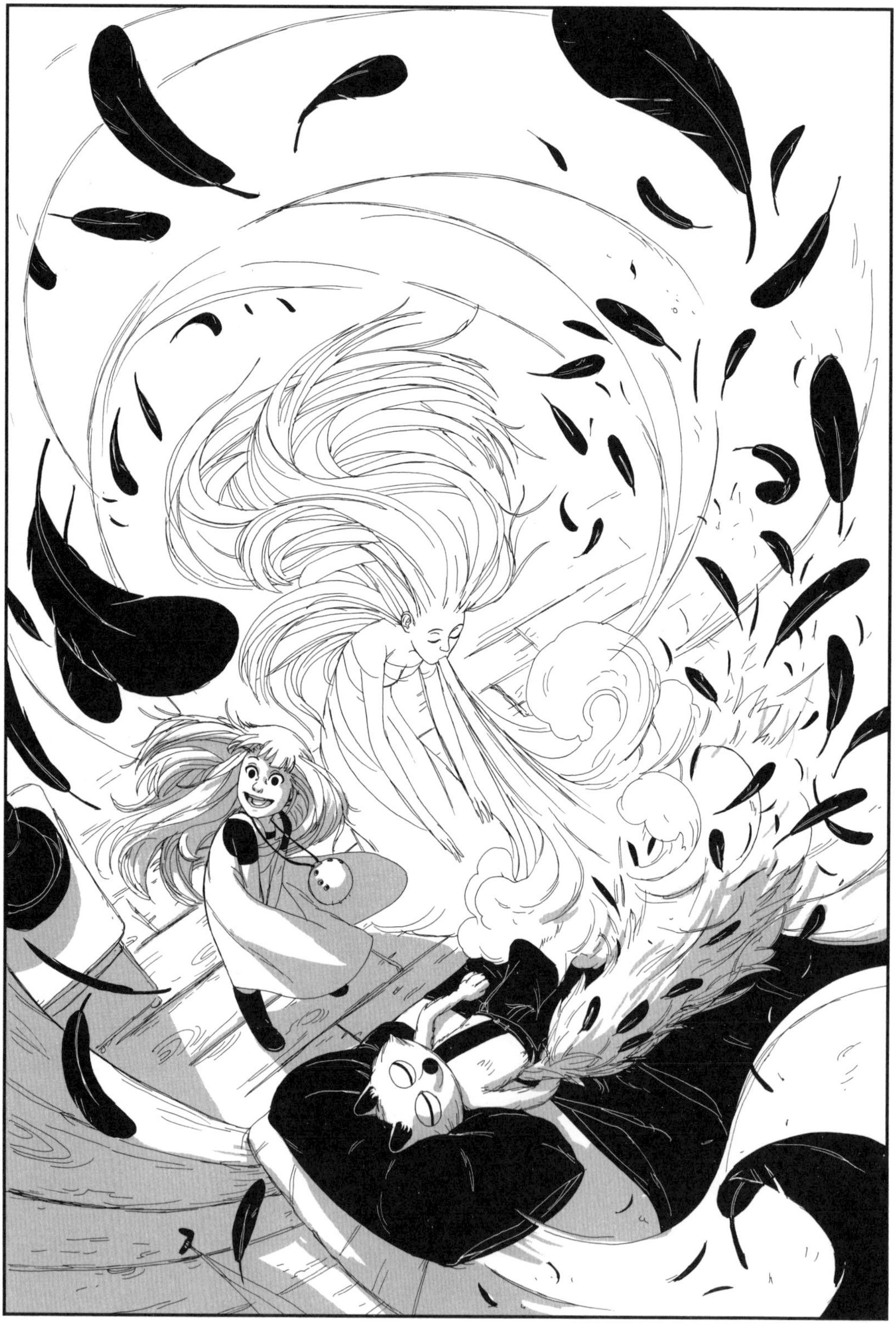

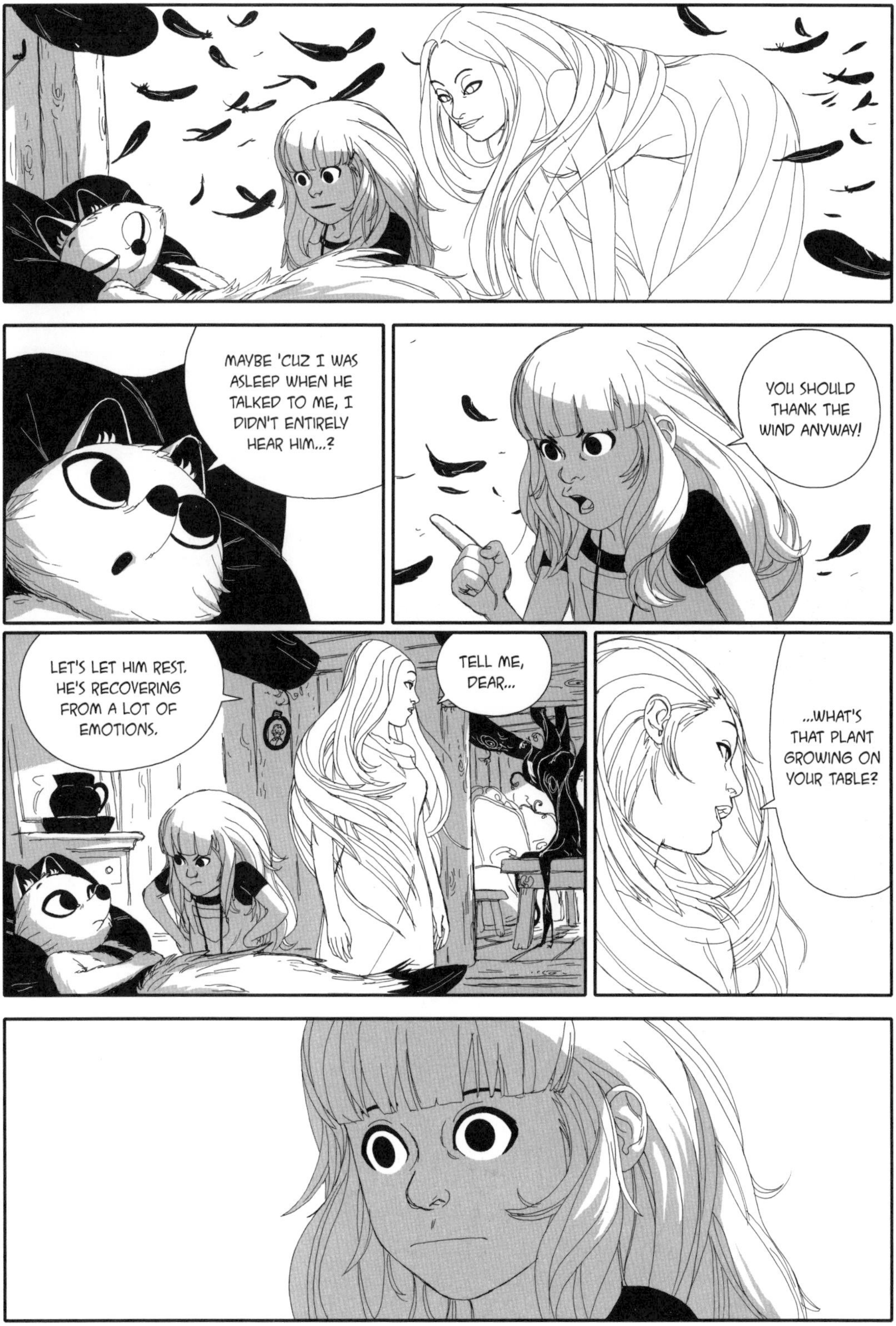
MAYBE 'CUZ I WAS ASLEEP WHEN HE TALKED TO ME, I DIDN'T ENTIRELY HEAR HIM...?
YOU SHOULD THANK THE WIND ANYWAY!
LET'S LET HIM REST. HE'S RECOVERING FROM A LOT OF EMOTIONS.
TELL ME, DEAR...
...WHAT'S THAT PLANT GROWING ON YOUR TABLE?

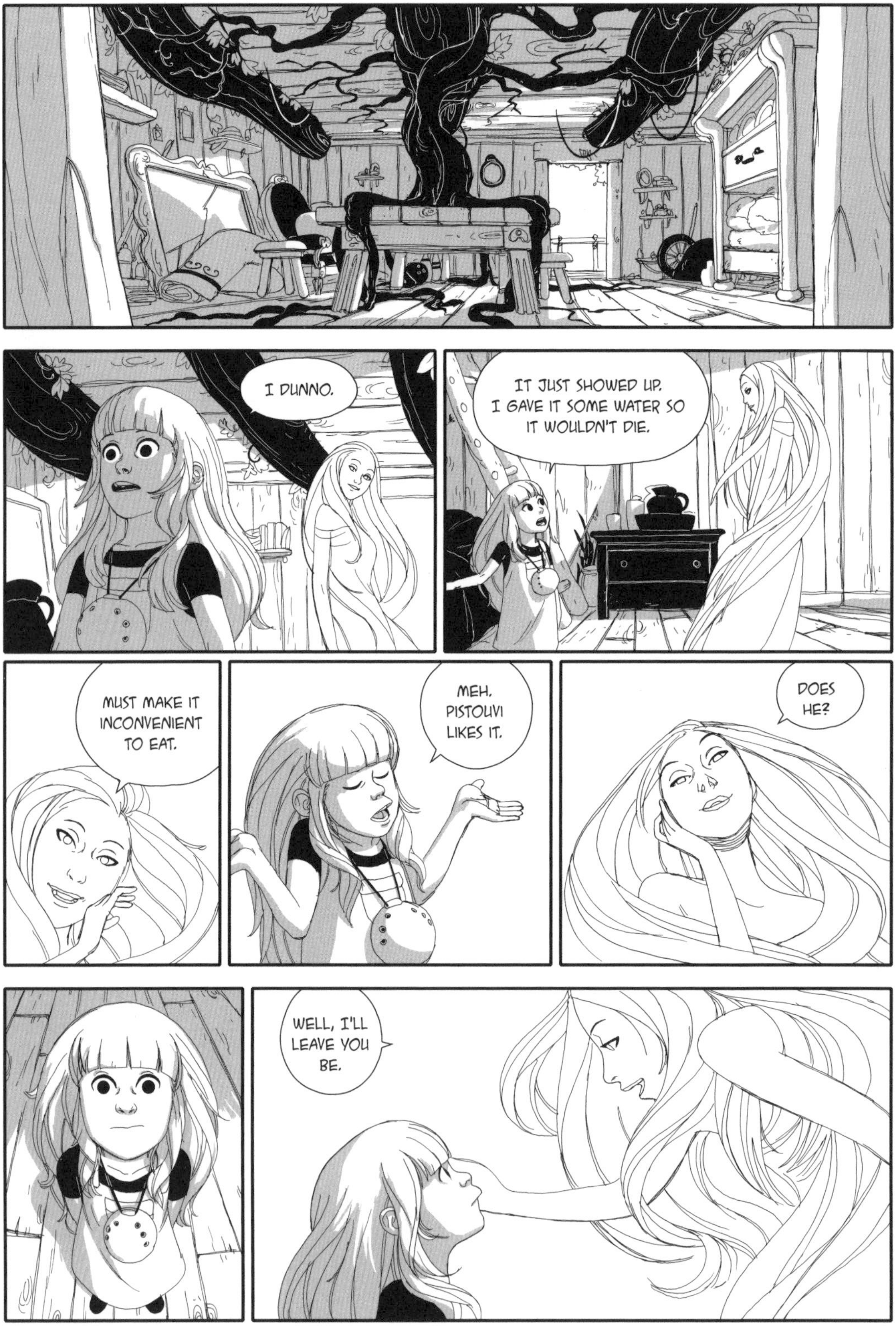
I DUNNO.
IT JUST SHOWED UP. I GAVE IT SOME WATER SO IT WOULDN'T DIE.
MUST MAKE IT INCONVENIENT TO EAT.
MEH. PISTOUVI LIKES IT.
DOES HE?
WELL, I'LL LEAVE YOU BE.

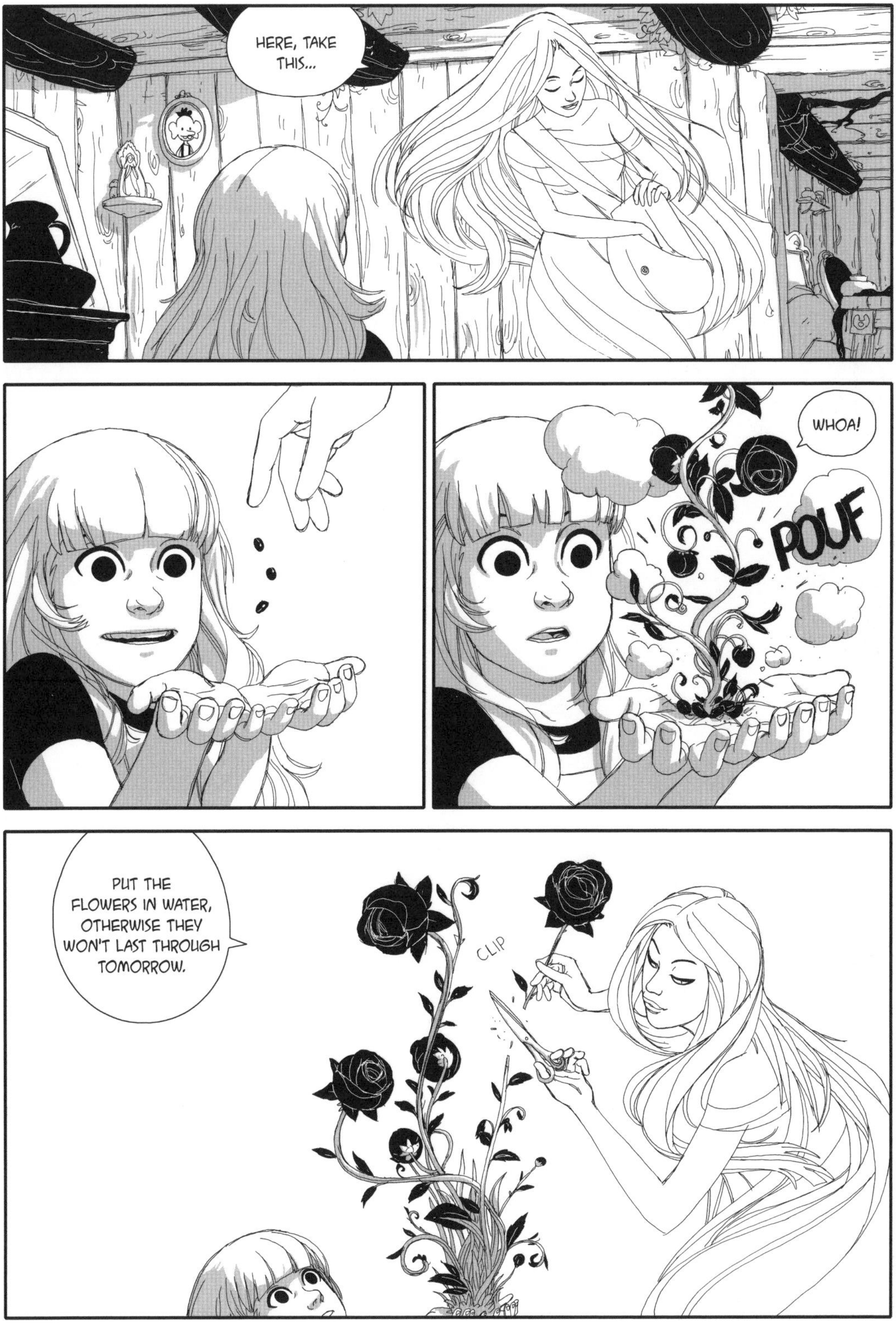
HERE, TAKE THIS...
WHOA!
POUF
PUT THE FLOWERS IN WATER, OTHERWISE THEY WON'T LAST THROUGH TOMORROW.
CLIP

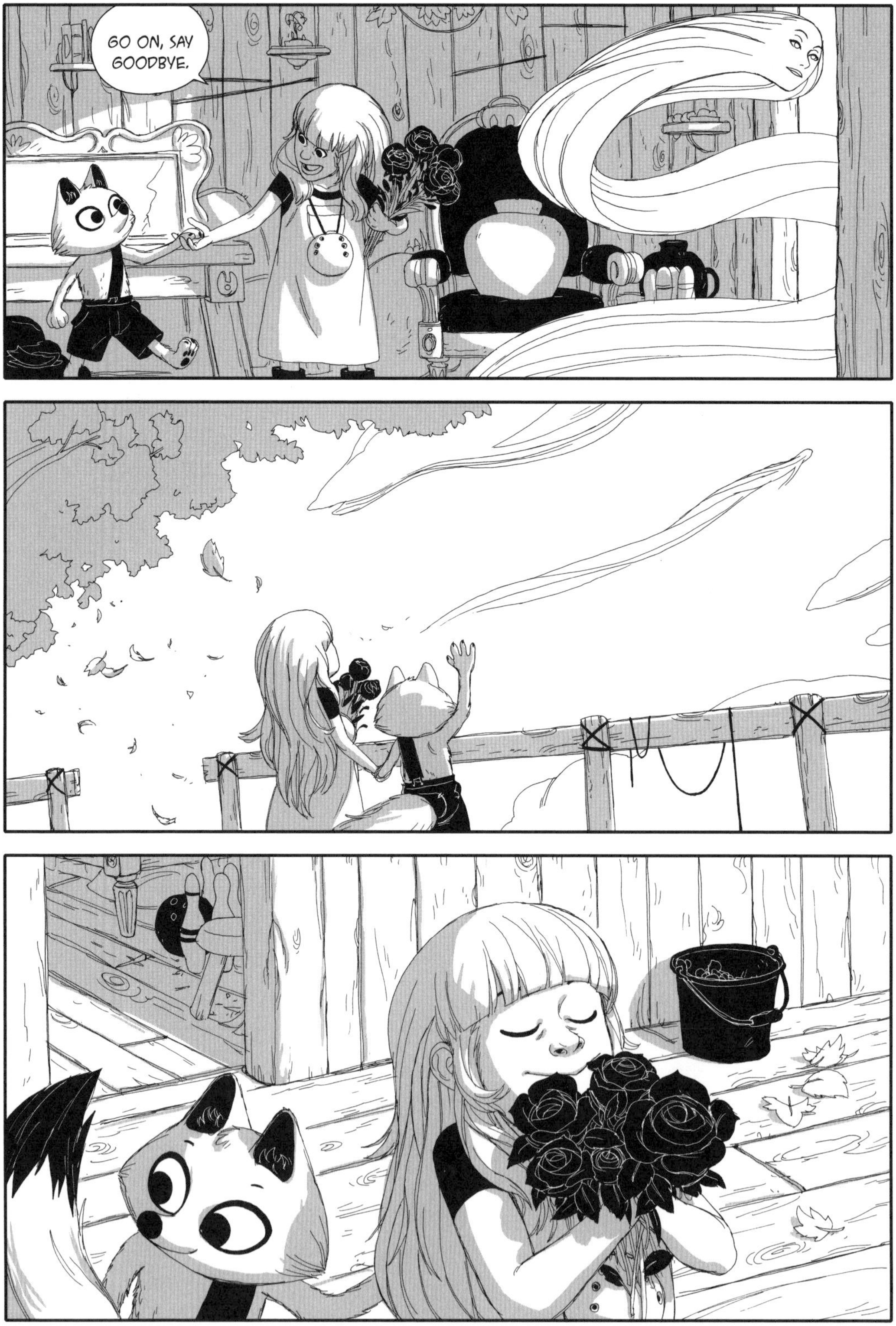
GO ON, SAY GOODBYE.

Chapter 5

ALWAYS

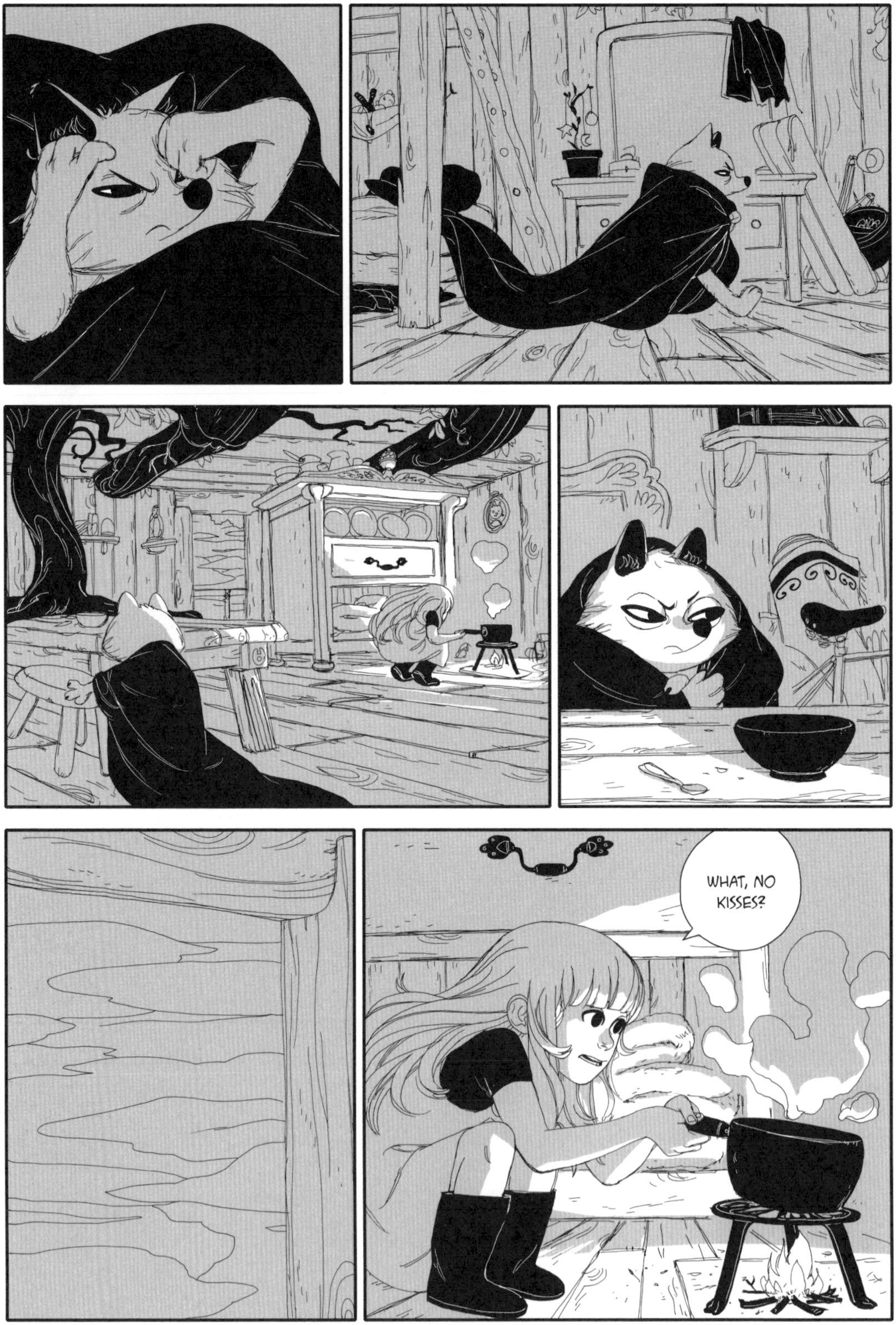
WHAT, NO KISSES?

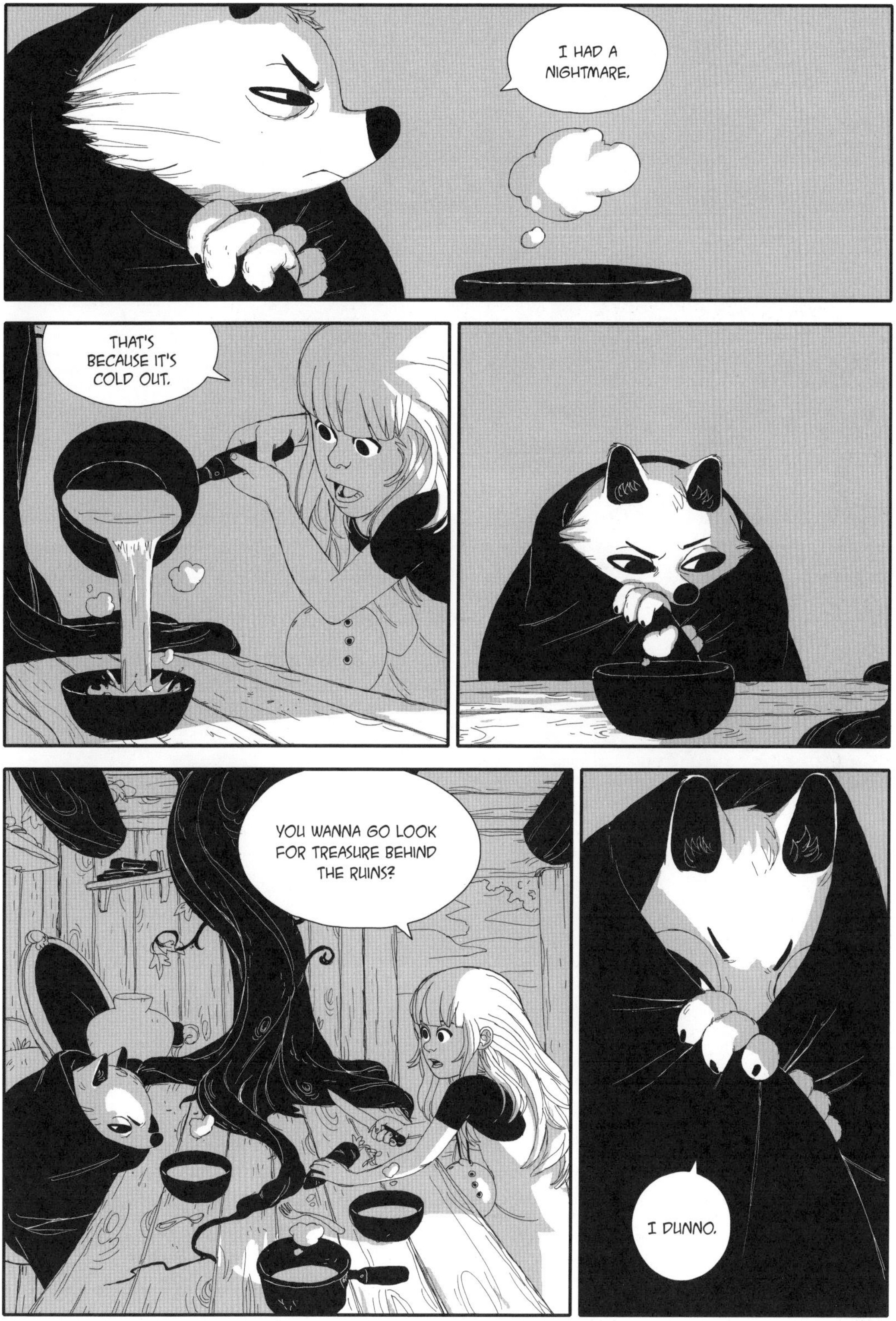
I HAD A NIGHTMARE.
THAT'S BECAUSE IT'S COLD OUT.
YOU WANNA GO LOOK FOR TREASURE BEHIND THE RUINS?
I DUNNO.

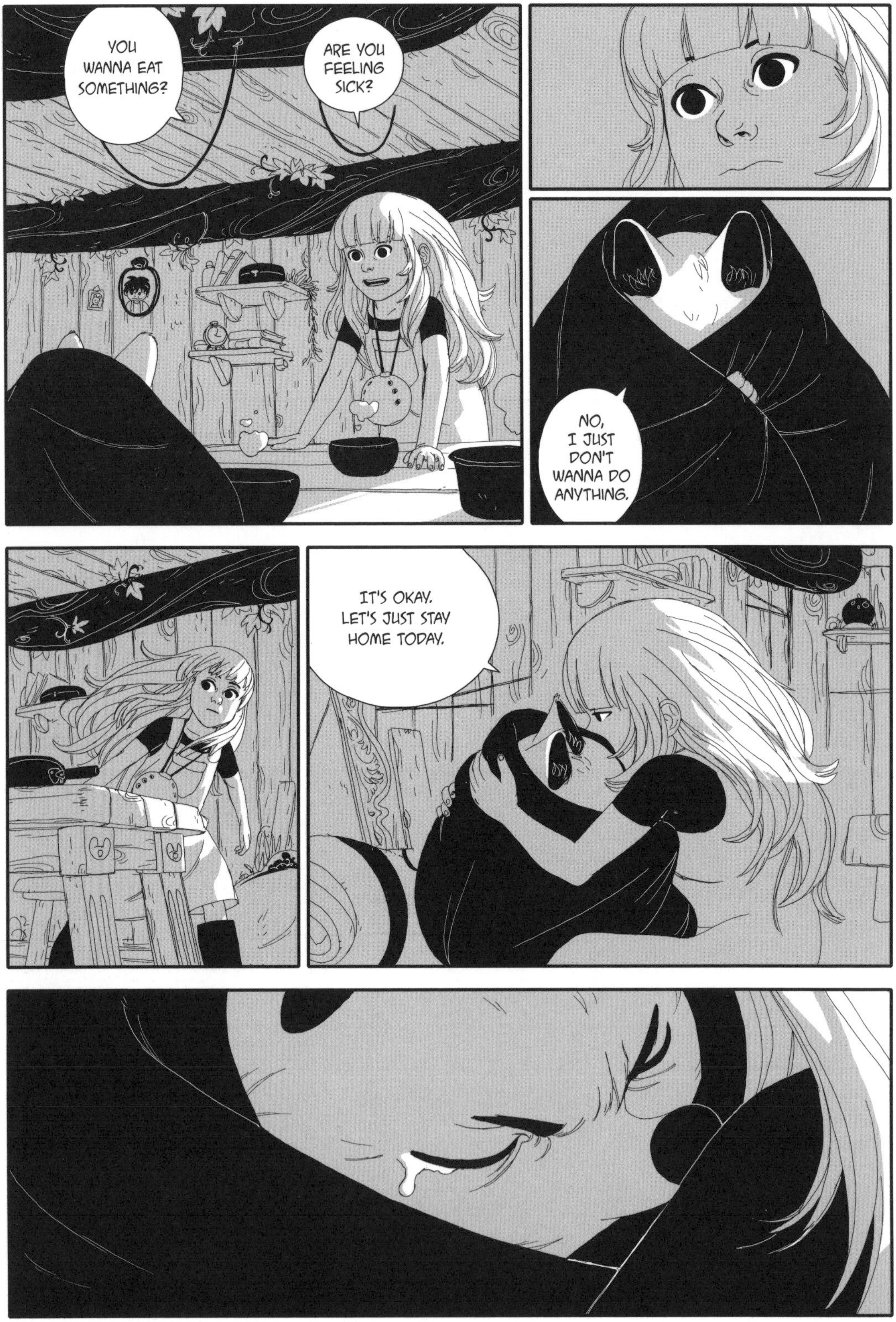
YOU WANNA EAT SOMETHING?
ARE YOU FEELING SICK?
NO, I JUST DON'T WANNA DO ANYTHING.
IT'S OKAY. LET'S JUST STAY HOME TODAY.

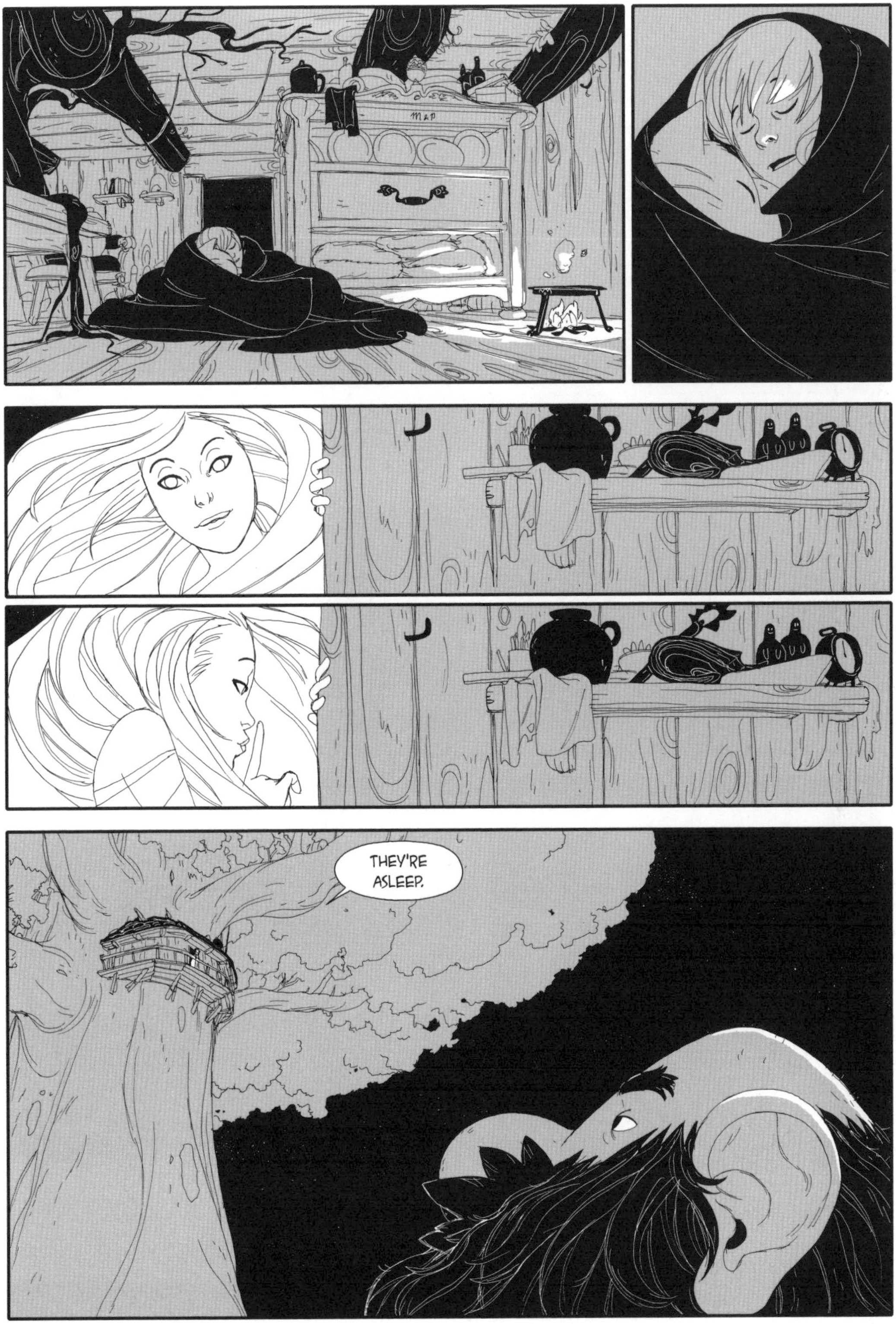
THEY'RE ASLEEP.

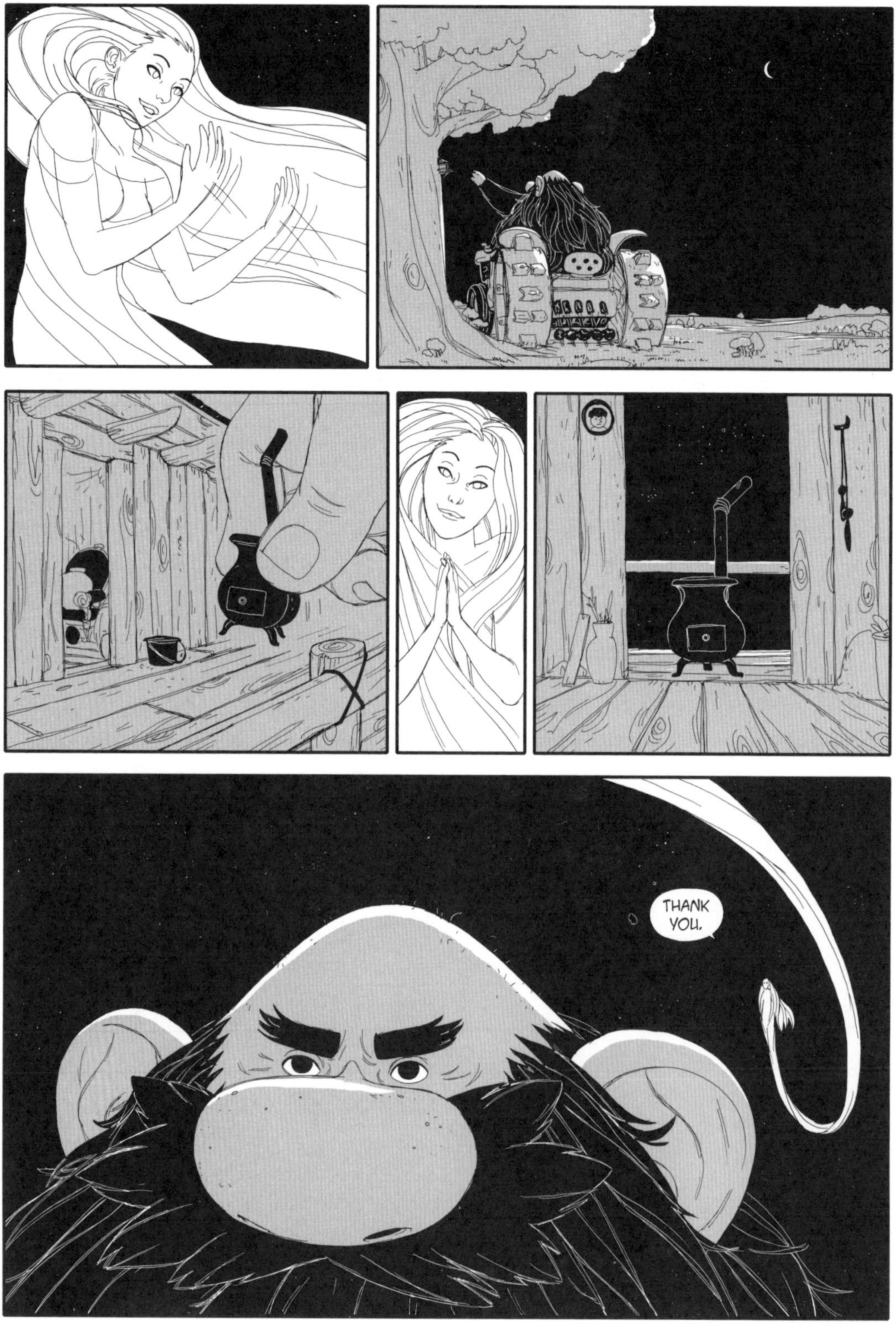
THANK YOU.

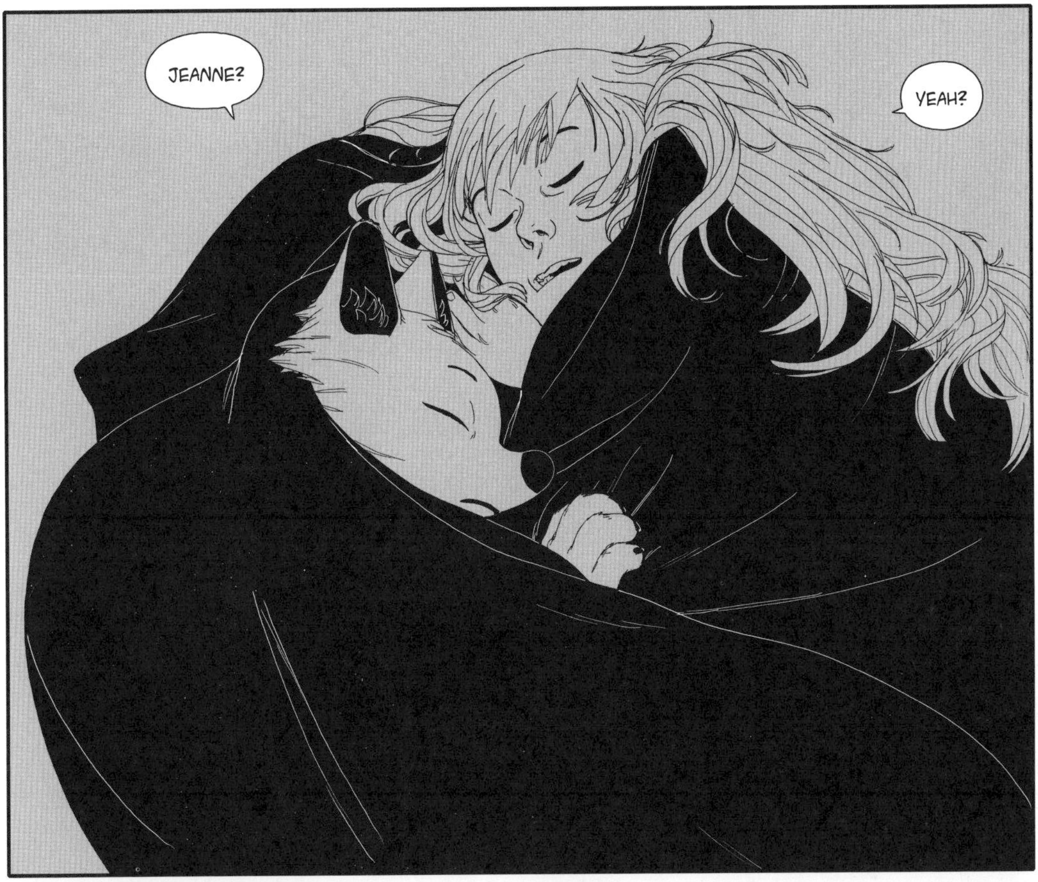
JEANNE?
YEAH?

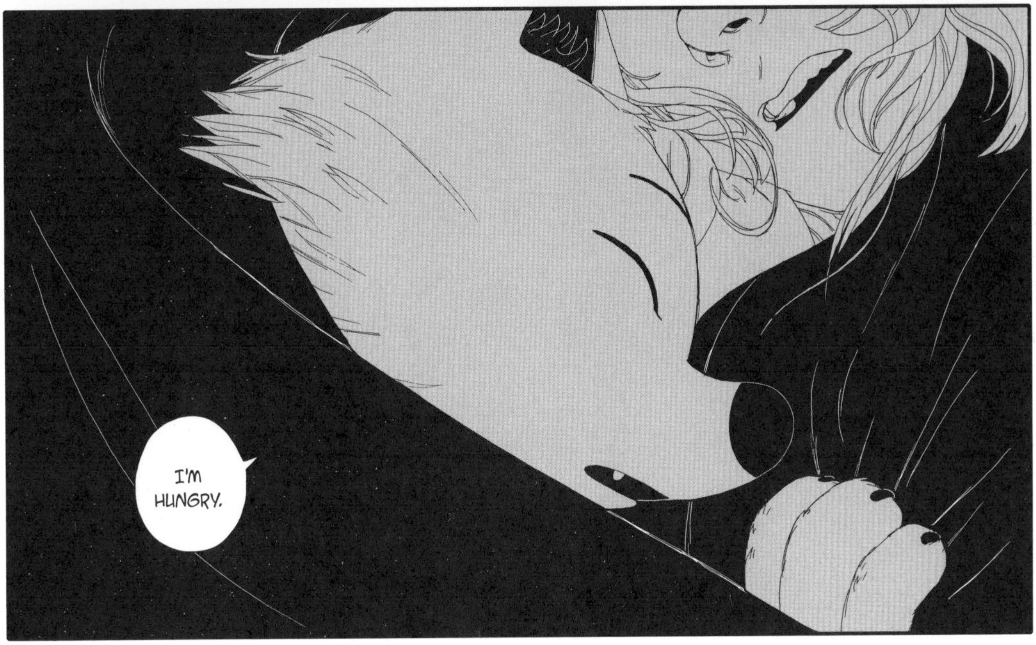
I'M HUNGRY.

Chapter 6

TOGETHER

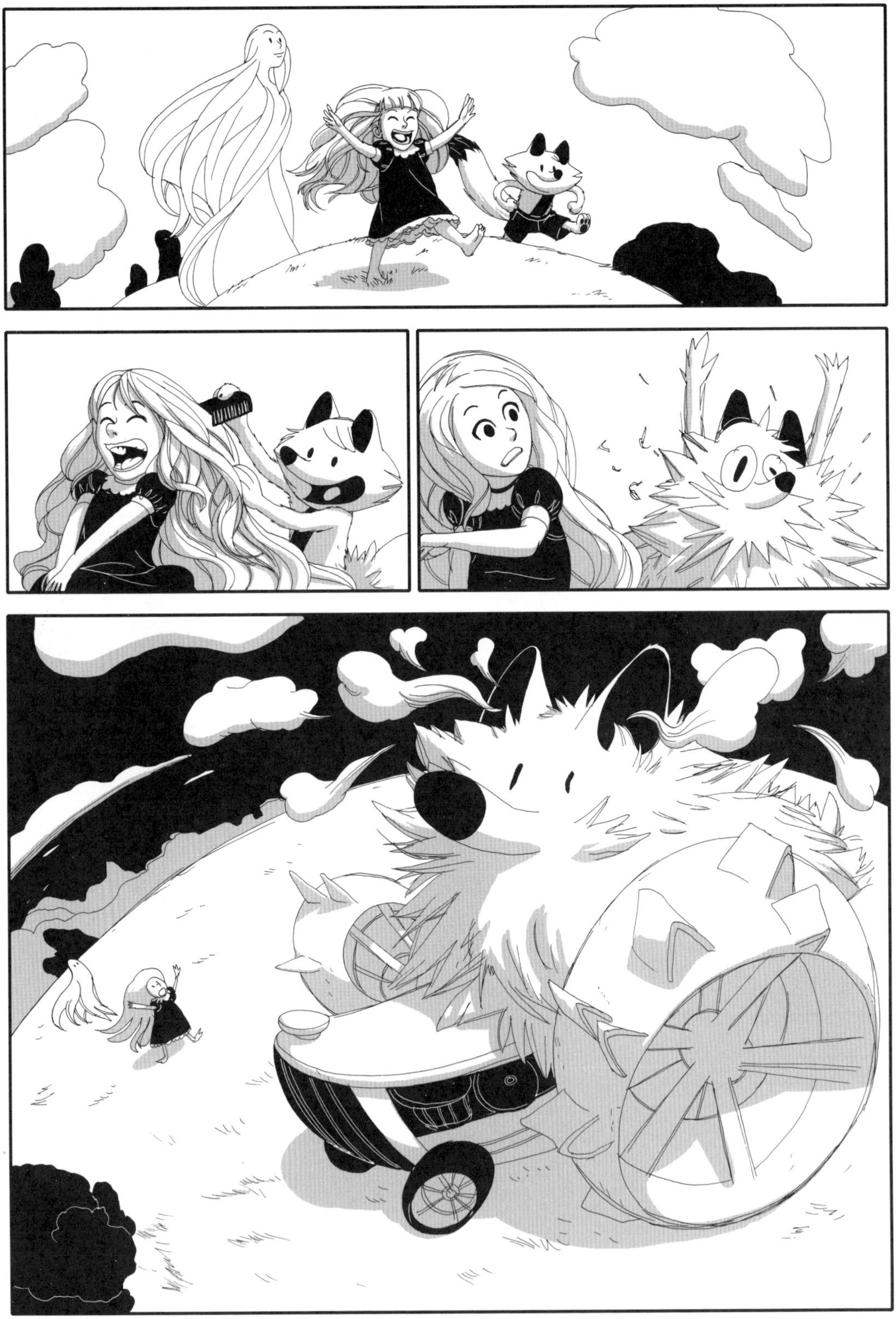

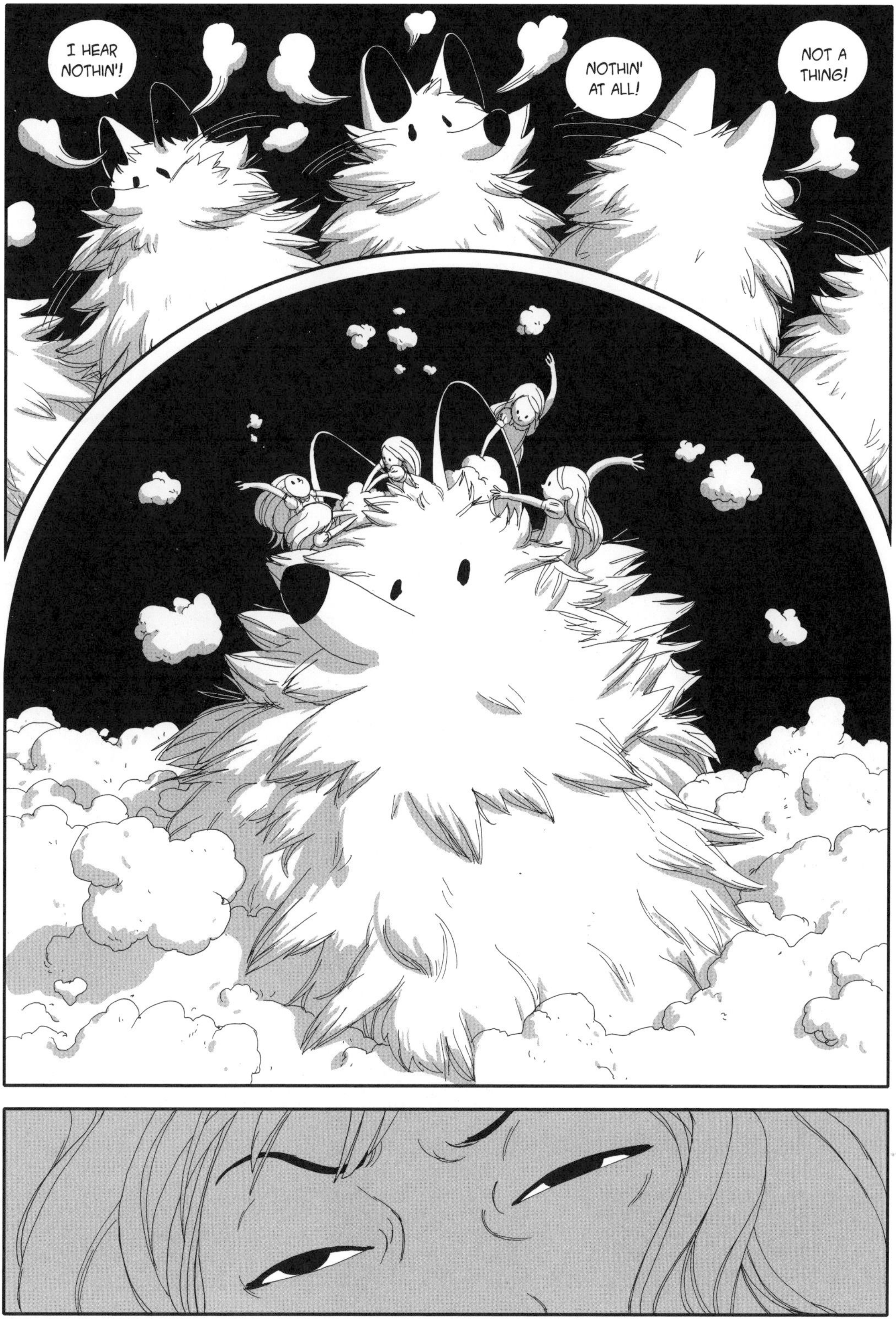
I HEAR NOTHIN'!
NOTHIN' AT ALL!
NOT A THING!

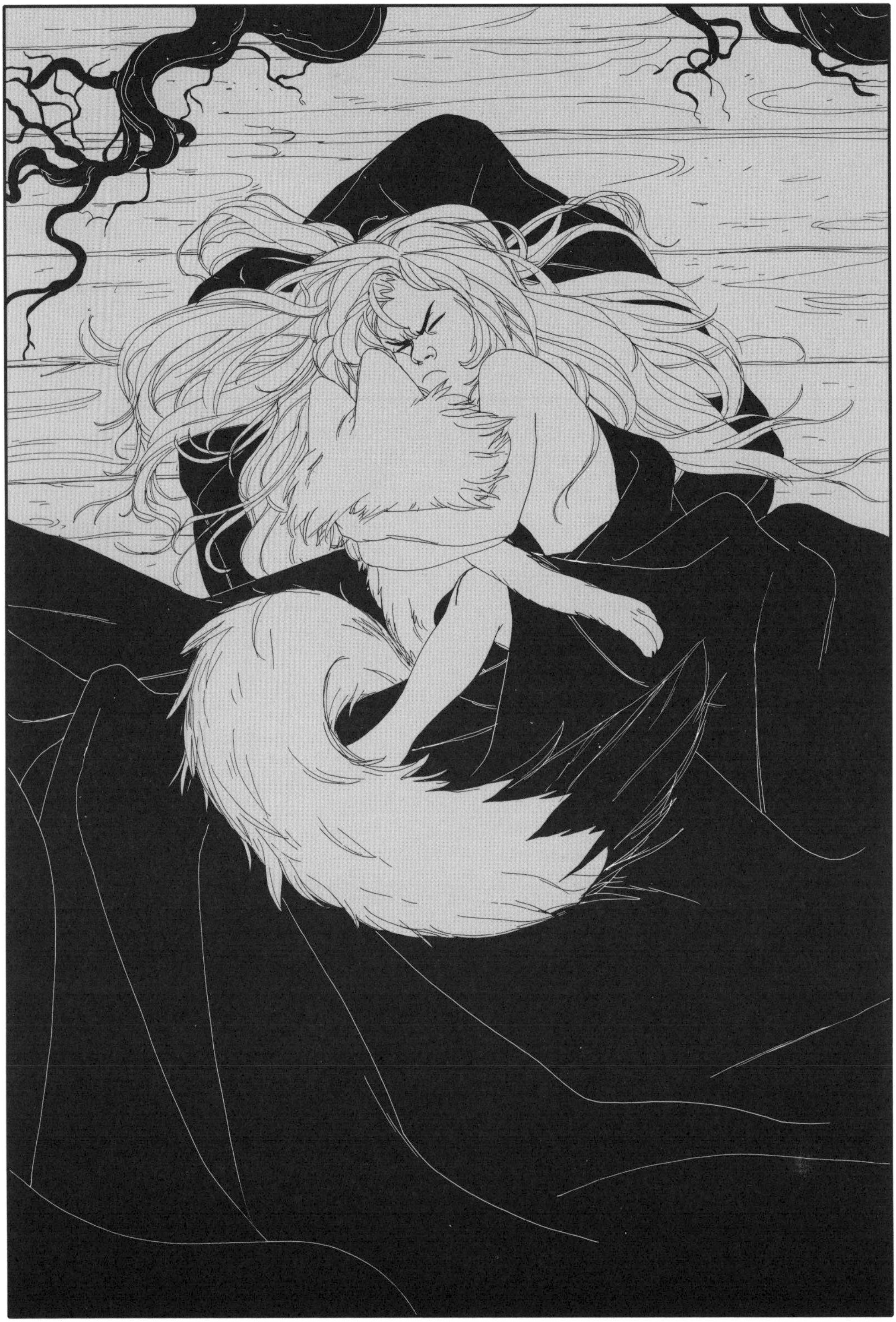

Chapter 7

NEVER

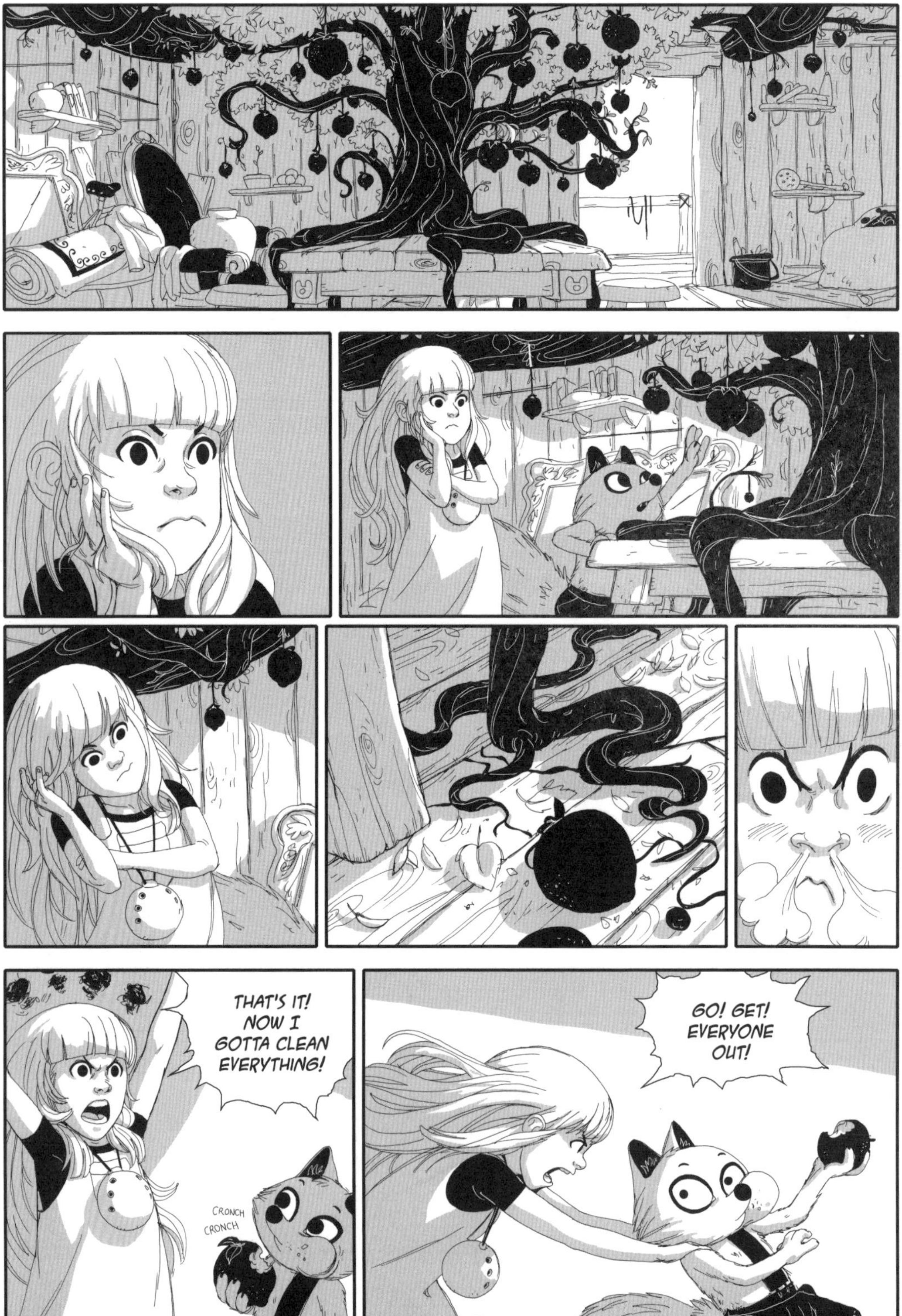
THAT'S IT! NOW I GOTTA CLEAN EVERYTHING!
CRONCH CRONCH
GO! GET! EVERYONE OUT!

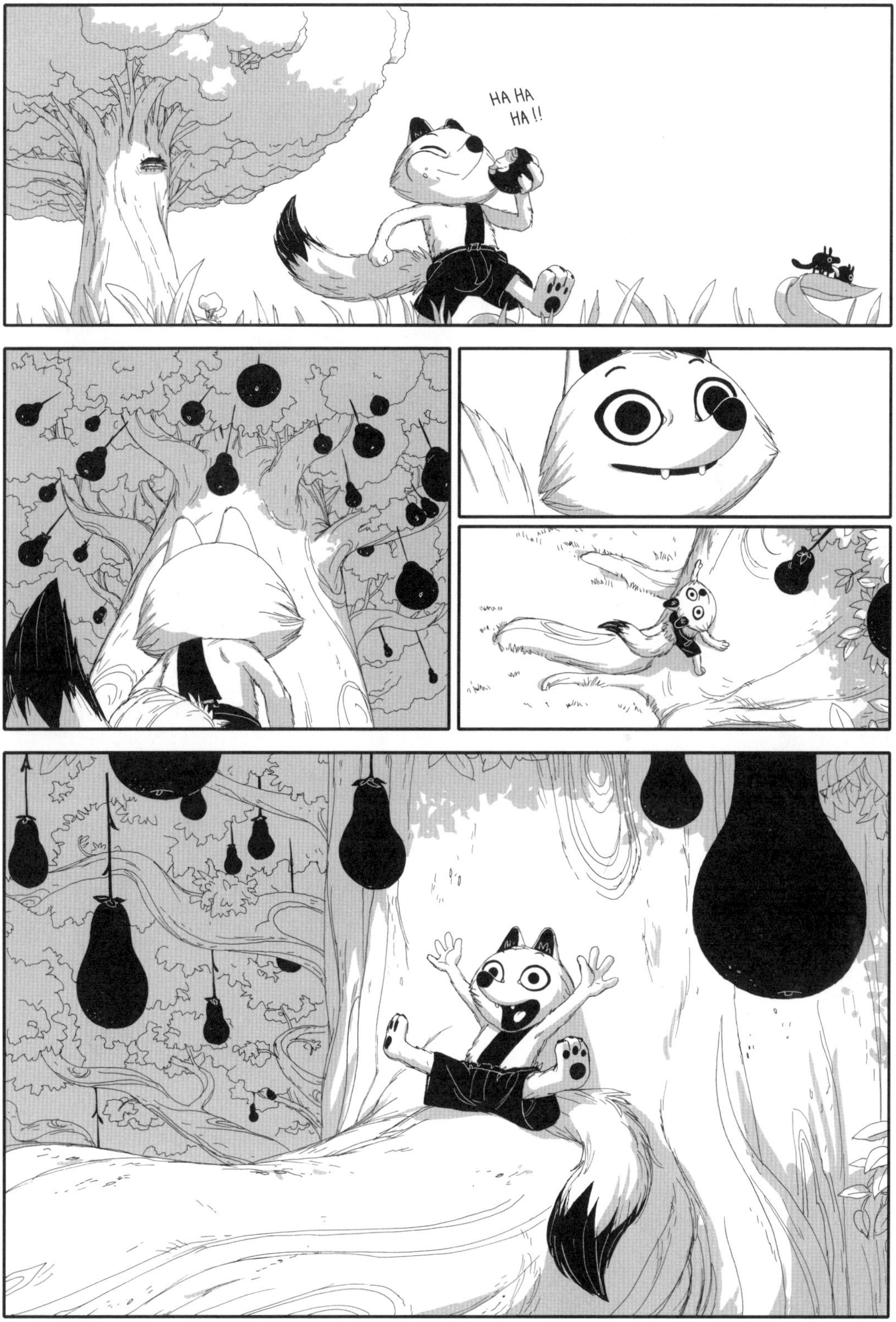
HA HA
HA !!

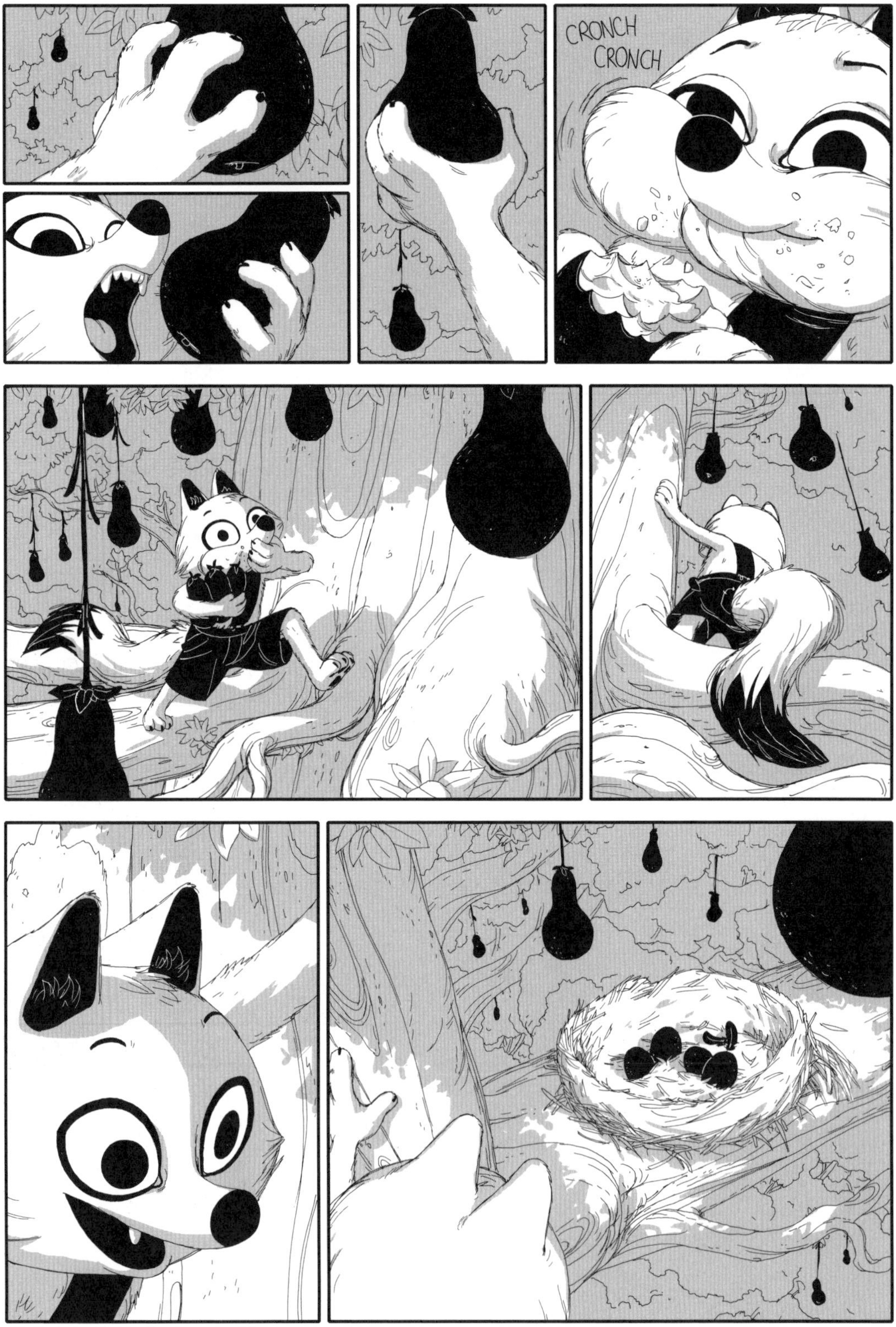
CRONCH
CRONCH

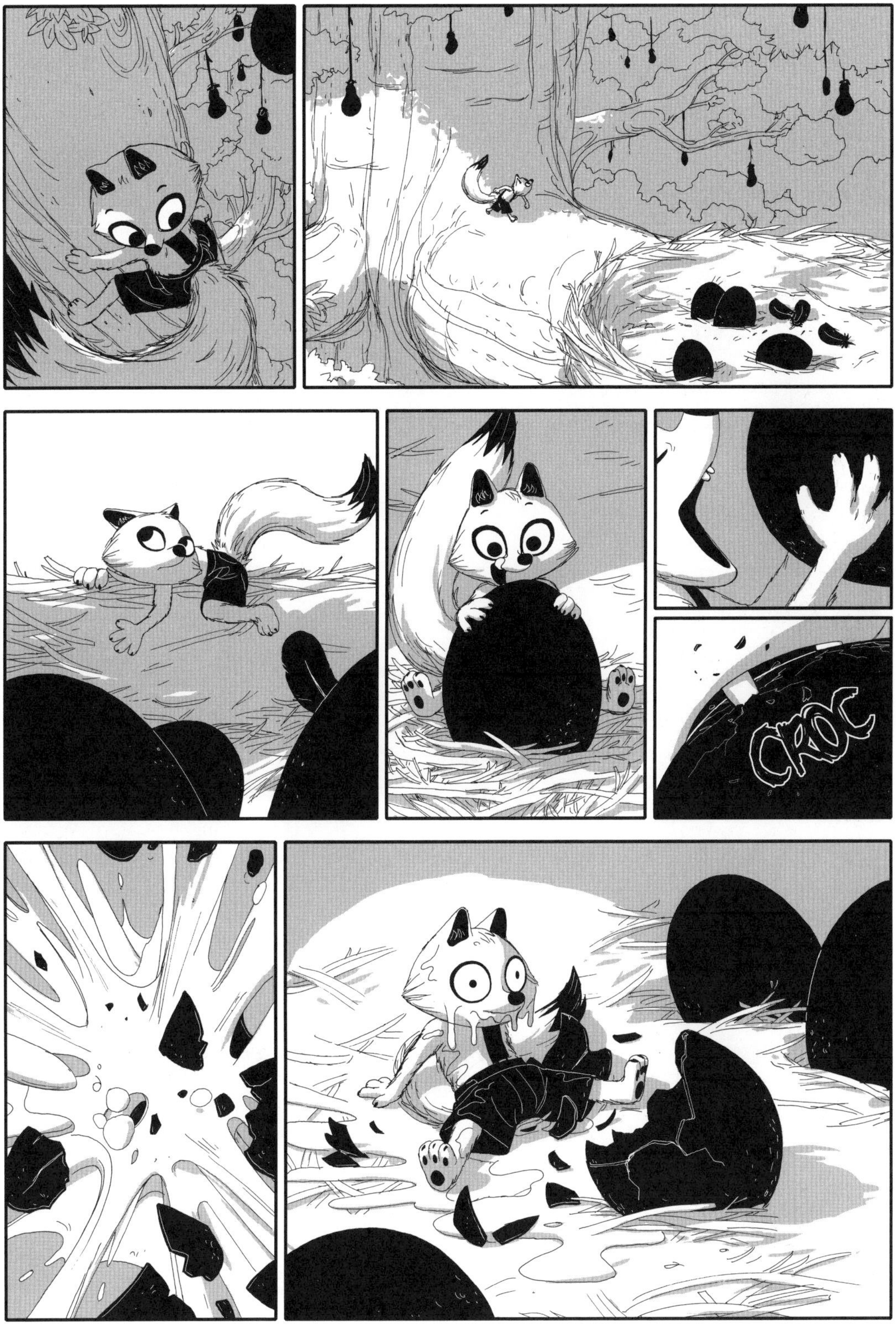
CROC

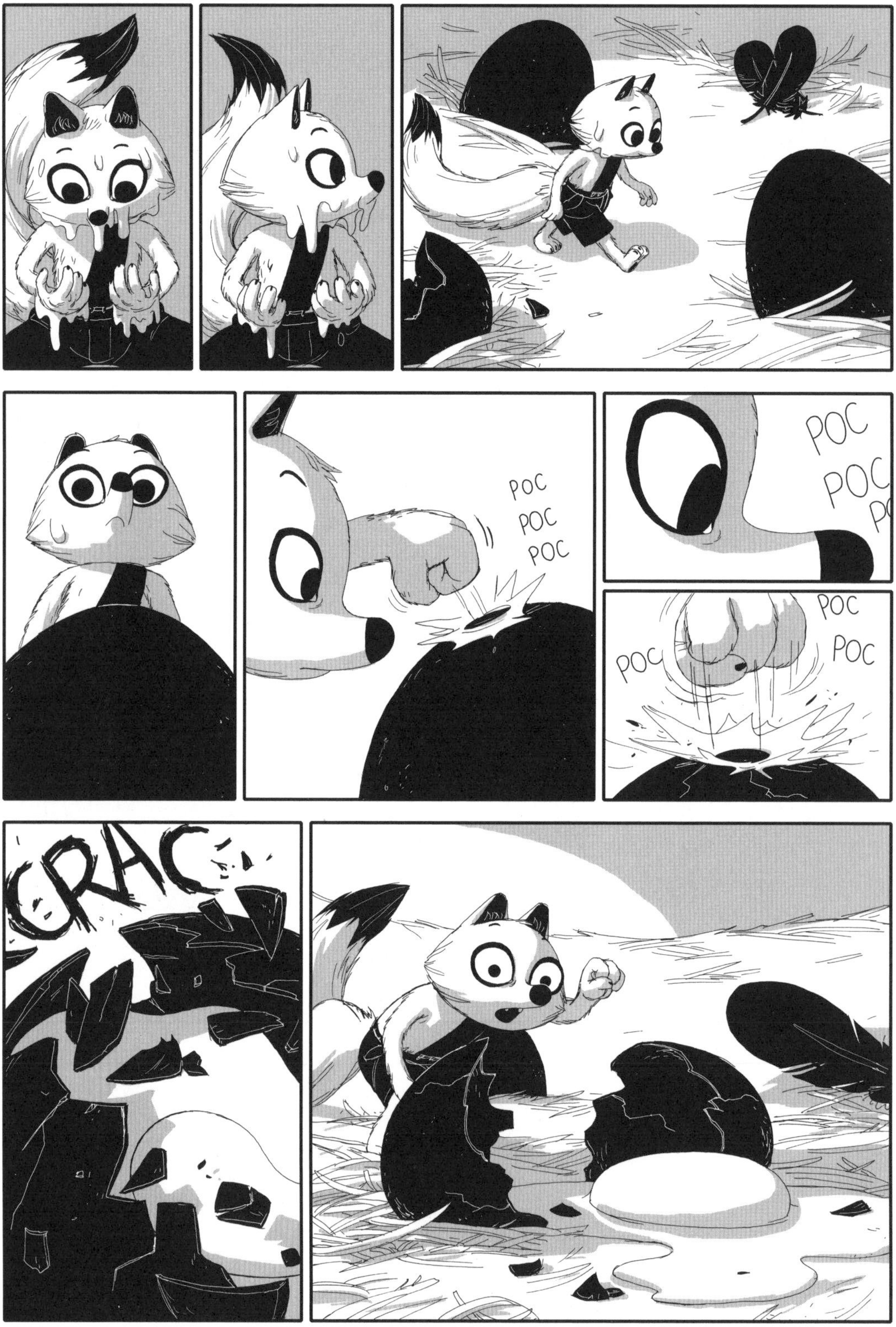

POC
POC
POC
POC
POC
POC
POC
POC
CRAC

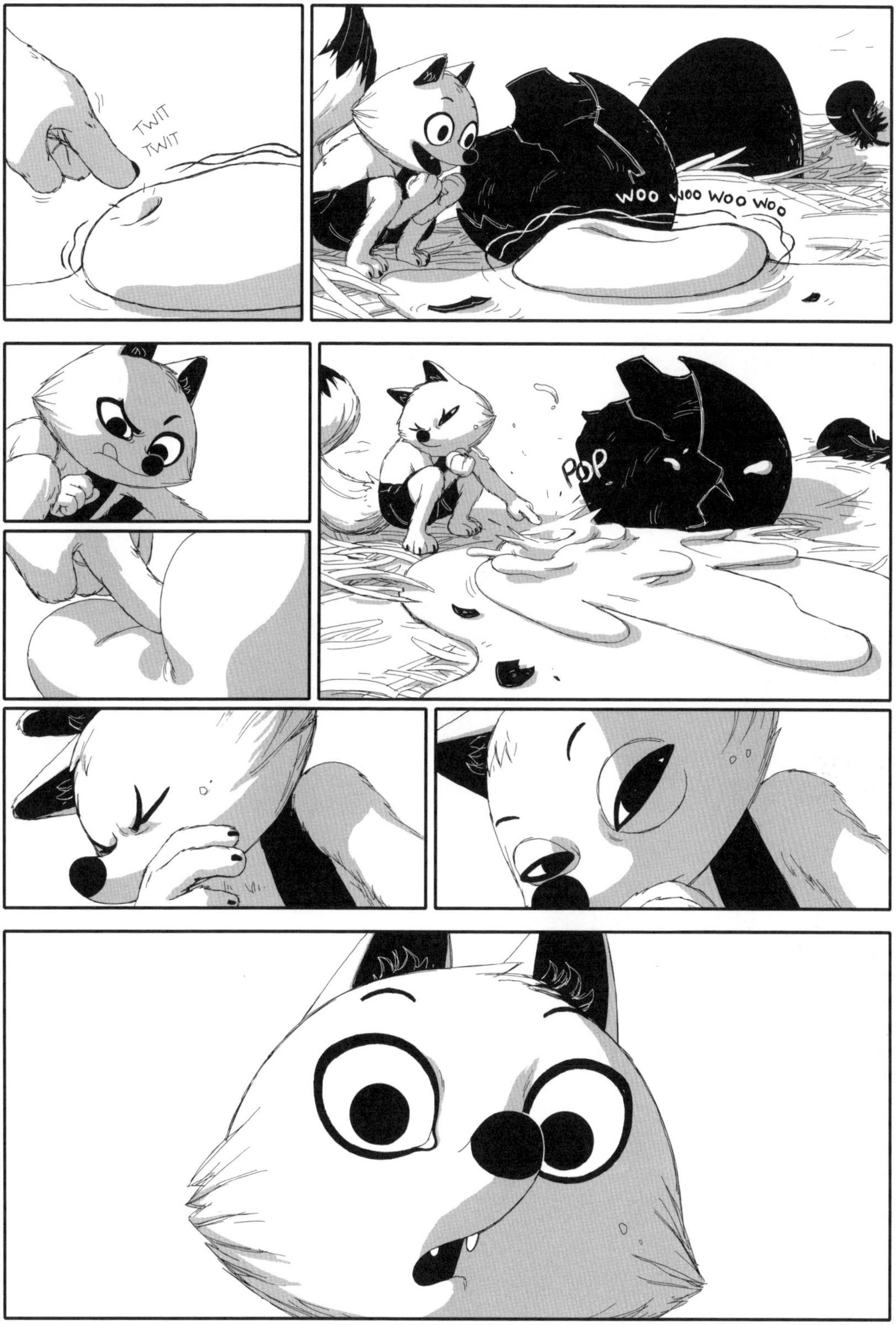
TWIT
TWIT
WOO WOO WOO WOO
POP

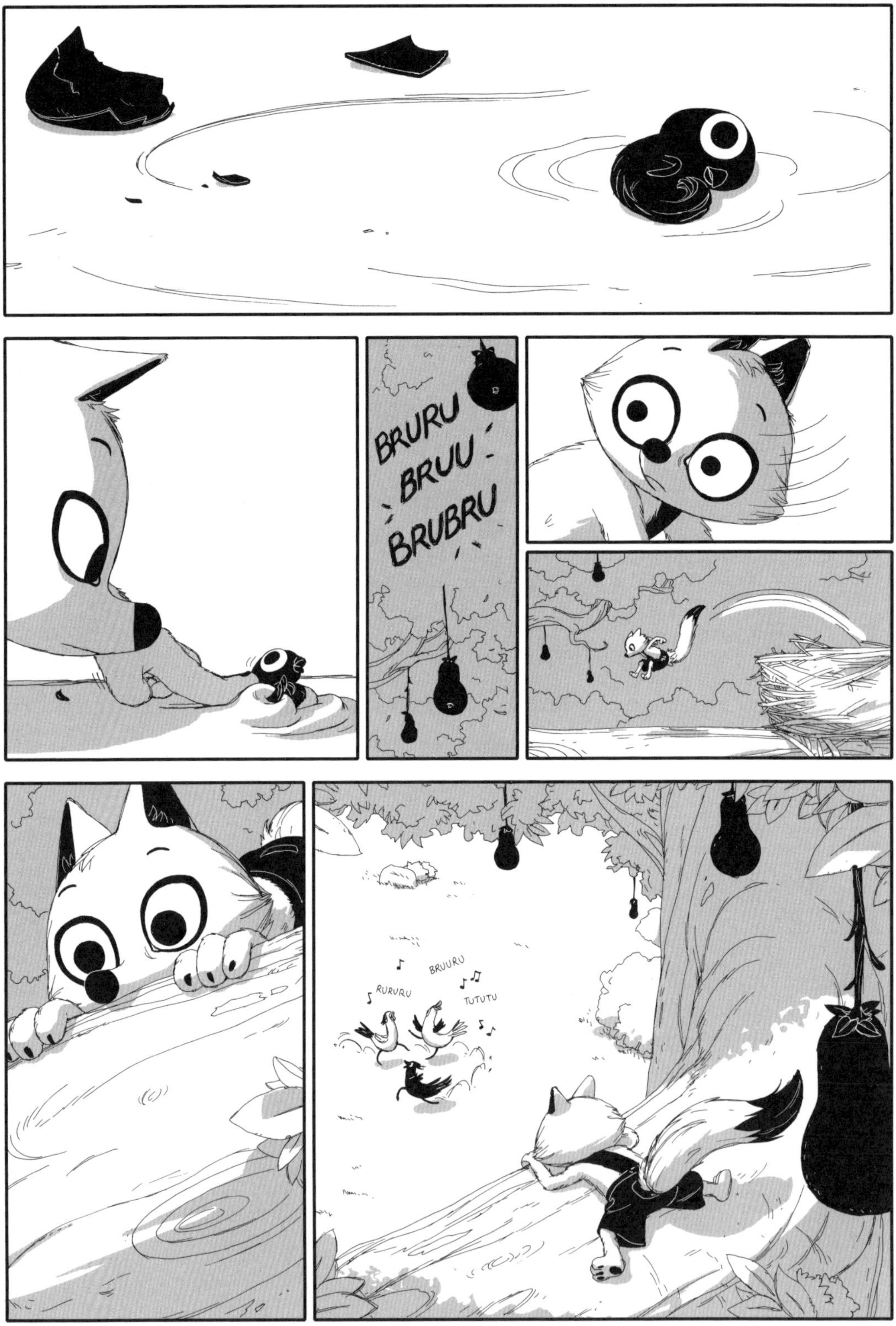
BRURU
BRUU
BRUBRU
RURURU
BRUURU
TUTUTU

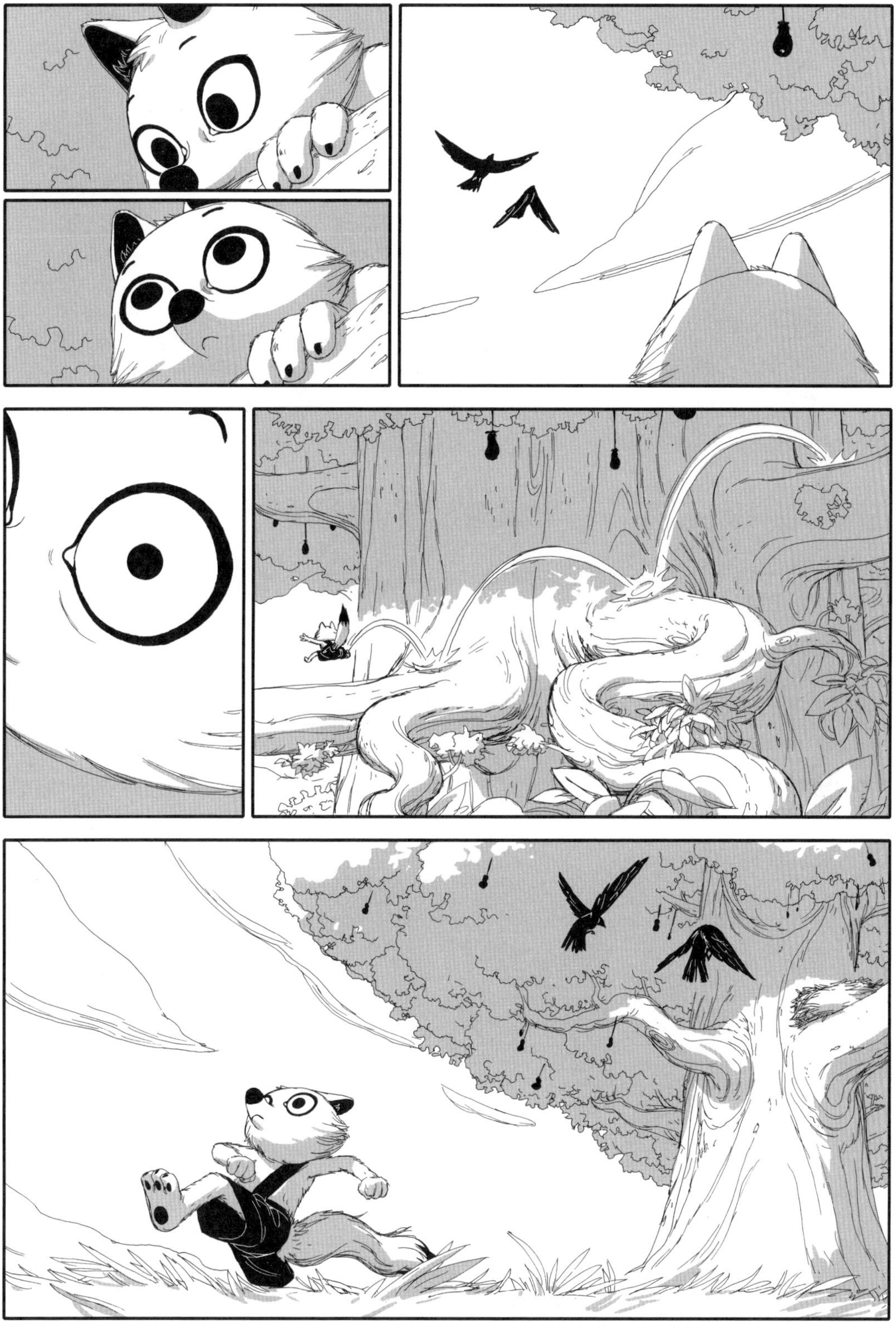

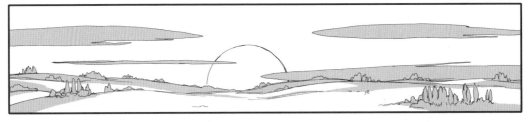

What've you been up to?

I went for a walk.

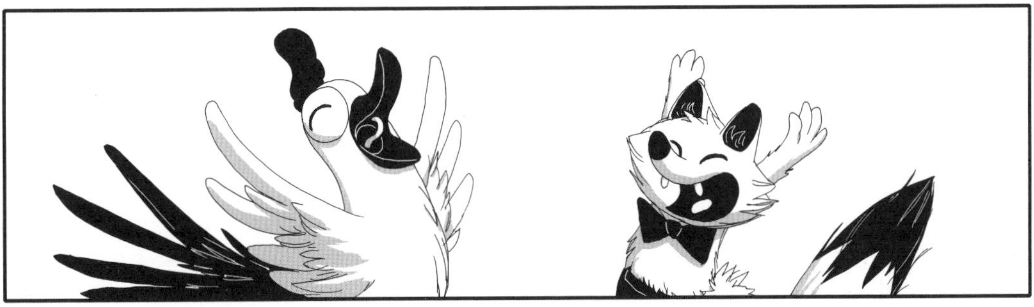

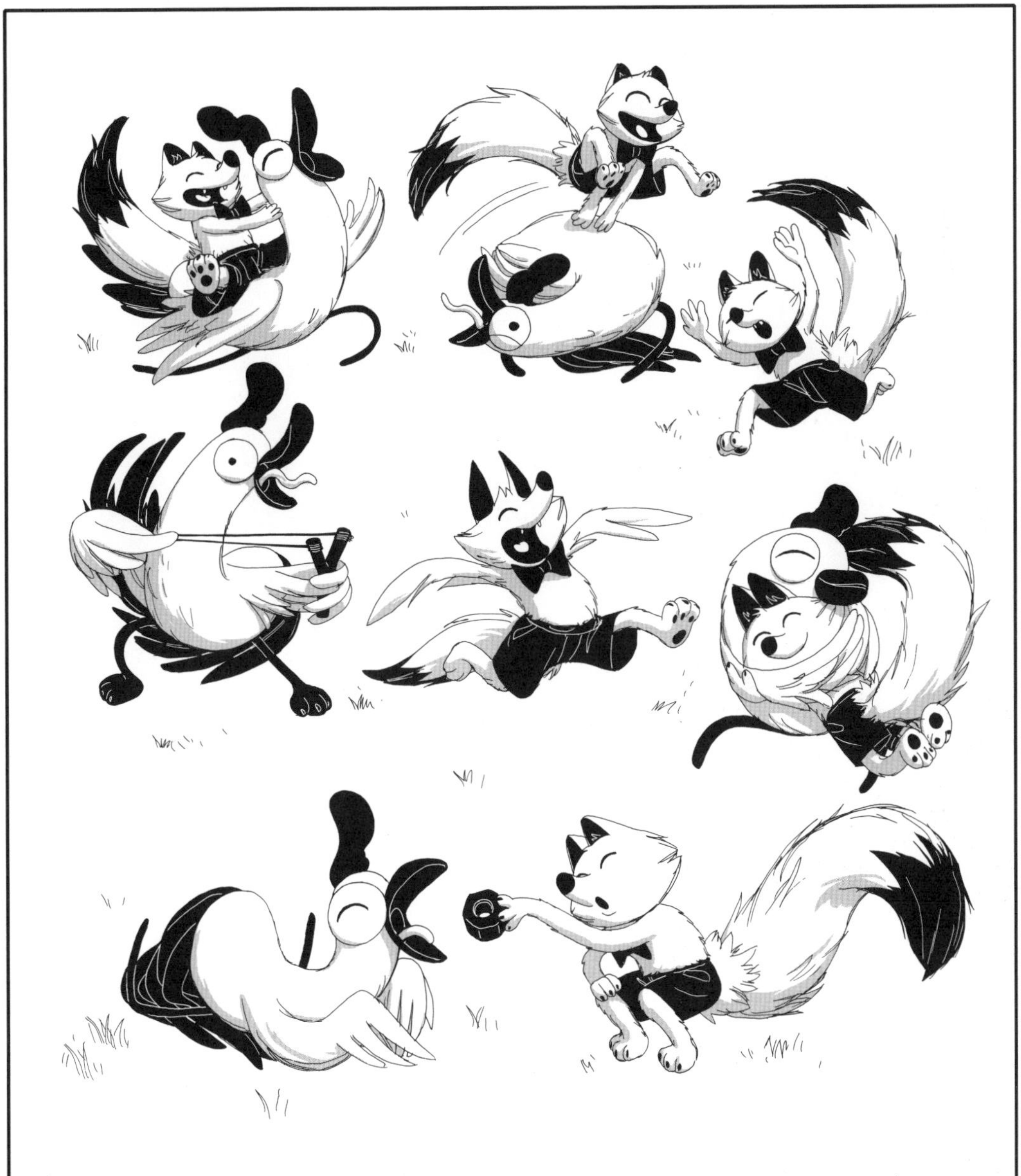

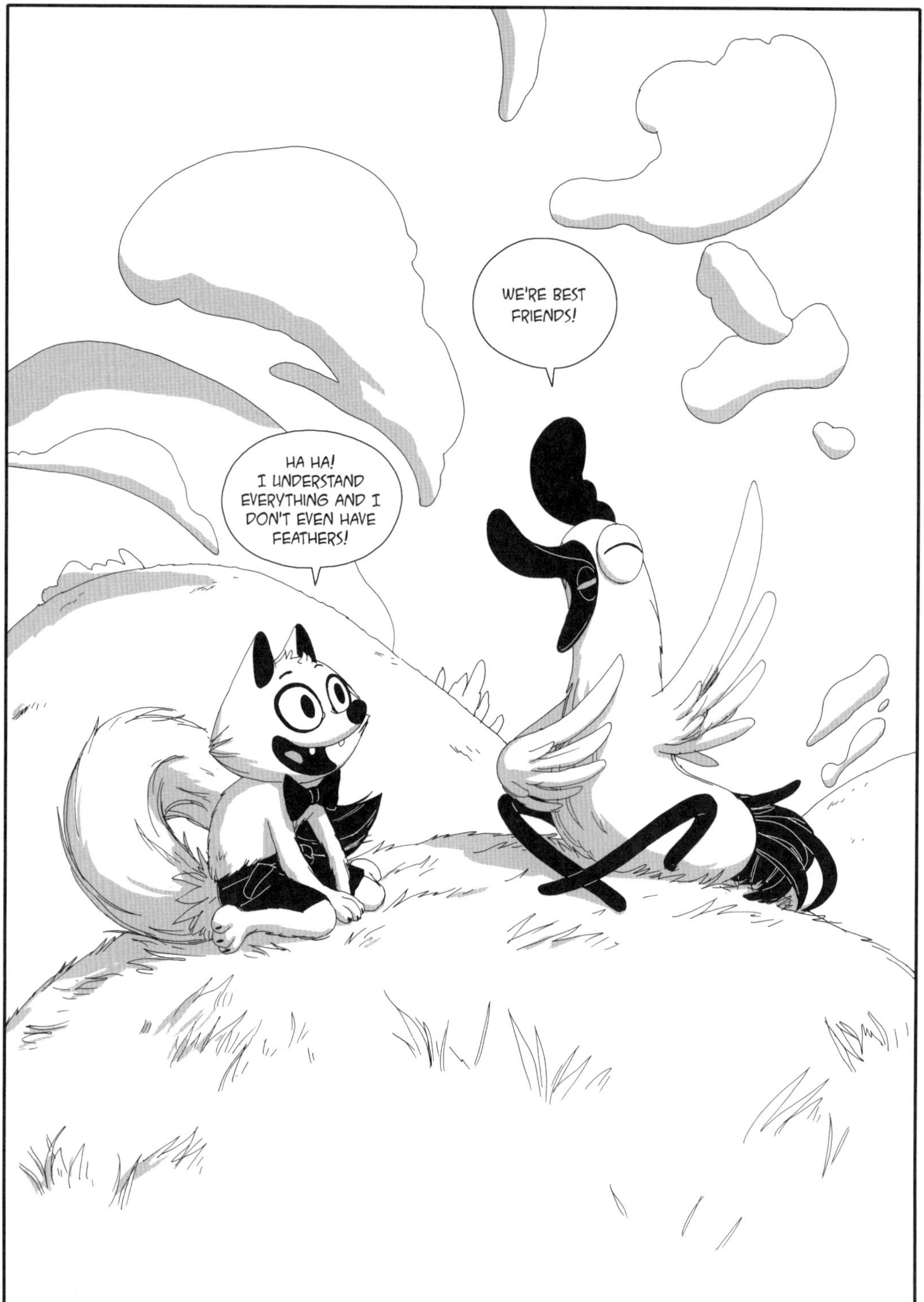
WE'RE BEST FRIENDS!
HA HA! I UNDERSTAND EVERYTHING AND I DON'T EVEN HAVE FEATHERS!

Chapter 8

NIGHT

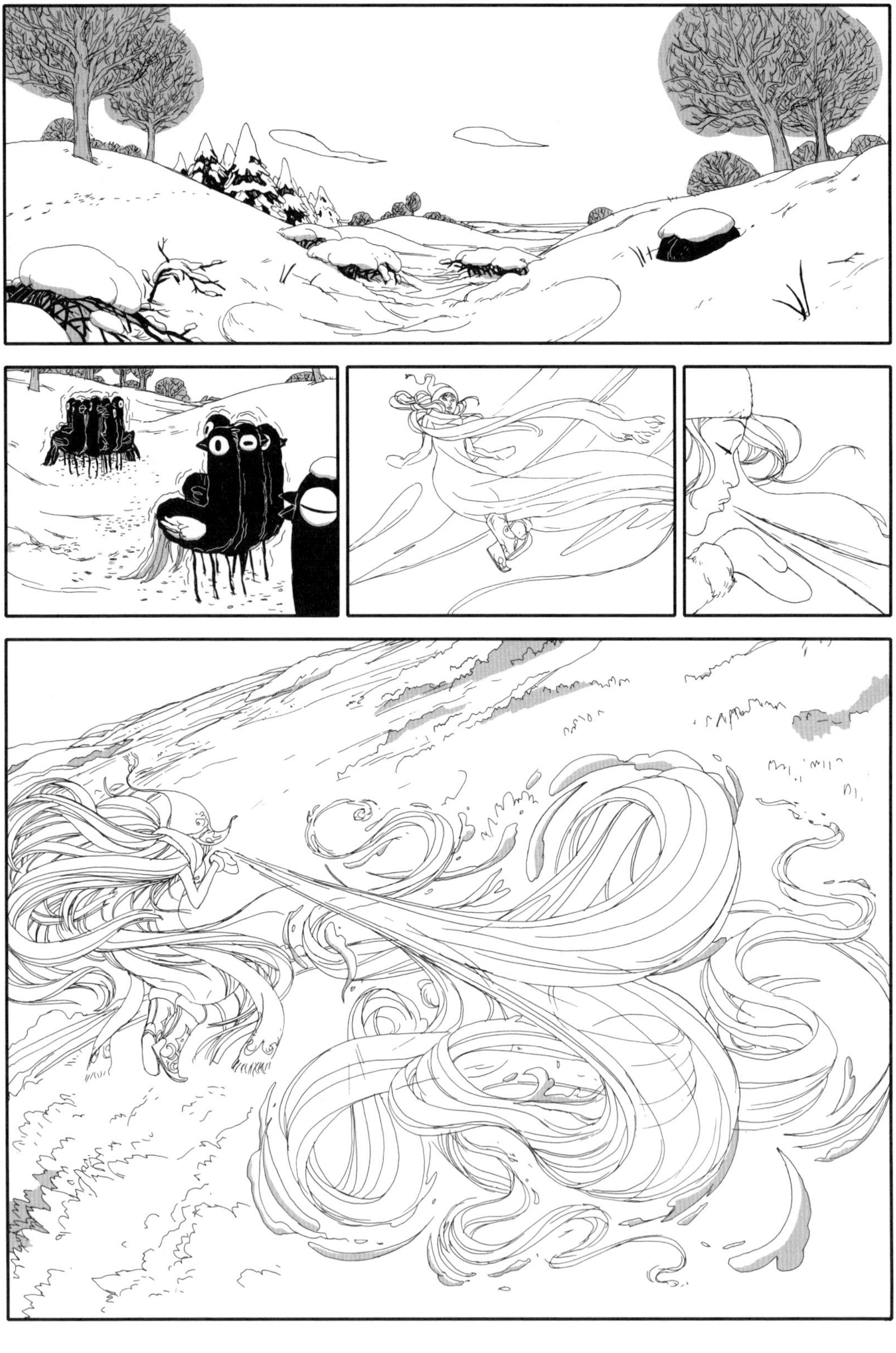

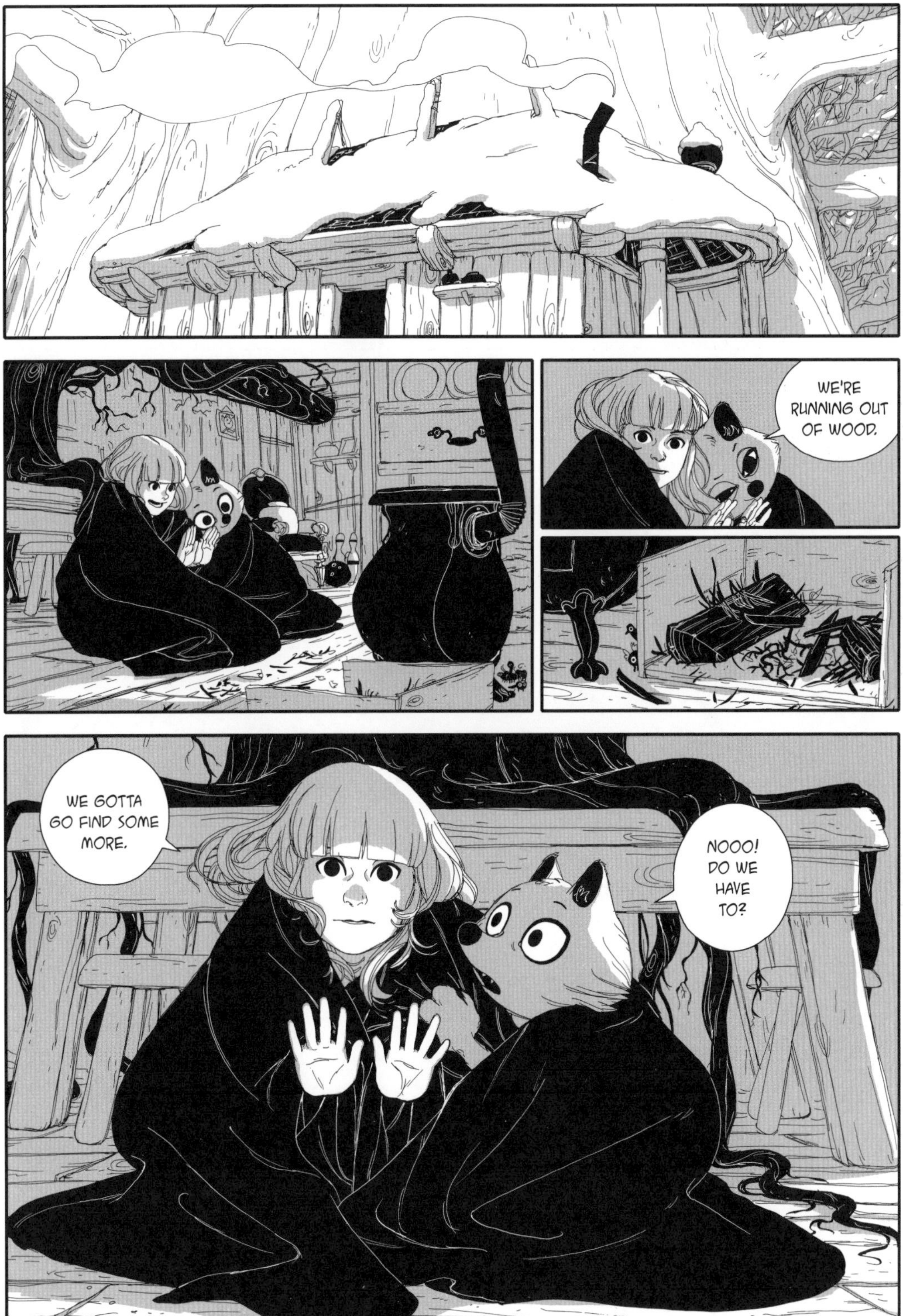
WE'RE RUNNING OUT OF WOOD.
WE GOTTA GO FIND SOME MORE.
NOOO! DO WE HAVE TO?

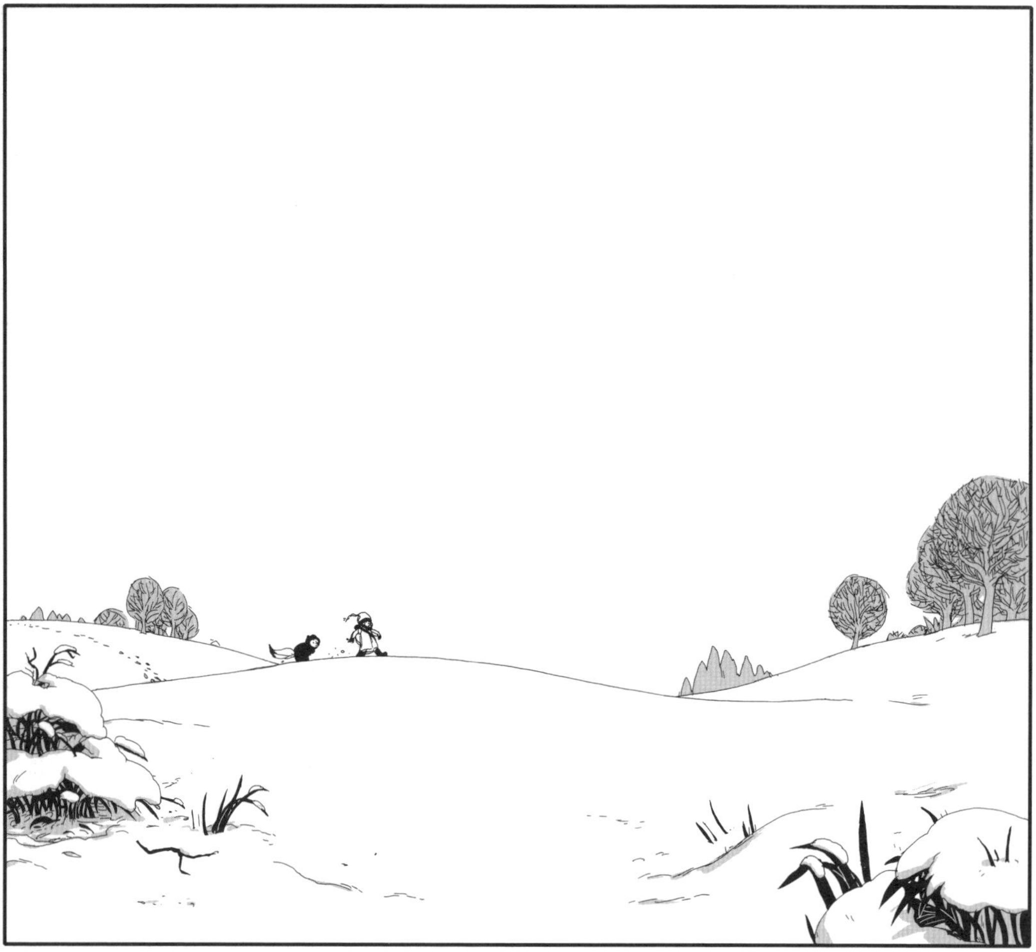

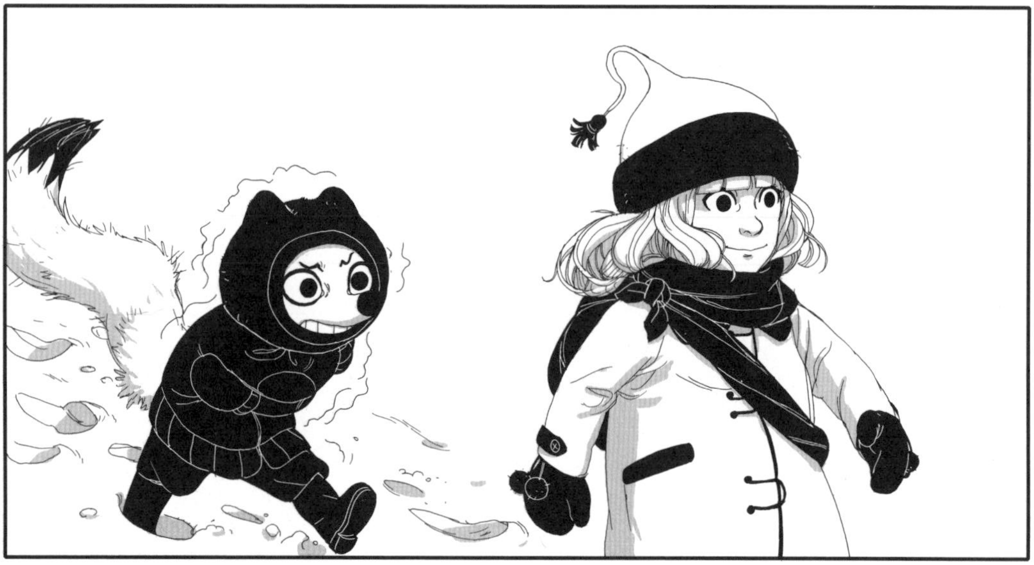

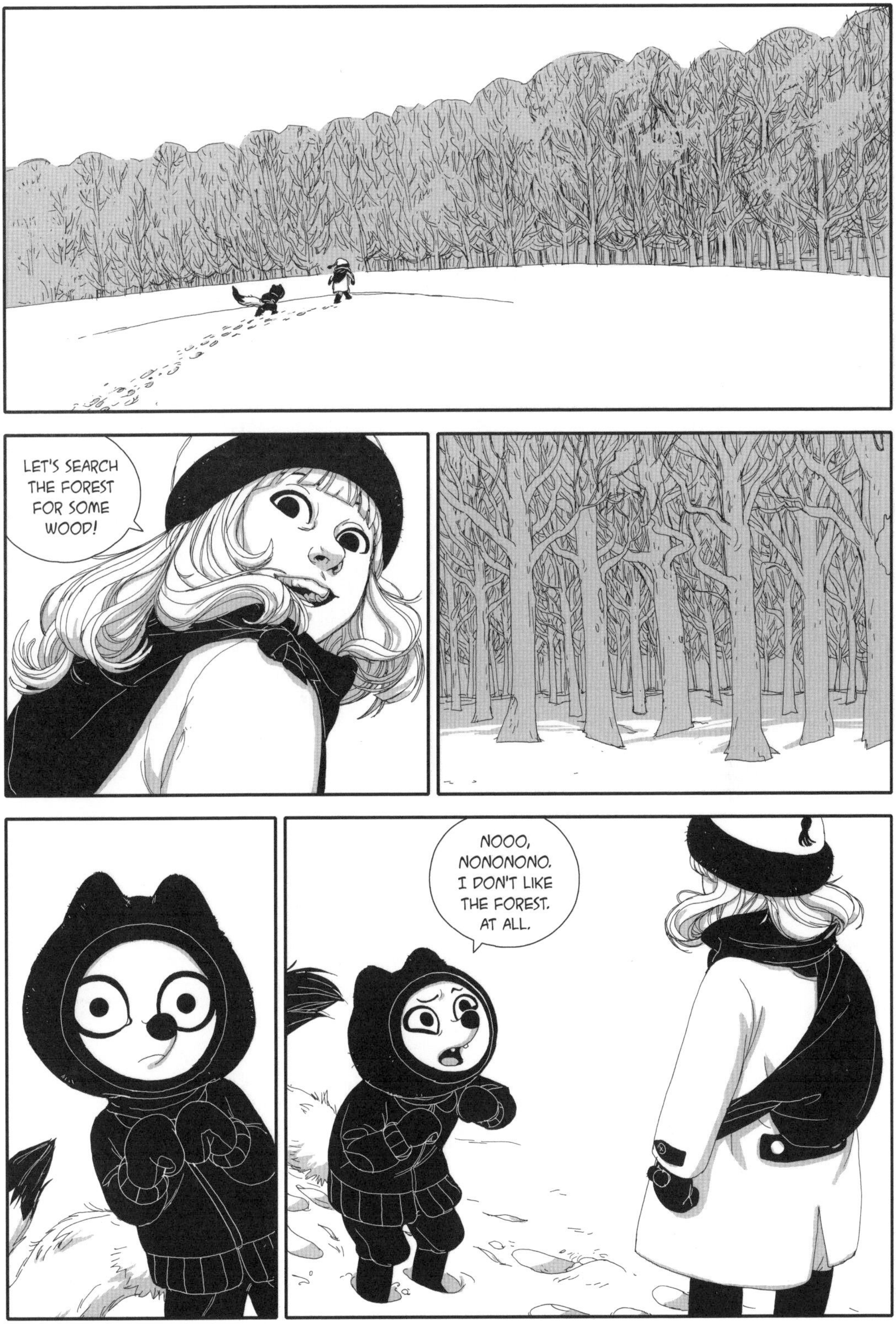
LET'S SEARCH THE FOREST FOR SOME WOOD!
NOOO, NONONONO. I DON'T LIKE THE FOREST. AT ALL.

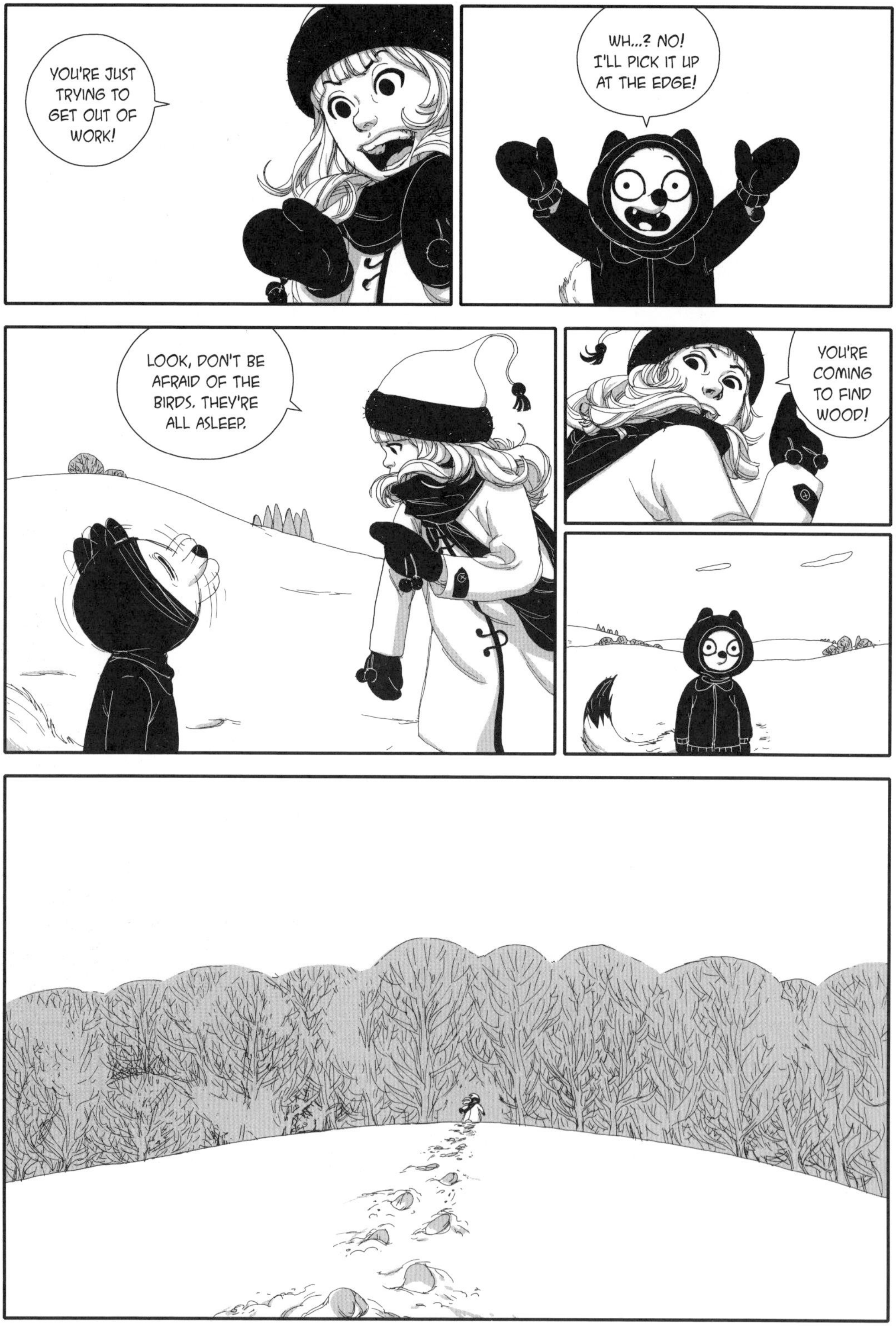
YOU'RE JUST TRYING TO GET OUT OF WORK!
WH...? NO! I'LL PICK IT UP AT THE EDGE!
LOOK, DON'T BE AFRAID OF THE BIRDS. THEY'RE ALL ASLEEP.
YOU'RE COMING TO FIND WOOD!

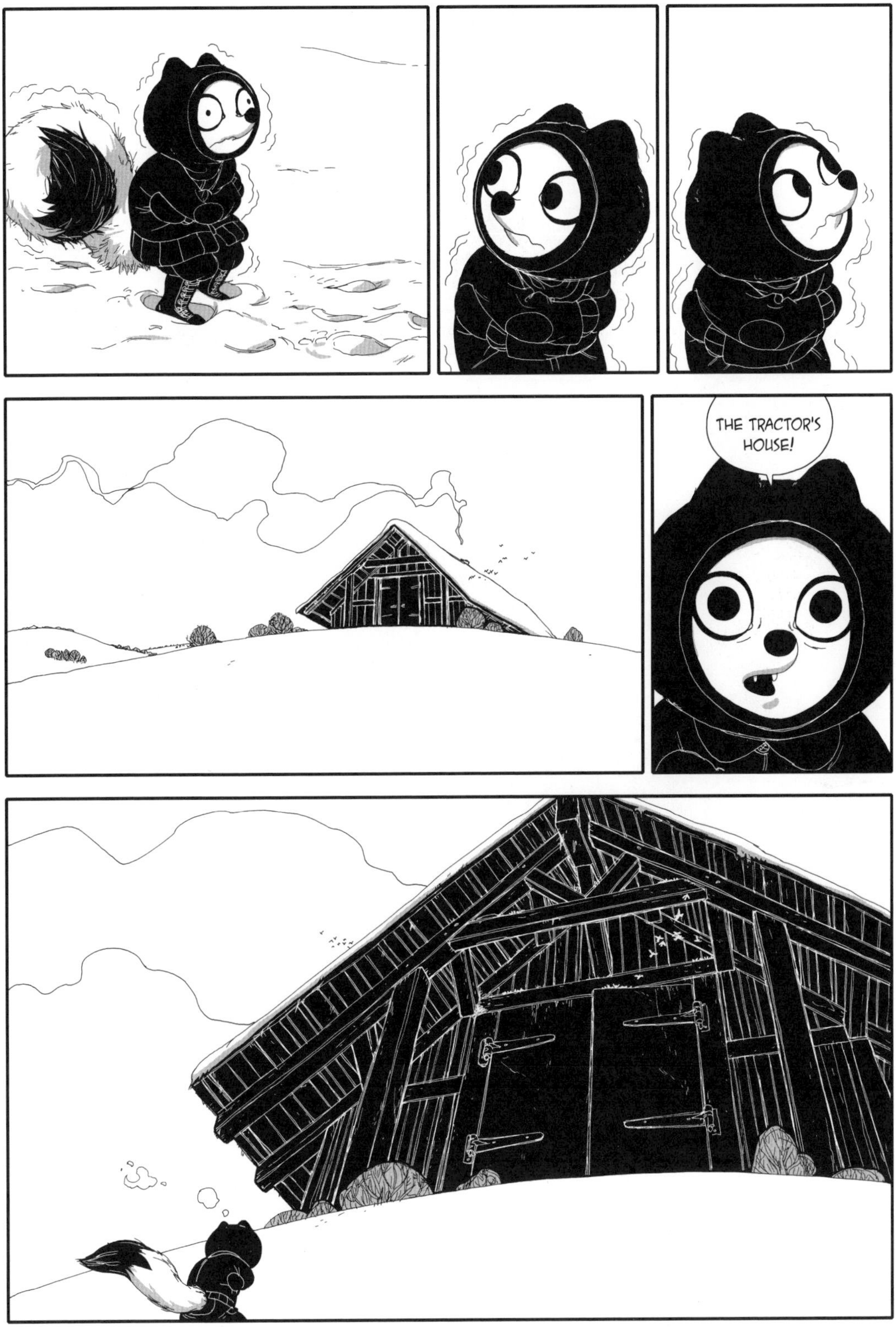
THE TRACTOR'S HOUSE!

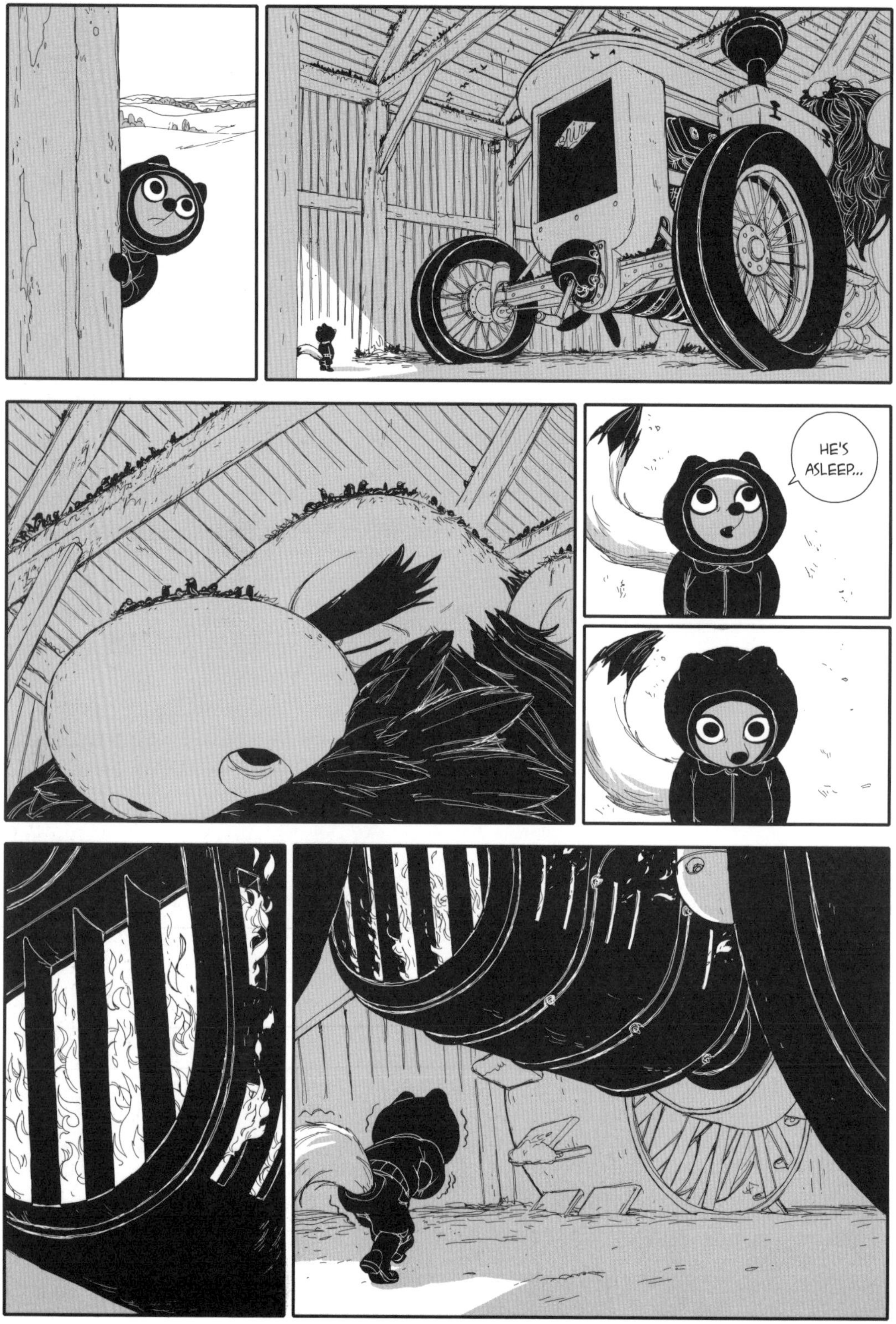
HE'S ASLEEP...

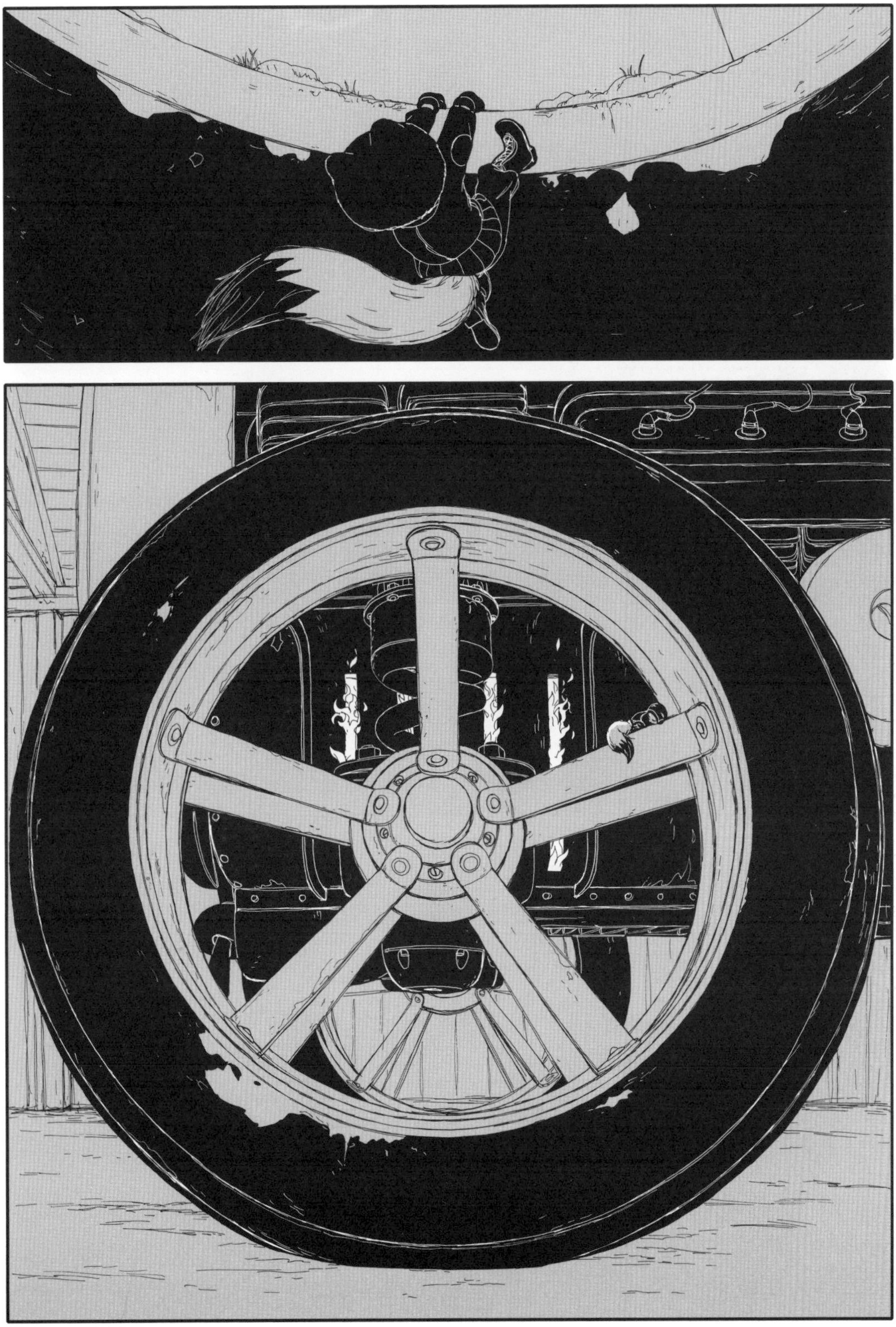

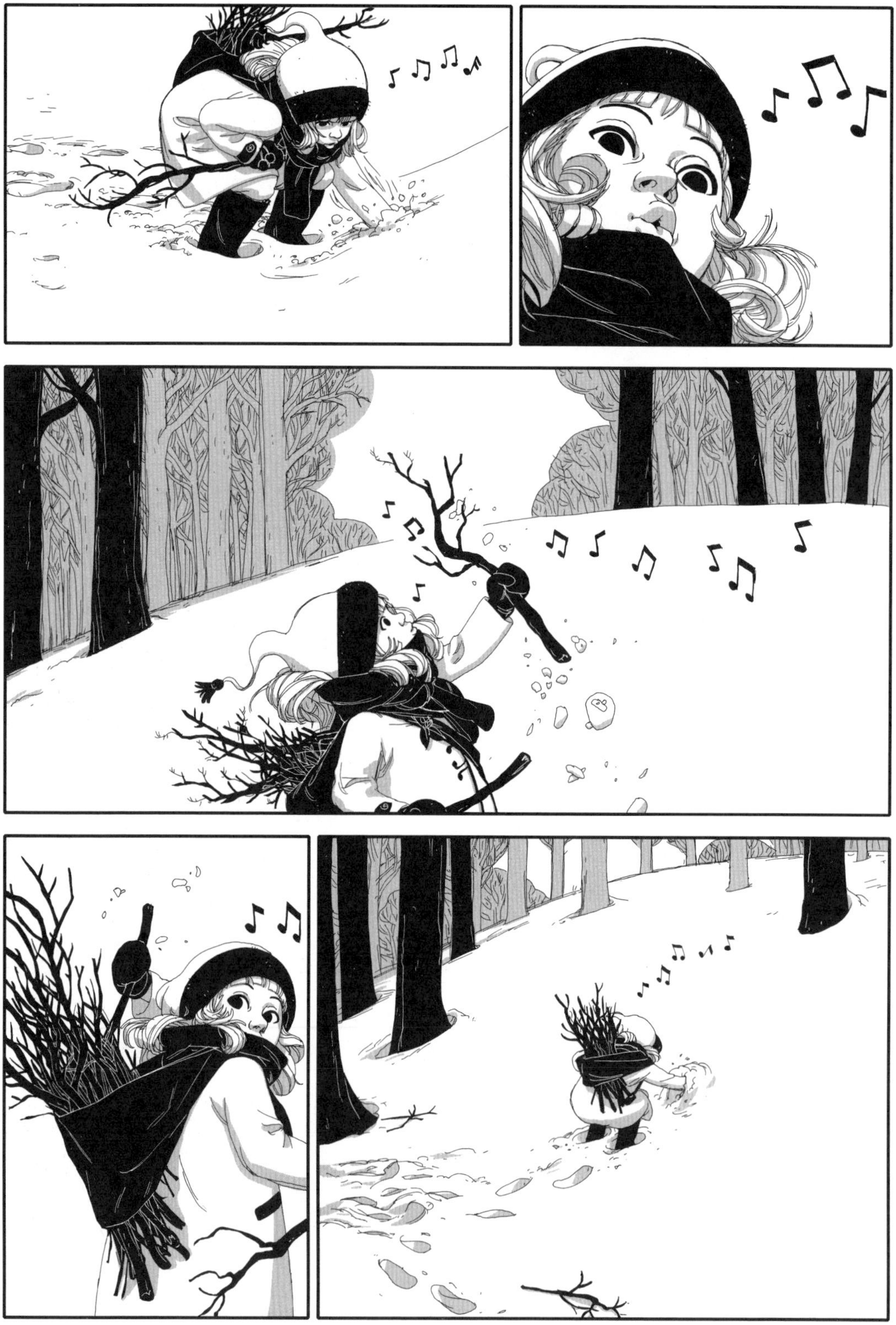

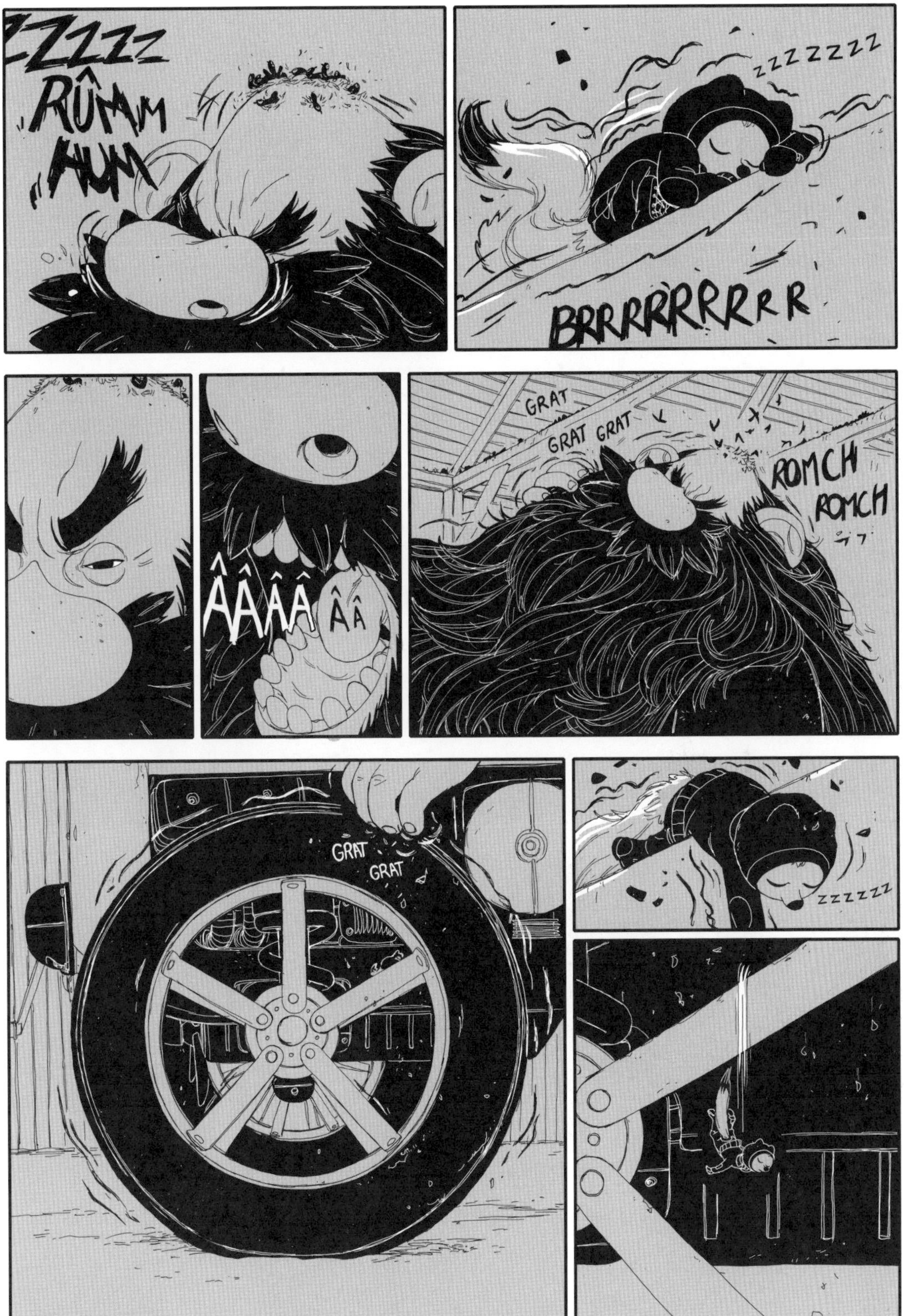
ZZZZZ
RÛÂM
HUM
ZZZZZZZ
BRRRRRRRRR
ÂÂÂÂ ÂÂ
GRAT
GRAT GRAT
ROMCH
ROMCH
GRAT
GRAT
ZZZZZZ

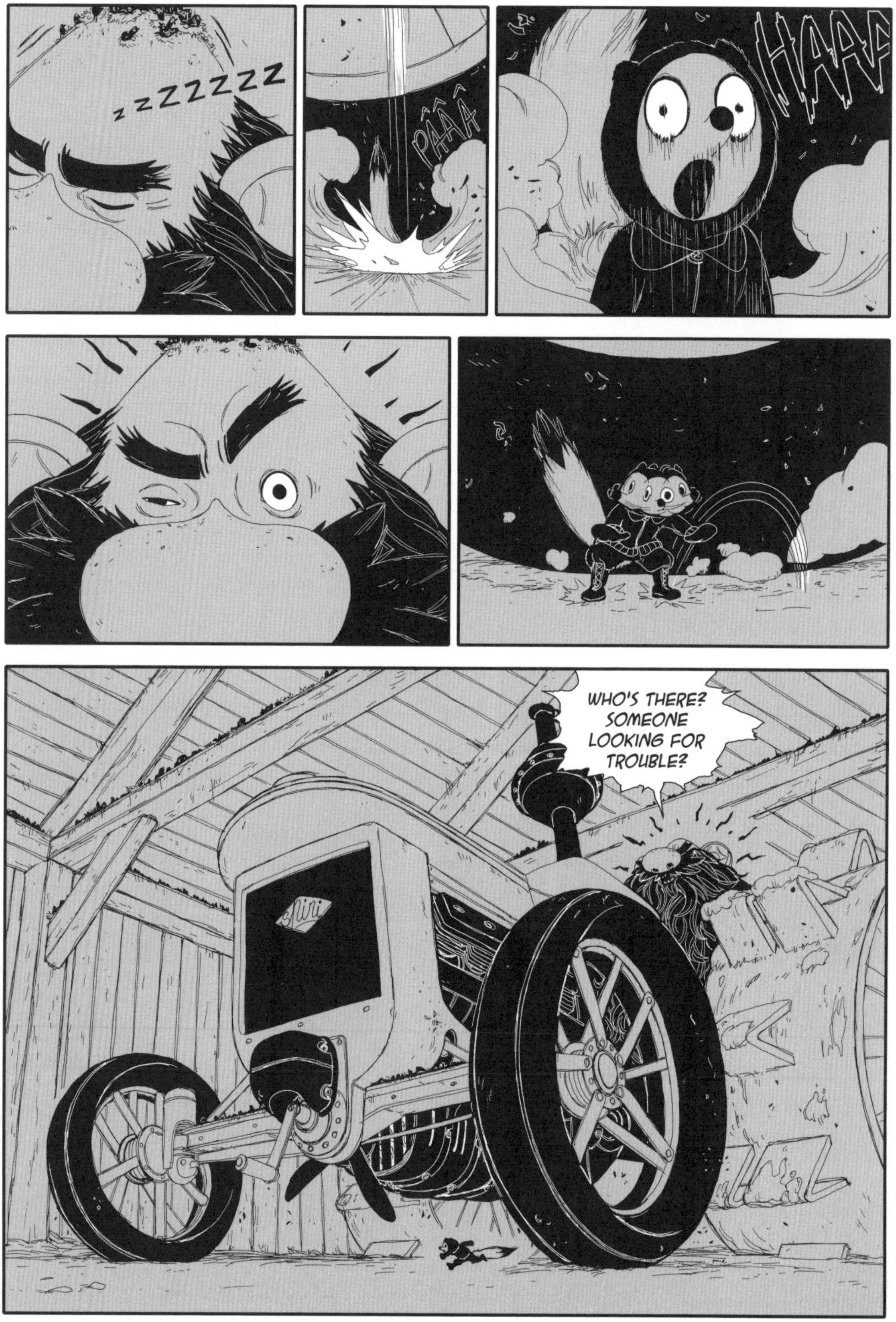
zzZZZZZ
PÂÂÂ
HAAA
WHO'S THERE? SOMEONE LOOKING FOR TROUBLE?

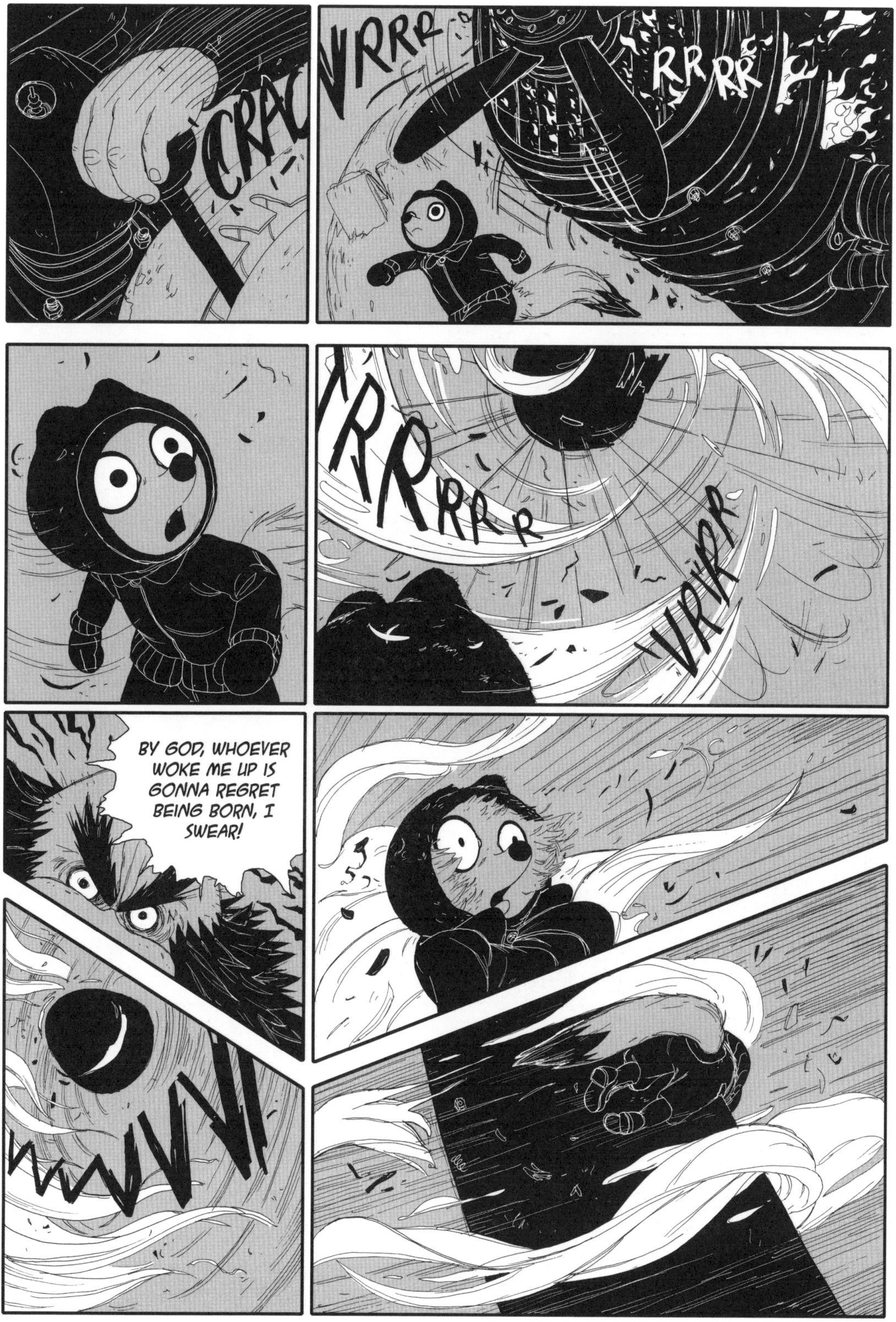
CRACK
VRRR
RRRR
RRRRRRR
VRRR
BY GOD, WHOEVER WOKE ME UP IS GONNA REGRET BEING BORN, I SWEAR!
WWVVV

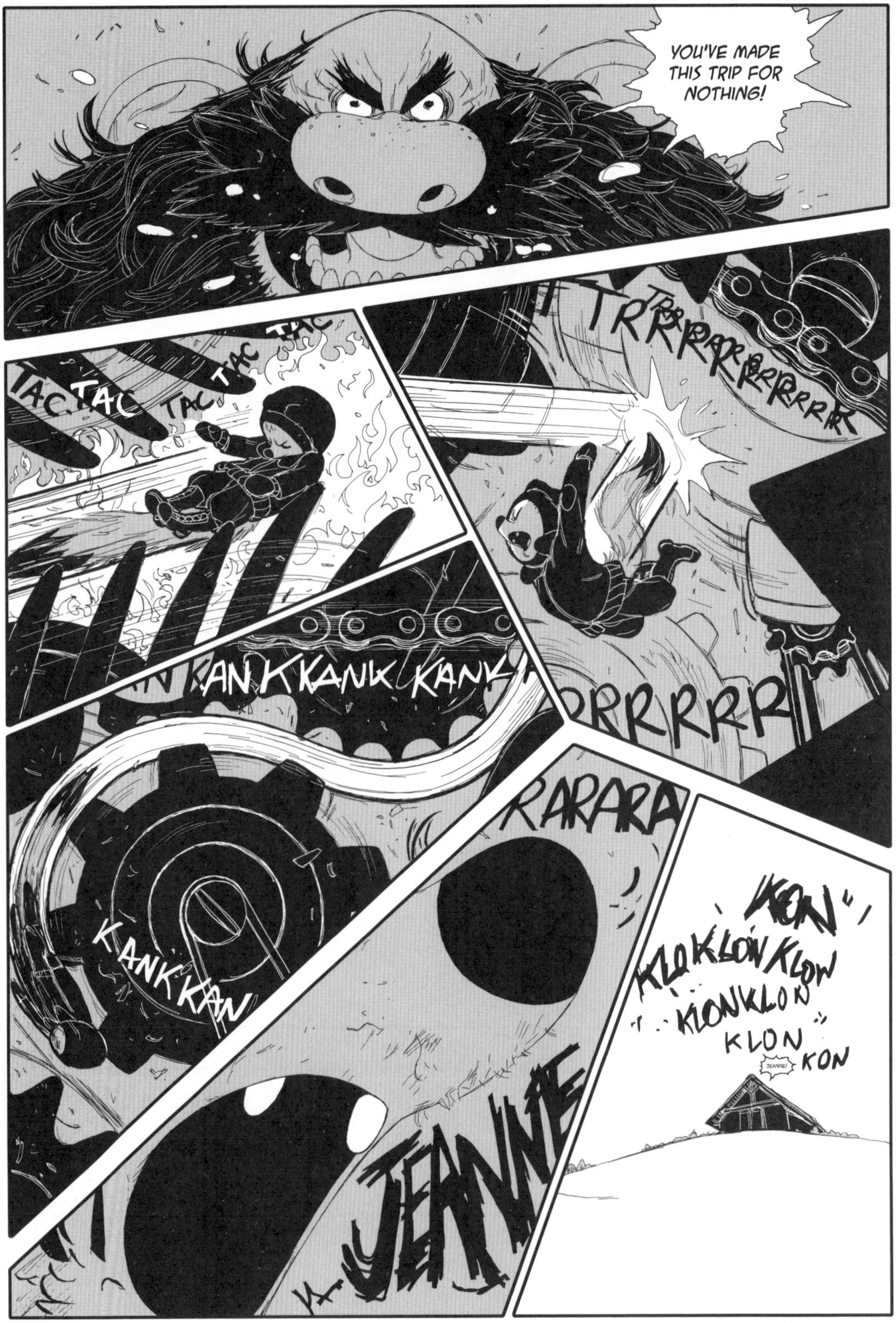

YOU'VE MADE THIS TRIP FOR NOTHING!
TAC TAC TAC TAC TAC
KANK KANK KANK
RRRRRRR
RARARA
JEANNE
KON
KLON KLON KLOW
KLONKLON
KLON
JEANNE!
KON

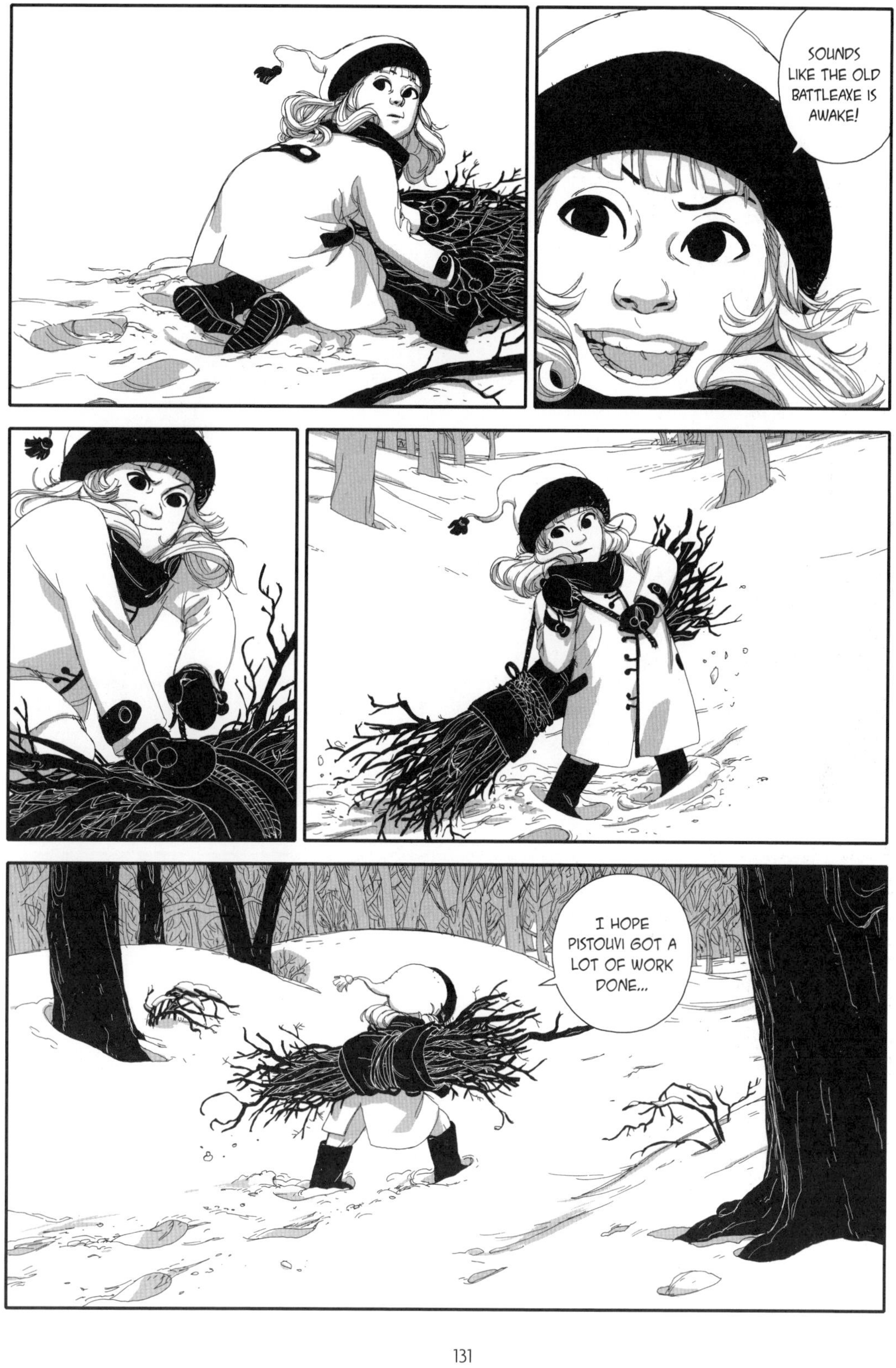
SOUNDS LIKE THE OLD BATTLEAXE IS AWAKE!
I HOPE PISTOUVI GOT A LOT OF WORK DONE...

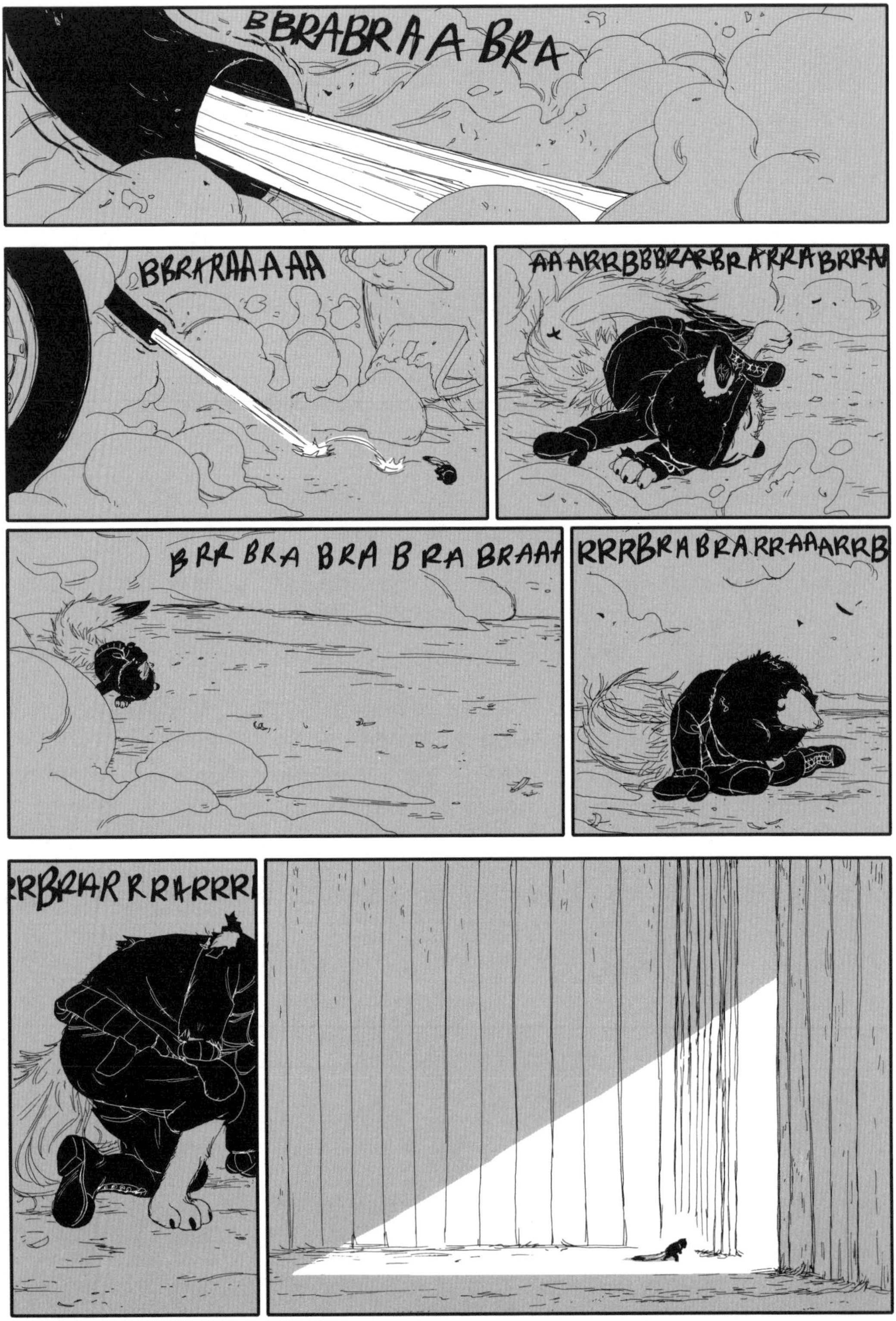
BBRABRA A BRA
BBRARAAAAAA
AA ARRBBBRARBRARRABRRA
BRR BRA BRA B RA BRAAA
RRRBRABRARRAAARRB
RRBRARRARRRR

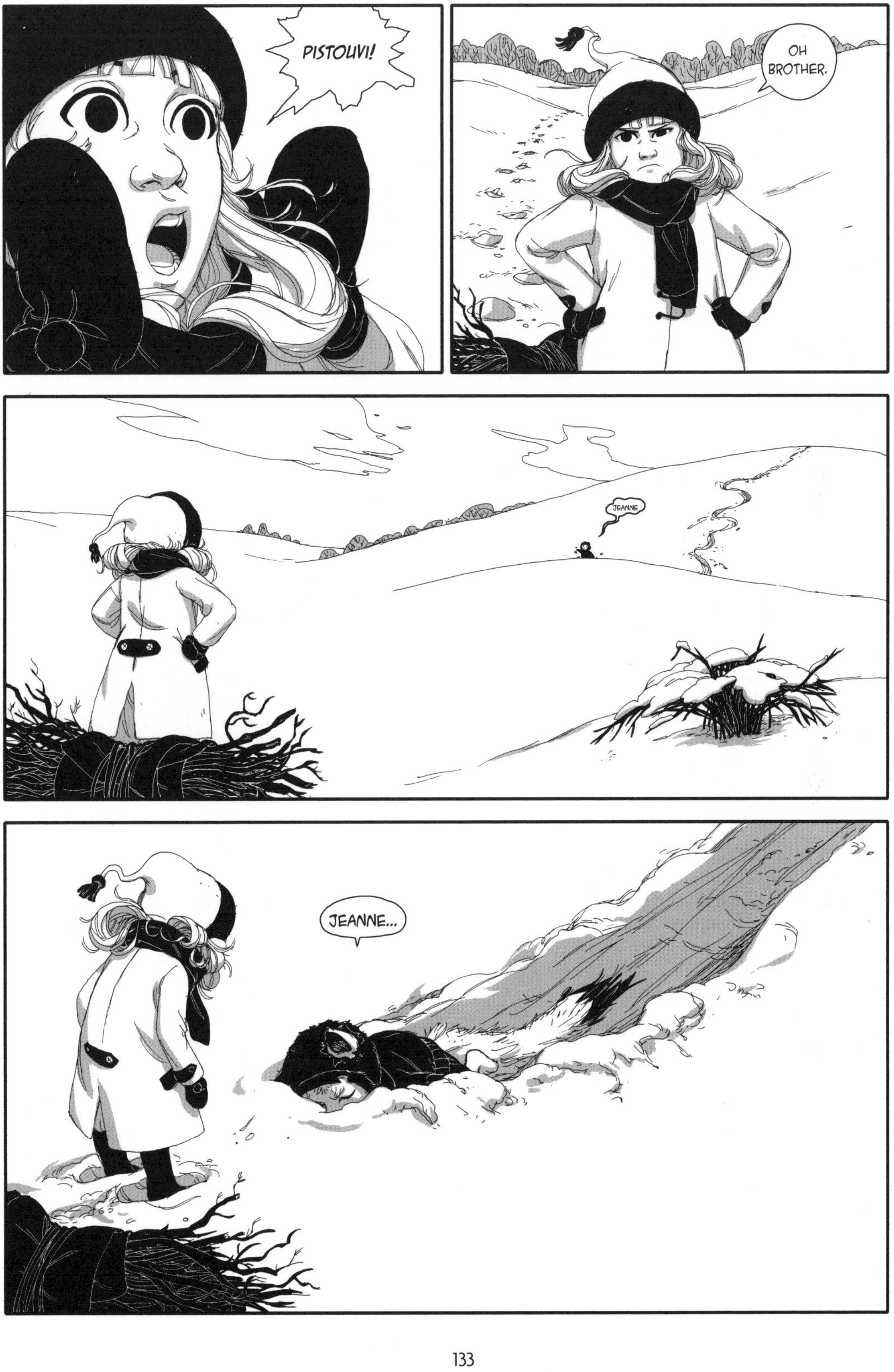
PISTOUVI!
OH BROTHER.
JEANNE
JEANNE...

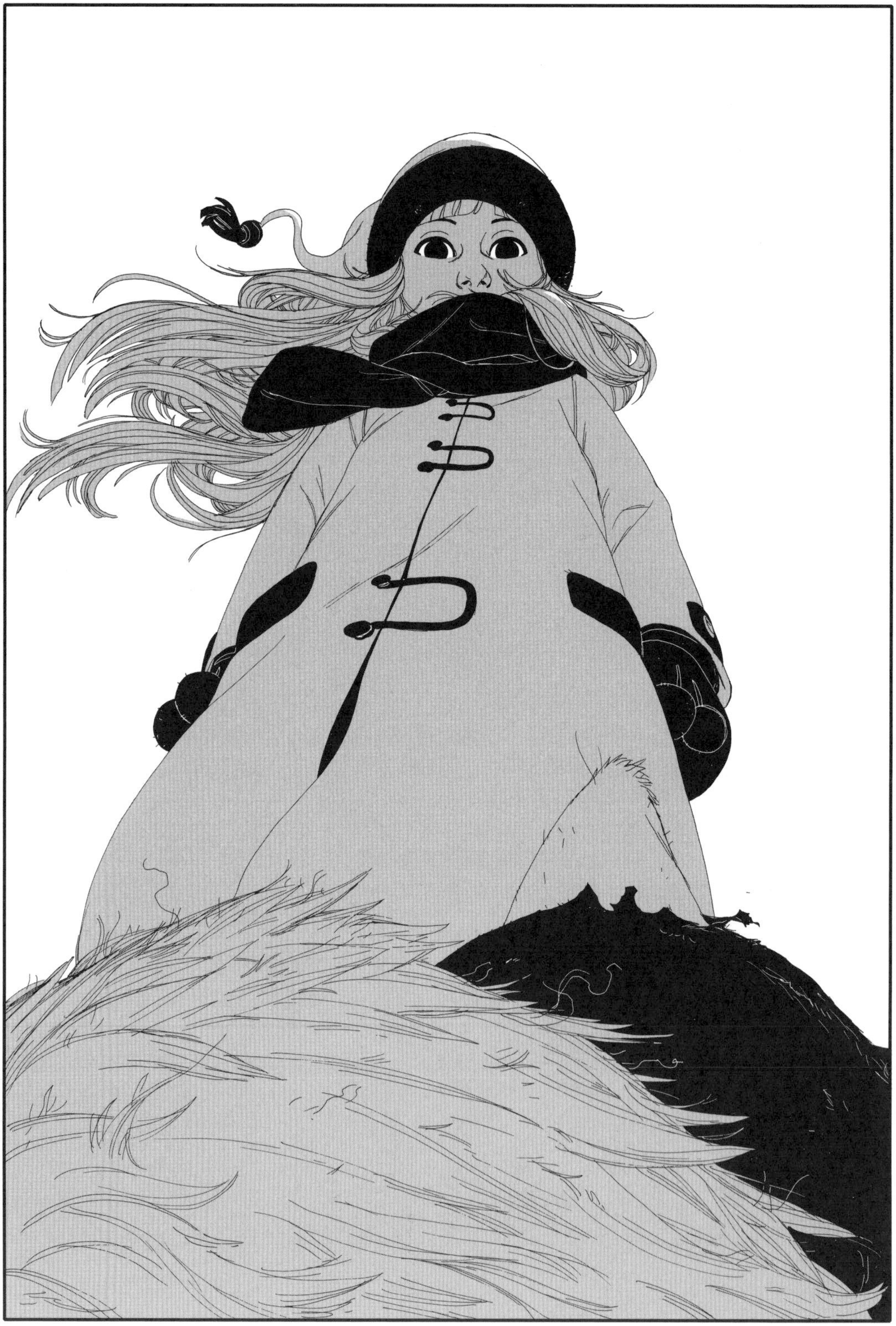

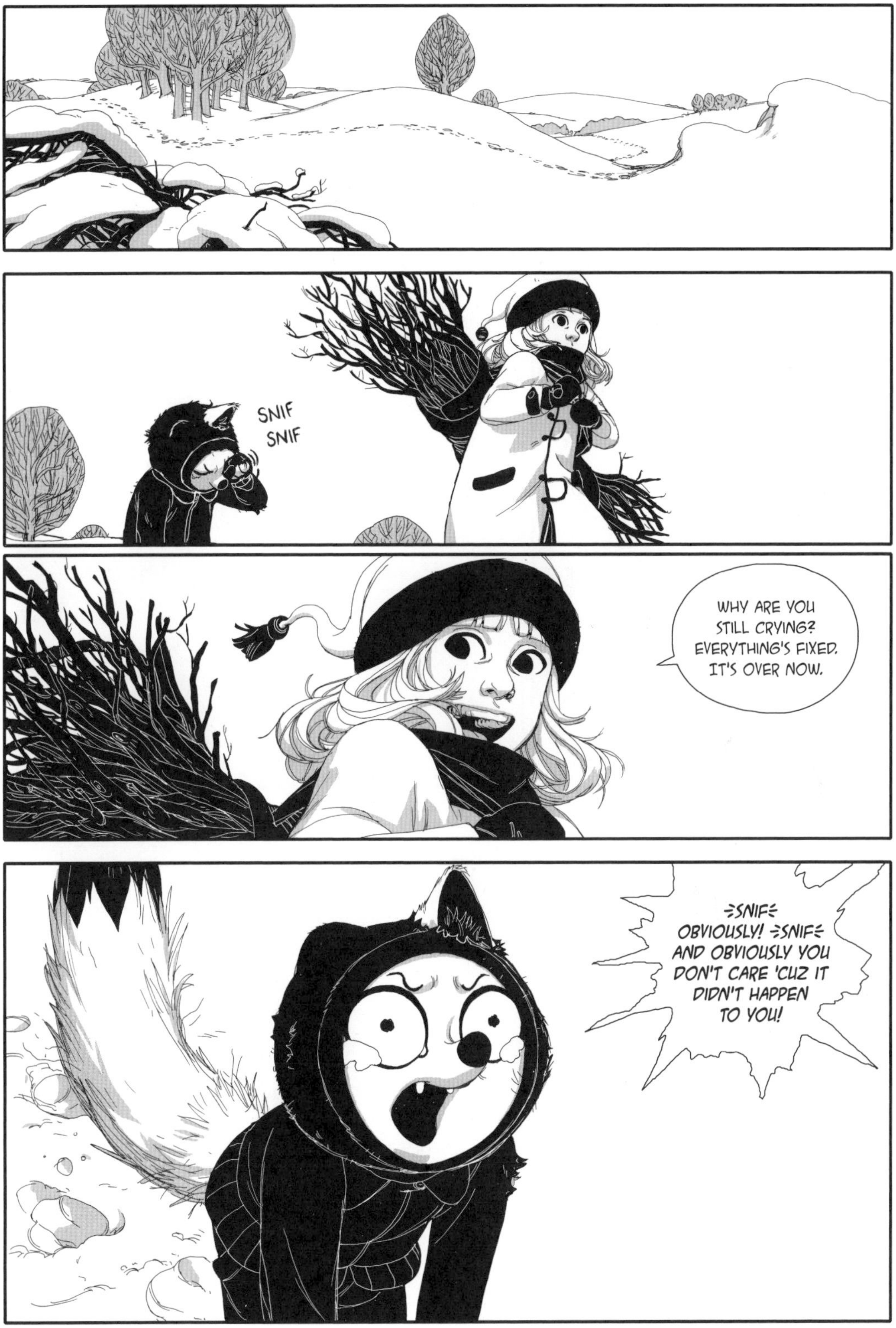
SNIF
SNIF
WHY ARE YOU STILL CRYING? EVERYTHING'S FIXED. IT'S OVER NOW.
≈SNIF≈ OBVIOUSLY! ≈SNIF≈ AND OBVIOUSLY YOU DON'T CARE 'CUZ IT DIDN'T HAPPEN TO YOU!

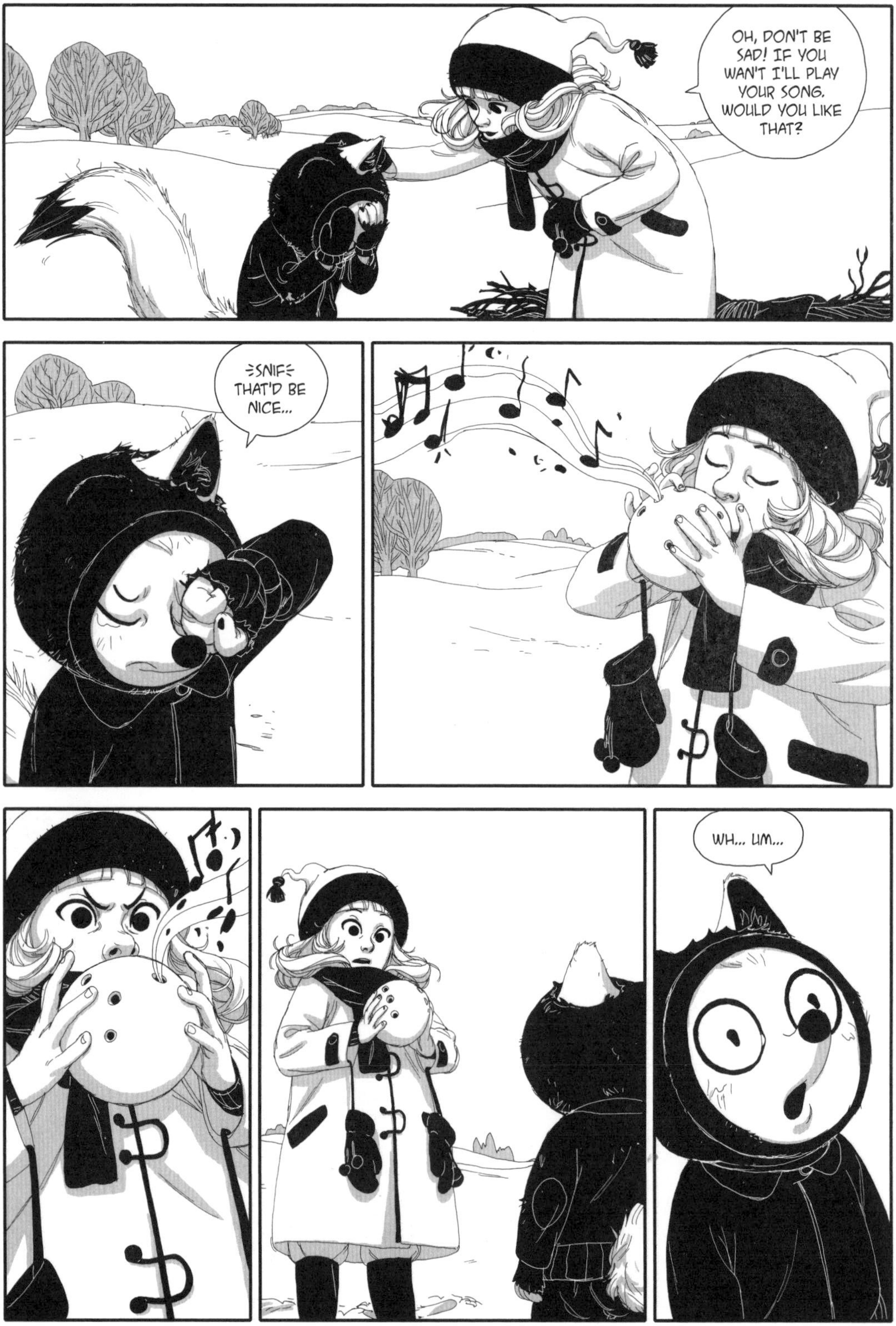
OH, DON'T BE SAD! IF YOU WAN'T I'LL PLAY YOUR SONG. WOULD YOU LIKE THAT?
≡SNIF≡ THAT'D BE NICE...
WH... UM...

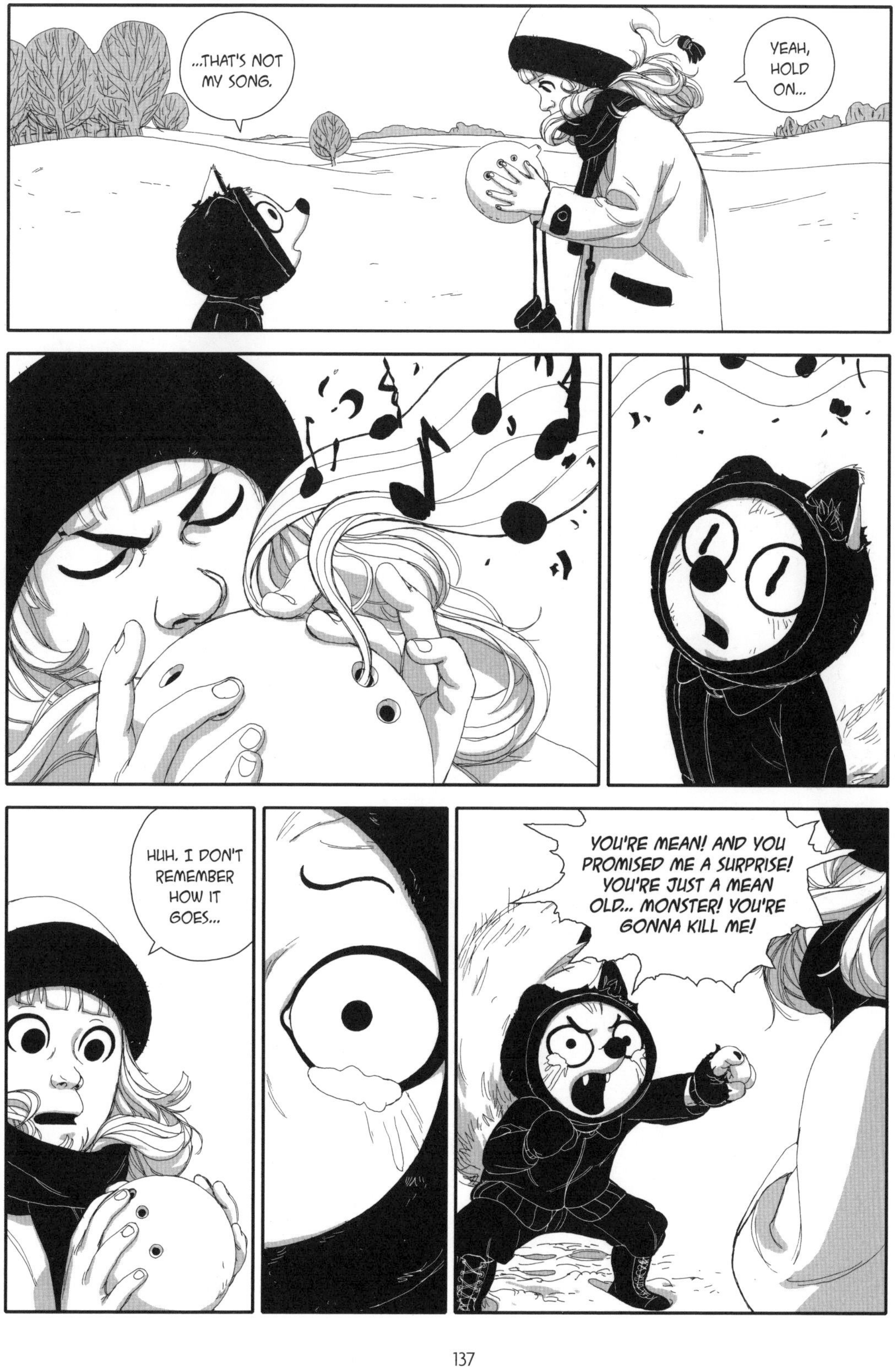
...THAT'S NOT MY SONG.
YEAH, HOLD ON...
HUH. I DON'T REMEMBER HOW IT GOES...
YOU'RE MEAN! AND YOU PROMISED ME A SURPRISE! YOU'RE JUST A MEAN OLD... MONSTER! YOU'RE GONNA KILL ME!

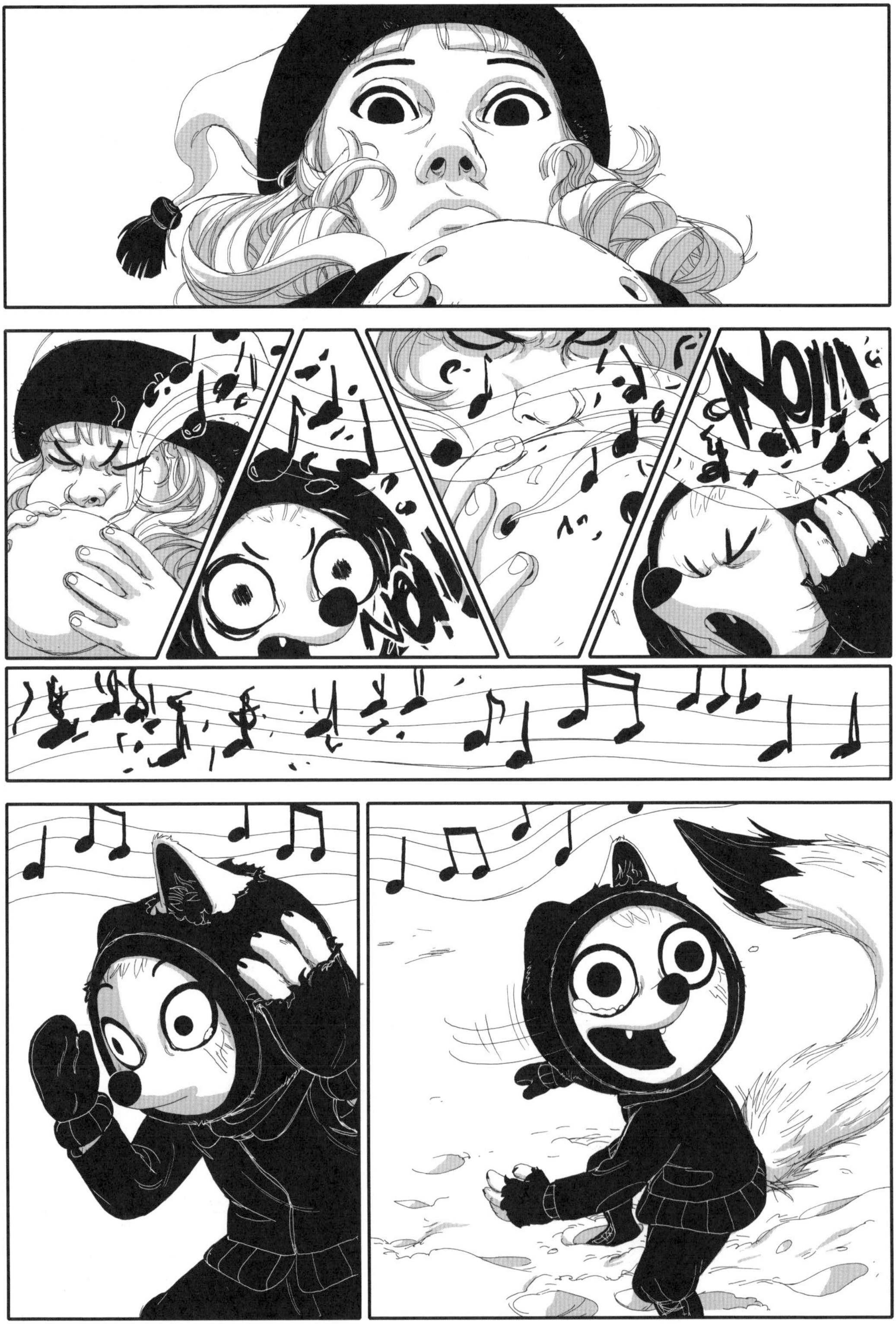

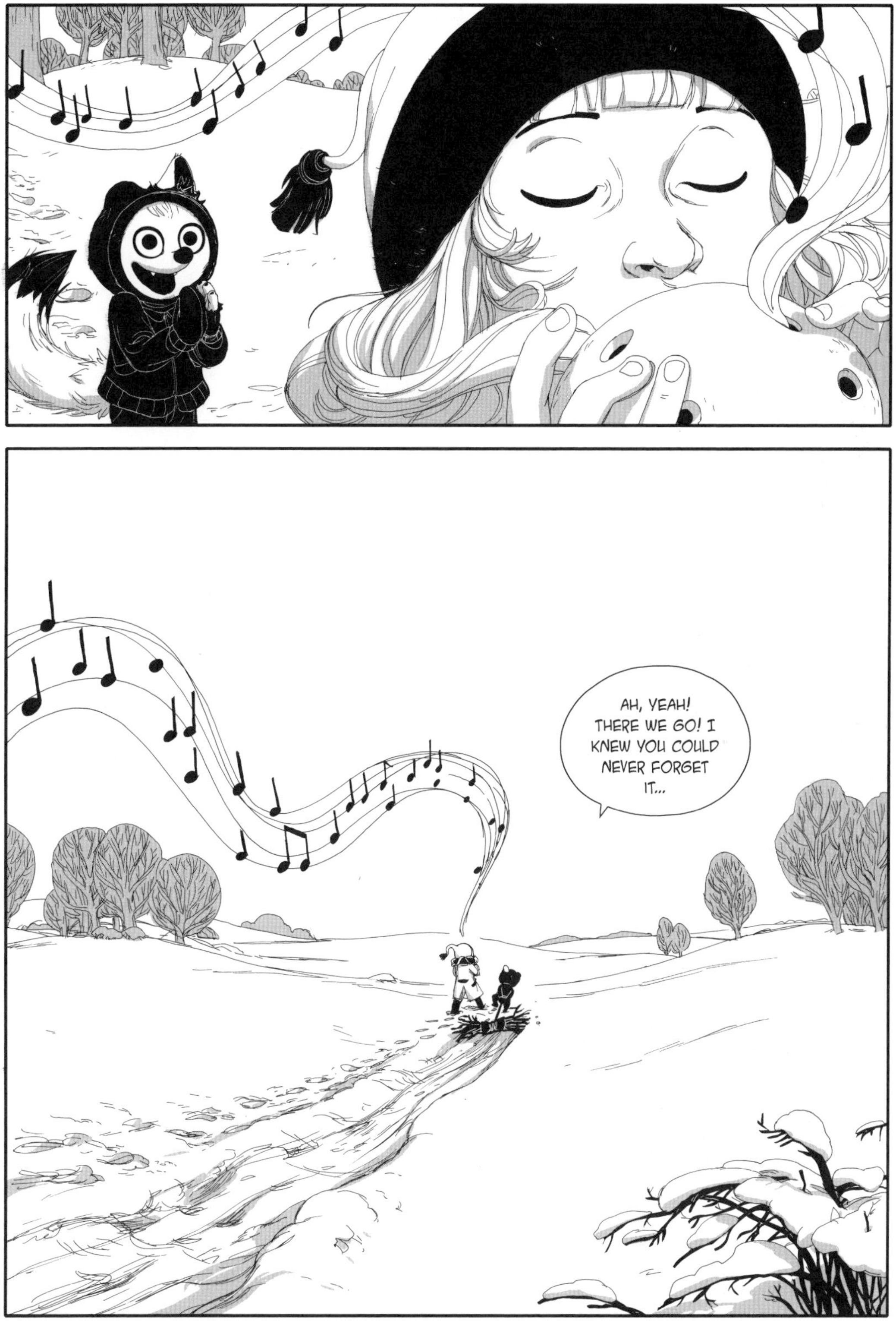
AH, YEAH! THERE WE GO! I KNEW YOU COULD NEVER FORGET IT...

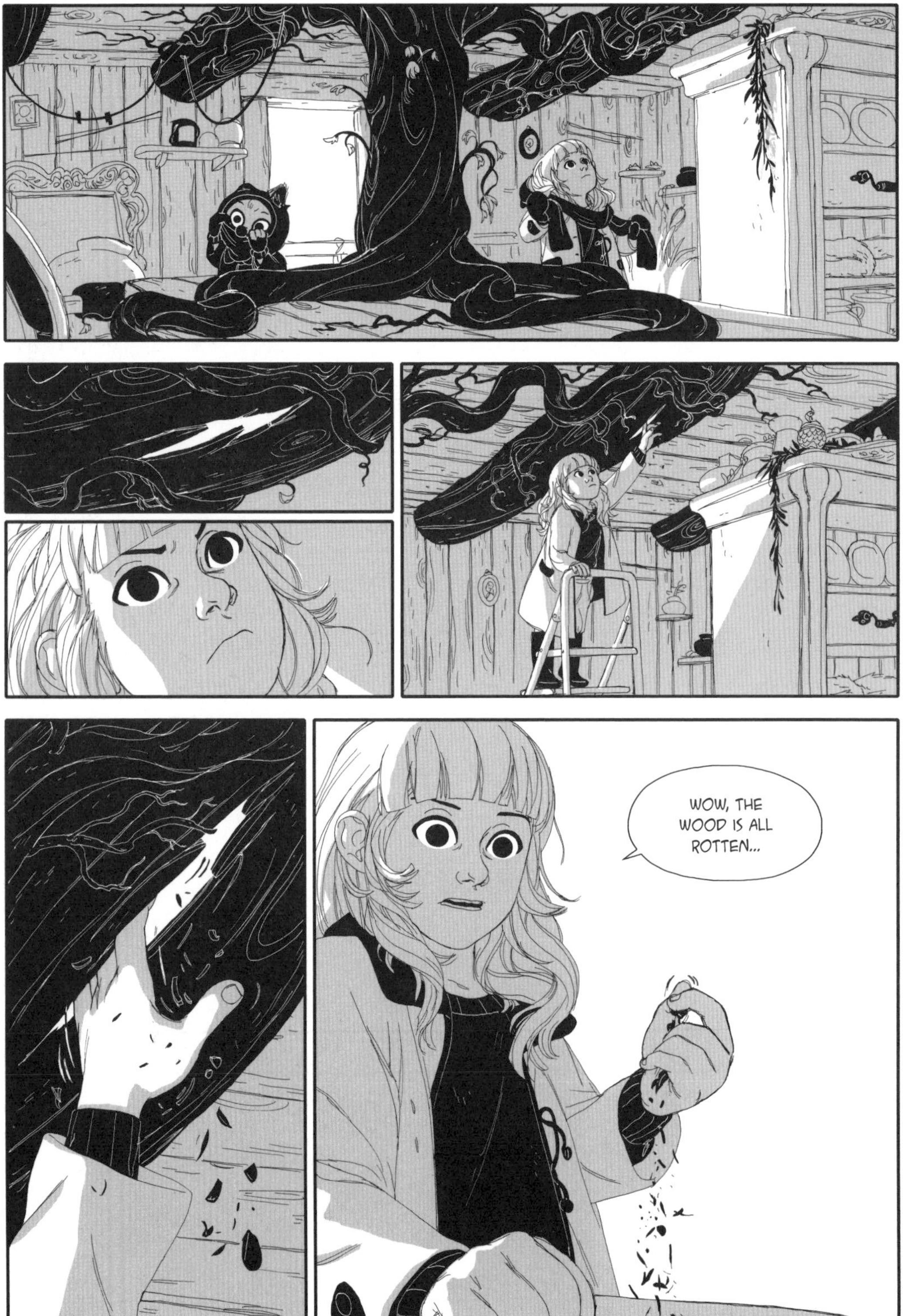
WOW, THE
WOOD IS ALL
ROTTEN...

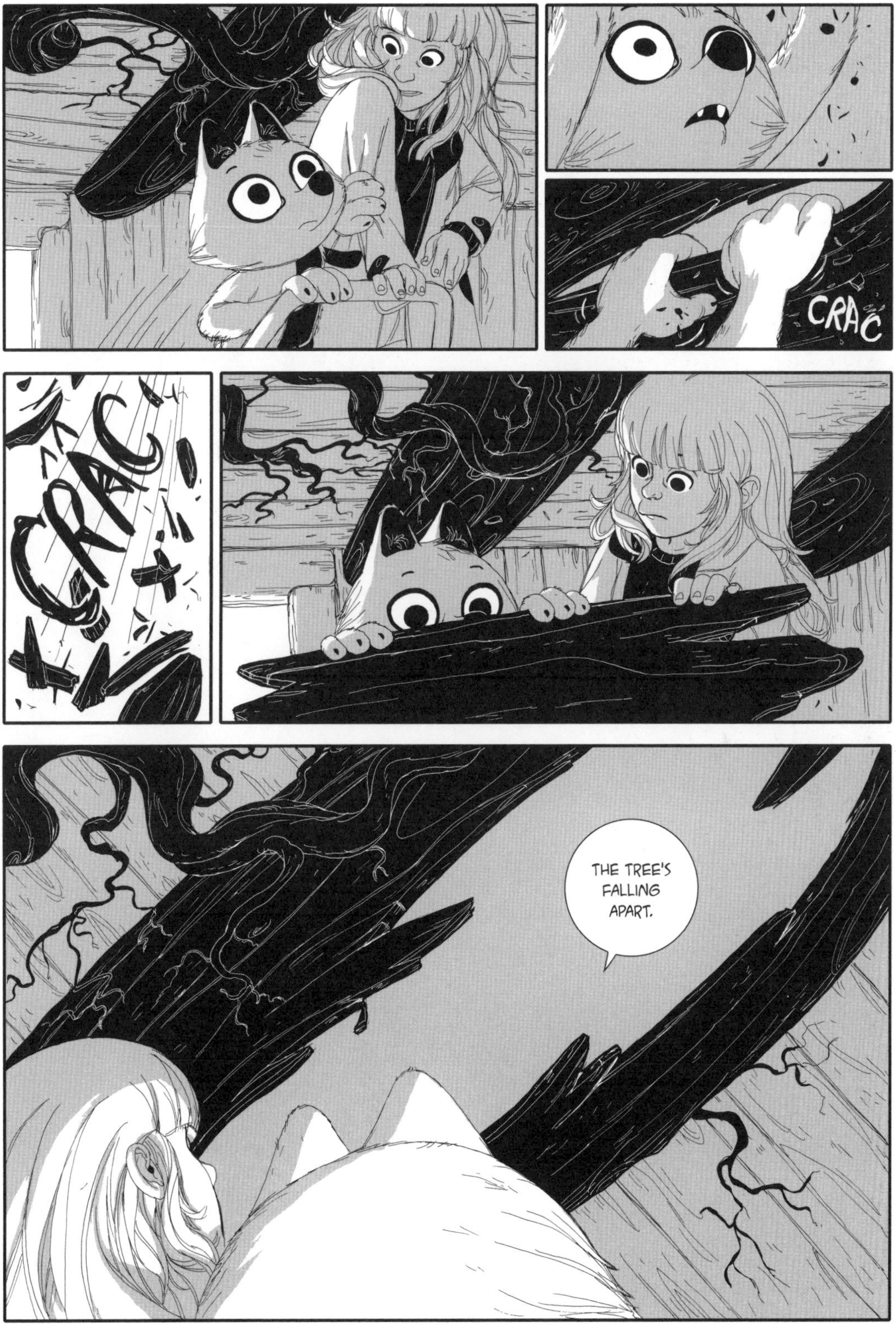
CRAC
CRAC
THE TREE'S FALLING APART.

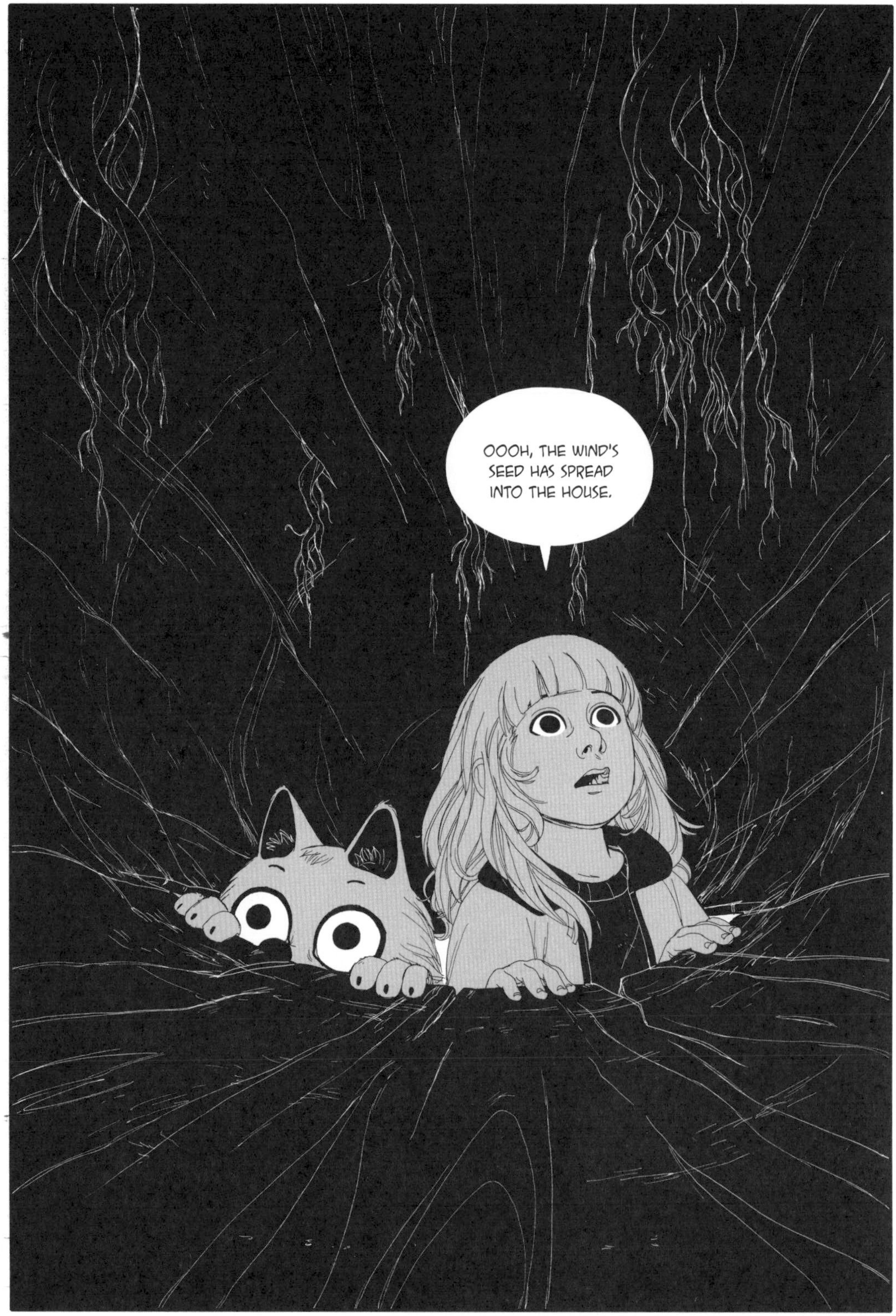
OOOH, THE WIND'S SEED HAS SPREAD INTO THE HOUSE.

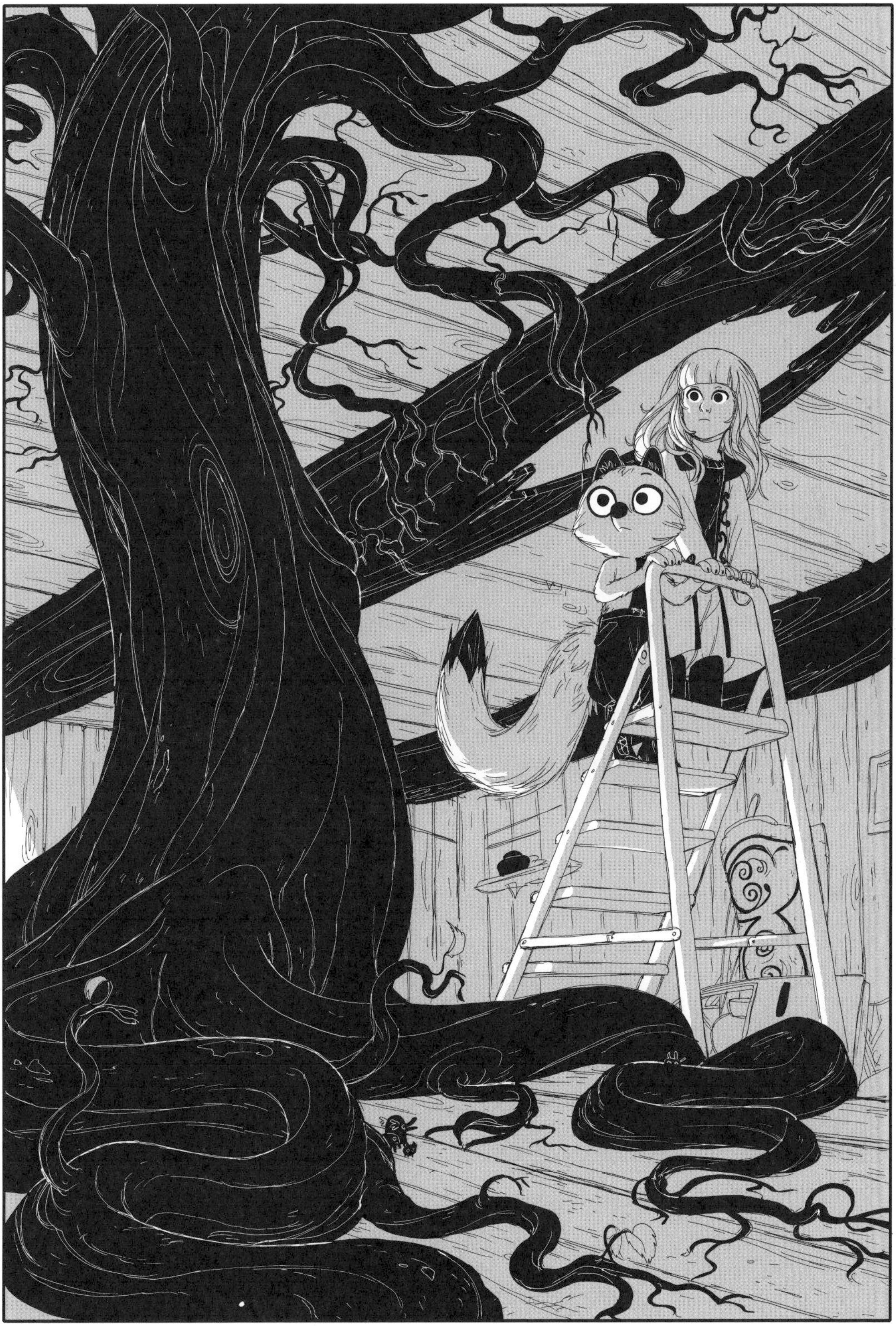

Chapter 9

PUNISHMENT

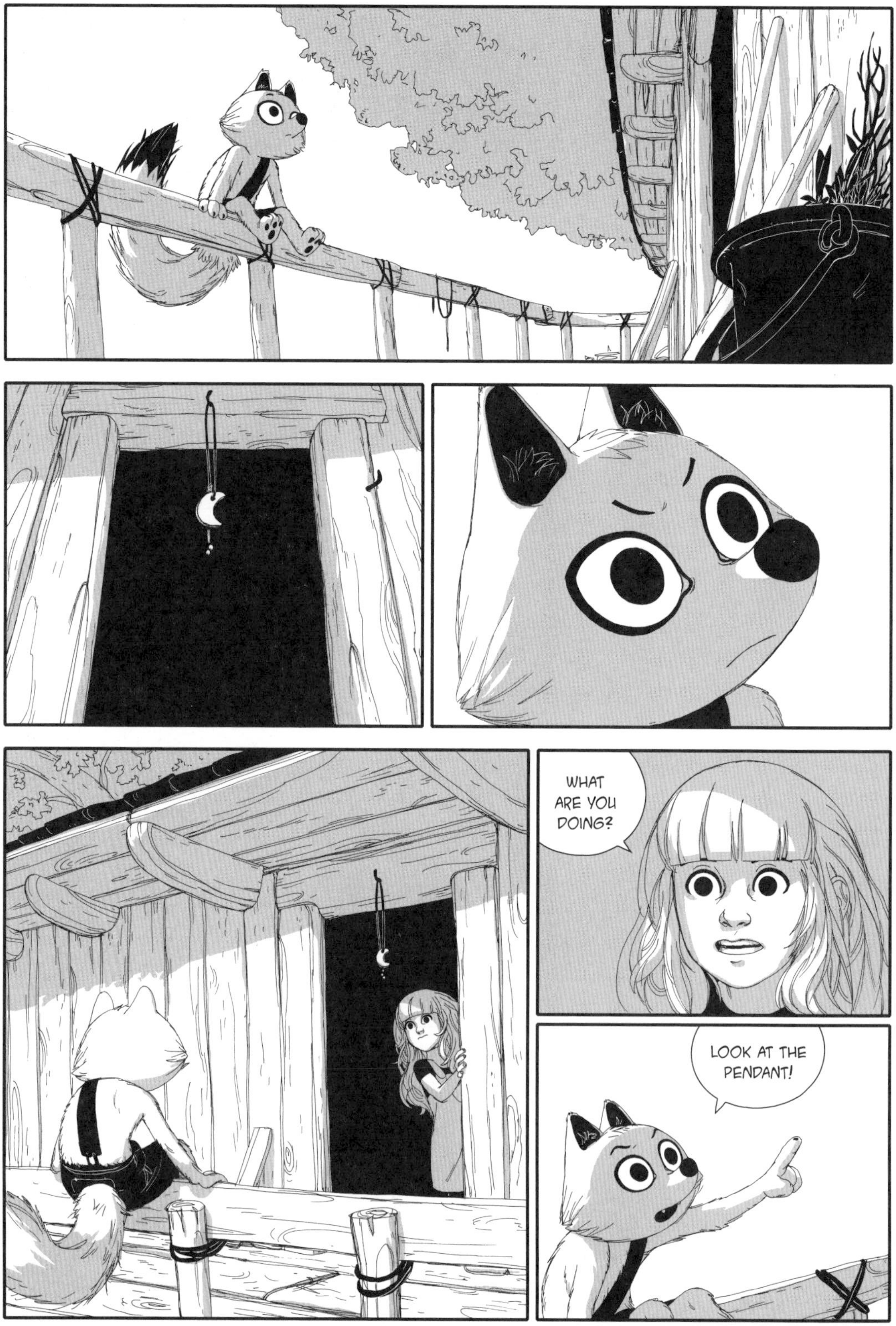
WHAT ARE YOU DOING?
LOOK AT THE PENDANT!

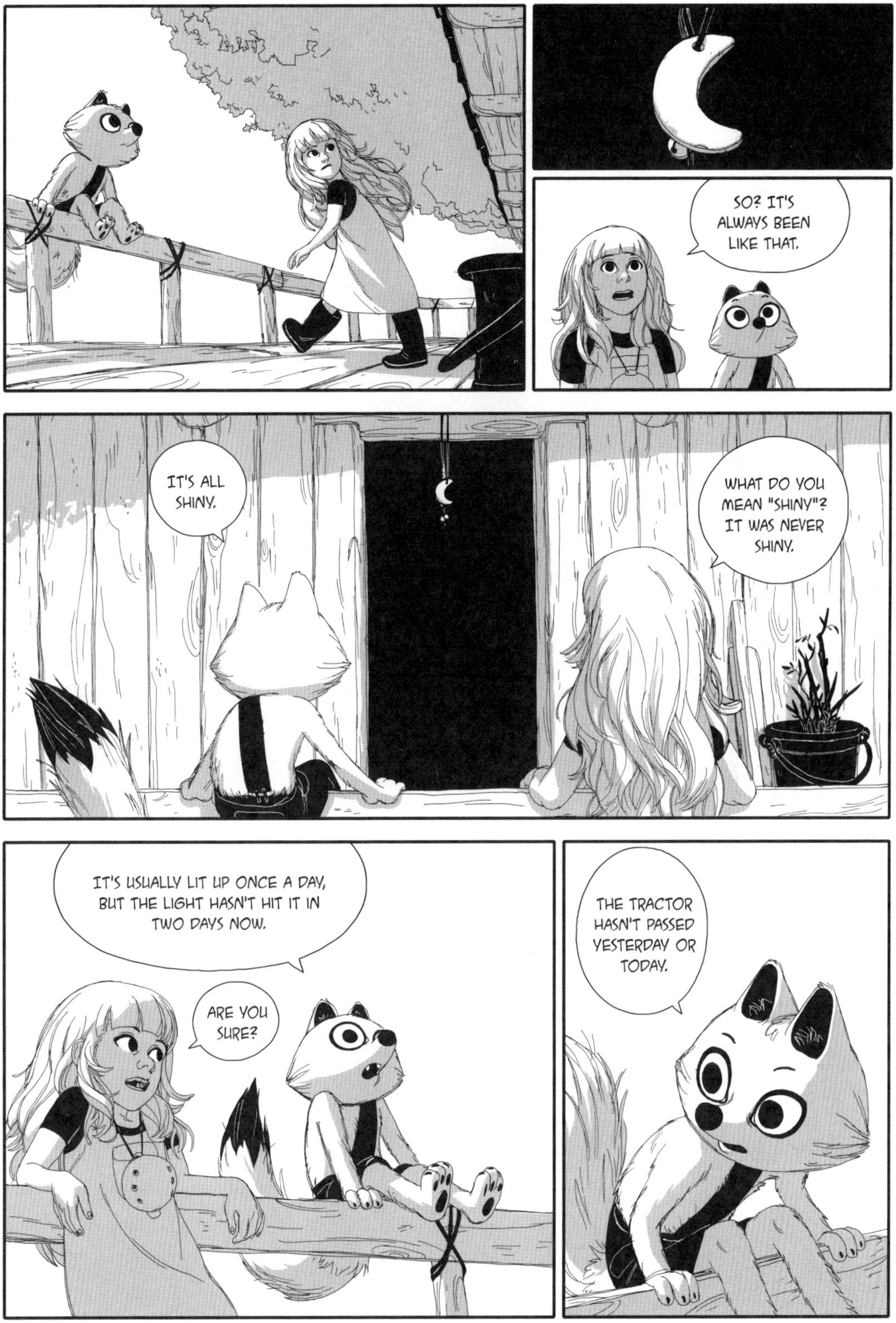
SO? IT'S ALWAYS BEEN LIKE THAT.
IT'S ALL SHINY.
WHAT DO YOU MEAN "SHINY"? IT WAS NEVER SHINY.
IT'S USUALLY LIT UP ONCE A DAY, BUT THE LIGHT HASN'T HIT IT IN TWO DAYS NOW.
ARE YOU SURE?
THE TRACTOR HASN'T PASSED YESTERDAY OR TODAY.

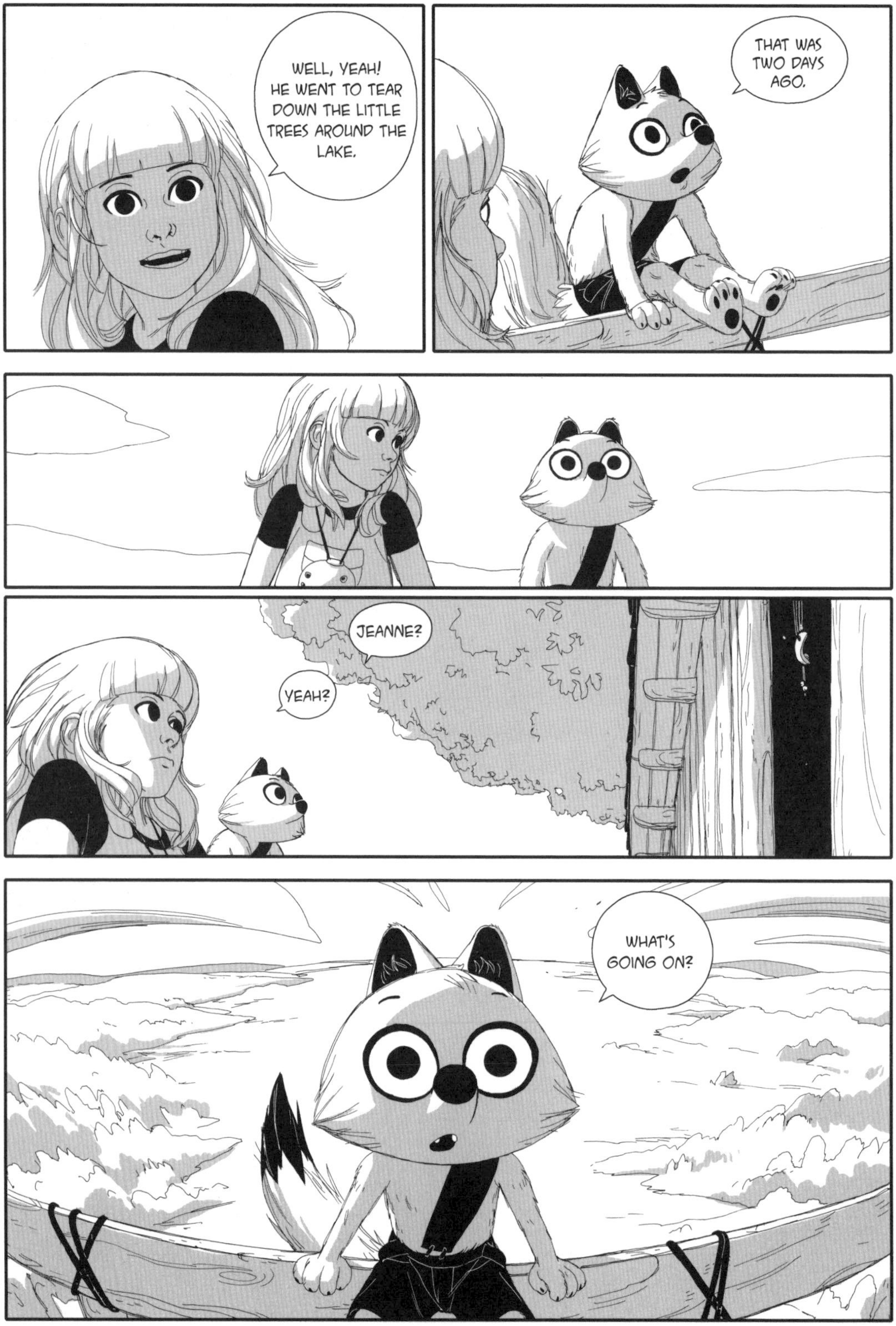
WELL, YEAH! HE WENT TO TEAR DOWN THE LITTLE TREES AROUND THE LAKE.
THAT WAS TWO DAYS AGO.
JEANNE?
YEAH?
WHAT'S GOING ON?

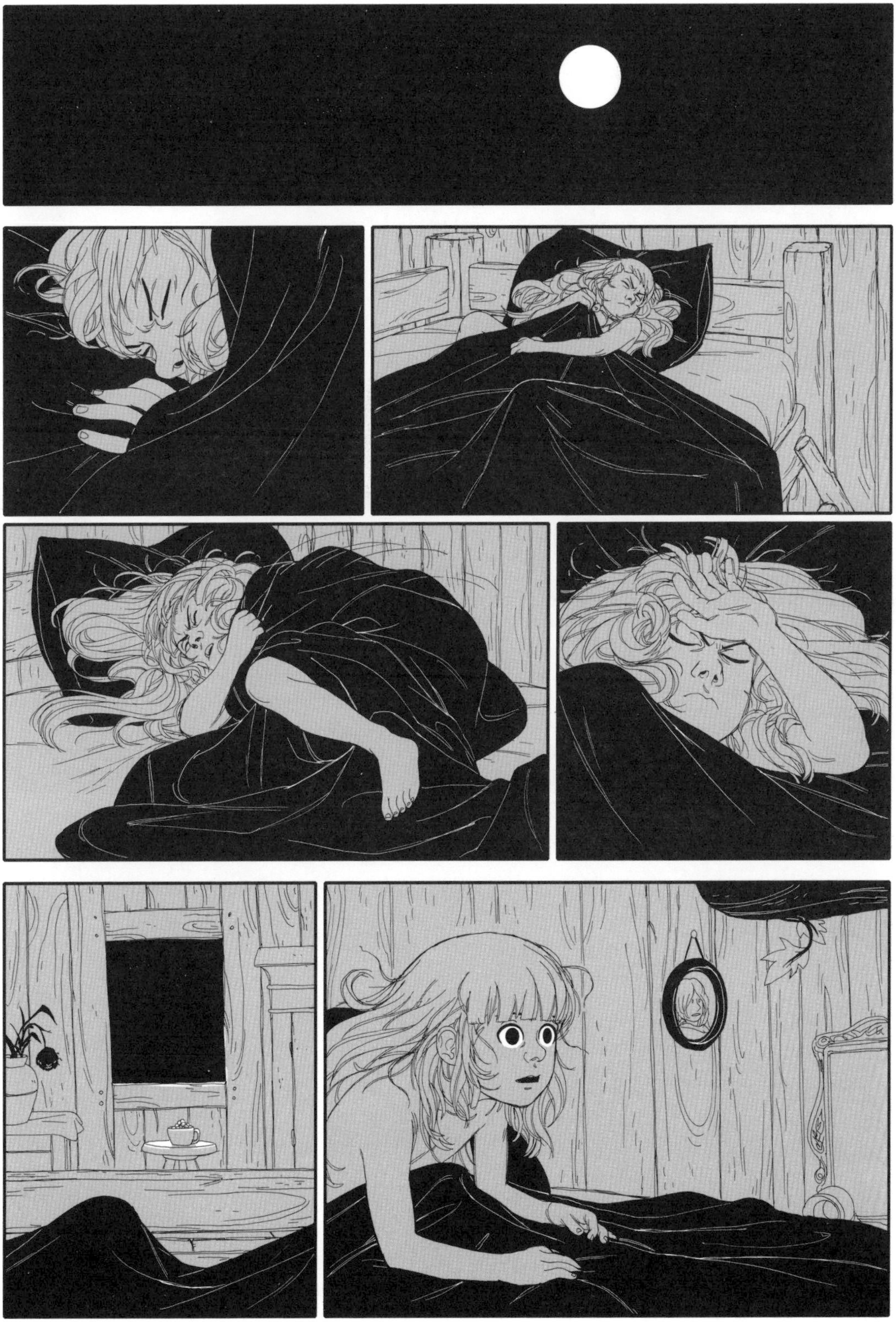

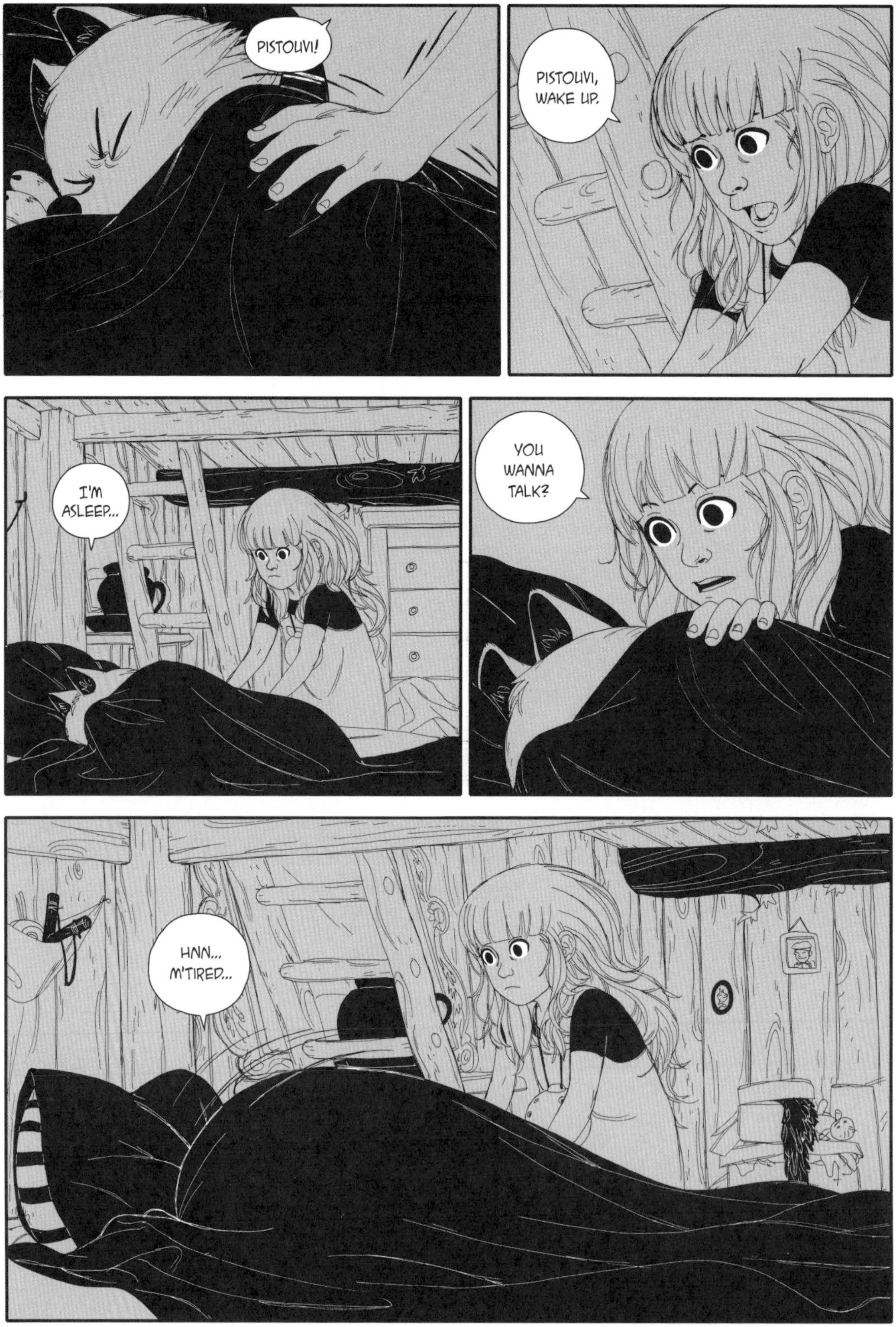

PISTOUVI!
PISTOUVI, WAKE UP.
I'M ASLEEP...
YOU WANNA TALK?
HNN... M'TIRED...

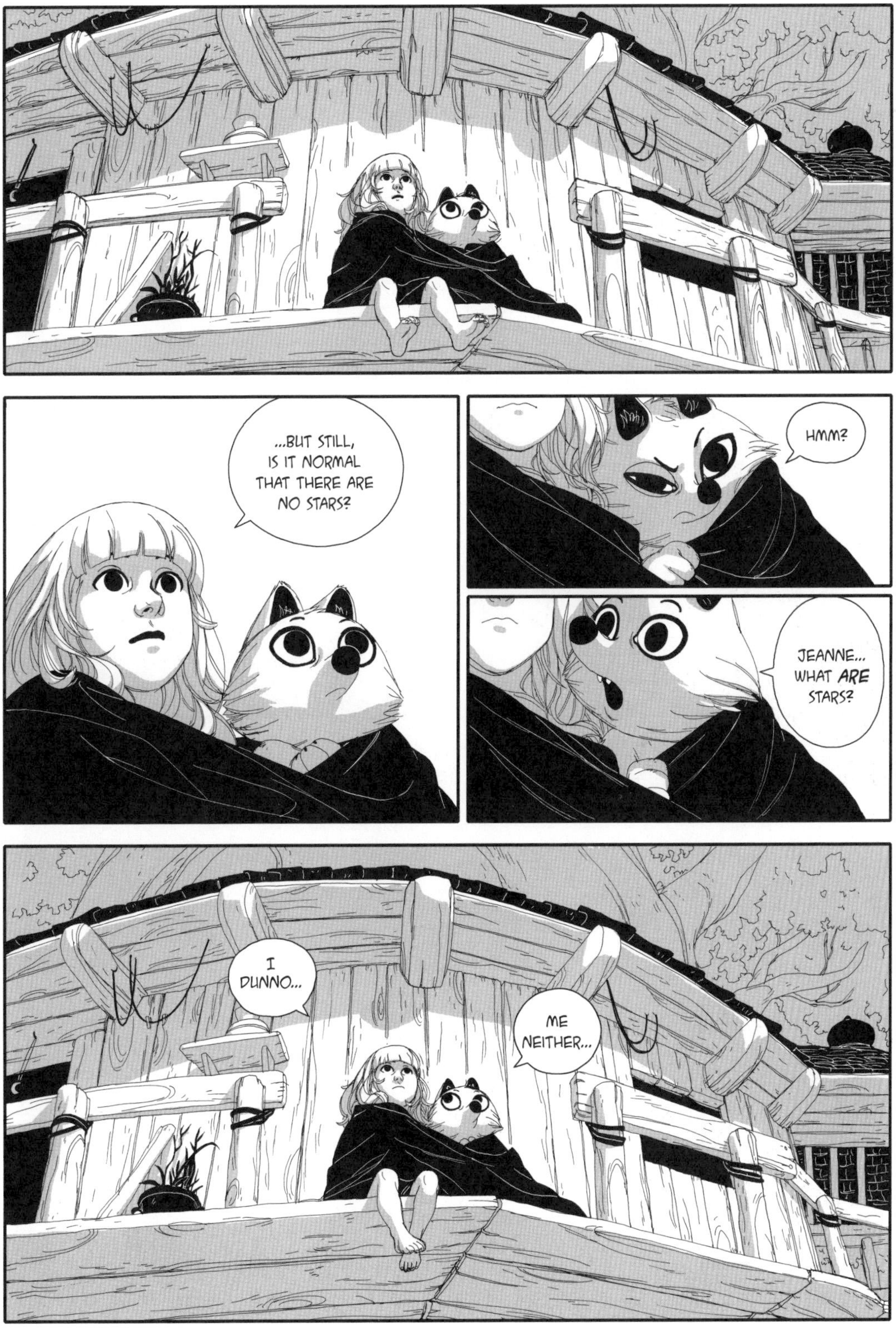
...BUT STILL, IS IT NORMAL THAT THERE ARE NO STARS?
HMM?
JEANNE... WHAT *ARE* STARS?
I DUNNO...
ME NEITHER...

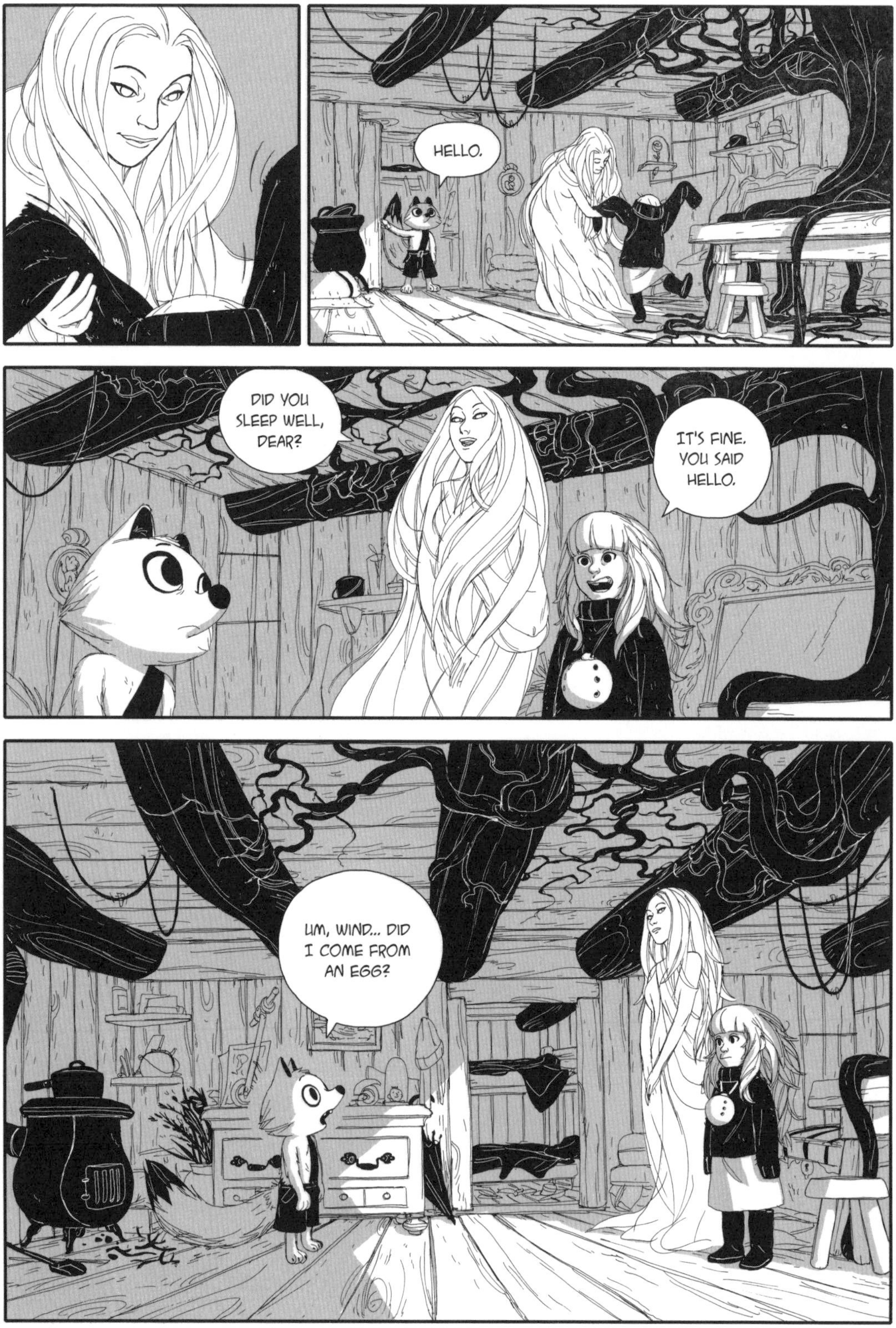
HELLO.
DID YOU SLEEP WELL, DEAR?
IT'S FINE. YOU SAID HELLO.
UM, WIND... DID I COME FROM AN EGG?

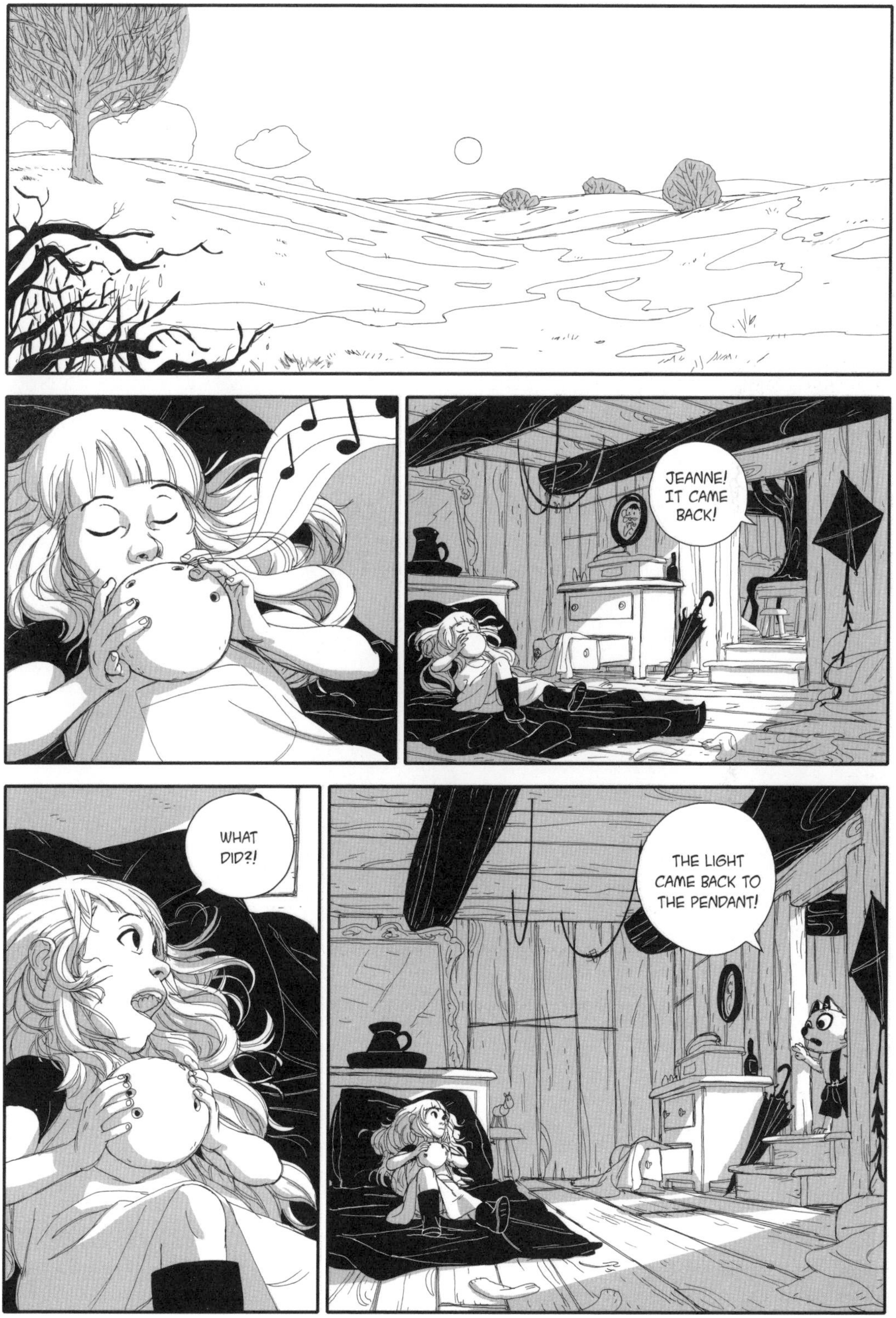
JEANNE! IT CAME BACK!
WHAT DID?!
THE LIGHT CAME BACK TO THE PENDANT!

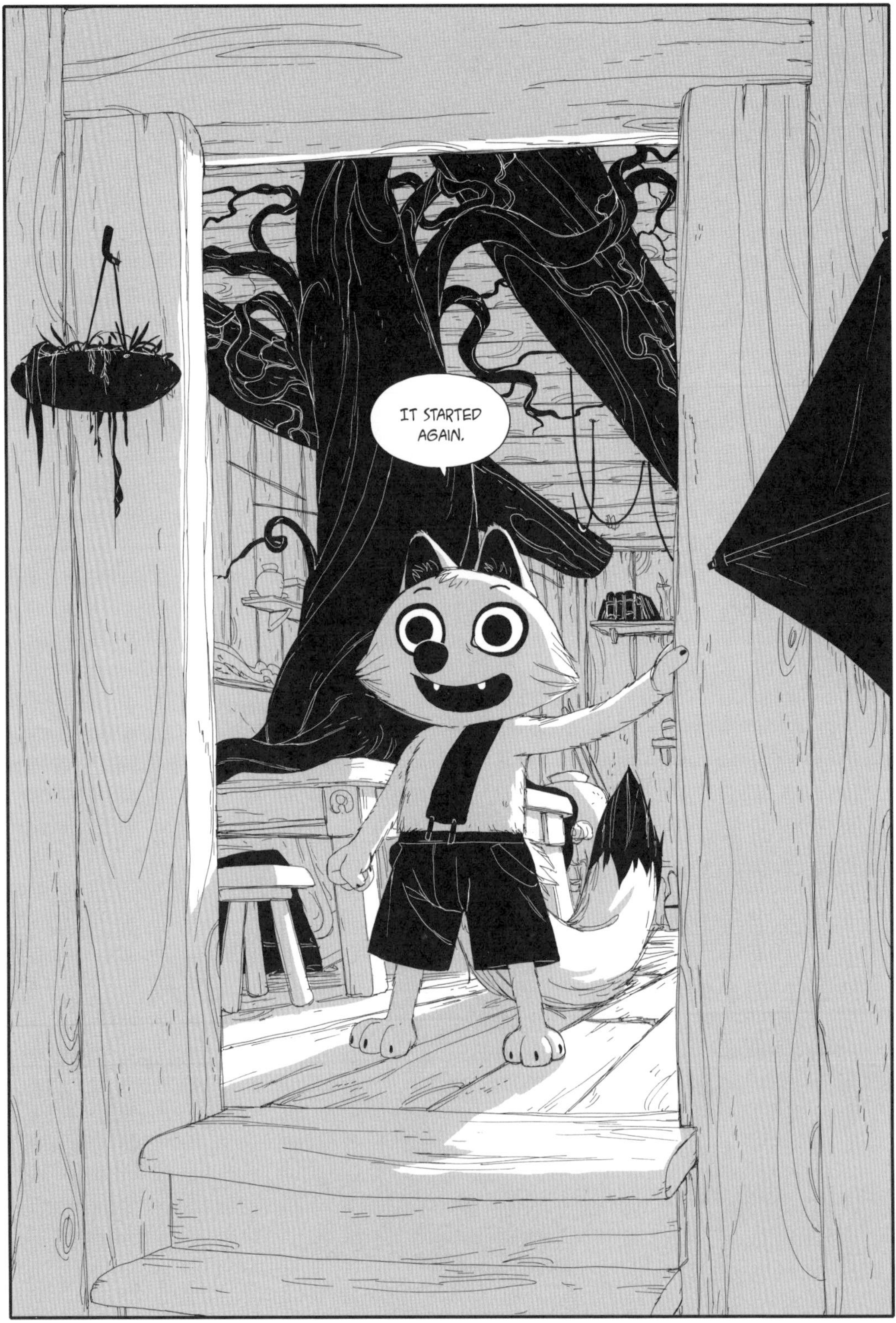
IT STARTED
AGAIN.

Chapter 10

WEDDING

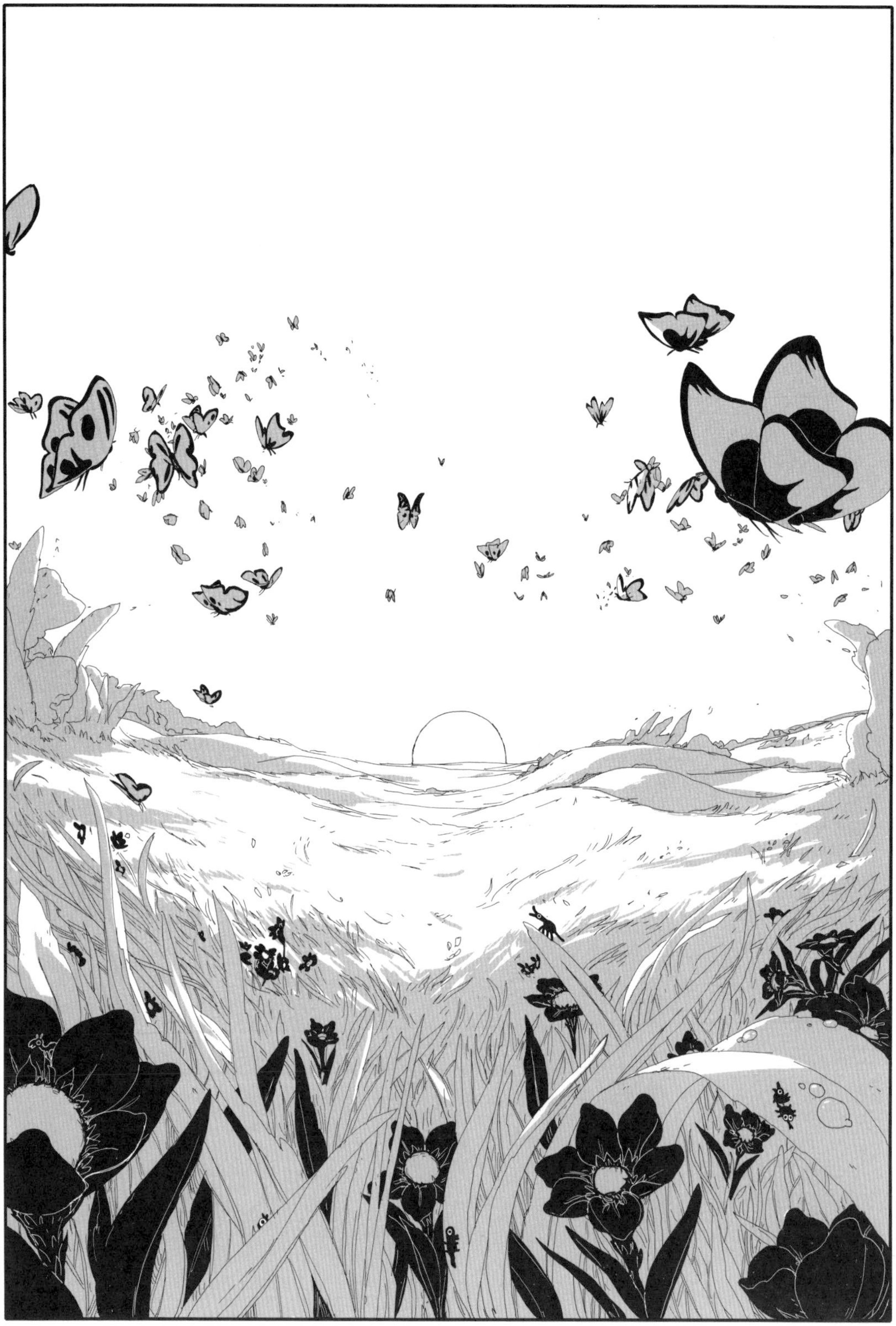

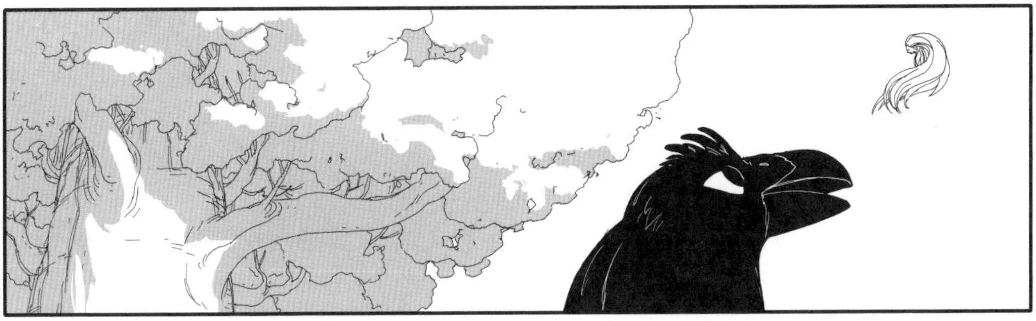

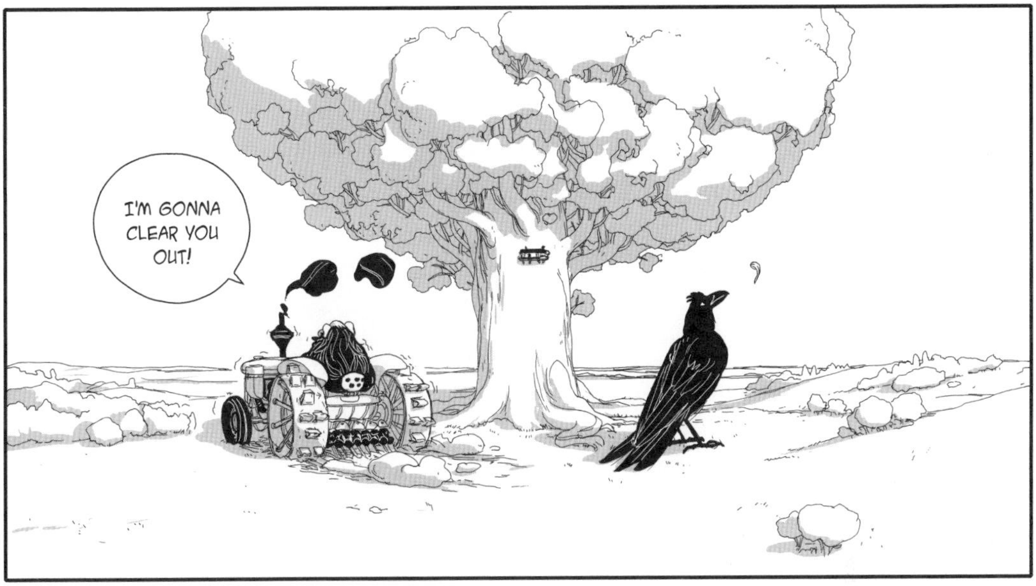
I'M GONNA CLEAR YOU OUT!

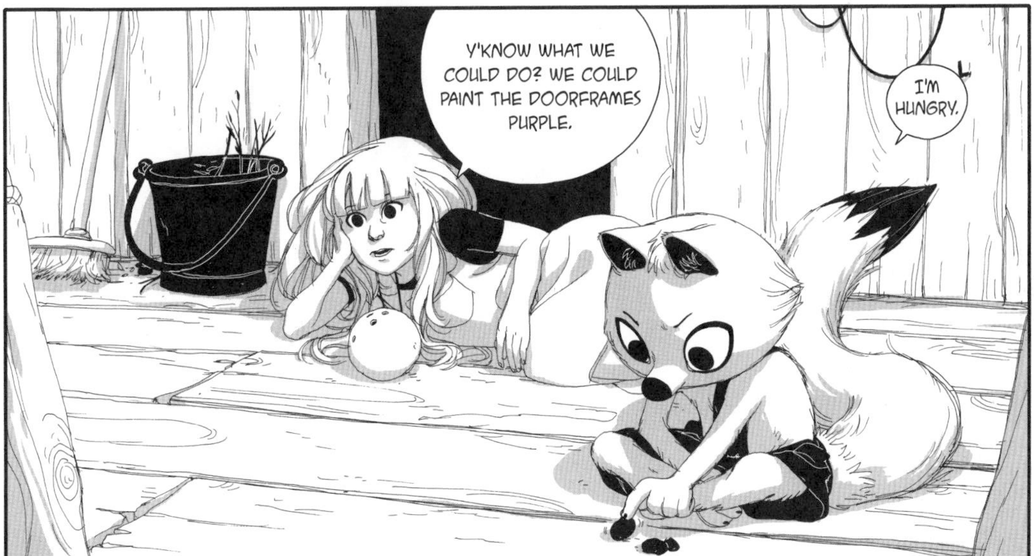
Y'KNOW WHAT WE COULD DO? WE COULD PAINT THE DOORFRAMES PURPLE.
I'M HUNGRY.

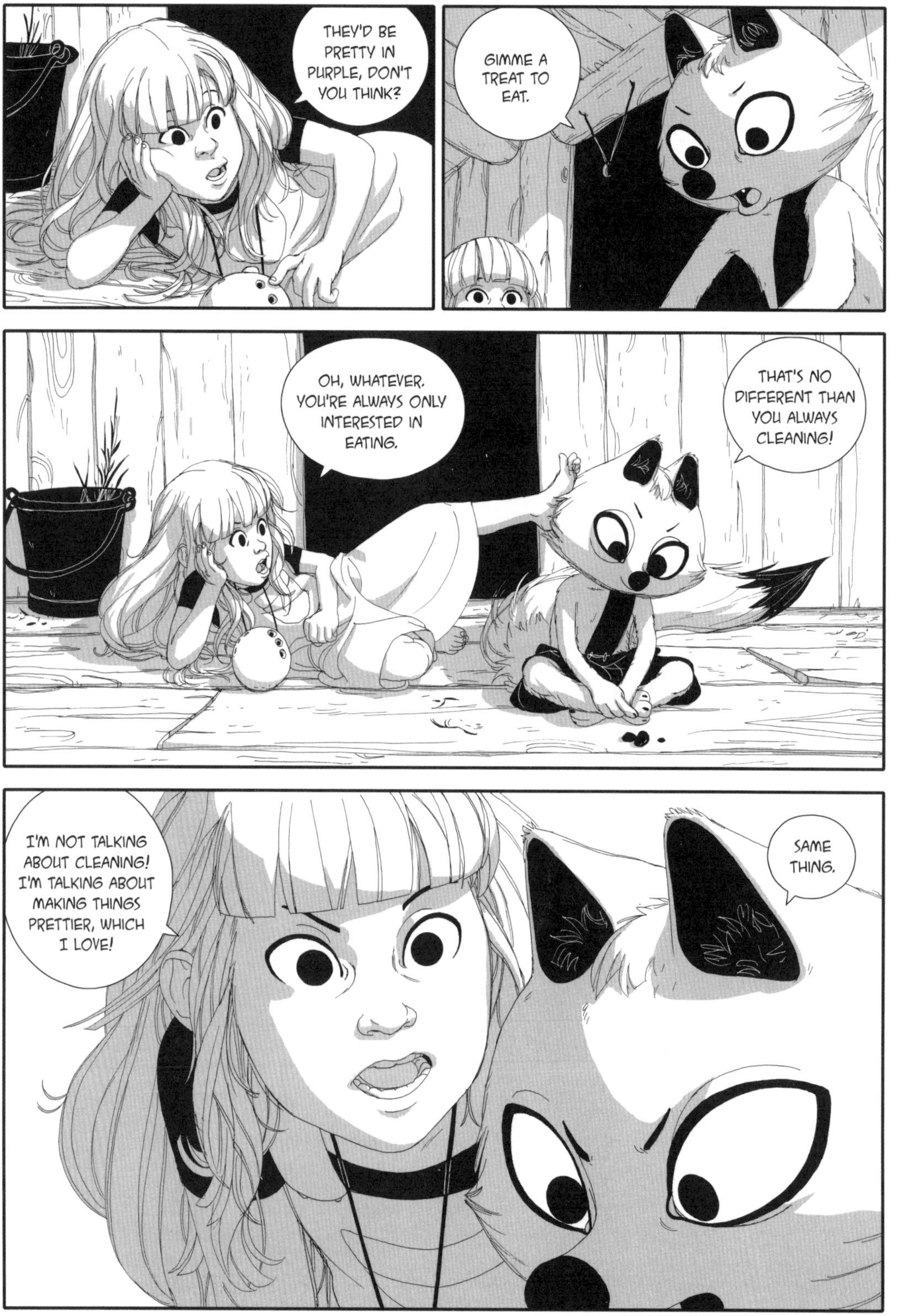
THEY'D BE PRETTY IN PURPLE, DON'T YOU THINK?
GIMME A TREAT TO EAT.
OH, WHATEVER. YOU'RE ALWAYS ONLY INTERESTED IN EATING.
THAT'S NO DIFFERENT THAN YOU ALWAYS CLEANING!
I'M NOT TALKING ABOUT CLEANING! I'M TALKING ABOUT MAKING THINGS PRETTIER, WHICH I LOVE!
SAME THING.

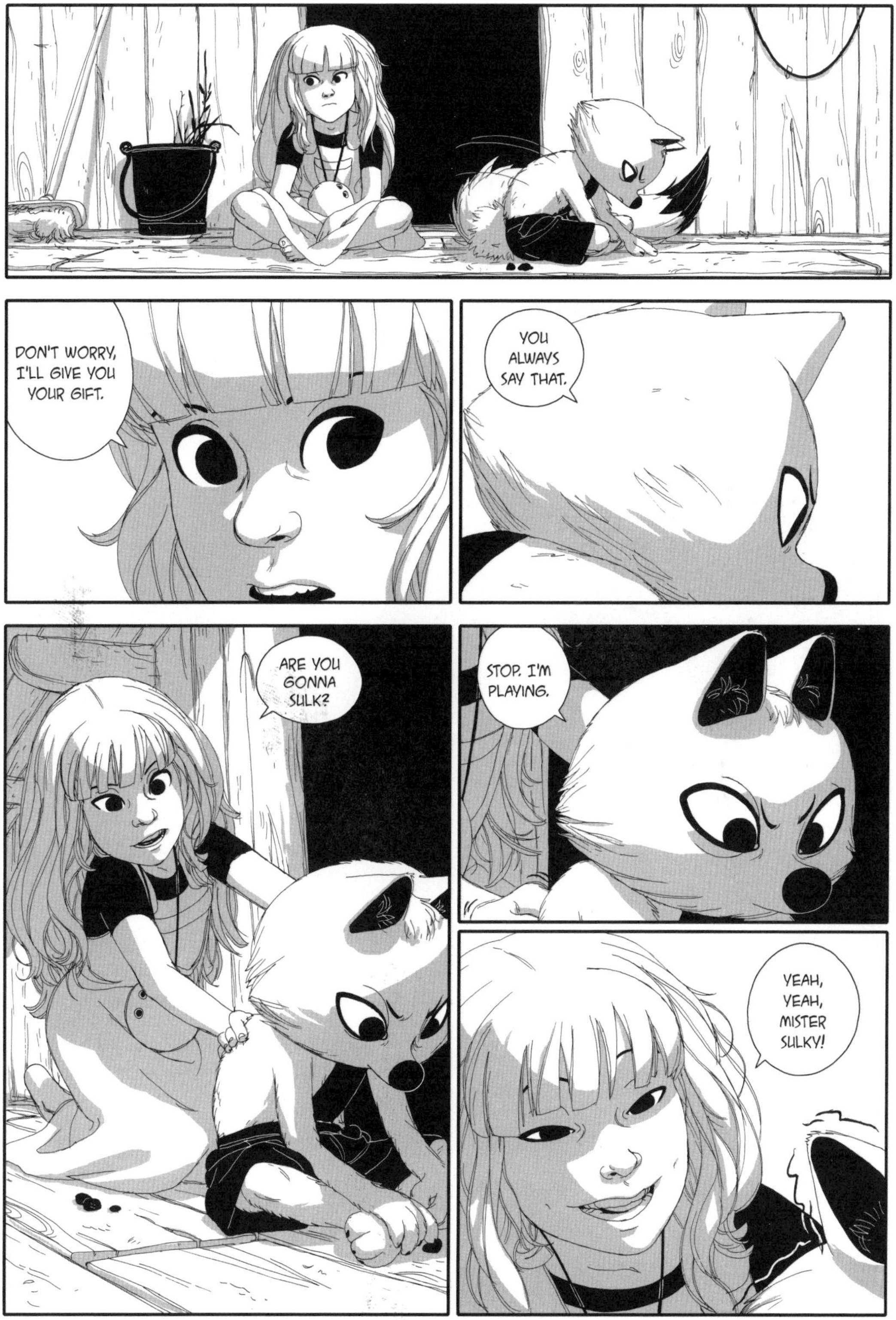
DON'T WORRY, I'LL GIVE YOU YOUR GIFT.
YOU ALWAYS SAY THAT.
ARE YOU GONNA SULK?
STOP. I'M PLAYING.
YEAH, YEAH, MISTER SULKY!

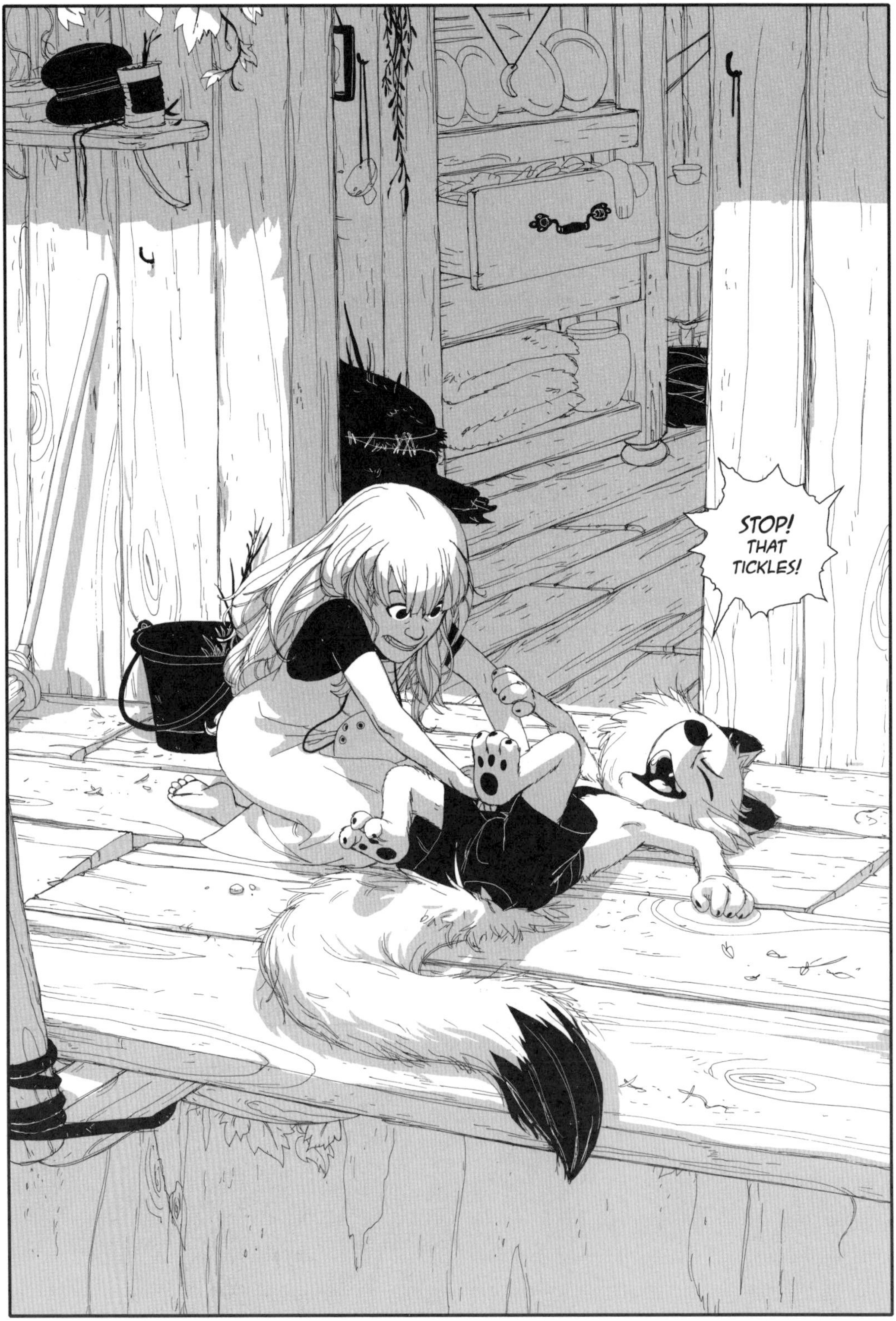
STOP! THAT TICKLES!

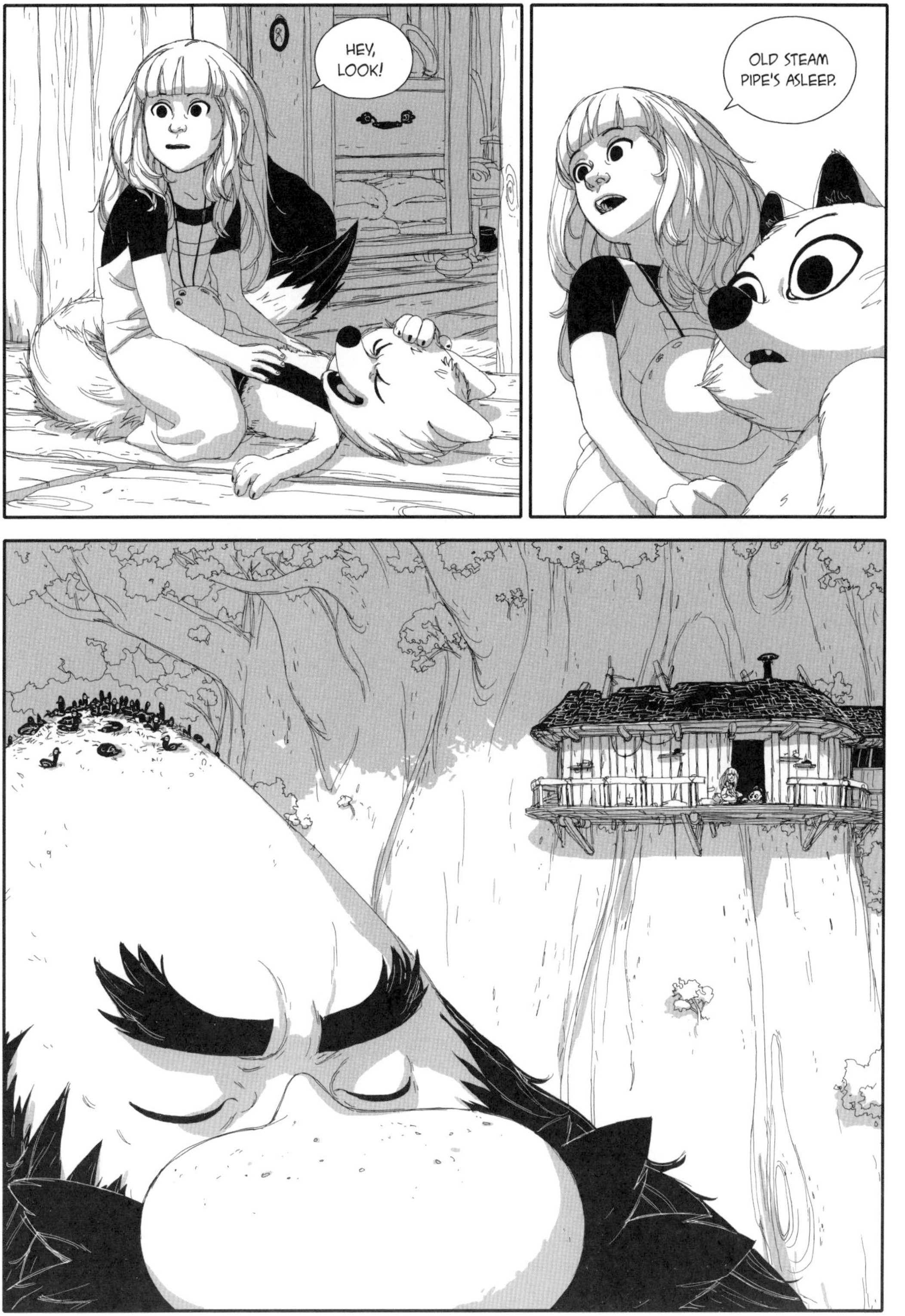
HEY,
LOOK!
OLD STEAM
PIPE'S ASLEEP.

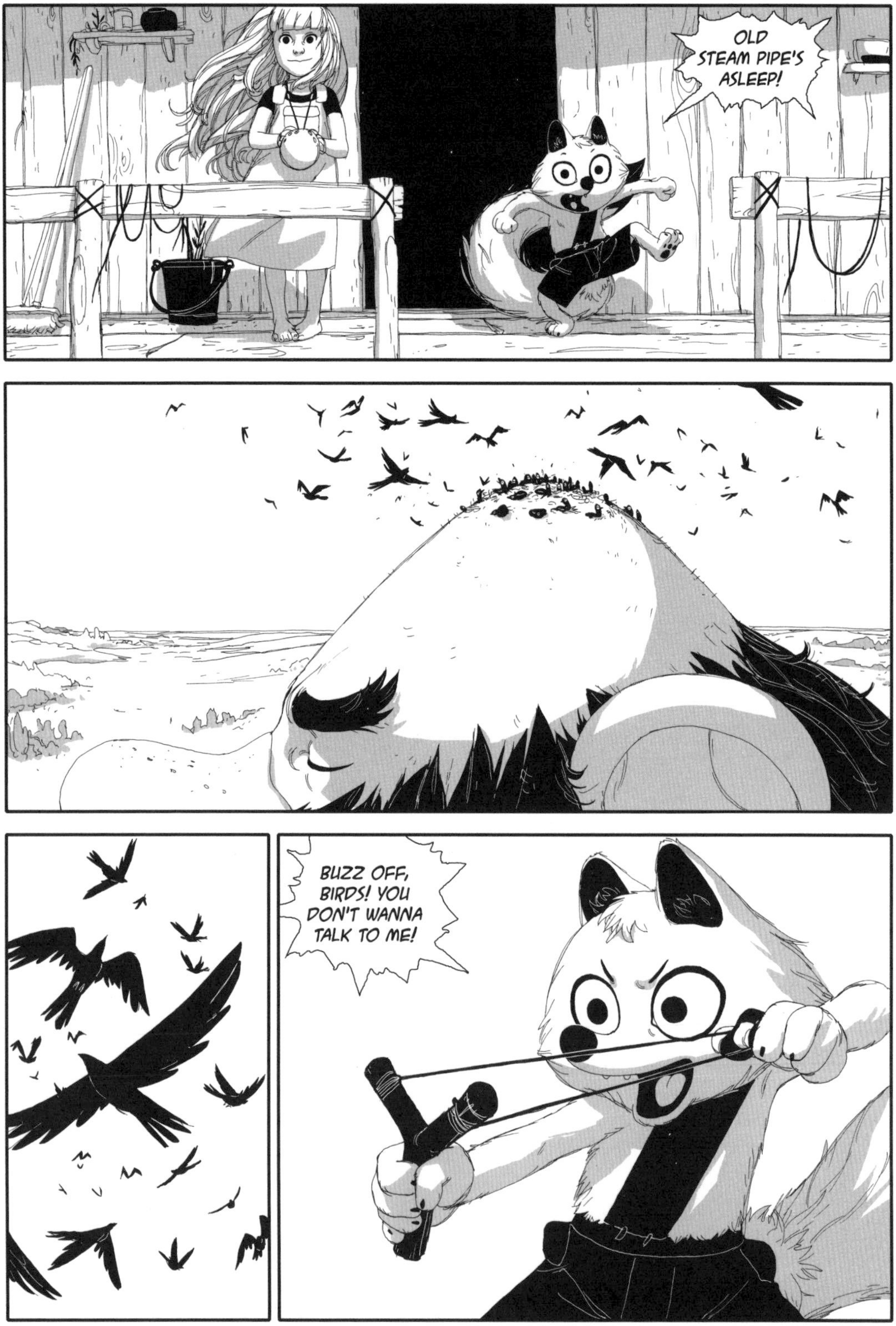
OLD STEAM PIPE'S ASLEEP!
BUZZ OFF, BIRDS! YOU DON'T WANNA TALK TO ME!

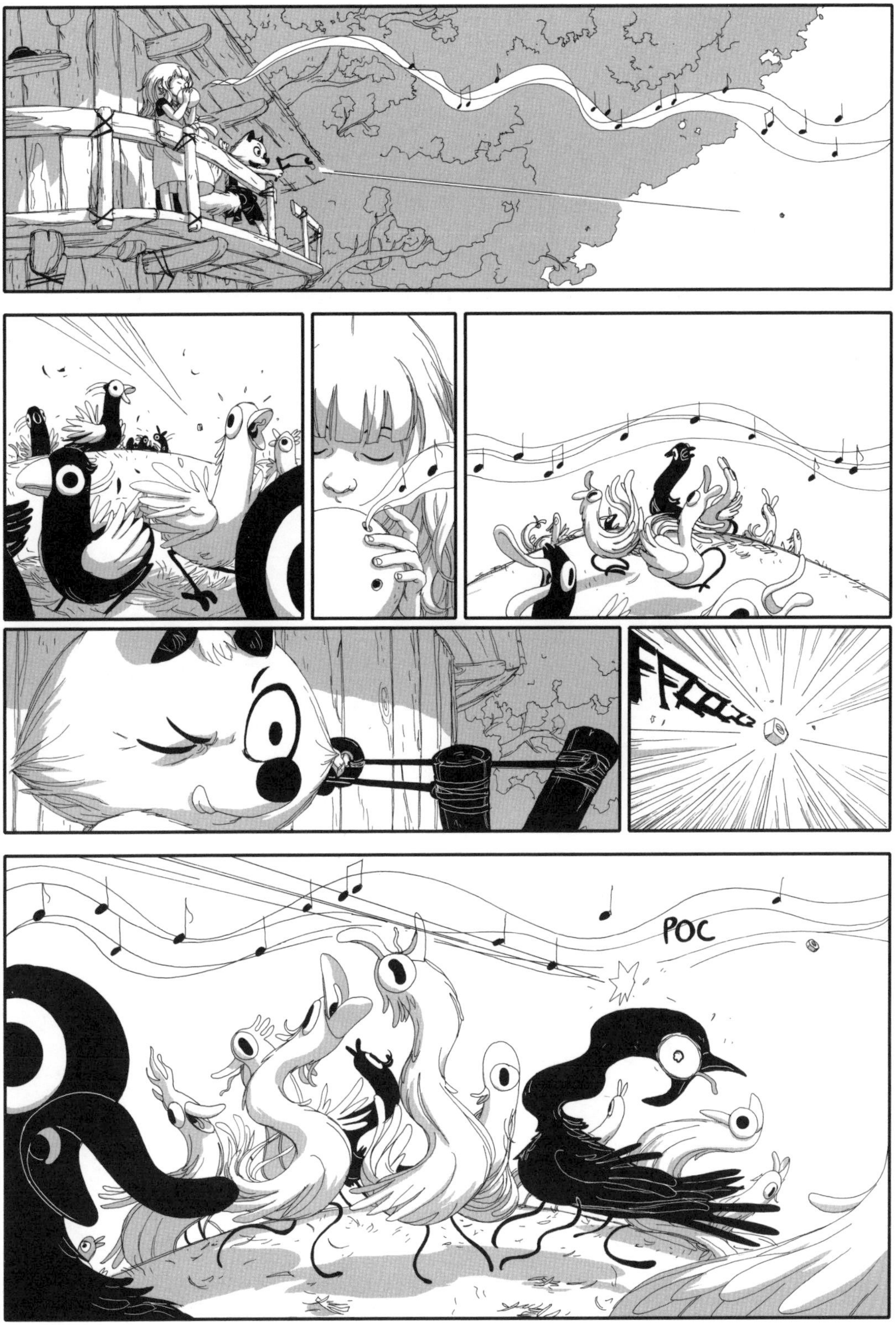
POC

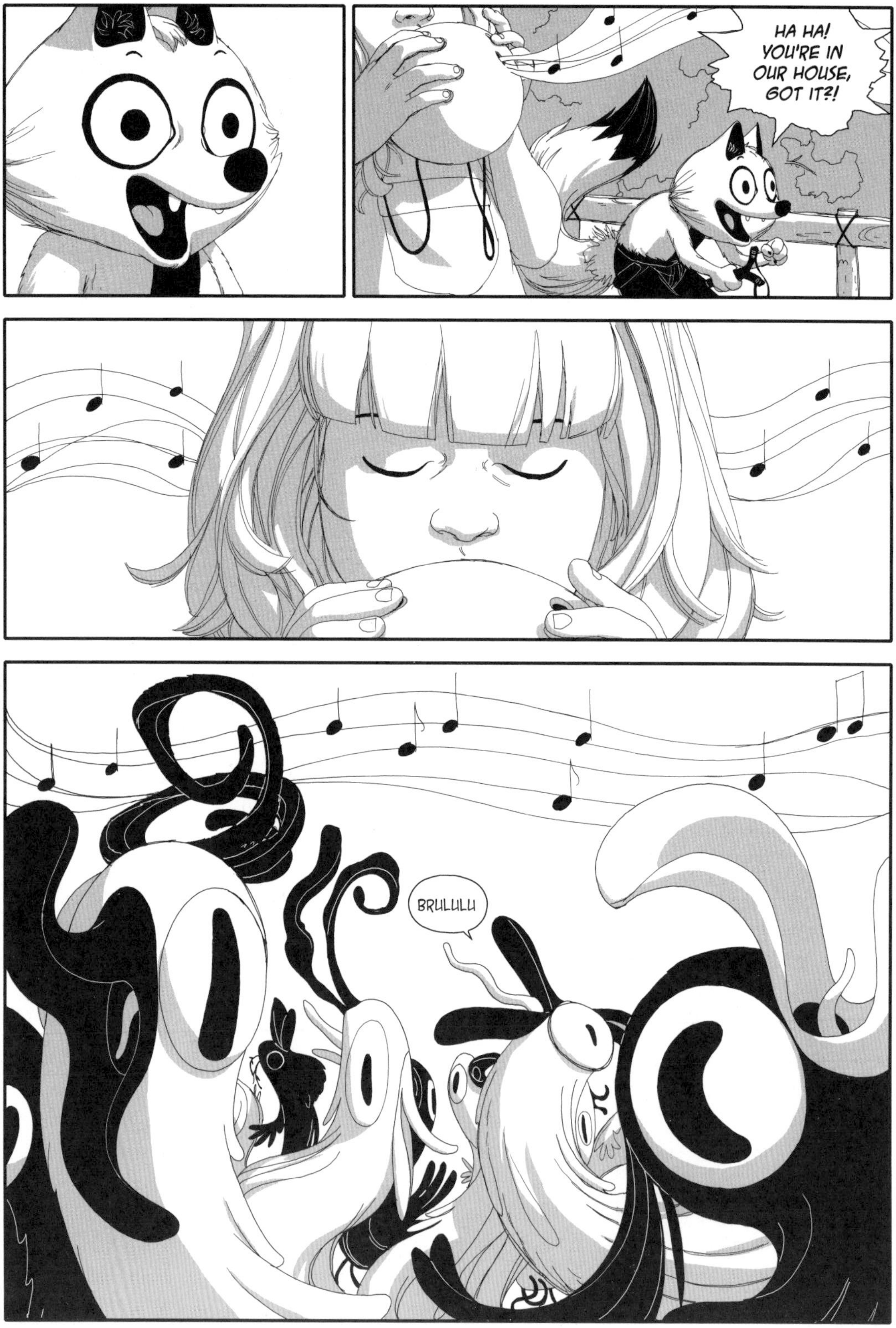
HA HA! YOU'RE IN OUR HOUSE, GOT IT?!
BRULULU

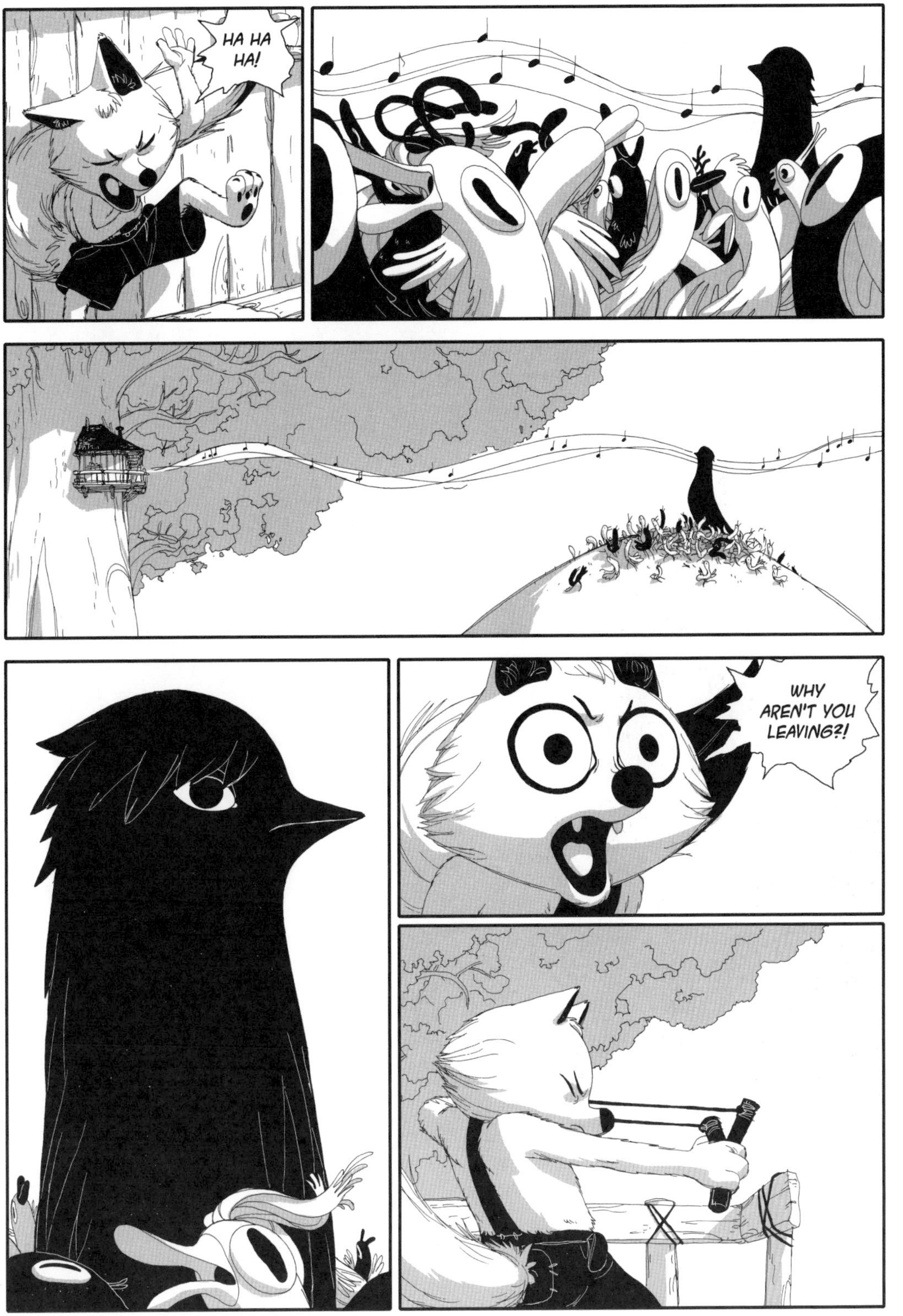
HA HA HA!
WHY AREN'T YOU LEAVING?!

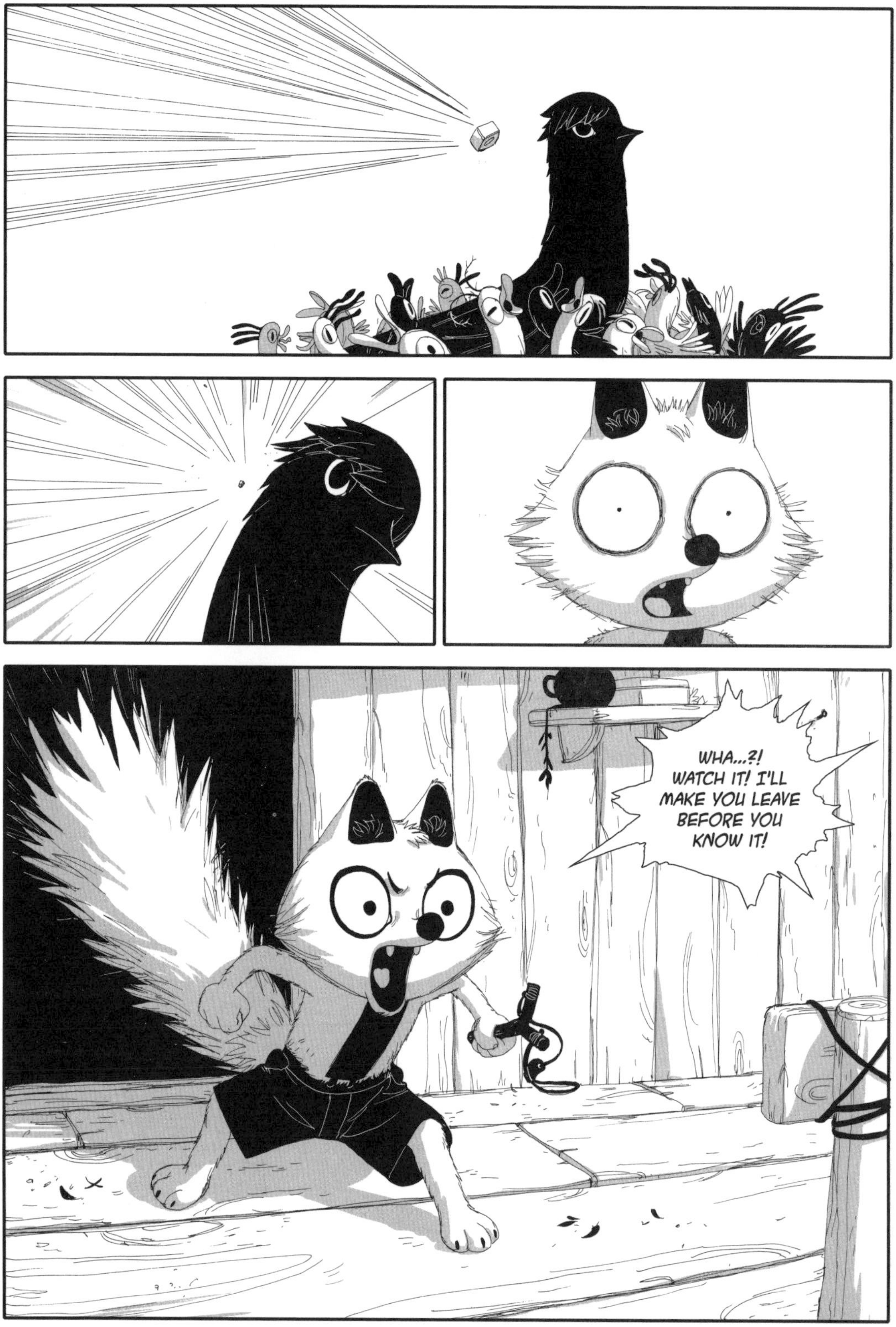
WHA...?! WATCH IT! I'LL MAKE YOU LEAVE BEFORE YOU KNOW IT!

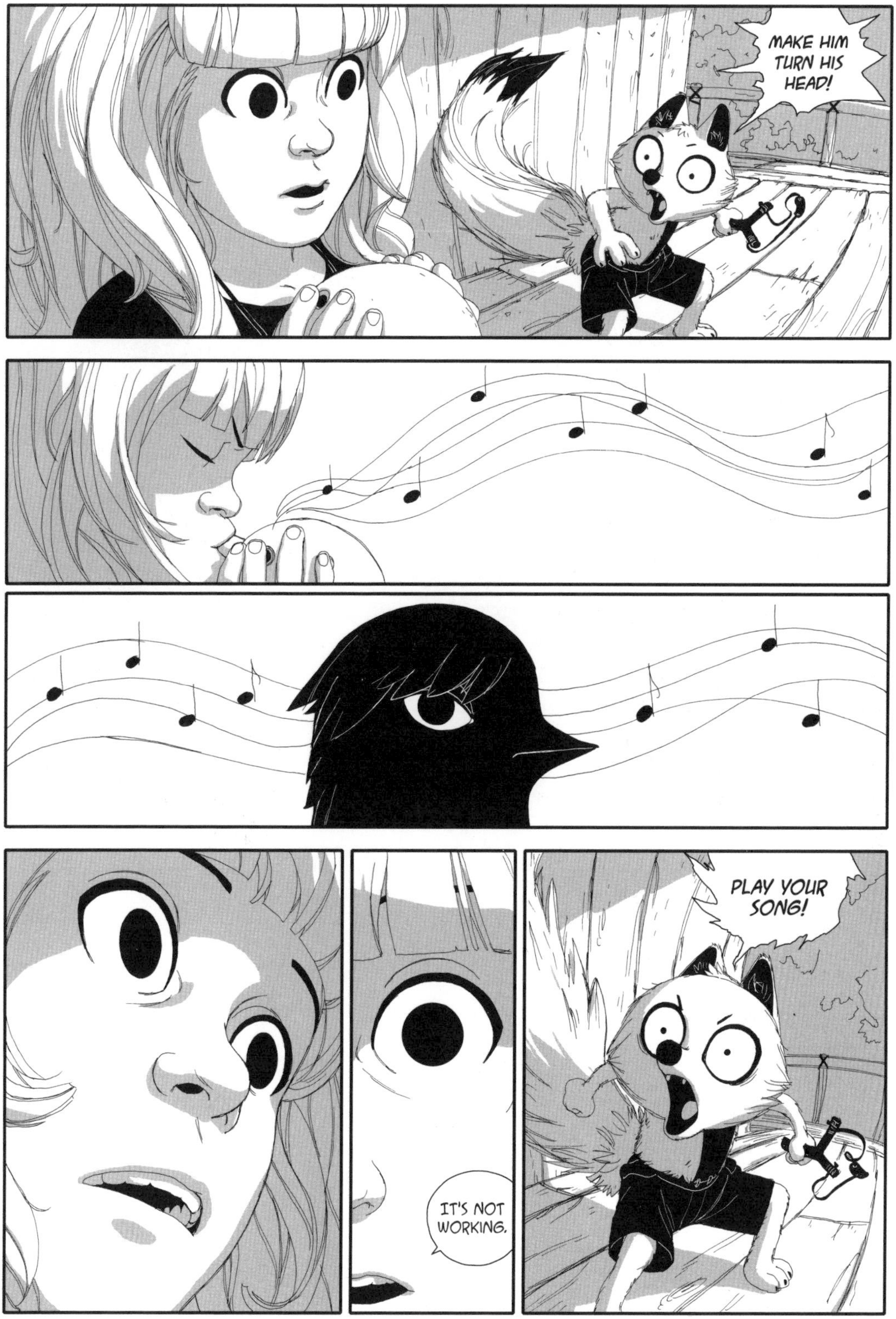
MAKE HIM TURN HIS HEAD!
IT'S NOT WORKING.
PLAY YOUR SONG!

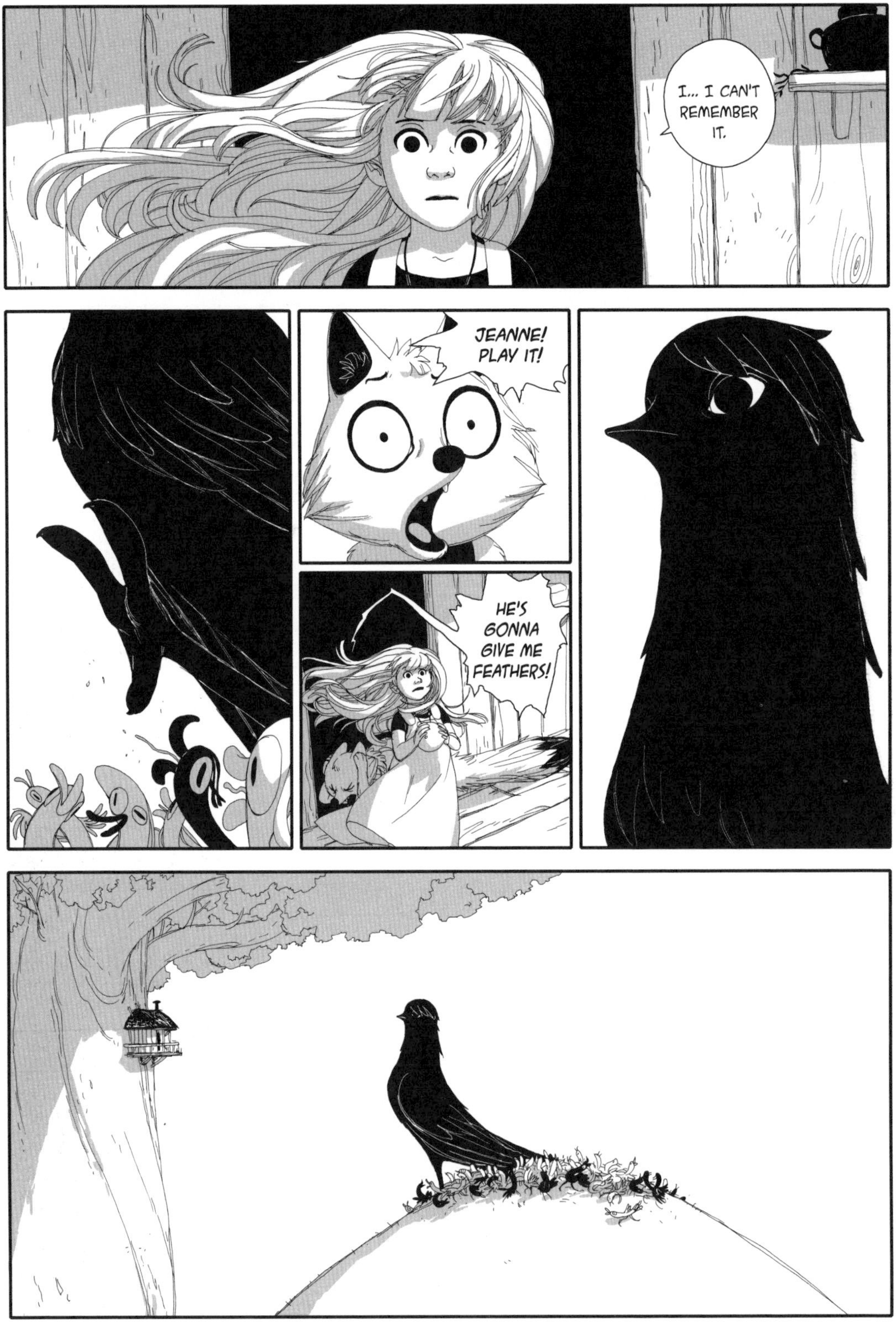
I... I CAN'T REMEMBER IT.
JEANNE! PLAY IT!
HE'S GONNA GIVE ME FEATHERS!

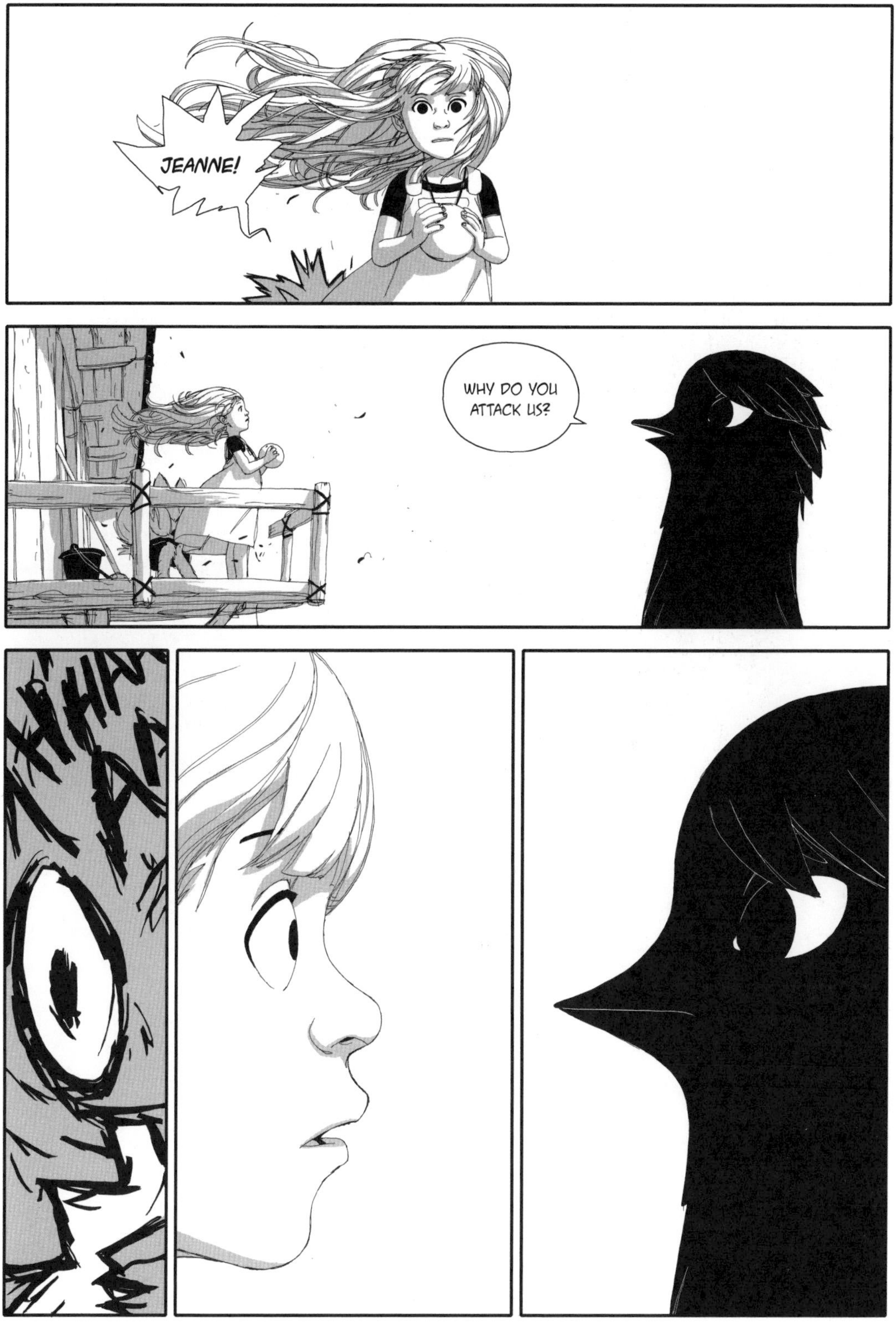
JEANNE!
WHY DO YOU ATTACK US?

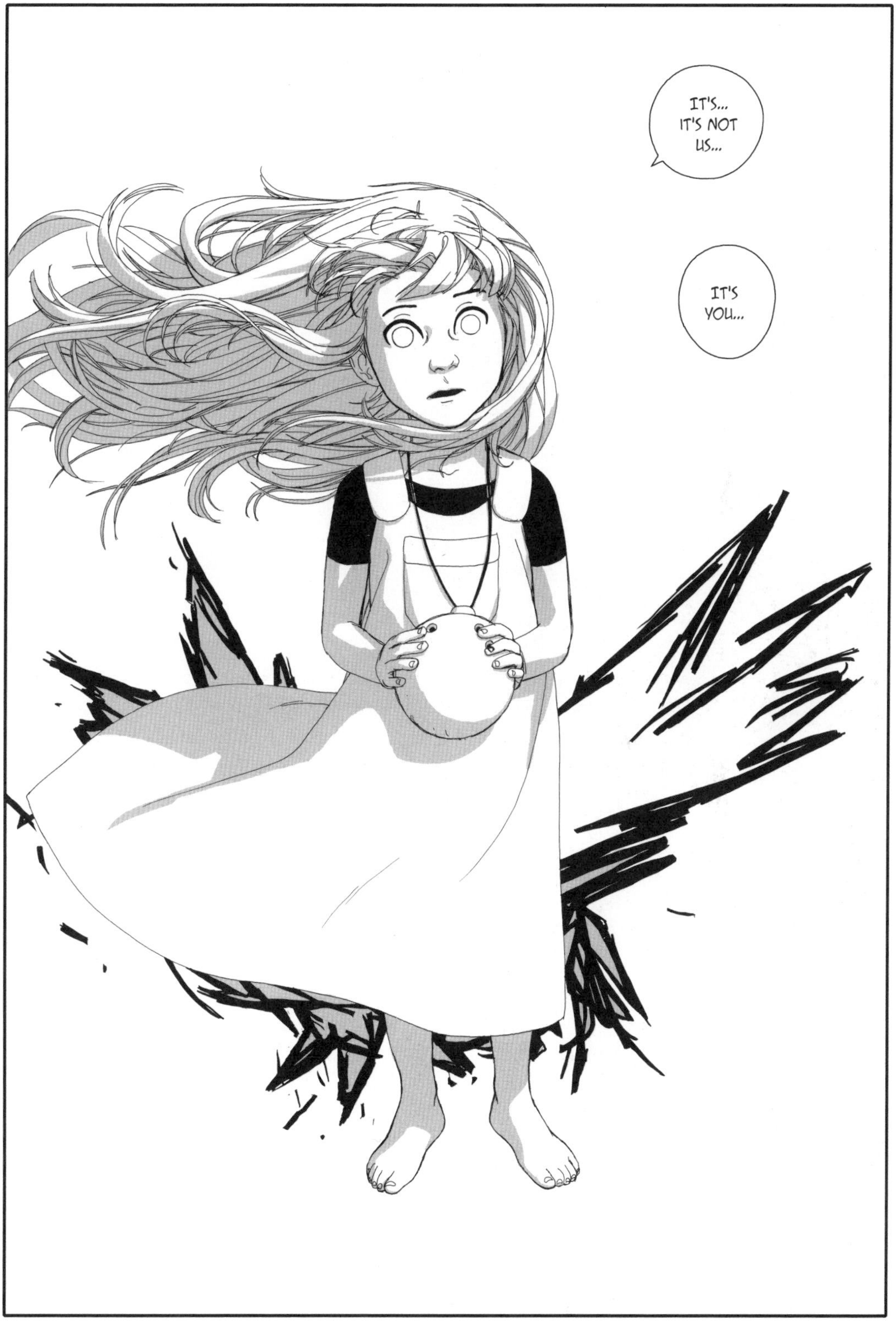
IT'S... IT'S NOT US...
IT'S YOU...

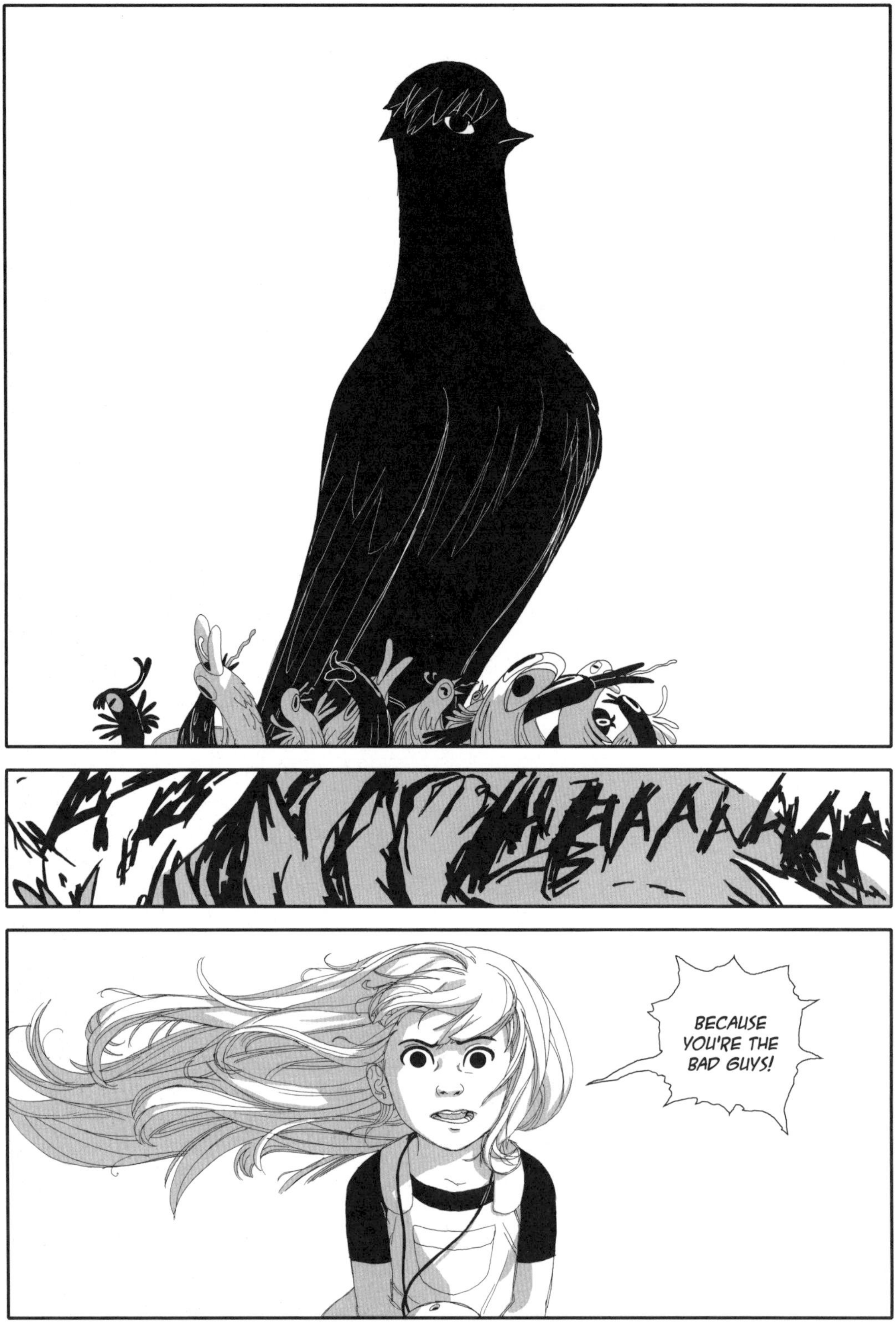
BECAUSE YOU'RE THE BAD GUYS!

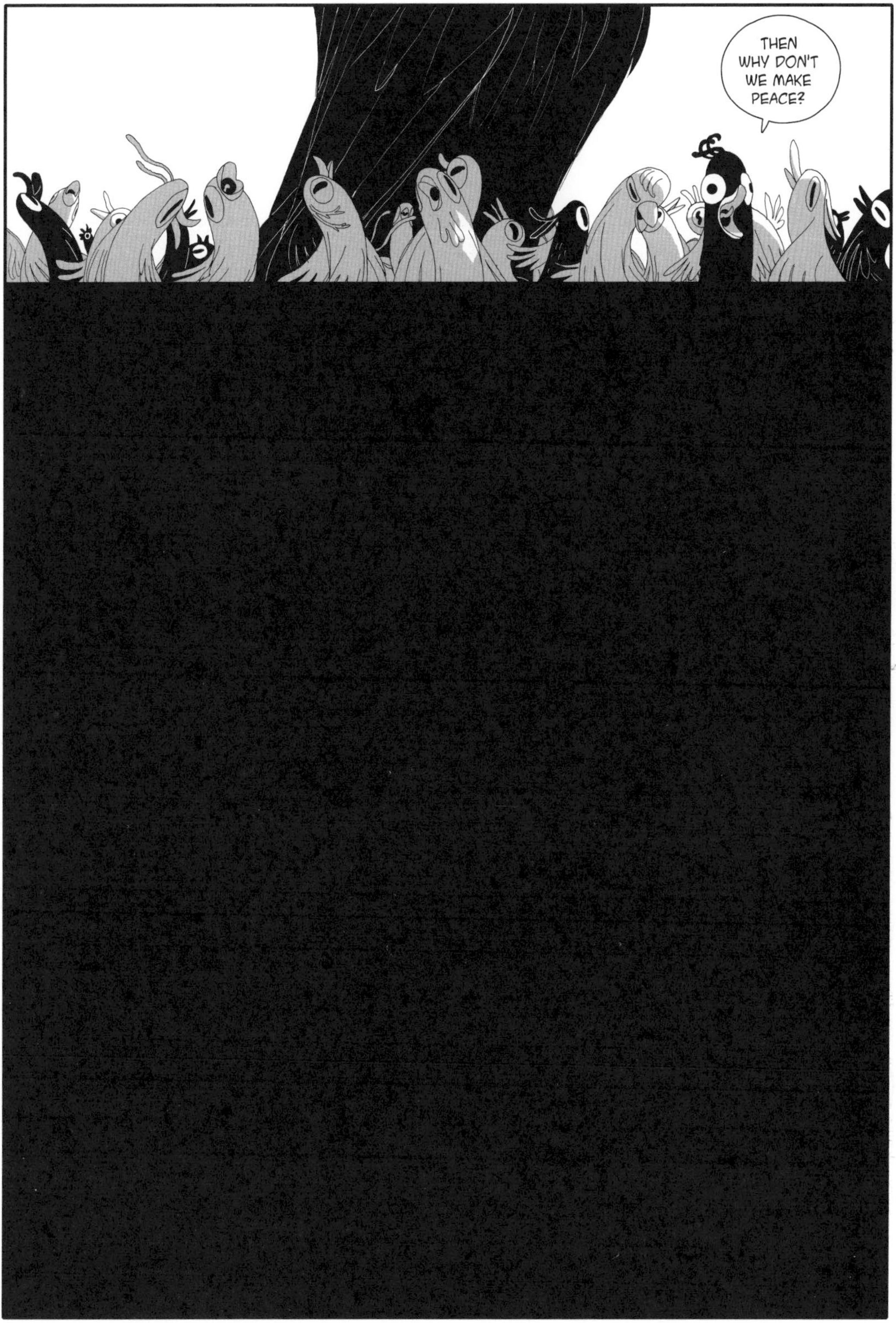
THEN WHY DON'T WE MAKE PEACE?

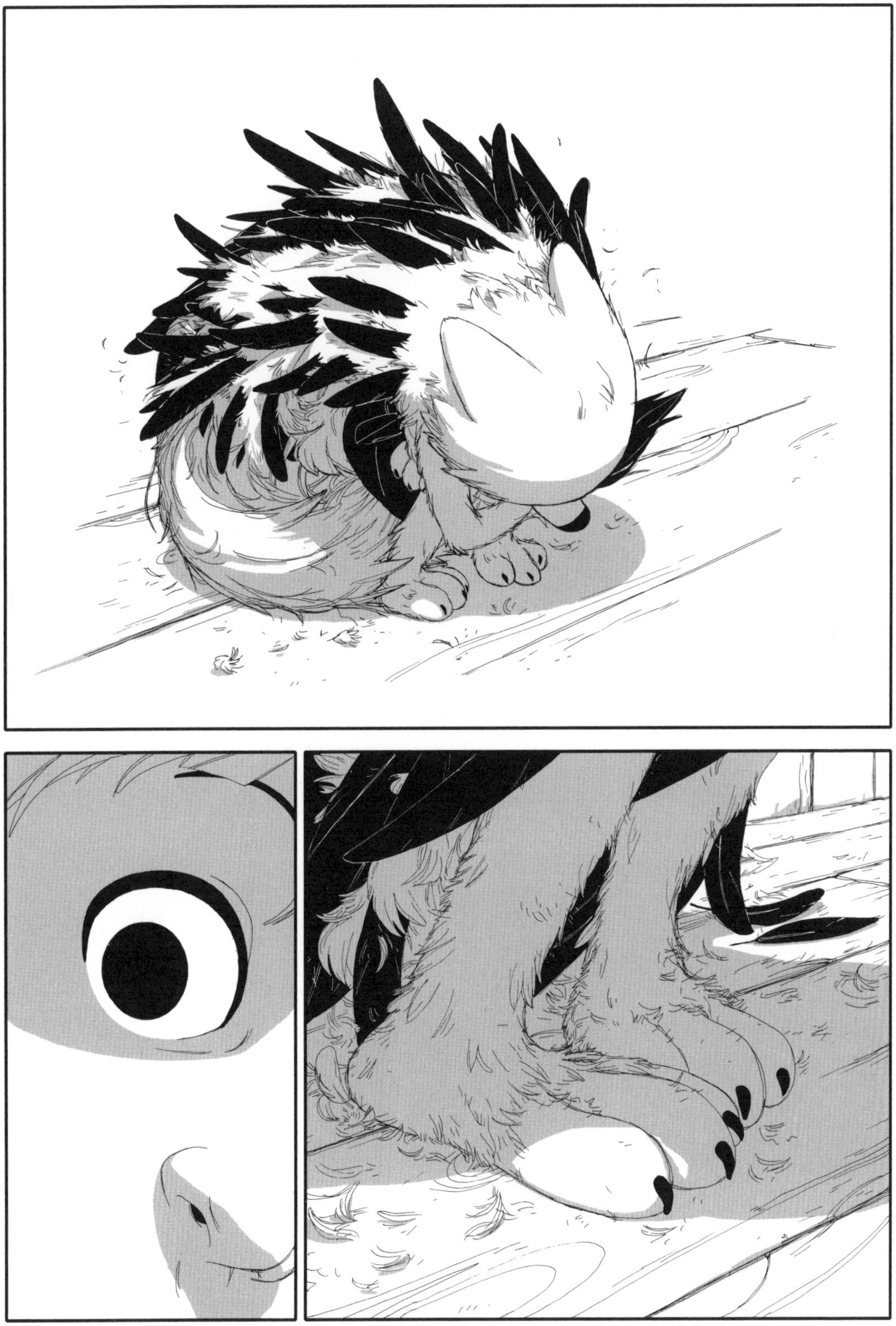

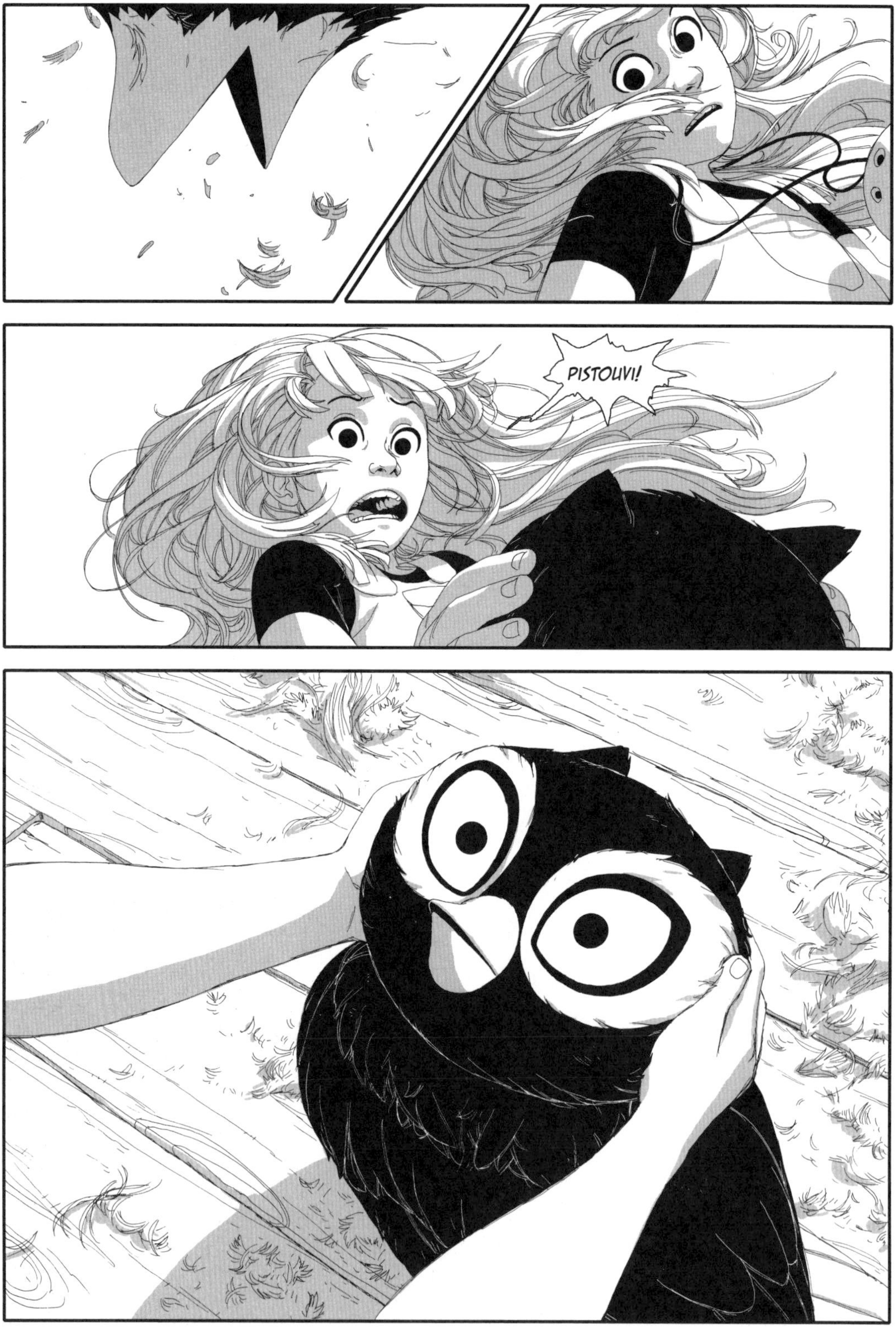
PISTOUVI!

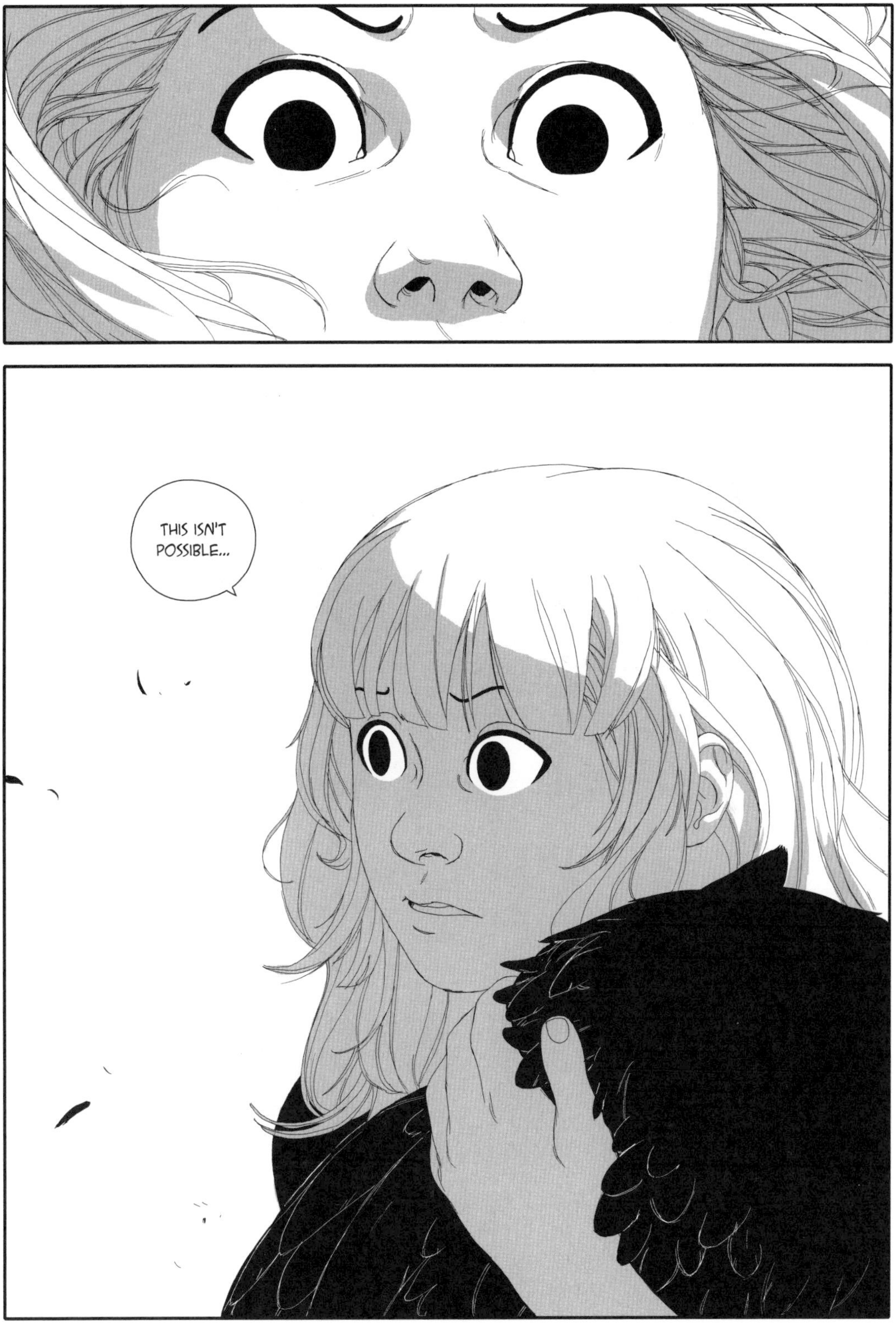
THIS ISN'T POSSIBLE...

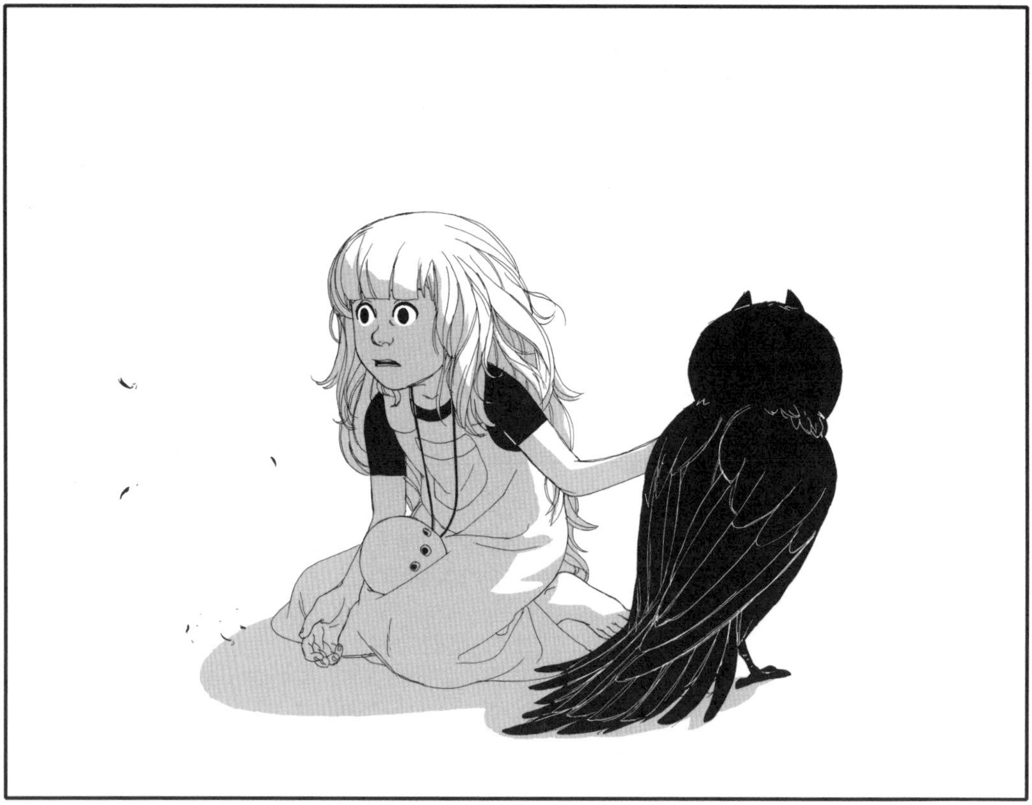

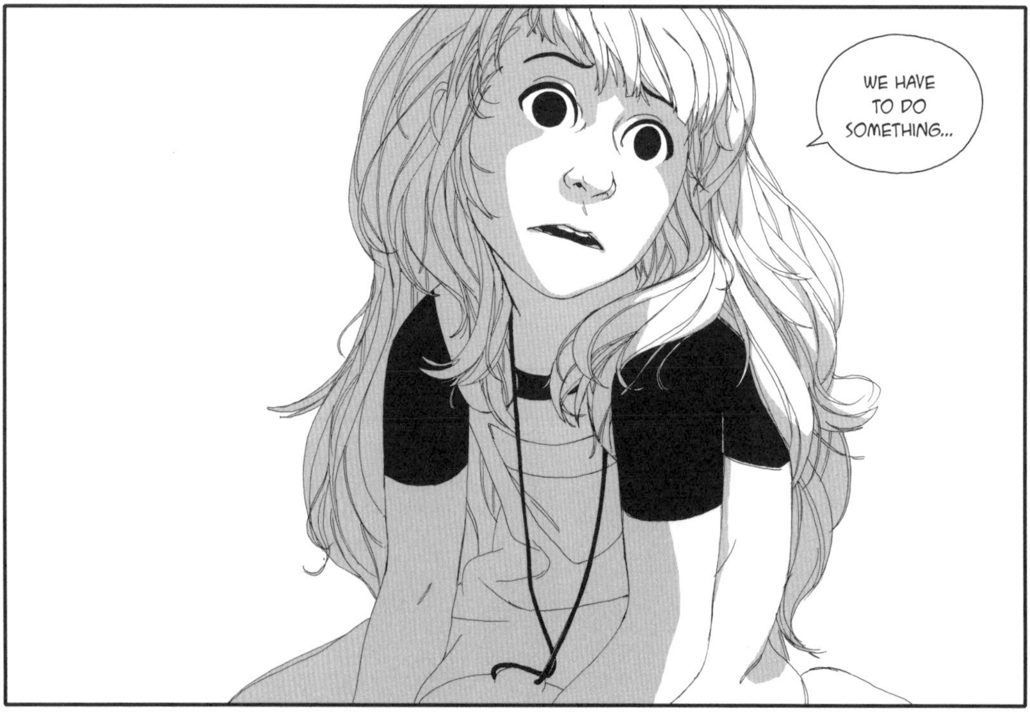
WE HAVE
TO DO
SOMETHING...

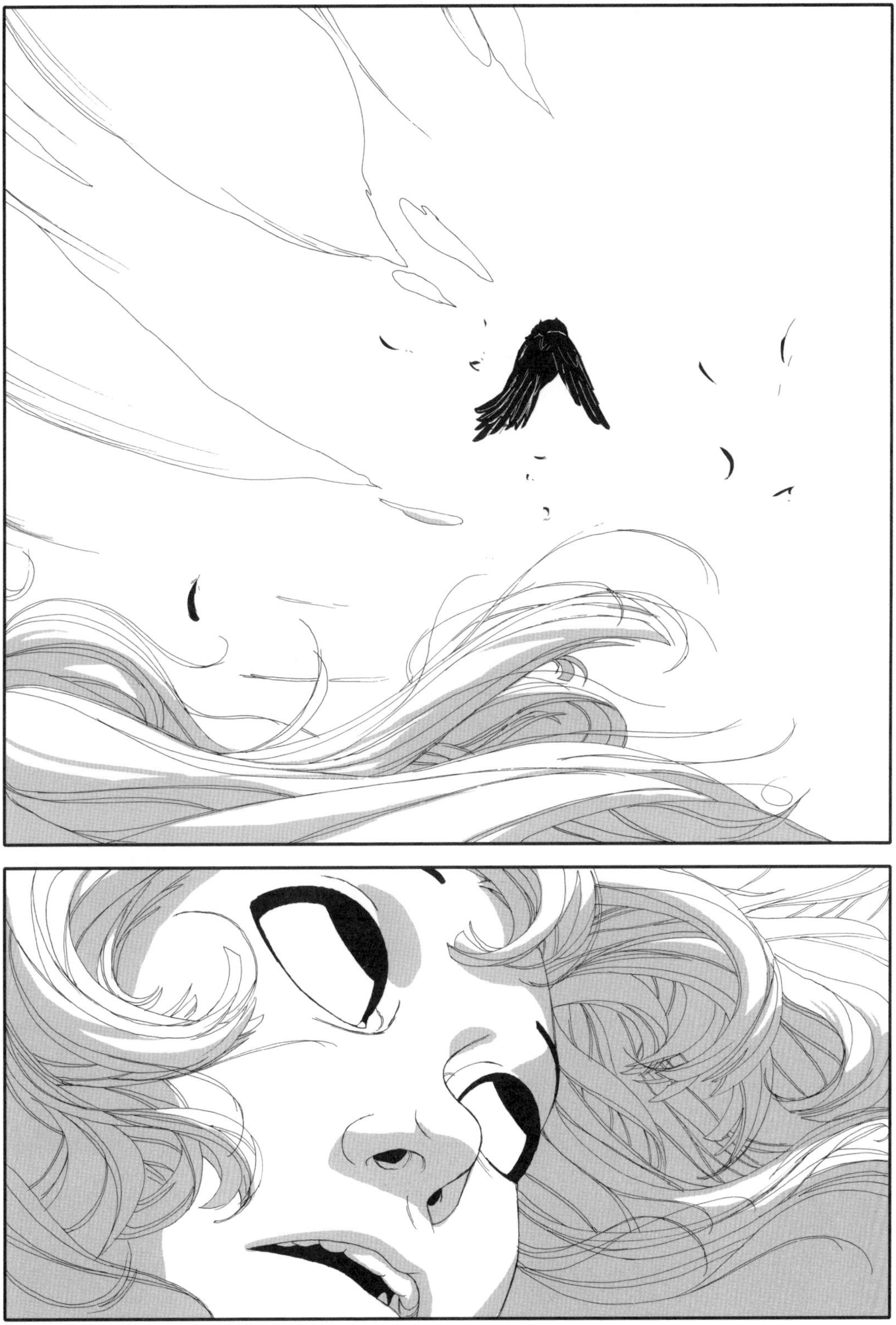

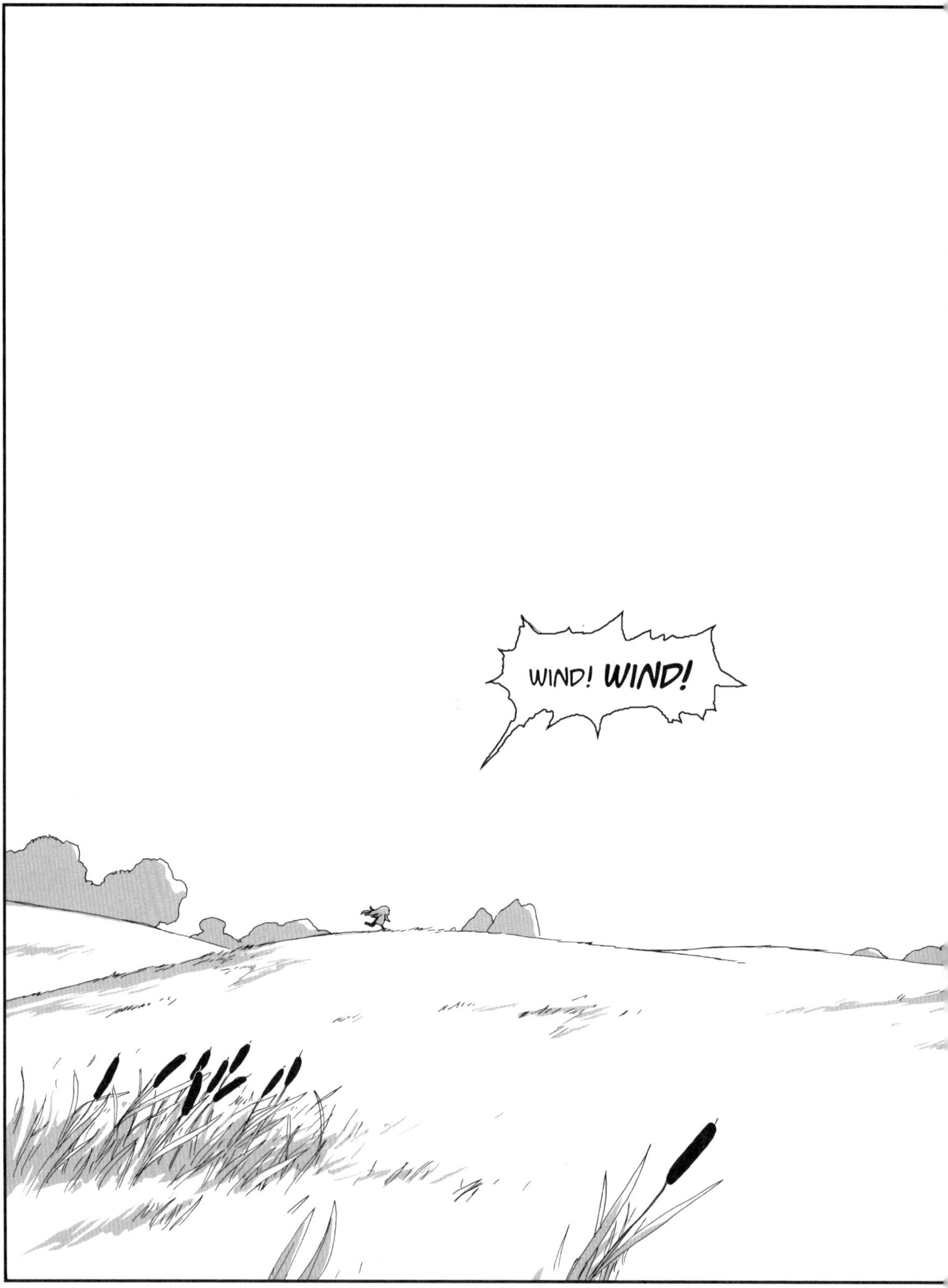
WIND! WIND!

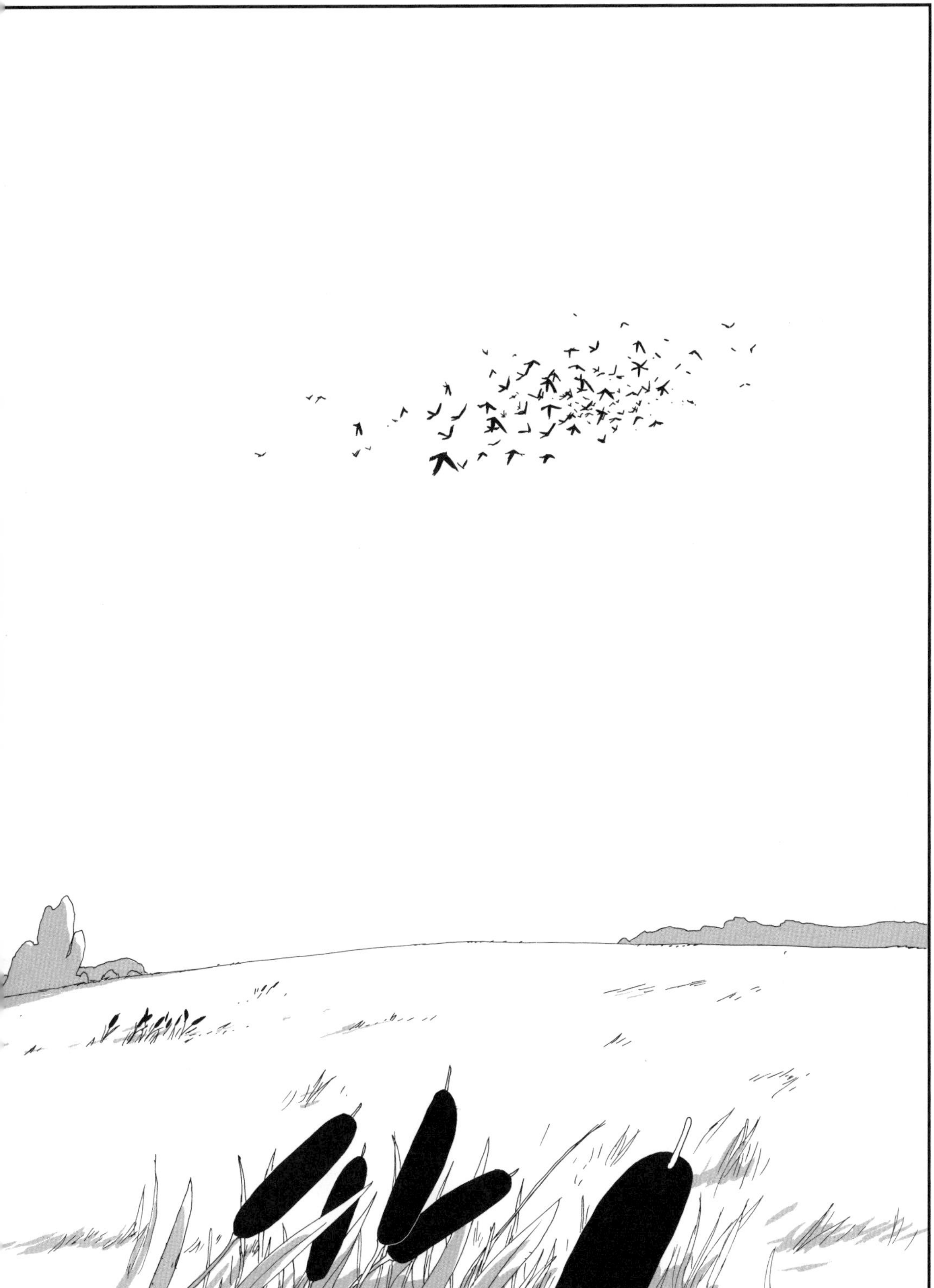

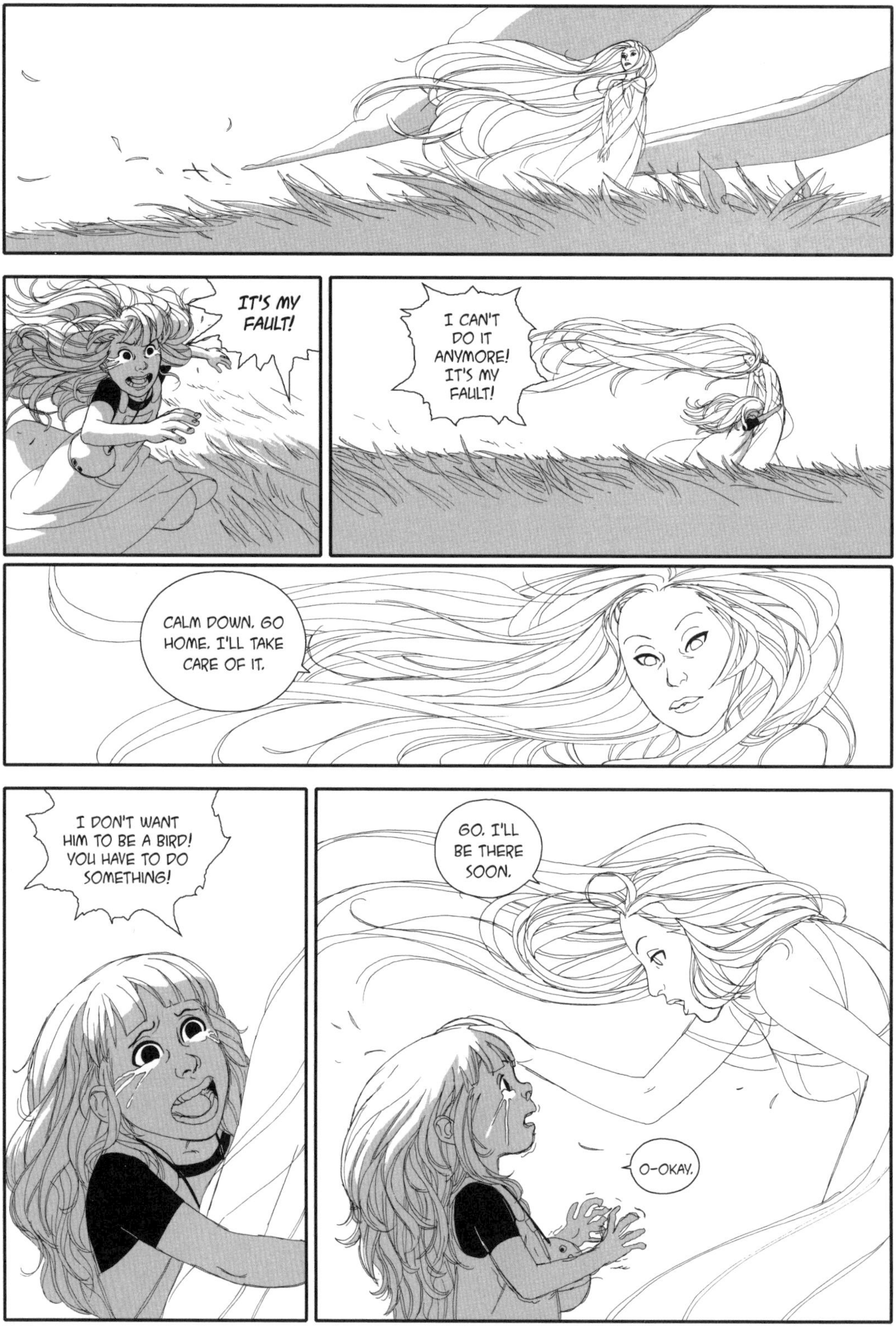
IT'S MY FAULT!
I CAN'T DO IT ANYMORE! IT'S MY FAULT!
CALM DOWN. GO HOME. I'LL TAKE CARE OF IT.
I DON'T WANT HIM TO BE A BIRD! YOU HAVE TO DO SOMETHING!
GO. I'LL BE THERE SOON.
O-OKAY.

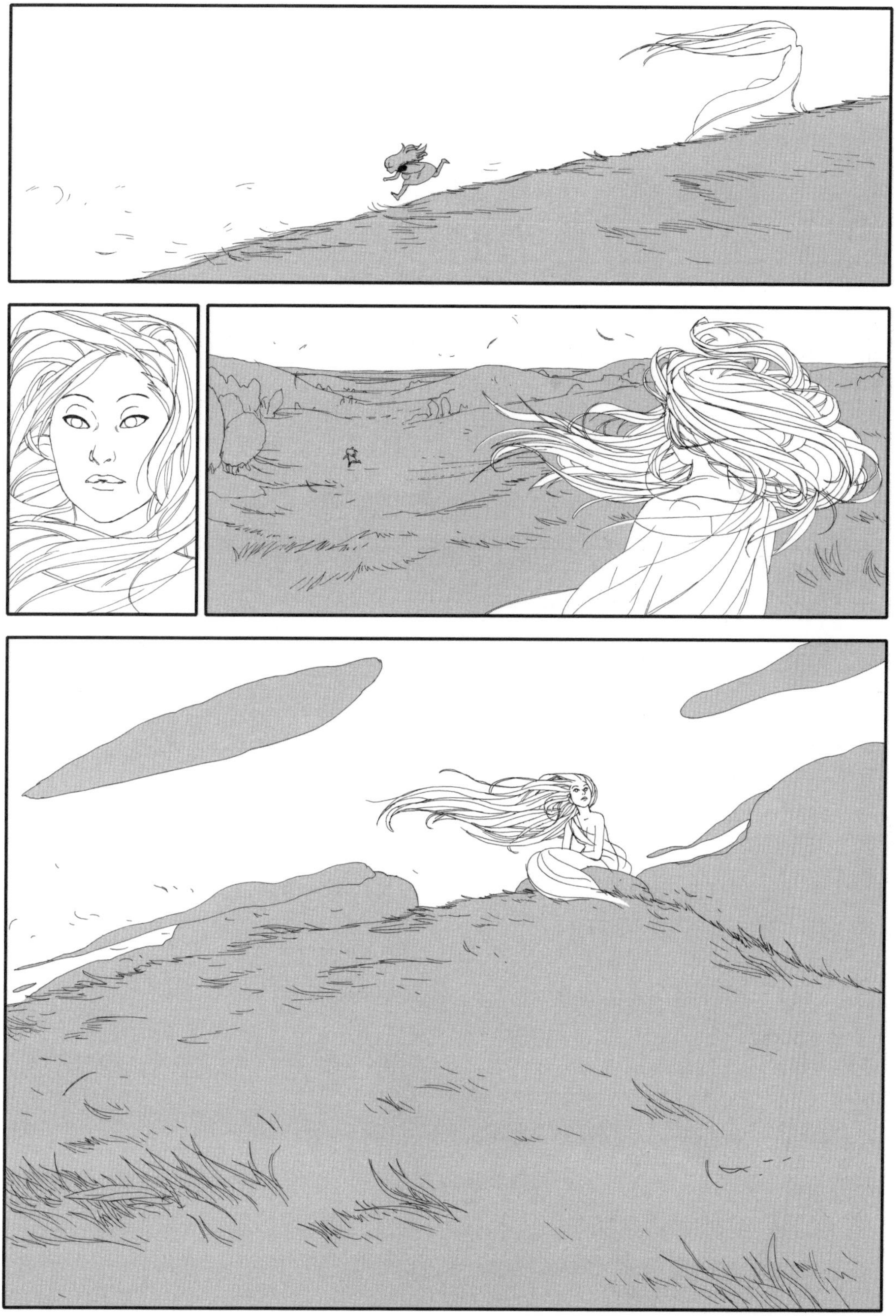

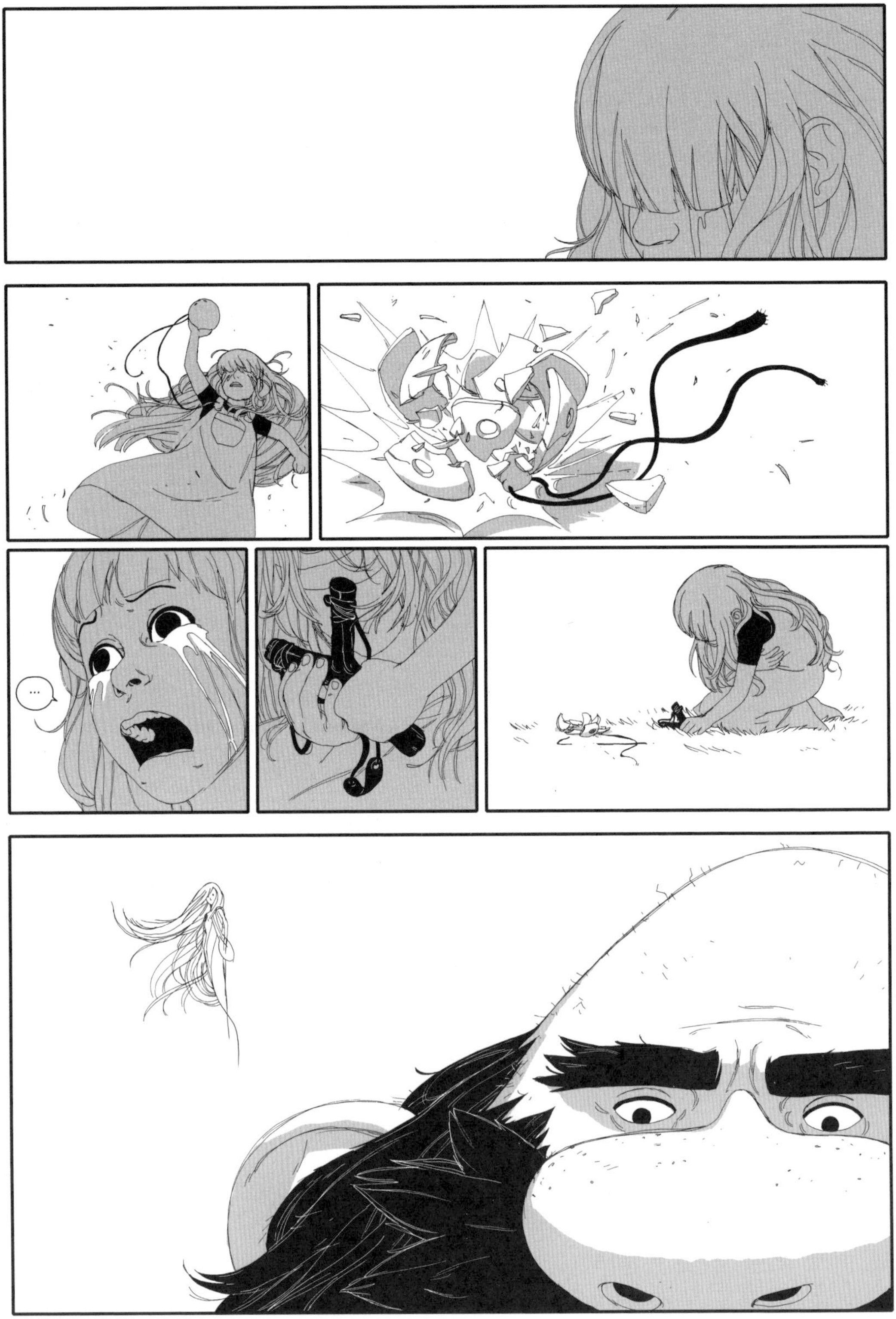
...

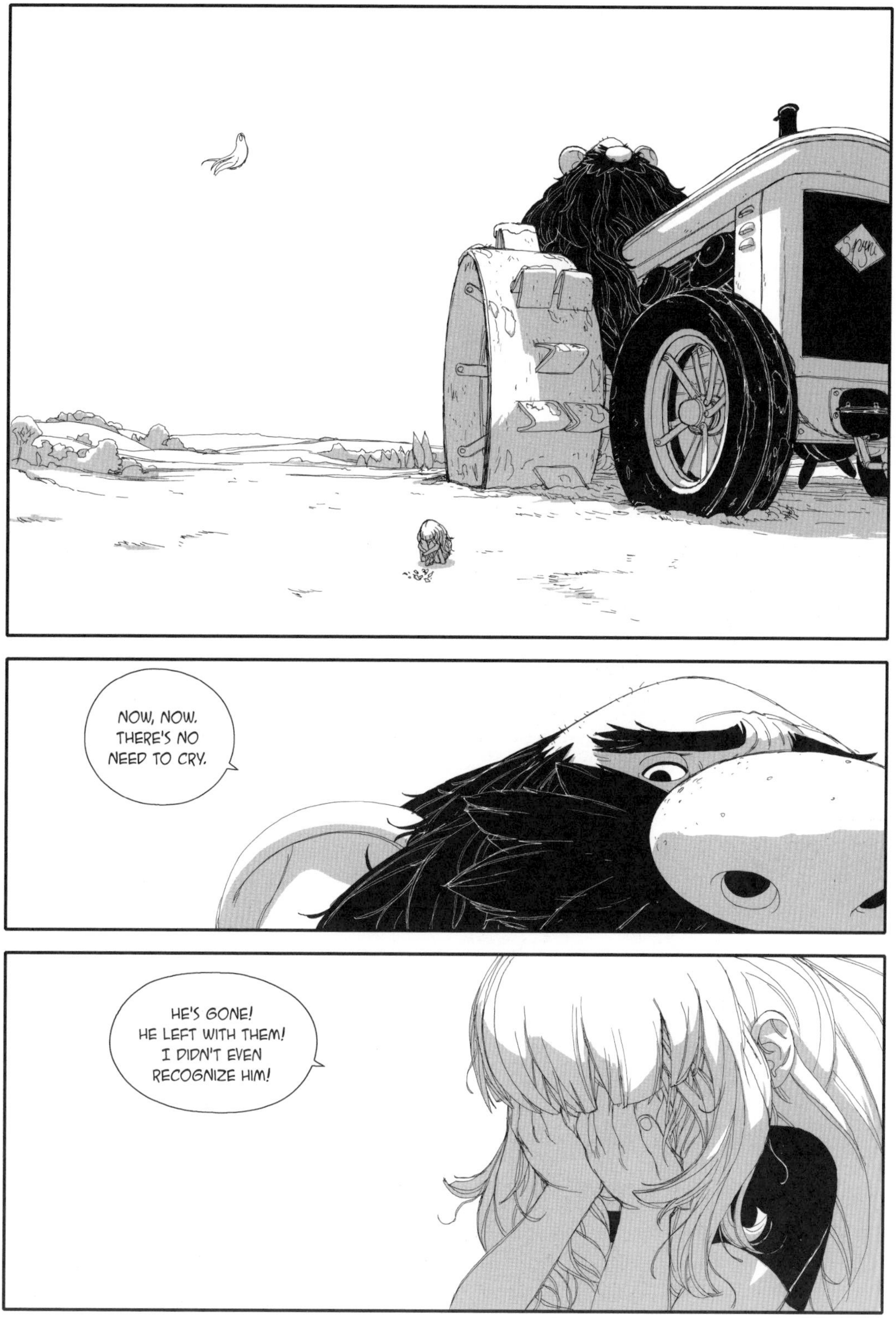
NOW, NOW.
THERE'S NO
NEED TO CRY.
HE'S GONE!
HE LEFT WITH THEM!
I DIDN'T EVEN
RECOGNIZE HIM!

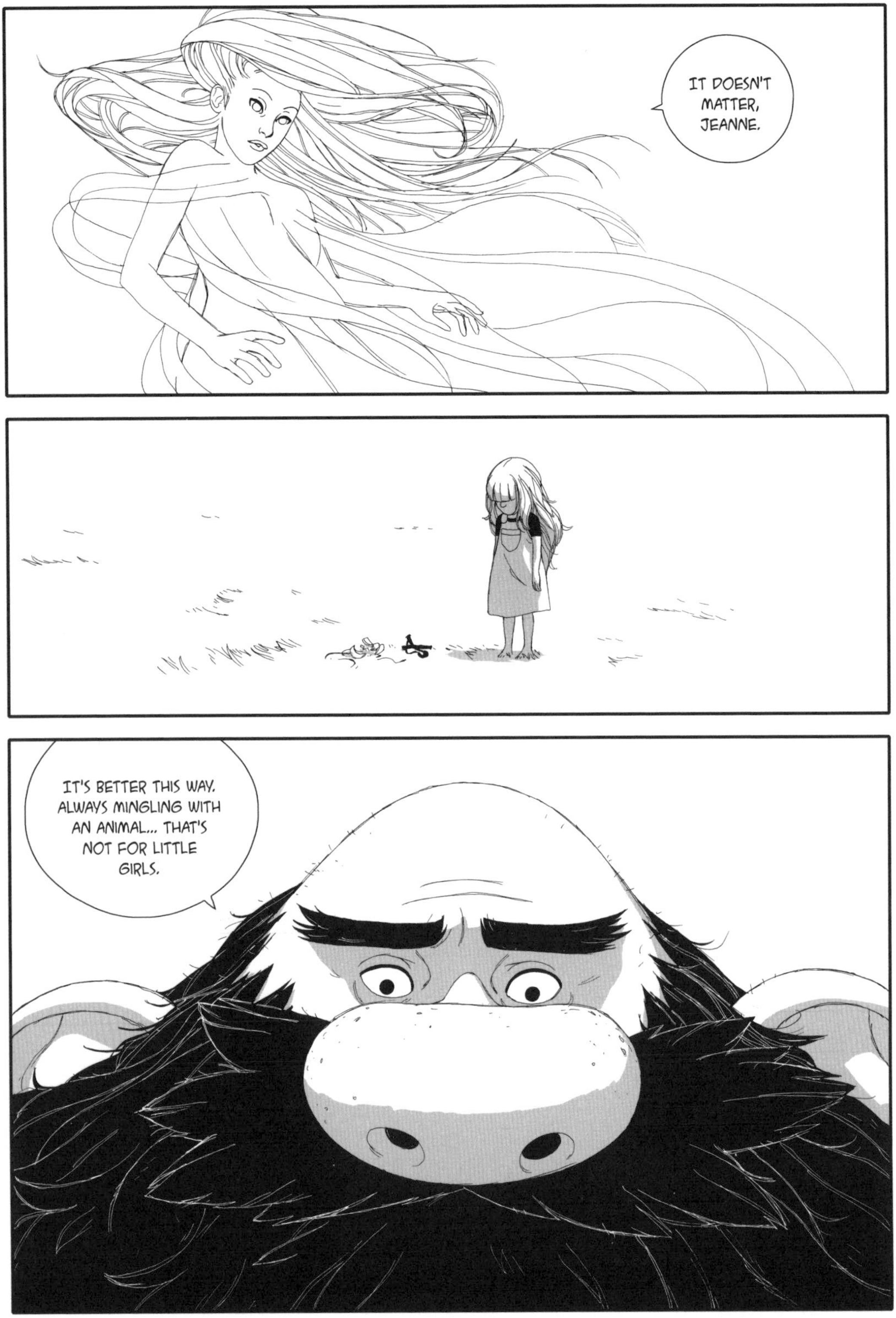
IT DOESN'T MATTER, JEANNE.
IT'S BETTER THIS WAY. ALWAYS MINGLING WITH AN ANIMAL... THAT'S NOT FOR LITTLE GIRLS.

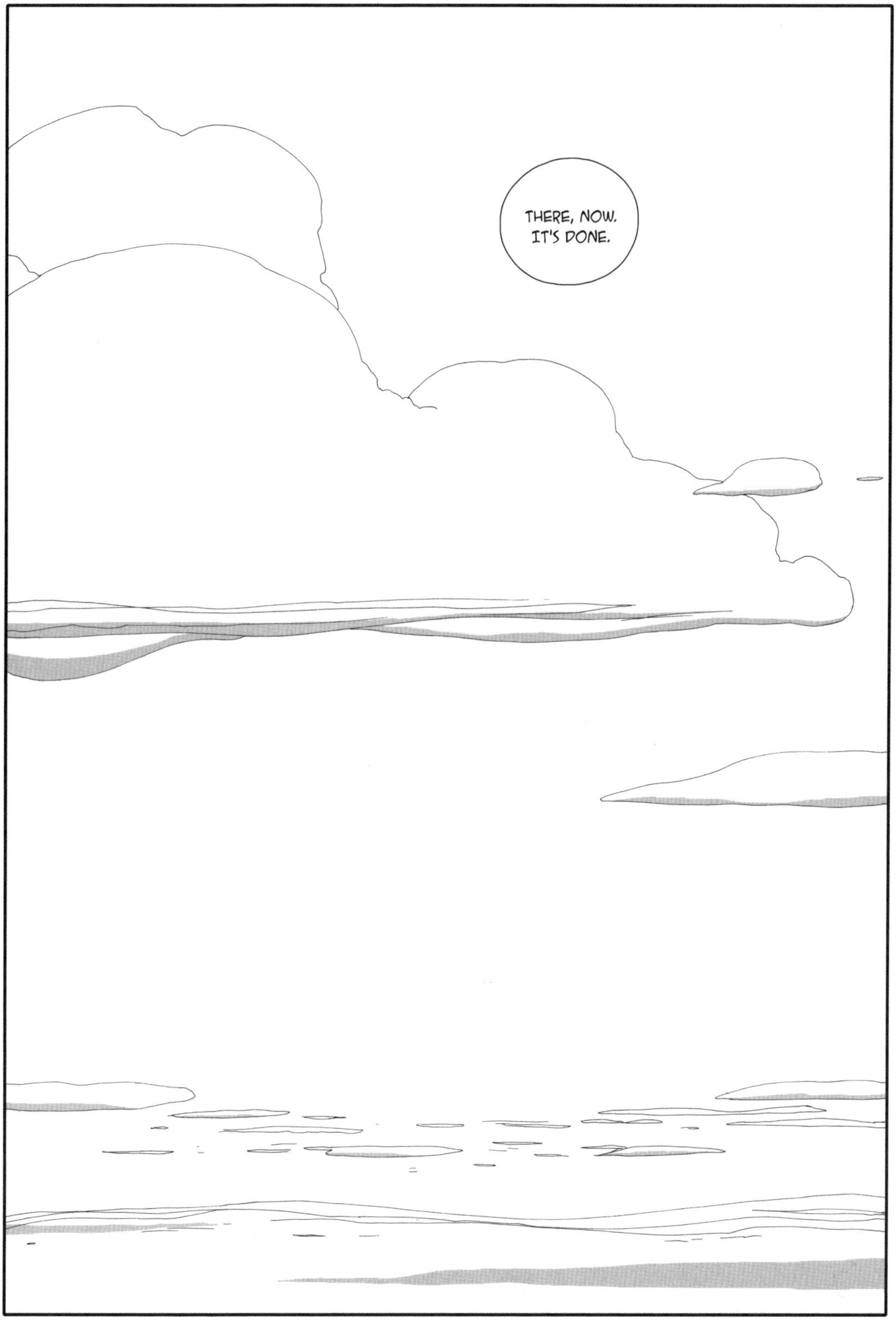
THERE, NOW. IT'S DONE.

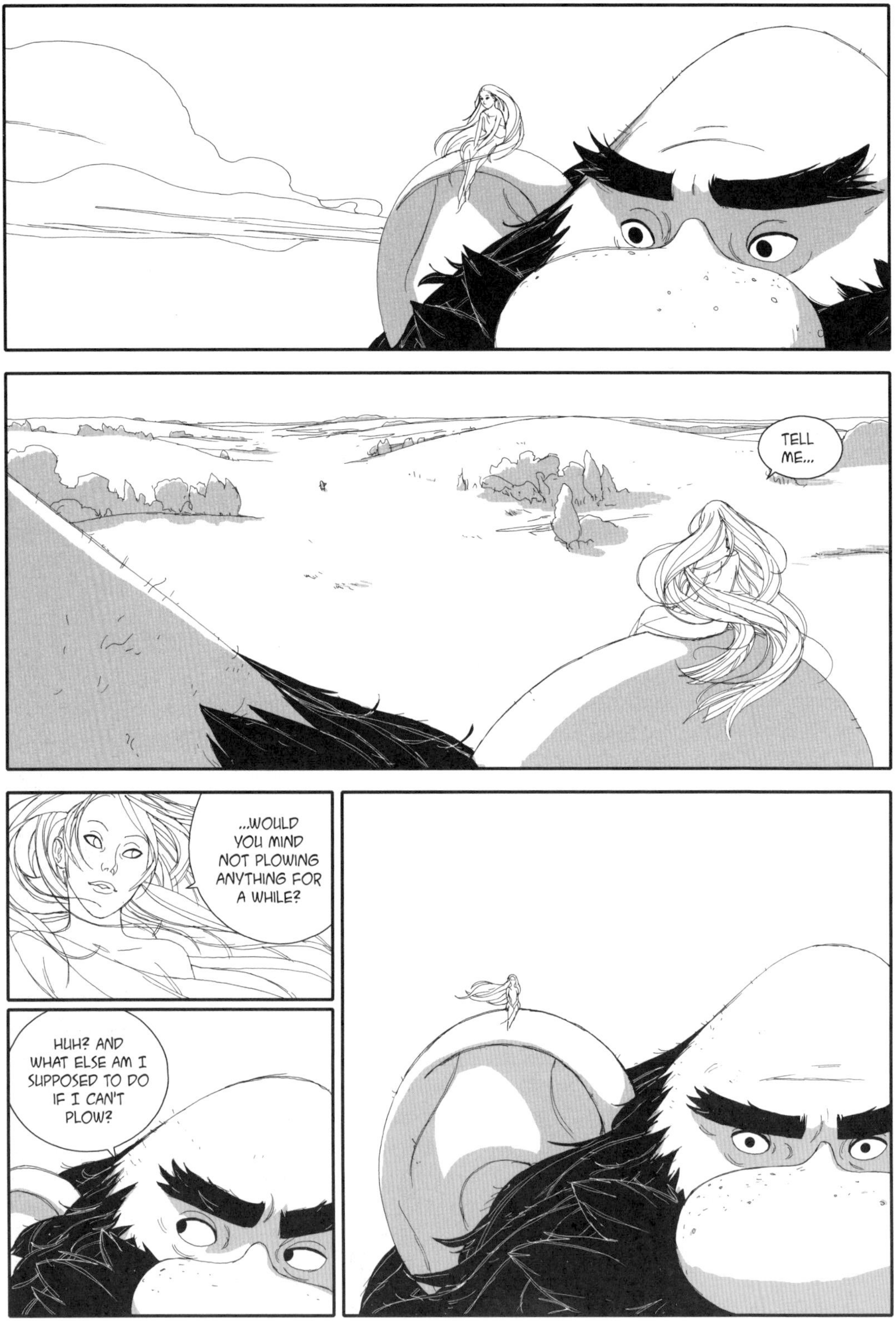
TELL ME...
...WOULD YOU MIND NOT PLOWING ANYTHING FOR A WHILE?
HUH? AND WHAT ELSE AM I SUPPOSED TO DO IF I CAN'T PLOW?

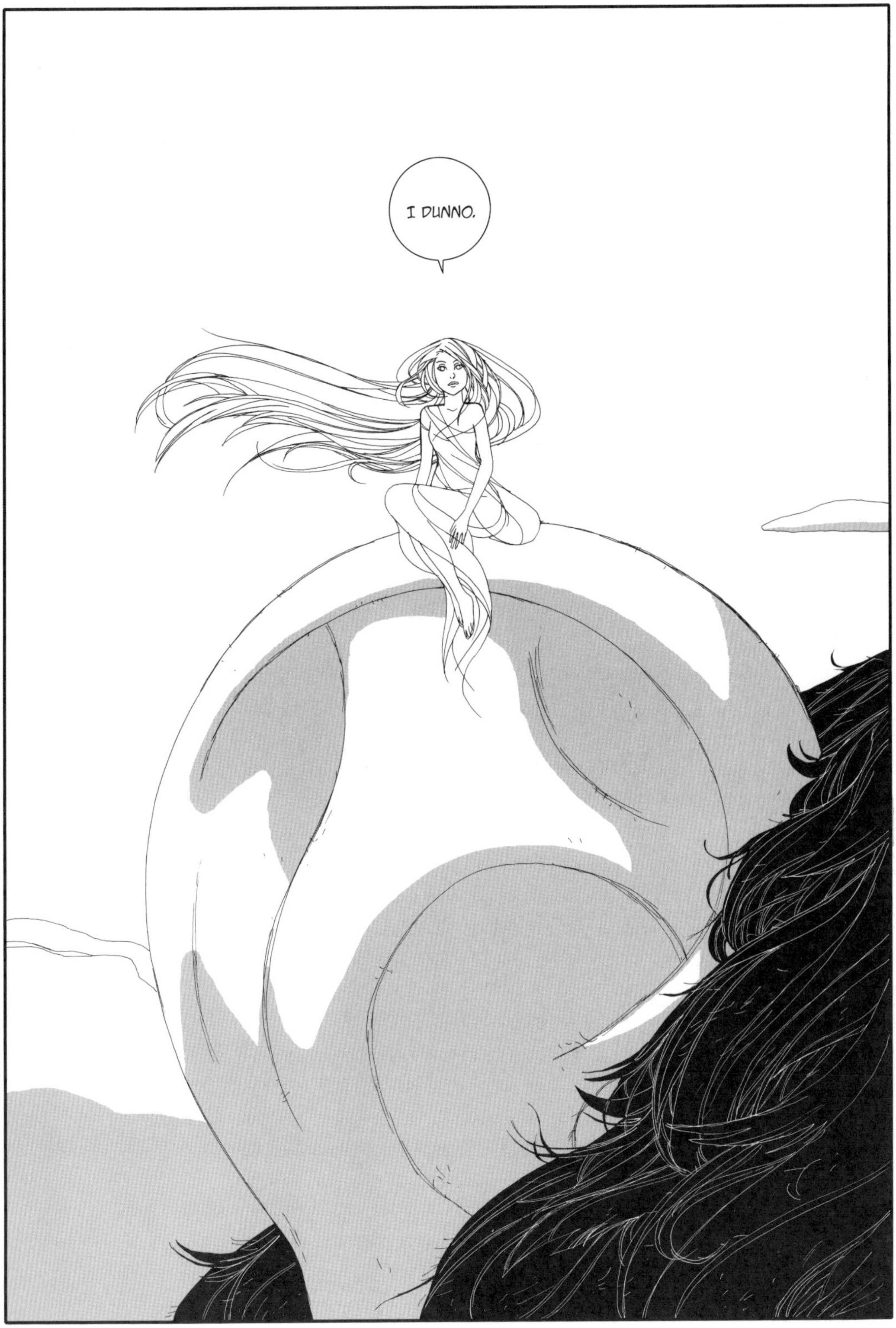
I DUNNO.

*Thanks to my mother, my brother, Merwan, Sandrine and Amélie
who were there when the ship sank.*

Bertrand

Thanks to Bertrand for his total involvement.

Merwan

Written by Merwan,
Designed and directed by Bertrand Gatignol.

English translation, layout, and editing by Mike Kennedy.

MAGNETIC™

ISBN: 978-1-942367-95-6
Library of Congress Control Number: 2020911866

Pistouvi published 2020 by Magnetic Press, LLC.

Printed in China.

10 9 8 7 6 5 4 3 2 1